SONS OF THE
TEXAS STAR

ALSO BY JEFFERSON GLASS

Conor Armenta Mystery Series

The First Light of Dawn

Shifting Sand

SONS OF THE
TEXAS STAR

A CONOR ARMENTA MYSTERY
BOOK THREE

JEFFERSON GLASS

WOLFPACK
PUBLISHING
— EST 2013 —

Sons of the Texas Star
Paperback Edition
Copyright © 2024 Jefferson Glass

Wolfpack Publishing
1707 E. Diana Street
Tampa, FL 33610

wolfpackpublishing.com

Paperback ISBN 978-1-63977-547-7
eBook ISBN 978-1-63977-546-0
LCCN: 2024947053

PRAISE FOR SONS OF THE TEXAS STAR

"Jefferson Glass offers plenty of intrigue, twists and surprises in his third Western mystery."

— THOMAS D. CLAGETT, WILL ROGERS
MEDALLION AWARD-WINNING AUTHOR OF
BLOOD WEST

"Jefferson Glass delivers an engaging historical mystery set in 1930s Las Vegas, where suspense, courtroom drama, and a heartfelt love story intertwine. With skilled storytelling and a deep sense of historical detail, *Sons of the Texas Star* weaves together murder, mystery, and the human heart, offering readers a journey through the tension and danger at the crossroads of the Old West and the dawn of modern America."

— CHRIS MULLEN, AWARD-WINNING AUTHOR
OF *ROWDY*

"*Sons of the Texas Star* paints a vivid portrait of early Las Vegas and the surrounding desert...flashbacks and leaps forward in time tell threads of the story, which come together by the end of the book. In that way, it's a bit like a John Dos Passos novel."

— JOHN G. BLUCK, AUTHOR OF THE LUKE RYDER
SERIES

Dedicated to those romantic cowboy stars of the early silver screen who mesmerized their audiences.

Some survived the evolution of the industry to have long careers in the Wild West. Others rode off silhouetted against blazing sunsets and waving their hats from the backs of rearing ponies never to return.

SONS OF THE
TEXAS STAR

1

"Where's my share of the money, Clay?" his twin brother asked as he burst through the front door.

"What share?" he replied.

"My half from selling the herd."

"It'll take every cent we made on the herd to pay off Dad's debts against the ranch, Bob," he retorted. "There won't be any money until we sell this place."

"I'll take my share now, Clay," he snarled as he drew the six-shooter from his holster.

The man called Clay drew his gun a tenth of a second faster. Both guns fired almost simultaneously as the two brothers fell on the tile floor of the foyer.

"Cut! Cut! Cut!" movie director Hugh Parker screamed. "Get these doors open and clear the smoke out of here! Get up off the floor, Matt, so we can shoot this again! You won this gunfight! Don't you remember anything? How can you forget the whole damned plot?"

Mark McCoy regained his feet as a grip knelt over his brother. "Get up Matt," he whispered as he tried to prod him. "You've really got Parker riled this time."

"Wayne!" Parker yelled for the technical director who, unknown to him, had already left the smoke-filled foyer. "I thought you coached these idiots! I don't have time for this!" Parker ranted, throwing his hands and script into the air as he stormed out. An assistant scurried to collect the scattering pages, as the director paced the floor of the sitting room.

Mark McCoy picked up his pistol and holstered it, then walked out into the courtyard away from the lingering smoke of the black powder cartridges.

"Matt," the grip continued in a normal voice. "C'mon now, the joke's over," he said, as he grabbed the actor's shoulder and shook it, he noticed the growing bloodstain on his chest. "Hey!" he yelled at the motionless body of Matt McCoy. "Help!" he yelled, looking around to see if anyone paid attention. "I think he's dead!"

A half-dozen cast and crew members converged on the prostrate Matt McCoy. Wayne Garrard who knelt by his side, took charge of the situation. The retired legendary US Marshal worked on the movie as a technical director.

"Grab a sheet or blanket," Garrard ordered one of the grips. As he covered the body along with the victim's pistol at his side, he glared at the director. "Make yourself useful, Parker, and call the sheriff."

* * *

Deputy Bennett Neilly arrived on the scene at twelve fifteen followed by Sheriff Conor Armenta five minutes later, almost exactly forty-five minutes after receiving the call.

"Watch the gate, Ben," Con told him. "Don't let anybody leave 'til I tell you."

"Yessir," Ben confirmed as Con walked toward the familiar front door of the hacienda.

"Marshal Garrard," Con acknowledged as he entered the open door. The foyer still reeked of burnt gunpowder.

"I'm retired, Sheriff," he replied as the two lawmen exchanged a firm grip. "My name is just Wayne now."

"Con Armenta. What happened?" he asked.

"Bad guy pulls his gun; good guy is faster on the draw and shoots the bad guy a split second before the bad guy's gun goes off into the floor. Cut...everybody's s'posed to get up and go to the commissary tent for lunch and live happily ever after. Trouble is, the good guy never got up. I took the liberty of securing the set within minutes of the occurrence."

"Who's the bad guy?"

"Mark McCoy," Garrard replied. "Good kid. Been working as my personal assistant for about a year on these make-believe shoot 'em ups. Finally got his big break acting in this one. Now this."

"Mark McCoy? Grew up out northwest of town here? About twenty-five?"

"You know him?"

"Know of him and his twin brother. They were little kids when I went to work in the gypsum mine. They'd gone off to California to strike it rich by the time I became a deputy. His brother's done pretty well from what I hear."

Wayne Garrard looked at Con with a twisted face through

one squinted eye. Without saying anything, he nodded toward
the corpse.

Con hesitated then knelt down and lifted the blanket. "This
is not good," he said as he looked at the glazed eyes of Matt
McCoy staring blankly at the ceiling.

"Never is, Sheriff."

When Garrard's eyes shifted toward the door, Con's
followed. "Hal," Con greeted the aging coroner as he shuffled
in the front door with a handful of evidence bags and a camera
around his neck.

"Con," he returned, then stopped staring blankly at
Garrard.

"Wayne," Con offered. "Dr. Harold Martin, our coroner."

"You know who he is?" Hal asked Con incredulously.

"Yeah. Wayne Garrard. Nice guy. You'll like him."

"This is Marshal Wayne Garrard. Arizona. Back in the
'80s...he's famous, Con."

Garrard offered Hal his hand.

"It's a pleasure to meet you, Marshal," Hal exuberated as
he pumped his hand.

"Like I told Con, I'm retired. Call me Wayne. Can I call you
Hal?"

"Whatever you like, sir."

"Very well, Hal." He looked at his watch. "The victim died
about sixty-five minutes ago."

Hal pulled back the blanket. "Holy smokes! It's Matt
McCoy." He reached into his pocket for a flashbulb.

"Take as many pictures as you like, Hal. They should also
have everything on film, three cameras rolling, I think."

"How soon could we see them?" Con asked.

"Hank?" Wayne called to a man standing nearby. "How
long to get the film developed that you shot today?"

"Hank is the lead cameraman," he told Con and Hal as the man approached.

"I can send them on the train to the darkroom at the studio. Probably have them back by Friday sometime."

"I have a darkroom," Hal offered.

"Different process and chemicals than still film," Hank informed them.

"I'll have a deputy hand-carry them, if you can arrange for someone to pick him up and bring him back to the station," Con told them.

"We can arrange that," Wayne told him.

"Where's Mark McCoy?

"In the sitting room," Wayne answered. "Co-stars don't get their own tent. I told him to sit tight until someone came to talk to him."

"The gun?"

"Locked in a prop box over here," Wayne waved Con to the side. "This is the chest where all of the guns are stored at night. I had the prop manager bring it in from the truck after the incident."

"Hal," Con beckoned. "Get photographs. Collect whatever you consider evidence."

The sheriff looked at Wayne. "I need to use the telephone."

"In there," Garrard motioned toward the study.

"I know," Con answered to Wayne's surprise and opened the door. He stepped into the study to encounter a man in his midforties wearing what Con assumed to be considered casual attire in the city. He leaned back in the leather upholstered chair behind what had been Brice Campbell's desk with the phone to his ear and a cigarette dangling from his lips. Ashes fell carelessly to the floor as the manufactured smoke bobbed when he spoke.

"Who are you?" Con demanded.

"I'm on the telephone," he answered.

"Hang up."

He kept talking.

"Now!" the sheriff commanded.

"This is business!" the man exclaimed as Con took the receiver from his hand and placed it on the cradle.

"Leanora Campbell doesn't permit smoking in this house. Anywhere in this house," Con growled, "and you haven't answered my question."

"That was Dave Fredericks!" the man interrupted. "Who the hell do you think you are?"

"I'm Sheriff Conor Armenta!" he answered. "Now, for the last time, who are you?"

"I don't have to answer anything."

Con drew his 1911 Colt automatic before the man knew what was happening. "This isn't a toy and it's not loaded with blanks," he informed the arrogant man as he pulled back the hammer. "Stand up and turn around," Con ordered, realizing then, the nearest handcuffs he had were in the glovebox of his pickup. "Whoever you are, you're under arrest for conspiracy to commit murder and interfering with a criminal investigation."

All color left the man's face. "But..."

"Too late. Shut up," he ordered. "Now hold up your hands and quietly walk out the front door."

"Everything okay, Con?" Garrard asked when they entered the foyer.

"It is now, Wayne," he answered as he escorted his captive across the room and out the door.

Everyone's eyes were clearly on Con and his prisoner. Once outside, Con stopped him. "Now, put out that butt."

The man did not speak nor attempt to lower his hands. He pushed the cigarette from between his lips with his tongue and ground it into the stone walkway beneath him. "Walk to that pickup with the star on the door," he told the man. He immediately proceeded.

"Stop right there," Con ordered as the man reached the right front fender of the truck. He walked past him and reached through the passenger window without lowering his gun. Fumbling by feel, he recovered two sets of handcuffs from the glovebox. Con slipped one set into the left hip pocket of his blue jeans.

"Give me your left hand," he told him and with his own, Con slipped a cuff around the slender wrist. As he moved behind him, Con silently released the hammer on his pistol and dropped it into his holster. He reached up and brought the right wrist behind the man and cuffed it to his left. The sheriff then ushered his prisoner to the rear of the pickup and lowered the tailgate.

"Have a seat," he told the man as he half lifted him up to the bed with his feet dangling off the back. He then used the other set of cuffs to secure him to one of the chains for the tailgate.

"You're in the shade," Con told him. "Just sit here nice and quiet. I'll be back to take you to jail when I'm finished."

He started to protest, but surrendered when Con held his finger to his lips and shushed him.

"Stupid cowboy." Con heard him mutter under his breath as he walked back toward the hacienda.

Con ignored the comment. *Bigheaded city-boy* he thought to himself and continued on.

The sheriff admired the architecture of the Campbell family's opulent estate as he reentered the main compound. Brice and Leanora Campbell had come from Wyoming after a few years in Utah a decade earlier. They built the entire compound in the Spanish style that many areas of the southwest were known for. He could only wonder what prompted Leanora Campbell, perhaps the wealthiest woman in the county, to lease it to the movie company. Her husband died a tragic death in the side garden only a few months ago. Now, a well-known actor has died, both violently and mysteriously in the foyer.

"What did the uppity pipsqueak do that got him into trouble, Con?" Wayne asked with a grin when the sheriff reentered the foyer.

"He wouldn't tell me who he was. Said he didn't have to. I arrested him," Con explained.

"What's the charge?"

"Conspiracy to commit murder and interfering with a criminal investigation."

"Whoa! Felony. That should have gotten his attention."

"Who is he? Some sort of bigwig?"

"You could say that," Wayne replied. "Hugh Parker. He's the director. The boss. Everybody out here answers to him."

"Not everyone, Wayne," Con answered. "I don't."

"What happened?"

"He was on the phone. Dropping ashes on the floor of Brice Campbell's study. Said he was busy. I told him to hang up. He wouldn't. I hung up for him."

"Who was he talking to?"

"Dave somebody."

"Dave Fredericks? David Whitfield Fredericks? Famous movie star? Founder of the studio?"

"Well…" Con blushed. "That's probably who it was. Didn't make the connection when he said, Dave." He reflected a moment. "I might be hearing from at least one of our county commissioners before this is over."

"Maybe, Con." Wayne winked, then busted into a hearty laugh. "I wish I'd been in there. Nobody likes Parker."

At that instant, Deputy Jesse Slater entered the foyer. "Who's the guy cuffed to your truck?" he asked.

"The director," Con's answer brought a bewildered expression from the deputy. "Long story," he added. "I'm glad you're here. I haven't even had a chance to begin questioning witnesses. Oh, and Jesse, this is Wayne Garrard. Wayne, Deputy Jesse Slater."

"*The* US Marshal Wayne Garrard?" Jesse clarified.

Wayne blushed. "That's me, but don't believe everything you've heard. And I'm retired. So, Wayne is just fine."

"Well, it's certainly an honor to meet you, sir," Jesse said as he vigorously shook Garrard's hand.

"Your crew is certainly respectful, Con," Wayne commended to the sheriff as he flexed circulation back into his fingers.

"No more so than I am," Con admitted. "Your reputation precedes you. I thank you for your assistance and am proud to work with you."

"Well, the feeling is mutual, Sheriff. I've read the papers and heard the talk around town. You've got a pretty hefty reputation of your own," the old marshal replied in admiration. "Faced down a Thompson machine gun with a .45 automatic...and won? Not too many folks get to live and talk about a thing like that."

"It wasn't nearly as romantic as it sounds," Con blushed, "and I wouldn't be able to talk about it, if Jesse here hadn't managed to haul my carcass to the hospital and got me sewed back together before I bled out."

"We'll need to sit down over a glass o' whisk…uh, soda pop and talk about that some evening," Wayne offered.

"Right now, I could use your help," Con asked.

"My pleasure, Con," Wayne began, "but I'm an eyewitness. I can't assist in the investigation."

"Could you introduce Jesse around and keep an ear to the ground while he questions these folks? I still need to use the telephone."

"I'd be honored."

"I'll question Mark McCoy myself," Con added.

"Sure, but there is one more thing you should probably know; without Parker, you won't get that film developed." Wayne touched his right index finger to the brim of his hat in salute and led Jesse across the foyer to the group of cast and crew who awaited them.

* * *

Sheriff Armenta entered the study and closed the door behind him. The room reeked of stale cigarette smoke not dissimilar to that of a poorly ventilated billiard hall. He wished he could leave the door open but opted to open a window instead. Mr. Parker had obviously been using the closed-up room for his office for several days. The abundance of ashes covering the terracotta tiles on the floor and the dozen butts ground into its surface among them, confirmed his suspicion. The despicable little man's pompousness disgusted Con. He picked up the phone and dialed.

"Clark County Sheriff's Office," the matronly female voice answered. Hazel Corbyn had worked for the sheriff's office for as long as Con could remember. Other than occasional misguided attempts to influence his personal life, Con could find no fault in her motherly persona. Her abilities in managing the office were impeccable.

"Hazel, this is Con. When does the next train to Los Angeles come through?"

"Passenger or freight?"

"Either."

Con could hear a muffled shuffling of papers. "Just a minute," returned the voice and the sound of the receiver being placed on her desk as footsteps walked away, then returned.

"Passenger at two o'clock. Freight at four forty-five."

"We're too late for the two o'clock. The freight train will be all night getting there."

"Yes, probably so," Hazel agreed. "What do you need?"

"I need there to be three of me."

"Besides that?"

"Who's on tonight?"

"Whitney and the new guy."

"Call Whit and tell him to come out to the Campbell's place as soon as he can get here."

"Anything else?"

"Make sure he has eating money for a couple of days. He's going to LA."

Con loathed having to ask a favor of Hugh Parker, but he needed to have the film of the shooting developed as soon as possible. He also knew he needed to secure the film, with or without the cooperation of the movie crew. He called District Court Judge William Tucker.

"What do you need, Con?" the judge asked.

"A search warrant for the Campbell estate and any vehicles or equipment on it."

"What are you looking for?"

"Evidence relating to the death of Matt McCoy."

"What?" Judge Tucker exclaimed. "What happened?"

"He was shot while filming a gunfight in this movie."

"*Sons of the Texas Star?*"

"Is that what it's called?"

"I read the book," the judge commented. "Good story. This happened when the brothers shot it out at the end?"

"Probably so," Con replied. "I don't know the story."

"So, who was playing the bad brother?" Tucker asked.

"Mark McCoy."

"Holy cow! When do you need the warrant?"

"Right now."

"I'll have a clerk run it over to your office as soon as I can get it written out."

"Give it to Hazel, Judge. I'll have a deputy bring it out here."

"Consider it done, Sheriff."

Con hung up and called Hazel back so she could have Whit bring the warrant. He walked to the window to get a breath of fresh air while trying to figure out a way to get the film developed without involving the director. When he recalled an acquaintance in California, he dialed the operator.

"Sheriff Armenta," he told her. "Can you connect me to the Bureau of Prohibition in Los Angeles?"

"Yes, Sheriff."

A couple of minutes later the telephone rang on the other end.

"Agent Michael O'Sullivan please," he asked the receptionist when she answered.

"May I ask who is calling?"

"Sheriff Conor Armenta, Las Vegas, Nevada."

"Is he expecting your call?"

"No ma'am," Con answered.

"One moment please," she replied, and the phone went silent.

"How are you, Sheriff?" the agent greeted when he came on the line. "All healed up?"

"I'm feeling fine," Con replied, "but I need a favor."

"If your brother wants to sell that horse of his, I'm your man." O'Sullivan chuckled.

"No," Con controlled a snicker. "As a matter of fact, he belongs to me as of a couple of months ago."

"Well, I'm a bit disappointed, but I suppose congratulations are in order."

"Thanks, but…"

"But that's not why you called," O'Sullivan interrupted. "What's going on?"

Con gave the agent a brief rundown on the investigation, "What I need is someone to develop the movie footage of the shooting. I need it done quickly and if possible, without the studio being involved."

"Which one?"

"Unified Stars."

"Okay. I know some of the folks over at the FBI office. Let me do some checking. I'll call you back."

* * *

The Las Vegas telephone directory lay among the mess on the desk. Con found the number for Fremont Construction and dialed the phone.

A sweet young female voice answered, "Good afternoon, Fremont Construction, this is Amy,"

"Amy, this is Sheriff Armenta. Is Newton Campbell in?"

"Yes, he is, Sheriff. Just a minute."

Seconds later, a vibrant male voice came on the line. "Newt Campbell, Sheriff. What can I do for you?"

"Where can I find your mother?" Con asked.

"She's in Wyoming visiting her sister for a couple of months. Is something wrong?"

"I'm sitting in your father's study with a dead movie star in the foyer."

"I'll be right there," Campbell replied and hung up before the sheriff could respond.

* * *

Con returned to the foyer and located Hank, the lead cameraman.

"Can you get the film ready to take to Los Angeles for me?"

"I sure can," he told the sheriff. "I'll need to take the cameras out to the truck to keep from exposing the footage when I open them up."

Hal was taking photographs of the layout of the room when Hank and two other cameramen came over to haul the three big cameras out the door.

"You got the pictures you need?" Con asked him.

"I think so," the coroner confirmed.

"Can these fellas take the movie cameras out to their truck now?"

"Yep. I've got the floor marked, a map drawn and pictures from four angles."

"Good," Con answered. "They're going to unload the film for us. Why don't you tag along and see how it's done?"

"I'd love to."

Con caught the doc's sleeve as he started out the door behind them and whispered. "Make sure they don't accidentally expose that film before it makes it into the canisters."

"I get your drift." Hal winked and hurried to catch the trio just as a 1929 Auburn Speedster pulled up to the outside gate in a cloud of dust. Con grinned as he saw the tall, handsome driver step out and talk to Parker at the rear of his sheriff's pickup truck. A scowl developed on the driver's face, then he strode toward the open front door of the estate. Con crossed the foyer to meet him.

"Howdy Con," the man greeted.

"Newt," the sheriff acknowledged.

"What happened?" Newton Campbell asked as he looked at the blanketed body on the foyer floor.

"As I understand it, the good guy was supposed to outdraw the bad guy, then... Cut! Then everybody breaks for lunch. That would have worked out fine, except the bad guy had real bullets."

"You're joking, right?"

"If I was, we wouldn't be standing here."

"Wow!"

"Exactly."

"So, who's that?" Newt nodded toward the body.

"The good guy."

"I got that. I mean, who is it really."

"You've got to keep shut up about this until I release it."

"Sure," Campbell agreed, still staring at the mound beneath the blanket. When the sheriff failed to continue, Newt looked back into leery eyes. "Seriously. My lips are sealed."

"Matt McCoy."

"You aren't kidding, are you?"

Con shook his head.

"Then who shot him?"

"Mark McCoy."

"His own brother?"

Con nodded. "Just like in the movie, except backwards of how it was supposed to happen," Con eyed Newt Campbell. "Understand now why you have to keep your mouth shut?"

"Yeah…yes, I do," Newt contemplated. "If Mark McCoy shot him, what's the deal with Parker out there?"

The sheriff proceeded to review the sequence of events leading up to Hugh Parker's arrest. Campbell was appalled.

"That little imp swore to my mother that when they left here, she wouldn't even know they had been around." He shook his head in disgust. "I should have never suggested it."

"Suggested what?" Con asked.

"When the movie people got to town, they found out I about my little herd of longhorn cattle. Much of the story involves a cattle drive from Texas to the railhead at Dodge City. My longhorns were perfect candidates to play the role. Those guys can make sixty head look like six thousand on film. Anyway, they rented them from me and trucked them out to Mike McCoy's ranch where they shot the roundup, then to Moapa. They drove them around in the desert and across Muddy River, all making it look like the Red River and Oklahoma in the movie. Indians from the reservation stampede the herd, rustlers, all the drama of an epic trail drive."

"So how did your mother's house get involved?" Con pressed.

"When they came to look at my cattle, they saw this house and fell in love with it. Said it would be the perfect setting for the Texas ranch in the movie. They wanted to lease it. It all sounded good to me, so I brought them to meet Mother. She agreed to their terms and decided to take an extended vacation in Wyoming while they filmed the movie. They took panorama shots of the cattle grazing around the house, cowboys herding them around with the house in the background, everything to make it look authentic before they loaded them up and took them out to McCoy's place."

As Newt Campbell concluded his explanation of how he and his mother were involved with the movie company, a deputy sheriff's patrol car came to a halt behind the Auburn in the driveway. Campbell's eyes followed the sheriff's gaze to the new arrival.

"Since you got here in about ten minutes, I suspect you passed my deputy on the way out here?"

"Yes, I believe I may have," Newt recalled as he watched the deputy's approach.

"Whit," Con acknowledged as they met.

"Sheriff," he replied as he glared at Campbell. "Here's the search warrant you requested," he added as he handed it to Con.

"Newt, this is Deputy Whitney Ellis," Con began, "he was with us on the raid of the moonshiners a few days after your father's death. He's a very capable lawman and operates strictly by the book."

"Excuse me," a woman wearing slacks interrupted as she approached. "Sheriff Armenta?"

"Yes," Con answered.

"There's a call for you. An Agent O'Sullivan?" she offered. "I heard the telephone ringing, so I answered it."

"Thank you, Miss."

Conor turned to his companions. "I believe the two of you may have met...in passing...about a half hour ago? You should take the next few minutes to get better acquainted."

Con turned on his heel and headed to the study.

2

MONDAY, JUNE 16, 1930

"**W**hat are you looking for?" Dutch Wagner demanded as he stared at the search warrant the sheriff just handed to him.

"Anything I want. Anywhere I want," Con replied through gritted teeth.

"I don't understand," Dutch stammered. "I run a perfectly legitimate business here."

"You'll understand soon enough," Armenta told him. "Let's start with that safe, there," he pointed to the wall-safe behind Dutch's desk.

"That's private. The contents of that safe are strictly personal."

"That warrant doesn't provide an exemption for personal. Open it."

"Uh, I don't, uh, remember the combination."

"You'll remember it quick enough or I'll have somebody in

here with nitroglycerin to blow the door off it. Take your pick."

Dutch turned around and began spinning the dial between glimpses over his shoulder.

"Don't fret about me," Con told him. "I'm not very good with numbers. I won't remember the combination. Oh, and by the way, step back so I can see both of your hands when you open it."

Dutch turned around and to one side, then reached with his right hand to turn the handle and pull the door open. The compartment was small, without a shelf. Two tall stacks of greenbacks sat atop a ledger. The ledger was cocked up on one side. Con leaned over to see what was under it in the dimly lit room. It wasn't the pistol he hoped to find but appeared to be the briarwood bowl of a pipe.

"I almost forgot to tell you, I've got another warrant here," he pulled an arrest warrant from his pocket with his left hand and held it out to him. As Dutch reached for it, Con continued.

"Gary D, Wagner, Jr., you are under arrest for felony extortion of the late Brice Campbell and for felony extortion of the late Katherine Wagner."

Dutch's face paled as his hand dove into the front pocket of his trousers. Before he could get ahold of the little pistol, he heard the ominous click of the hammer being pulled back on Armenta's 1911 Colt. He looked up into the barrel of the .45 only a few inches from his nose.

"I hope that's the .25 automatic that killed your mother and Jimmy Garza," Con said calmly. "My day would become so much more gratifying."

Wagner did not move or answer.

"Take that gun out of your pocket real slow and easy,

Dutch. If it went off, it might startle me. I could accidentally jerk my trigger finger and make a mess of your office."

Wagner carefully extracted the .25 automatic from the front pocket of his trousers and laid it on the desk in front of him.

"Hands in the air, Dutch," Con ordered.

He complied.

"Jess," the sheriff called to his deputy standing near the bar outside the door.

"Yeah, Sheriff. What do you need?"

"Is everything all right out there?"

"Yessir."

"Call Ben inside, then send him in here for me."

"Got it," Jesse replied and backed toward the front door keeping the bartender and both stairways covered with his shotgun.

"Everything clear out there, Ben?" Jesse hollered.

"Sure is, Jess."

"Good. Come in here and assist the sheriff in the office."

Ben came through the door carrying his shotgun and paused beside Jesse for a moment to let his eyes adjust from the bright sunlight outside.

"Right past the end of the bar there," Jesse told him. "I'll cover you."

Ben proceeded cautiously toward the office door. Jesse followed a few paces behind him, resuming his former position near the bar.

"Right behind you, Sheriff," Ben announced when he reached the door.

"Come on in, Ben," Armenta told him, still keeping his Colt in Dutch's face while he stepped to the side of the desk. "Point that shotgun right at his belly. I don't want any stray pellets hitting me."

"Yessir," Ben announced. As he stepped forward to hold the short-barreled 12-gauge pump a foot from Dutch's stomach, Con stepped behind Wagner ensuring his safety. Dutch became nauseous. Cold sweat trickled down his cheeks as the sheriff cuffed him.

"Load him in Jesse's car," Con told Ben as he checked him further for weapons. "Here's the warrant. Take him to the jail, then come back here."

As Ben ushered Wagner out the door, Con advised the young deputy, "Dutch thinks he's a dangerous man." The comment brought a sardonic smile to Wagner's lips. It quickly disappeared when the sheriff added, "Don't give him a chance to prove it...shoot first."

"Yessir."

* * *

Sheriff Conor Armenta leaned against the front of Dutch Wagner's desk contemplating his next move as he looked out the door. Glaring light entered the open doors of the main entrance to Dutch's Oasis, a gentleman's club in the notorious Block 16 district of Las Vegas. The bar on the ground floor served soft-drinks and sandwiches surrounded by a half-dozen billiard tables. Wide stairways led both upstairs and down.

The upstairs consisted of a bordello. Listed as female boardinghouses in the city directory, brothels were perfectly legal as long as they kept in accordance with state health standards.

The basement offered other audacious entertainment. In reality, more moonshine than soda pop probably crossed the bar downstairs where patrons were offered a wide selection of illegal gambling choices. In addition, the upstairs girls wandered the room provocatively soliciting their wares to potential customers. The elevator at the rear of the room could whisk a client to the upper level quickly and discretely for a private interlude.

The innerworkings of Dutch's shameless enterprise were of little consequence to the sheriff, legal or otherwise. He left those concerns to the city marshal. Sheriff Armenta's interest was far deeper and more sinister than what took place under this roof on a daily basis.

A couple of months before, Con uncovered two solid counts of extortion. Over the last few weeks, he found enough additional evidence to justify an arrest warrant. He believed it would soon help secure a conviction. The vilest aspect of these crimes was that Katherine Wagner, one of the victims, was Dutch's own mother. To further the intrigue, both Katherine and one of Dutch's employees, Jimmy Garza, were recently murdered in separate incidents. Executed might be a better term.

In a letter to her daughter, Katherine Wagner predicted her own demise and named Dutch as the perpetrator. Circumstantial evidence reaped the search warrant of the Oasis in hopes of uncovering additional proof of Dutch's accountability.

He picked up the phone on Dutch's desk and dialed the coroner's office.

"Coroner," the gruff voice on the other end answered.

"Hal, this is Con."

"What's going on?"

"I need you to grab some evidence bags and your camera and come over to Dutch's Oasis."

"You get tired of messing around and kill him?"

"Not yet. He's in jail and I've got a search warrant."

"I'll be over in a jiffy."

* * *

Con left the office door open as he walked to the bar. Jesse stood at the far end standing vigil over the room. Con motioned to the bartender who leaned against the backbar polishing a glass with a towel midway between the two. He casually wandered over at Con's beckoning.

"Who's in charge of this place when Dutch isn't here?" Con asked.

"Nobody," he answered.

"Just sort of runs itself, does it?"

"Yeah, pretty much."

"Everyone just does what they please?"

"Well…Sal kinda keeps an eye on things."

"And the girls upstairs?"

"Nah. Pearl takes care of them."

After just seeing his boss hauled out in handcuffs, the bartender was less than cooperative. Con tried not to show his irritation. He pulled a photograph from his pocket of the former employee found murdered two weeks earlier.

"You know this guy?"

"I've seen him."

"Recently?"

"A while back."

"Does he work for Dutch?"

"Not here."

"Somewhere else?"

"Maybe."

Con took a deep breath and slowly let it out. "Where will I find Sal?"

"He left."

"When?"

"About when you got here."

Con looked toward the back door. "This way?"

The bartender grinned and nodded as Con opened the door. "Everything okay out here, Whit?" he asked, glancing back at the bartender in time to see the grin suddenly disappear.

"Just fine, Sheriff," Whit called back from behind the deputy's sedan. "The big fella over there in the shade is just taking a nap."

"You must be Sal," Con stated as he walked toward the handcuffed man lying face down in the alley.

"I never killed that kid," Sal blurted out as he turned his head to the sheriff. "I liked him. We were friends."

Sal's unexpected disclosure caught Con momentarily off guard. The situation raced quickly through his mind as he continued to approach the man. He suspected Sal, unaware of his boss's arrest, thought Dutch had used him as a scapegoat for Jimmy Garza's murder. He obviously had been involved.

"Not very friendly, tying him to the belly of a rail car so he would be dragged by the train. We picked up parts of his body for a quarter mile." Con's anger suddenly welled up inside him. "Maybe you'd like to explain what a good friend you were to his parents; how sorry you are that there was nothing in the coffin they could recognize as their son."

"That was Dutch's idea," Sal pleaded. "I's just following orders."

Con had closed the distance to within a few feet when Sal closed his eyes and turned his face away. He winced in anticipation of boots breaking ribs, a punishment he himself had doled out to several victims in his grim career, or worse, receiving a bullet in the head.

"What's the matter, Sal? Can't face what's coming?" Con stopped himself one step away from unleashing his fury on the helpless thug. Instead, he kicked a bit of loose rocks and dirt at him and stopped.

"Any weapons, Whit?"

"I only checked his belt when I cuffed him. Didn't figure he could reach anything else for the meantime."

"Give me a hand here."

Whitney leaned his shotgun against the car and came over. Each officer grabbed an arm. Sal let out a yelp as they pulled him to his knees.

"Stand up you cowardly trash," Con rumbled as they hoisted him to his feet. "What's the rest of your name, Sal?"

"Nothin'."

"Well, Mr. Nothin'," Con pressured, "you can either tell me now or sit an extra month in jail while I wait for fingerprints to get back so I know who you really are."

"Rizzo," Sal responded. "Salvatore Rizzo."

"Salvatore Rizzo," Con began, "you're under arrest for the murder of Jimmy Garza."

Sal's face grew pallid. "But I never killed him," he whined. "Dutch did it."

"You can explain that to the judge," Con told him. "Or you and Dutch can work it out between yourselves while you're drawing straws for who goes first into the gas chamber."

Sal hung his head like a whipped schoolboy standing in front of the principal while Con removed a Colt automatic nearly identical to his own from a shoulder holster. "Anything else?" he asked.

"Inside my left pant leg," Sal answered.

Con lifted the leg of his loose trousers to reveal a Remington derringer in an ankle holster. He followed up checking pockets. "Take him to jail, Whit," he told the deputy. "Tell them to do a complete search there, then come back here."

Whitney stuffed Rizzo into the back of the patrol car. Con reentered the back door to the club as the sedan pulled out onto Ogden to proceed the half block down 2nd St. to the Clark County Jail.

Hal and Ben came through the front doors together as Con reached the bar.

"Ben," the sheriff began, "position yourself here. You need to cover both doors, both stairways, and the bar. No one leaves without my say-so."

"Yessir."

"Hal," Con addressed the coroner as he pulled the automatic and derringer from his waistband. "These were removed from the person of Salvatore Rizzo. He's on his way to jail right now."

Dr. Martin slipped both pistols into separate evidence bags with numbered tags and scribbled into his notebook. He slid them down the bar. "Keep an eye on those, too," he told Deputy Neilly.

Hal and Jesse followed Con into Dutch's office.

"Photograph the entire room before you touch anything," Con told them. "The .25 on the desk came out of Dutch's pants pocket. No one's touched it but him," he said as he moved behind the desk. "Dutch opened the safe. I want a record of exactly how it looks right now," he said. "The two of you need to count the money. Both of you sign a note stating the amount you put in the bag. I want to see the ledger book before you bag it. Beneath the book appears to be a briarwood pipe. It may have belonged to Brice Campbell. Dust it for fingerprints. I need to show it to Leanora Campbell for identification."

"Anything else?" Hal asked.

"Check every inch of this room," he answered. "Take anything that might be evidence. Whit will be back from the jail before long. Have him join Ben watching the main lounge. I'm going downstairs. Stay here 'til I get back."

* * *

Con descended the wide stairway into what seemed the bowels of hell. At this hour the nearly vacant room smelled of last evening's cigars and cigarettes. A loan gambler sat at a blackjack table as the dealer flipped cards mumbling the play in a drowsy monotone. The gambler sipped on a glass of amber liquid and tossed a couple of chips forward on the table anticipating the next round of cards.

The middle-aged bartender wiped a white towel absent-mindedly across the counter. Arm garters at his elbows held his sleeves above the wrists. Ringlets of curly blond hair dangled haphazardly down his brow when he looked up at the sheriff coming down the stairs. A woman seated at the bar turned around on her stool to face the intruder when the bartender spoke to her. She held a burning cigarette in her right hand and a glass of dark liquid in her left that she sucked through a straw before returning it to rest on the bar. A somewhat plain looking woman in her late forties Con guessed. She wore slacks and a modest blouse. Medium length wavy brown hair surrounded the pale face, scrubbed clean except for the brilliant red lips that stained the end of her smoke.

Con slid the photograph of Jimmy Garza across the bar. "You recognize this fella?"

The bartender picked up the snapshot and studied it for a moment. "Nah, doesn't look familiar, but I see a hundred different faces in here every night." He handed it to the woman. "What do ya' think, Pearl?"

The mention of her name immediately caught Con's attention. If the main-floor bartender told the truth, Pearl and Sal were the only two employees of the Oasis that had any authority besides the owner.

"He's been upstairs a time or two," she offered. "Not a regular," she added as she handed the picture back to Con.

"Seen him recently?" he asked.

"He was in a few weeks ago…early, I think."

"Maybe two weeks ago? On a Saturday?"

"Could be."

"He was murdered that night."

The announcement clearly shocked the bartender. If it troubled Pearl, her expression failed to display it.

"He ate dinner in here that night," the bartender suddenly revealed after claiming ignorance just moments before. "Sat right here at the bar. Around seven o'clock," he unexpectedly recalled. "The place was just starting to fill up."

"Are you willing to testify to that if needed?"

"Sure, I guess," the bartender agreed. "You know who killed him?"

Pearl Lewis shifted in her seat, clearly uncomfortable with the bartender's sudden recovery from amnesia.

"I will in a few days when I get the ballistics back on the murder weapon. Anything else I should know?" Con asked the bartender.

"No. Just ate his dinner, had a couple of drinks, and left."

Pearl rolled her eyes as the bartender admitted to presumably serving liquor to someone, obviously Indian, who later was murdered.

"Where did he go?"

"Upstairs."

"Took the stairs?"

"The elevator."

Pearl could hardly believe how freely the bartender spilled his guts out to the sheriff. "Why don't you just tell him what size underwear you have on, Bob?" she asked incredulously.

"He didn't ask," Bob answered, not understanding a connection.

Con stifled his urge to grin and turned his attention to the madam. "I've already arrested Dutch on other charges that will send him to prison for several years. Is there something you'd like to add that happened that night, Pearl?"

This bit of news clearly set her on her heels. "What charges?"

"Extortion. Cut and dried case."

Pearl's demeanor took on a much more serious tone. "Pour me another drink, Bob," she ordered, "and whatever the sheriff would like."

The bartender looked questioningly to Con.

"Coca-Cola," he stated.

"Bring them over," Pearl told Bob, then turned to Con. "We need to talk privately," she told him as she snuffed out her cigarette and led the way with the remainder of her current drink to a table across the room. She emptied her glass as she walked and sat it on the table when she took her seat. Con sat down across from her as she lit up another cigarette. Pearl had yet to utter a word when Bob brought their drinks a moment later. She took a long sip through her straw. Con opted suspiciously to refrain from drinking his Coca-Cola, wary that Bob may have slipped him a Mickey Finn. Pearl did not seem to notice.

"You weren't surprised when I told you he was murdered." Con tapped on the pocket containing Jimmy Garza's photograph.

"Jimmy came up early, around eight o'clock," she began. "He'd been drinking, which was rare for him because he couldn't hold his liquor, but he wasn't drunk. I sent him to Janet. They'd been together before. Jimmy was gentle. Janet doesn't like rough." Pearl puffed on her cigarette and took another sip of her drink.

Con knew he had not mentioned Jimmy Garza's name. Pearl obviously knew him.

"I knew we'd be busy soon, so I decided to go down to the bar on the ground floor and have a sandwich while we were still slow," the madam continued. "I had finished my sandwich and was drinking a glass of tea when Jimmy came down the stairs about eight thirty. He went straight to the door of Dutch's office and knocked, then went in. It was already getting noisy and I didn't hear Dutch invite him in from where I sat." Pearl took a long draw on her cigarette and flicked ashes into the ashtray beside her drink as she slowly exhaled the smoke. She started to pick up her drink, then sat it back down.

"A few minutes later, Dutch came out of his office. He put something into his pants pocket as he closed the door behind him." She paused and took a sip of her drink. "There was blood on his right hand. He wiped it off with his handkerchief. I thought he'd bloodied Jimmy's nose. He went into the restroom." Pearl toyed with her cigarette in the ashtray and Con thought her eyes looked moister than they had a moment ago.

"Are you okay?" he asked.

She nodded her head. "When Dutch came out of the restroom, he went straight downstairs. A minute later, Sal came up. He glanced around the room, then went into Dutch's office and closed the door. A little while later, the door opened. I could see Sal's hand on the knob. He had Jimmy over his shoulder and I could see Jimmy's feet through the doorway. Sal must have been trying to see if anyone was watching. I looked away. A second later, I looked again. Sal was rushing toward the backdoor with Jimmy over his shoulder. There was blood on the back of Jimmy's jacket collar."

"Then what?" Con asked.

"I came down here and got a drink." She held up her glass. "Coca-Cola with a shot of whiskey," she added as she took a swallow without the straw. "More than one actually. Dutch was drinking straight bourbon, the good stuff, by the glassful. He doesn't usually stick around down here on Saturday night, but he did that night. He drank a lot and gave away a lot of free drinks. He made sure everyone in the place knew he was here."

"An alibi," Con stated flatly.

"Absolutely," Pearl agreed. "When Sal showed back up at midnight, Dutch hung around for another half hour, then went upstairs to his apartment."

"You know I'll want you to testify too."

"Yes," she answered. "I will."

Con assessed his next move with the investigation. "I'll need to search Dutch's room upstairs," he told her.

"It's locked."

"Anyone have a key besides Dutch?"

"Not that I'm aware of."

"We'll break the door in," he told her as she raised an

eyebrow. "I have a search warrant," the sheriff added and pulled it from his pocket to show her. He then changed directions. "Is the Janet who was with Jimmy that night, Janet Rae?" Con asked.

"Why, yes. You know her?"

"Yes, I do. Her brother got into some trouble a while back. She helped him out," he explained.

"She's here," Pearl noted.

"I'll need to talk to her too."

* * *

Pearl followed Sheriff Armenta as he climbed the stairs back to the ground level of the club. Jesse and Hal sat at the bar drinking iced tea.

"Everything go all right?" Con asked as he motioned Ben and Whit to join them.

"Sure did," Jesse responded.

"How much money?"

"Seventeen thousand dollars and change," Hal answered. "Jesse and I thought about claiming a bonus from the county, but decided against it." He chuckled. "Figured we'd just end up going out and making fools of ourselves with that kind of cash in our pockets."

"Good call," Con agreed. "Hal, we need to take the rug from Dutch's office and check it thoroughly for blood stains. They will likely match those of Jimmy Garza."

"Gentlemen, this is Pearl," Con introduced. "She's in charge of everything upstairs."

Ben and Jesse blushed at the introduction.

"Pearl is going to take you upstairs to Dutch's apartment. The door is most likely locked and we don't have a key. You'll

break the door in and conduct a similar search of the apartment as we did in Dutch's office. There is little chance of
further need to guard the premises. Ben, Whit, you can join
Hal and Jesse in the search," Con paused a moment, "and
boys, same as the cash in the safe, there will be no sampling of
the merchandise while you're up there."

Ben and Jesse both turned a darker shade of red while Hal
and Whit grinned and nodded.

"Pearl, could you send Janet to the bar downstairs to talk
to me while these fellas finish up their work upstairs?"

"Certainly, Sheriff," she replied.

* * *

Con sat at the bar drinking his second Coca-Cola when Janet
Rae came down the elevator. She wore a casual skirt and
blouse with her hair pulled back into a ponytail and no
makeup. Her eyes were red and swollen. She'd been crying.

Bob sat a glass of iced tea on the bar near the sheriff before
Janet could cross the room.

"Good afternoon, Miss Rae," Con offered as he stood to
meet her. She offered her hand and Armenta accepted and
shook it.

"Pearl told me that Jimmy was murdered the other night
after we had been together," she began.

"That's true," Con responded. "Can you tell me about that
night?"

She glanced around the vacant room.

"Let's go over here," Con suggested, motioning toward the
area where he and Pearl had talked earlier.

"It was early," she said as they sat down across the table
from one another. "I hadn't even gotten ready yet when Pearl

knocked on my door and said I had a visitor. When I opened the door and saw it was Jimmy, I wasn't worried. He had been drinking, which I'd never seen before, but he was still his same sweet self. I asked him what he was celebrating and he told me he was mourning. Someone he cared a lot for had died a few weeks earlier and he was still sad. I told him that I would try to make him happier.

"He never wanted to just...you know...do it. We got undressed and laid naked together, just holding each other... for a long time. He was always so gentle. I looked at his face and he was crying. I felt terrible. I asked if he wanted to stop. I told him I wouldn't charge him, but he said no. I finally got him interested and he said he was okay when we finished. We went over our time a little, but nobody cared. I never saw his sweet smile the whole time. He said he was going back to Moapa and probably wouldn't see me again. Then he got dressed and left.

"I had no idea that something terrible was wrong or that somebody wanted to kill him. Maybe I should have...I don't know," she started to cry again. She was a nice young girl who under difficult circumstances had chosen the short way out only to discover that there was no future and no turning back. Now someone she cared for in this repulsive profession had been murdered, and there was nothing she could do about it.

"Miss Rae," Con interrupted her remorse.

"Yes, Sheriff?" She returned to the present. Janet admired this man sitting across the table from her. She respected him and seemed for some unknown reason to be respected by him, though she certainly felt undeserving of it. He just seemed to understand how hard life is and did not shun her for the poor choices she had made that landed her where she now was.

"A couple of hours ago, I arrested Dutch for blackmailing

Brice Campbell and his mother. I promised you a few months back that I would never ask you to do this, but—"

"You want me to testify against him," she interrupted.

"I've got a real solid case against him, but if it comes down to push and shove, your testimony could make a difference. You don't need to answer right away but think about it." He watched the wheels turning in her head. "Not that it's directly involved with the extortion, but I'm almost certain he murdered Jimmy Garza, too."

"But, why?"

"I think Dutch murdered his mother and Jimmy knew it, maybe witnessed it. He was in the way."

"The person who died that Jimmy was sad about?"

"Yes."

"I'll testify," she answered firmly.

"You don't have to—"

"Yes, I do," Janet Rae interrupted. "What do I have to lose? My dignity? My job?" She burst back into tears. "Oh, my God, what have I done?" she wailed, "How could I have sunk so low? I swear, I'll repay you."

3

Sheriff Armenta returned to the foyer to find Newton Campbell and Deputy Whitney Ellis in a heated, yet controlled conversation.

"How are you two doing? Getting to know each other?" he asked them.

"Do you have any idea how fast he was driving when he passed me?" the deputy asked his boss.

"Oh." Con thought about it a moment. "Sixty…maybe seventy miles-per-hour. Does that sound about right?"

"Yeah, but it's not all right," Ellis objected.

"Newt," the sheriff redirected the conversation, "how long would it take you to get to LA in your Auburn?"

The question puzzled Campbell. "Eight hours, I suppose."

"If you're in a hurry?"

"Six," Newt replied. "Maybe less."

"Are things terribly busy at work today?"

"What do you have in mind?"

"Deputy Ellis here needs to get three rolls of undeveloped movie footage to the FBI in Los Angeles tonight," Con suggested. "I think you should make it your civic duty to chauffeur him and the film there."

"Right now?" Campbell asked.

"And back tomorrow as early as possible."

"I'll need to stop by the office before I go," Newt told the sheriff with a grin. "Let Amy know when to expect me back."

"Sure," Con answered, returning the smile.

"Don't I have any say-so in this?" Whit balked.

"No," Con replied as he placed his arm on his deputy's shoulder. "Whitney, you're going on a training mission. You'll learn the difference of what it's like to travel very fast in a car that's engineered to drive that speed compared to herding a car down a road at thirty or forty miles-per-hour that was built to drive twenty-five like the one you're used to."

"The guy's a maniac," Ellis complained without conviction.

"I know," Con agreed in mock consolation.

As if on cue, Hal and the cameraman, Hank came across the courtyard with three film canisters. Hank demonstrated how the latch mechanism on the canisters worked that helped to avoid accidental opening and subsequent exposure of the film.

"Just to confirm to you the legality of our taking these movie reels," Con told Hank as he showed him the warrant. "Here's our search warrant for the Campbell estate."

"I don't need to see that," he told them. "I know you're doing everything necessary to find out what happened."

"I appreciate your support, Hank," Con thanked him, "but someone here may not want us to figure out what happened."

As Sheriff Armenta shook his hand, Hank's understanding

of Con's insinuation led to an abrupt change in the cameraman's expression. He suddenly realized that what he had perceived as an accident, may have been murder.

Con accompanied Newton Campbell and Deputy Ellis to Newt's car with the canisters.

"Do you remember Agent Mike O'Sullivan from the Bureau of Prohibition, Whit?" he asked.

"Yeah, sure Sheriff."

"Here's his phone number." Con handed him a slip of paper torn from his tally book. "When you get close to LA, call him. He'll tell you where to meet him, then take you to the FBI to get the film developed."

"Yessir," Whit answered as he tucked the slip of paper into his wallet. After placing the canisters behind the passenger seat of the Auburn, he moved his sedan and parked it alongside the road out of the way. By the time he climbed from behind the wheel, Newt's car sat on the road beside him. They were moving almost before Whitney seated himself. Con watched and listened. The Lycoming engine roared as the Auburn Speedster accelerated, disappearing in a cloud of dust down the graveled road. He looked at his watch, two thirty, and returned to the house.

* * *

When Con opened the door to the sitting room, in spite of the open window, it reeked of cigarette smoke. Mark McCoy paced the terracotta-tiled floor among a dozen butts ground into it. His gun belt, with empty holster lay on the coffee table. When he turned to face the sheriff, he stood a good four inches taller than Armenta. A blotch of faux blood stained his shirt.

"Mark McCoy?" Con asked.

"Yessir, Sheriff," he answered.

Wayne Garrard described this man as a good kid. Con was not seeing it. The flagrant disregard people in this business had for others' property repulsed him.

"How old are you?" Armenta asked.

"Twenty-five."

"You put out your smokes on the floor of your own house?"

"No sir," Mark replied. "I don't smoke."

"Sorry," Con withdrew, caught off guard by McCoy's answer. "This is a fine home. It irks me to see it treated like a warehouse…or worse. Parker?" the sheriff asked, motioning to the floor.

Mark nodded in embarrassment. He was obviously upset and Con felt guilty for jumping to conclusions. This young man may have just murdered his brother. To the sheriff, he did not look like a murderer. He was, however, an actor. Maybe a very good one.

"Sit down, Mark," he told him, indicating to a low-slung leather chair. One that Con recalled to be uncomfortable from an earlier visit. Con took a seat across the coffee table from him in a chair constructed in a more upright design. He planned the seating arrangement intentionally, in order to appear taller to the younger man. A subliminal display of his authority.

"Tell me what happened."

"Everything was going fine. We'd made a couple of mistakes, but this take was just like we rehearsed. I came in and confronted Matt about the money. We argue. I pull my gun. He draws just a hair faster and shoots me. I shoot a split second later. Me and Matt practiced it for hours and had the timing down just perfect."

"But your gun turned out to have a real bullet and Matt is really dead."

Mark's face paled as his eyes overflowed. "Yeah."

"Wayne said your shot was supposed to go into the floor. How did you manage to shoot Matt?"

"I wasn't aiming at him," Mark whimpered. "I just pulled the trigger."

"How long did you have the gun?"

"What do you mean?"

When did you get it from the propman?"

"I got it from Jenny right after breakfast."

"Jenny?"

"Jennifer Vance. She's the assistant prop manager."

"And no one else had access to the gun before the shooting?"

"I belted it on and never took it off until I came in here. I picked the gun up off the floor after the scene and put it back in the holster. I went outside to get away from the smoke. Wayne was already out there. Then someone yelled Matt was dead and we came back in."

"How did the gun end up back in the prop box?"

"Wayne had taken charge and had Joe bring the firearms chest in. I handed it to Wayne, Wayne put it in the box and Joe locked it. Then he gave Wayne the key."

"Joe's the prop manager?" Con asked.

"Yeah, Joe Vance."

"Jenny's his wife?"

"His daughter."

"Then what happened?"

"Wayne told me to come in here and stay put. I opened the door and Mr. Parker was in here. I told him I was supposed to stay in here. We talked a minute. He told me to take off my gun belt. I handed it to him and he laid it here." Mark nodded to the coffee table between them. "He left and closed the door. I opened the window and been in here ever since."

"Did you notice anyone acting unusually toward you this morning? Trying to distract you, maybe?"

"No." Mark shook his head thoughtfully. "Like I said, everything was going great."

"How well do you know the other members of the cast and crew?"

"Really well, most of them," he answered. "I've been working as Wayne's assistant for about a year. Other odd jobs off and on around the studio for three years before that. It's mostly the same folks on every picture."

"What kinds of jobs?"

"Me and Matt both started out as stuntmen four years ago. We'd play getting shot off horses at a full gallop. Getting throwed out windows in saloon fights. Jumping off balconies." Mark's mood became almost joyful as he reminisced. His face beamed momentarily. "We had lots of fun."

"So, you guys fell right in?"

"It was hit-n-miss. Work a couple weeks and make thirty or forty dollars apiece. Then hope something else would come along before we ran out of money. If it got too far between jobs, we'd wash dishes, do yardwork, whatever we could find. Then we'd quit and go back to the studio whenever the call came."

"Matt became a big hit pretty quickly then? What was it like working with your brother?"

Mark laughed. "That's kind of ironic."

"What do you mean?"

"We were both working for Mr. Parker on *Silver Sundown*. I broke my ankle jumping off a cliff. There were a few more weeks on my contract and they weren't about to pay me without working. Since I could still hobble around, they had me shoveling horseshit in between sets of sitting in a saloon as an extra. When they got done filming, Matt got the axe. My ankle was healing up and they liked the way I worked around the horses, so they kept me on as a wrangler." He chuckled. "I had a full-time job for fifteen dollars a week and Matt was back busing tables at a restaurant downtown where all the bigwigs go to eat."

"So how did he become a star?"

"A couple of months later, he's getting thrown down the stairs in a brawl and gets knocked halfway out of his senses. He lands at David Whitfield Fredericks's feet seeing little birds flying around in his head. Mr. Fredericks helps him up and says, 'That was quite a stunt.' Matt says he was just trying to make it look real. Fredericks says, 'Don't I know you from somewhere?' Matt's not about to tell him he was cleaning tables in the restaurant where Fredericks was eating dinner with friends a week before, so Matt lies and tells him he had doubled for him in some film a year before. A week later, Matt has a couple of lines. By the end of filming, he's had lots of lines and is added to the opening credits. A month farther along, he's co-starring and two months after that he's a movie star."

"Did he ever tell Fredericks the truth?"

"I don't think so. If he did, I don't think Fredericks would care now. Unified Stars has made a ton of money off of him."

"Are you jealous?"

"Some, I guess," Mark admitted. "Always have been a little. He always had a way of charming the girls. Just naturally popular, I suppose. I've continually been the outsider. A bit of a black sheep of sorts," he recollected. "On the other hand, he bought a big house in Hollywood and had more money than he could spend. People always wanted their picture taken with him and autographs. I live for free in his guest house and get to attend all of the parties around the swimming pool. What do I care?"

"Wayne said you had a pretty good role in this movie."

"Yeah," Mark scoffed. "Parker thought it was perfect to have real twin brothers playing twin brothers in the movie. Especially since it wouldn't matter if the nobody twin brother got killed off in the end. That didn't work out so well, did it?"

"No, I suppose not," the conversation ended as abruptly as Matt McCoy's life had. There was nothing more to say. There was nothing more at all.

"Where are you staying?" Con asked finally as he stood and rolled up the gun belt around the empty holster from the table.

"Out at the ranch," Mark answered.

"And Matt, too?"

"Yeah." Mark nodded without looking up.

"Do you want me to tell him?" Con asked.

"Dad?" he asked, looking up at the sheriff.

Con nodded.

"No, I will."

* * *

When Sheriff Armenta returned to the foyer, Deputy Jesse Slater and Wayne Garrard were still interviewing witnesses at the far end of the room. He stepped out into the front courtyard to find Dr. Hal Martin sitting on a stone bench in the shade drinking lemonade on ice.

"Girl from the commissary tent brought it," Hal informed him before Con could ask its origin.

"You finished in there?" He nodded toward the doorway.

"Yep, just waiting for you before I move anything."

"You have Mark's gun?"

"Tagged and bagged," Hal told him. "Didn't figure the prop box as evidence since it arrived after the fact. Everything else is where I found it with a bag waiting for it."

"Anything I should know about?"

Hal looked past him. "There's a reporter about fifty feet behind you coming our way."

Con turned around. "Stanley Olsen. How did you find out about this?"

"Good afternoon, Sheriff," the young reporter from the *Las Vegas Evening Review* replied as he handed Con a typed page. "This came across the wire an hour ago."

Con began reading the article. Announced by David Whitfield Fredericks of Unified Stars Studios at twelve forty-five today...only minutes after he arrived on the scene.

"Parker," he muttered under his breath.

"I've got about ten minutes to change anything in that before it goes to press...if I can use a telephone that is," Olsen commented.

"No, Stan," Con said, handing it back to him without reading further. "Go ahead and print whatever they said. In a separate article, tell them Clark County Sheriff's Department has arrested Director Hugh Parker on charges of conspiracy to commit murder and interfering with a criminal investigation. Sheriff Conor Armenta stated the incident is under investigation."

"Are you sure, Sheriff?" Stan asked in disbelief.

"There is nothing in that article that I said," Con told him.

"I'm not responsible for misinformation. Go in the front door. The first door on your left is Brice Campbell's study. The telephone is in there. Don't talk to anyone or report anything that you see on this property until I tell you it's okay. Understood?"

"Yessir, Sheriff."

Hal tried to stifle a snicker. "I thought for a minute, he was going to salute you, Con," then they heard Stanley gasp when he entered the foyer. "I guess he's never seen a dead body before."

"Where's Mark's gun?"

"Okay," Hal grumbled as he struggled to his feet. "I'll get off my ass," he hobbled into the foyer and returned with a cotton draw-string sack. He spotted Con near the rear of his pickup truck and started that way.

* * *

Hugh Parker had squirmed his way as far across the bed of the sheriff's truck as he could, trying to chase the shade as the sun crept across the sky.

"Where do I find Joe Vance?" Con asked him.

"You can't treat me like this," Parker spewed.

"Where do I find Joe Vance?" Con repeated, struggling to control his ire.

"I deserve respect. You have no idea who I am."

"I know exactly who and what you are. You're the slime from the spittoon at the end of the bar that hasn't been dumped in a month. You're the bigheaded big city idiot who is doing everything in his power to hamper this murder investigation. You'll get my respect when you've earned it and not a minute before. Right now, you're sliding backward so fast no one will ever catch you," the sheriff was nearly shaking with rage. "Now, for the third and last time, where will I find Joe Vance?"

"That gray truck over there." Parker pointed with his head. "Now are you going to let me go?"

Con reached behind the director and unlocked the handcuff from the chain on his truck's tailgate. Without speaking, he lifted the little man down and stood him on the ground.

"Ben!" he hollered to his deputy by the gate and motioned him over to him.

"Yessir, Sheriff," Ben addressed as he approached.

"This is Hugh Parker, Ben. He's a *really* important movie director. Take him over to the commissary tent and get him something cool to drink. Get something for yourself while you're at it."

"Is that all, Sheriff?"

"No, Ben. After that, load him in your patrol car and take him to the county jail. When you get there, tell them he is under arrest for conspiracy to commit murder and interfering with a criminal investigation. Tell them he is to be held without bail until I have a chance to confer with Judge Tucker about further charges."

"Those are both felonies already, Sheriff."

"Yes, they are," Con agreed, "and I have more than enough evidence for convictions on both charges. I'm not sure about obstruction of justice and contempt. I've heard I'm just a stupid cowboy, but however I look at it, I'd be willing to bet money if someone bailed him out of jail, he'd be across the state line into California before you could blink...and out of the country within twenty-four hours of that."

Parker stood there trembling. His already pasty face showed no sign of color.

"Be careful with him, Ben. He's a slippery little devil. Something to do with spittoons. I can't recall."

* * *

"Joe Vance?" Con called to the man in the rear of the truck as he stood at the foot of the steps protruding from it.

"Yes, Sheriff," the stocky man of fifty replied when he turned and saw him. "What can I do for you?"

"I have Mark McCoy's gun and belt," Con told him as Hal carried the rolled up belt the sheriff had handed to him. The gun remained in the cotton evidence bag. "I'd like to hear what you can tell me about them."

"Sure," Joe replied as he came down the steps. "Let's get over here in the shade," he pointed to the side of the truck. "It's hotter than the dickens in there," he added, indicating the enclosed van body.

Vance accepted the evidence bag as Hal handed it to him and reached inside. "This is a single action Colt revolver. Serial number ends in forty-one-seventeen," he held the pistol away at arm's length, squinting to read the serial number. "Just a minute." He moved out into the direct sunlight and repeated the process. "This isn't Mark's gun," he said as he handed it to Con. "It's Matt's. Forty-one-twenty."

"You're sure?" Con asked as he verified the serial number.

"Positive. I bought four identical revolvers brand new, two years ago; consecutive serial numbers ending in forty-one-seventeen through forty-one-twenty," Joe Vance remembered. "Dave Fredericks got forty-one-seventeen. Matt McCoy was the new kid. He got the last one; forty-one-twenty."

"So, how did Mark McCoy end up getting David Whitfield Fredericks' gun?" the sheriff quizzed.

"Hand-me-down," Joe explained. "Dave said to give the kid that one and get him a new one."

"Surely you haven't memorized the serial number of every gun on the set?" Con questioned.

"No, nothing like that," Vance replied. "I've boxes full of old guns that all the other actors carry. I just keep close track on the ones that shoot. Can't have some old piece of junk blowing up in someone's face."

"What do you mean? The others don't shoot?"

"Firing pins are all filed off," he handed the gun to the sheriff.

Con hefted the pistol in his hand. "So, you're saying this isn't the gun that killed Matt McCoy?" he looked accusingly at Hal for a mix-up.

"Now, I never said that," the propman defended. "I just said that isn't Mark McCoy's gun. It's Matt's."

Con opened the loading gate on the revolver and began to roll the cylinder. "Why the red paint on the cartridges?"

"Fingernail polish," Joe responded. "Blanks."

He rolled the cylinder over to the next round. No red mark on the bottom of the Remington cartridge. The dimple left by the firing pin in the center of the primer clearly indicated it had been fired.

"Well, if we find an extra blank cartridge laying around, we'll know where it came from and the likely vicinity of where the cartridge swap took place."

"Not as easy as that. We always leave an empty chamber for the hammer to rest on," the propman told him.

"Even with blanks?" Con asked.

"The burning gunpowder that's expelled when discharging a blank cartridge is not only painful, but can easily start a fire," he explained. "It's just safer this way."

"If this was Matt's six-shooter, how could the two gun belts get switched?"

"Guns, not gun belts," Vance clarified. "That's Mark's belt." He pointed to Hal's handful. "That scrape on the tip of the holster came from Mark's horse falling with him last week."

"Anything else we should know about?" Hal asked as he handed Joe the belt.

Joe carefully examined the cartridge belt. "This first bullet," he pointed out the cartridge in the first loop on the right-hand side. "Not from this truck. It's a Peters Cartridge Company round. I only use Remington ammunition."

"Can you show me around the truck?" Con asked.

"Sure," Mr. Vance replied and led Con up the steps into the back of his truck that was jammed full of every possible item that might be needed to help portray a scene in a particular way. The sun beating down on the metal exterior of the unventilated van body made the cramped space feel like the inside of a furnace.

"Where would the chest in the foyer normally be kept?" Con asked.

"Right there," Joe pointed at a clean spot on the floor whose square outline clearly marked the position. A cigarette butt ground out in front of it caught Con's attention.

"Do you or your daughter smoke, Joe?" he asked as he knelt down for a closer look.

"No," he answered, puzzled by the question.

"Who else comes in here?"

"No one. I run a tight ship," the prop manager responded with pride.

"Who has keys to the chest?"

"Well, Me and Jenny...and Hugh Parker."

"Parker never comes in here?"

Joe chuckled. "He would never lower himself to set foot into this sweatbox."

"Hal," Con called to the coroner. "Could you bring your camera up here?"

"Whadaya need, Con?" he replied in question as he shuffled into the crowded van.

"A picture of the outline of the firearms chest and that cigarette butt. Bring the cigarette with you, when you come out."

Con's answer brought a gasp from Joe Vance. "What the hell?" he muttered as he looked over the sheriff's shoulder at the floor.

* * *

"What do you make of all that?" Hal asked as the two old friends walked across the courtyard to the open door at the front of the house.

"I honestly don't know," Armenta replied. "Either Hugh Parker was in that van recently or someone is trying to frame him."

"What about the six-gun mix-up?" Hal continued. "Joe Vance sure seems to keep a close rein on everything."

"But he completely missed the cigarette butt on the floor."

Hal nodded in agreement.

"Suppose the guns got switched accidentally yesterday," Con suggested, "or even last week for that matter and nobody checked them close enough to notice. Say, somebody wants Matt McCoy killed. They slip a real bullet into the empty chamber of what they think is Mark's gun, then roll the cylinder around to be in the right position to fire when Mark pulls the hammer back in the make-believe shoot out. Bang, bang. Both guns go off, Mark kills Matt accidentally and the real killer walks away scot-free."

"What if," Hal began, "somebody wants Mark killed. They slip the bullet into Matt's gun knowing he's supposed to kill Mark in make-believe, but before that can happen, somebody else swaps guns. Matt gets killed instead, and they still walk away scot-free. Just killed the wrong guy."

Con put together another scenario. "How about Mark wants to kill Matt. He knows about the Remington cartridge thing but can only get his hands on a Peters cartridge. He takes a Remington from his belt and puts it in the gun, then puts the Peters in its place thinking no one will look there; shoots his brother and pretends he didn't know the gun was loaded."

"What about the wrong gun?" Hal asked.

"Maybe that's the only true accident that happened in this whole big *accident*."

"Could be," Hal mused as they reached the door.

Con looked at his watch. "I've gotta get Mark out of here so he can talk to his dad before the newspaper comes out."

"I'll be right here," Hal responded and resumed his earlier position on the bench.

* * *

Sheriff Armenta opened the door to the sitting room to find Mark McCoy accompanied by a young woman in slacks. His facial expression obviously gave away his surprise.

"Oh! Sheriff," the startled McCoy exclaimed. "This is Jenny Vance."

"Miss Vance." Con tipped his hat. "How'd you get out here this morning, Mark?"

"I rode with Matt."

"Okay," Con responded as he closed the door and left the two alone.

Jesse had finished questioning his witnesses. He and Wayne Garrard were standing together talking across the foyer.

"Wayne?"

"Yeah, Con."

"Where are you staying while you're in town?"

"The Hotel Nevada," Garrard answered. "Why do you ask?"

"David Whitfield Fredericks called the newspaper in LA and announced Matt McCoy's death," Con told him.

"Jeez," Garrard said. "All these idiots can think about is free publicity."

"It came across the wire here a couple of hours ago and will be on the front page of the *Evening Review* this afternoon," Con began. "Mark wants to be the one to tell his dad and I can't get away yet. I can't let him take Matt's car and I gotta get him to the ranch before the paper hits the streets and someone calls Mike McCoy. Can you drive him?"

"Sure can, Sheriff."

"I'll meet you at the Mesquite Café at seven in the morning," Con told him. "It's only a couple of blocks from your hotel. I'll buy you breakfast."

"I've eaten there. Good food," Wayne agreed. "But I know how much most of you sheriffs get paid. I'll buy." He grinned.

"I'll let you." Con smiled back. "See you in the morning."

Wayne crossed the foyer to the sitting room. He and Mark McCoy came out a moment later.

"Wayne," Con hailed them. "The key to the chest?"

Wayne dug into his pocket, pulling out the key, and tossed it to him. "See you in the morning, Con," he hollered as he and Mark exited.

"I can take the key for you, Sheriff," Jenny Vance offered as she came from the sitting room.

"Thanks, but I'll be needing it," Con told her. She seemed a bit miffed at him for keeping the key. It roused his suspicion. He followed her to the front door. "You could help me out though," he beckoned.

"How's that?" she asked rather snootily.

"Which cars belong to Matt McCoy and Hugh Parker?"

"The blue Packard Roadster is Matt's." She pointed. "Mr. Parker has a maroon Cadillac Sedan," she added, looking around the area. "I don't see it. It must be by his tent,"

"And where would that be?"

"Over past the commissary."

"Thanks," Con offered to her back as she strutted away across the courtyard without response.

"C'mon inside, Hal," he said and returned to the foyer.

Deputy Jesse Slater crossed the foyer to meet them.

"How did it go, Jess?" Con asked.

"Okay, I guess. Marshal Garrard added a question or two."

"Did you take a statement from him?"

"Yeah," Jesse told him. "I interviewed him first. He said he didn't want any other stories to influence his account."

"Smart man."

"Yessir and really friendly too."

"I know both of you are mesmerized by him," Con began. "I am, too. But in his own eyes, he's just another lawman. His career has been long and at times exciting. Most importantly, he's lived through it. I am grateful for his assistance and have told him so. He *is* a material witness and he reminded me of that fact. Please accept his advice with grace and respect. His experience is invaluable. All that being said, it's still our case, not his. It is our responsibility to solve it and no one else's."

"Got it, Sheriff," Jesse acknowledged with Hal's nod in agreement.

"Jesse, that first door on the left is Brice Campbell's study. Use the telephone on his desk to call a tow truck. Whit's patrol car needs to be brought to town and we have some cars to impound."

Jesse disappeared into the study and Con turned to Hal. "What did you find?"

"Nothing very unusual," the doc replied, "except this." He reached down and lifted the blanket that covered the upper half of Matt McCoy's body. "What do you see?"

"The entry wound is just about a perfect heart shot."

"Bingo. You win the money. Two inches to the center and one inch down from the left nipple," the aging coroner evaluated. "You can't get much more fatal than that. He was dead before he hit the floor. Maybe before he even felt it."

"Wayne said Mark's shot was supposed to go off into the floor. No bullet actually but pointed at the floor anyway."

"The center of his chest was a heck of a long way from the floor!" Hal exclaimed.

"Mark said he just drew the gun out and pulled the trigger. He didn't point at anything."

"What's the odds of making a shot like that by accident?" Hal cried out in disbelief. "Maybe one in a million?"

"Or even ten million," Con added aloud, though it was more of a comment to himself.

4

TUESDAY, JUNE 17, 1930

Sheriff Conor Armenta sat at his desk examining the briarwood pipe taken from the safe in Dutch Wagner's office. It had been wiped clean of fingerprints other than a small portion of a thumbprint between the bowl and the angled stem. He managed to lift it and sent it to Carson City for the state crime lab to identify...maybe. The pipe met the description of the small and curved pipe Leanora Campbell mentioned being missing from her late husband's effects when he spoke to her last week. There was a chip in the rim of the bowl. It was not new. Smoldering tobacco had long since charred the interior edges of it. The ledger from the safe contained entries that seemed to reflect those found in Brice Campbell's ledger marked 'Dutch.' The two authenticated each other. He picked up the telephone and dialed.

"Campbell residence," the businesslike female voice answered.

"Is Mrs. Campbell in?"

"May I ask who is calling?"

"Sheriff Armenta."

"Just a moment, please."

The distinct sound of footsteps dissipating into the distance as the maid left the room followed that of the receiver being laid down on a hard surface.

After a slightly unusual click, a new voice came on the line. "Hello, Sheriff. This is Leonora Campbell," she introduced.

"Mrs. Campbell, we arrested Dutch Wagner yesterday on extortion charges," Con informed her. Then heard approaching footsteps in the background followed by the click of the first telephone being hung up.

"I read about it in last evening's *Review*," Mrs. Campbell replied. "The headline was more exciting than the vague column that accompanied it."

"Well..." Con chuckled, now more at ease that their privacy seemed secure. "I didn't give the reporter much to write about, but that's not the reason I called. We also had a search warrant for Dutch's Oasis. Following the arrest, we found a few things that attracted my attention and a couple that might also interest you."

The bait piqued her curiosity. "What might those be?"

"A ledger and a small, curved briarwood pipe," he heard a slight gasp.

Leonora Campbell quickly regained her composure. "Yes, that is very interesting."

"I would like for you to see them. Could I bring them out this evening?"

"Yes. I will be home."

"Would it bother you if Mrs. Sommers accompanied me?"

"Not at all," she replied. "She's a delightful girl." June

Sommers had come to work as a secretary for Mrs. Campbell's son-in-law five years earlier. Her addition to his law firm allowed Leanora's daughter to stay at home in hopes of starting a family. In the small town of Las Vegas, news spread rapidly when the thirtyish widow and the bachelor sheriff began seeing each other a few months ago. "Why don't you two join me for supper? I'm so tired of eating alone."

"Well, I uh…" he stuttered, unsure how to receive the sudden invitation.

"Seven thirty?"

"Yeah, sure."

"I shall see you then."

Con sat momentarily stunned behind his desk. The Campbells were a wealthy…beyond wealthy family. The Armentas were sheepherders. The family was a bit more than simply out of his league. They were from a different planet. The only reason he knew them at all was from his investigation into Brice Campbell's death two and a half months ago. He thought about that for a moment. If it had not been for that investigation, he never would have met June…or her daughter April. He never would have fallen in love with her. He'd only asked that she might join him because of the distance Mrs. Campbell lived from town. He thought June would enjoy the evening drive in the country. Now he was going to supper. The fear of being awkwardly embarrassed by his ignorance began to creep over him. He looked through the open door at the clock in the outer office. Four thirty. Three hours until…until the supper…or his execution. He dialed the telephone.

"Robert Westcott, attorney at law," the voice on the phone greeted him. He sat there a moment letting its sweetness replace his anxiety.

"Hello, darling," he finally replied after nearly too long of a pause.

"Hello, Conor," her tone beamed through the telephone. "How has your day been?"

"Somewhat surprising," he answered unsurely. "What are your plans for this evening?"

"Leftover meatloaf," she replied, slightly puzzled. "Why do you ask?"

"Since you mentioned supper, do you think Joyce could watch April tonight?"

"Probably. What do you have in mind?"

"We're invited to Leanora Campbell's for supper." He heard a slight gasp. "Seven thirty."

"Why?" June finally managed to ask in confusion.

"I spoke to her on the telephone a little while ago. I have some things for her to look at. So, I asked if I could bring them out this evening to show her. She said she'd be home. I thought you might enjoy the drive so I asked if you could join me. She says sure, then tells me she's tired of eating alone. The next thing I knew we're invited to supper."

"Casual?"

"I hope so. I barely know casual, let alone anything fancy."

June had a very clear understanding of her boyfriend. "Are you nervous?" she asked without needing to.

"That wouldn't begin to describe it."

"Everything will be fine. You have met her a few times before. She is very nice. Casual for her is pretty fancy for you. Wear your gray pinstriped shirt. The one with the white collar and cuffs. No tie. Your newest blue jeans…and no gun," she added and waited with no reply. "Okay?"

"Okay."

"Pick me up at six thirty."

"Yes, ma'am."

"I love you, Conor." She hung up before he could reply.

* * *

Con pulled his sheriff's pickup alongside his nearly new Chevrolet coupe behind his house. He set the cotton evidence bag behind the seat of the coupe, then unlatched his gun belt, and rolled it up. He paused in thought for a moment, then cached it beneath the seat. Too often recently, he had been caught unprepared in difficult circumstances. When he closed the door, he realized how dirty the car had become. After filling a bucket with soapy water, he stripped off his uniform shirt and dove in to wash the car from stem to stern. In the warm afternoon air, the soap dried nearly before he could rinse it off, but with a little diligence, it shined pretty nicely.

He grabbed a cold Coca-Cola from the refrigerator and downed half of it as he headed toward the bathroom. The clock on the mantel read five thirty when Con passed it en route. One hour to pick up June. He filled his shaving mug with hot water and started running more hot water to fill the bathtub. Con went into the bedroom and set out his clothes. He finished off the rest of his Coca-Cola as he sponged the dust from his boots without enough time to polish them.

Returning to the bathroom, he brushed his teeth and climbed into the tub of steaming water. Even in the heat of the day, the hot water soothed his body as he slowly immersed himself in it. When he washed his hair, he submerged his whole head and held his breath as he rinsed the suds from it. The clock on the mantel struck six as he climbed from the tub. Con poured the hot water from his shaving mug, then began whipping the warm soap into a lather with the brush.

Spreading the froth across his face, he made four swift strokes with his razor across the strop then scraped the whiskers from his cheeks, neck, and chin. By the time he wiped the excess soap from his face, he had dripped dry from his bath onto the bathroom rug. The alcohol from the splash of shaving lotion stung and refreshed at the same time, cooling his face as it evaporated.

Five minutes later, he tucked his stiffly starched shirt into his jeans and walked out the back door.

* * *

The black-fendered, chocolate-brown Chevrolet pulled up in front of the house on South 3rd Street at six twenty-five. Con bound up the steps to be met halfway across the porch by June's embrace. He breathed in the fragrance of her hair and kissed her, then backed away to take in her beauty. She wore a flowered summer dress that showed off her figure, and heels that elevated her to nearly eye level with Con in his boots.

"You look and smell wonderful, as always," he told her as he held her hand at arm's length.

"You look pretty spiffy yourself, cowboy…and I caught a hint of Donna's foo-foo juice, too," she added with a grin in reference to the shaving lotion his niece gave him the previous Christmas.

"Are we ready then?" he asked.

"April is spending the night at Joyce's. They are probably enjoying their own supper right now, or she would be on the porch yelling to us." She smiled as she looked to her neighbor's house.

"Joyce has been very accommodating lately," Con commented.

"As well as your sister," June added. "We should do something special for both of them."

"Yes, we should," Con agreed as he opened the car door for her.

She turned and kissed him again. "It feels so perfect to be in love with you, Conor. I cannot quit smiling or thinking of you."

"I feel the same way," he said as he pulled her close with his free arm and kissed her again. "I love you, June."

* * *

After a leisurely drive out Pine Canyon Road in the cooling evening air, Con turned the coupe into the gate of the Campbell estate. A quarter mile further, they passed through the adobe wall that contained the manicured grounds of the hacienda. Newton Campbell's tan Auburn Speedster rested on the flagstone drive in front of the arched entrance into the courtyard. The presence of her son's car somewhat relieved Con's apprehension of dining alone with Mrs. Campbell. He pulled up alongside it. The dark green fenders of the speedster showed the same layer of dust from Pine Canyon Road as did the black fenders of Con's coupe.

Con retrieved the cotton sack from behind the seat after holding June's door. The bag now seemed tacky among the tile-roofed elegance of the surroundings. The couple locked arms as they strolled across the courtyard to the front door.

"Here goes nothin'," Con mumbled as he raised his hand to the large iron clapper on the front door.

"Or everything," June added, briefly unmasking the tensions beneath her pleasant smile as she stood poised beside him.

The large door soon opened silently before them. "Good to see you again, Sheriff," Newton welcomed as he held out his hand. "Mrs. Sommers," he nodded to June. "Please come in," he invited after vigorously shaking Con's hand.

"Thank you, Mr. Campbell," Con replied as he removed his Stetson and followed June through the door.

"Please call me Newt. I won't know who you're talking to, otherwise." He chuckled.

"Okay, Newt," Con blushed awkwardly.

"You can hang your hat here." He pointed out the elaborate hall-tree inside the door. "May I call you Conor?"

"Or Con would be fine," he answered as he hung his hat and started to leave the evidence bag.

"Bring that with you, Con." Newt beckoned. "We're in the rear courtyard."

"Your mother has a lovely home, Mr. Campbell." June finally broke her silence as they followed Newt through the long foyer toward a pair of French doors at the rear of the house.

"Yes, she does, Mrs. Sommers." He stopped and turned to face them. "Can we drop the formalities for this evening?" he asked. "May I call you June while you're here?"

"Yes, Newton," she replied. "That would be fine while in Conor's presence. Your mother may consider it a bit too familiar elsewhere," she added.

Newt Campbell blushed behind a very broad smile. "Yes, I believe you have assessed her quite well, June." He laughed heartily. "My sister Amelia is worse," he added. "Charm school took all of the charm right out of her."

"Perhaps I have misjudged Mrs. Campbell then." June giggled. "I had supposed your sister had acquired her proper etiquette from your mother's influence."

"As she and Dad gained affluence, Mother became more aware of their position in society and worked hard to overcome the diction and manners she'd grown up with," he revealed. "Inside, she's like anyone else." He paused a moment and became quite serious. "Never let her know I told you that," he added then smiled and let out another laugh.

June began to realize that Newton Campbell was actually very charming. He seemed to have the natural ability to put others at ease. She could see Conor already beginning to relax in his company.

"I've never actually lived here," Newt continued as they approached the French doors. "I was away at college when they built it and returned to Wyoming when I graduated. "As you both are aware, I just moved to Las Vegas recently."

At that, he opened one side of the French doors and held it for the couple to pass through. To Con's surprise, Amy, the receptionist for the Campbell's Fremont Construction Company sat beside Leanora Campbell chatting.

"Con, you remember Amy, don't you?" Newt asked.

"Yes, I do." Con nodded to her.

"June," Newt continued, "this is Amy Slater. Amy, June Sommers."

"My pleasure, Miss Slater," June acknowledged curiously. "Why does your name sound so familiar to me?"

"Deputy Jesse Slater, maybe? He's my big brother."

Con and June were both surprised by the revelation. Con spoke first. "Jesse has spoken from time to time about having a *little* sister," he emphasized the word, "always in the context of a teenager. I guess whatever he has mentioned has always been reminiscing of years past. Without knowing otherwise, I expected you would be fifteen or sixteen."

"We're far enough apart in age that we really didn't grow

up together," she shared, smiling. "So, I suppose that makes sense."

June glanced back and forth between the second love of her lifetime and the cute, animated girl nearly a decade her junior. "So how do you two know each other?" She truly felt guilty for her flash of jealousy, but she really wanted to know.

"I'm the receptionist for Fremont Construction," Amy replied cheerfully. "Sheriff Armenta has been in a couple of times regarding his investigation into Mr. Campbell's death," she quickly glanced at Leanora Campbell, wishing she had not mentioned her late husband. Mrs. Campbell seemed not to be troubled by the comment.

"Thank you for coming all the way out here, Sheriff," Leanora Campbell joined in, "and it is good to see you outside of Robert's office, Mrs. Sommers. I hope that neither of you mind that I invited Newt and Amy to join us."

"Not at all," June chimed in, "and please call me June."

"Very well, June. Would either of you care for a glass of tea?" she asked. "Grace is busy with supper, but I can get it."

"That sounds very good, if it's not a bother," June answered.

"Keep your seat, Leanora," Amy nearly ordered her. "I'm sure you and Newt have things to discuss with Sheriff Armenta. June and I will get the tea," she added, as she led the way back into the house. Somewhat shocked by Amy's demeanor, June followed.

Amy closed the door behind them and started down a hallway. June could hear Grace working in the kitchen when Amy stopped abruptly in front of her and turned to speak in a lowered voice. "Don't worry about Leanora. Once you get to know her, she's not nearly as snooty as you think," she waited, listening to the noise from the kitchen, then added, "I've worked for Fremont for five years. I had no idea how nice she was until Newt and I...started...you know...seeing each other."

No, June did not want to *know*, but could easily surmise Amy's wide-eyed implication. She could feel her face reddening, certainly Amy noticed, but she kept quiet. June lived in Riverside, California until about the same time that Amy went to work at the construction company. The flapper craze grew in Los Angeles a decade earlier. Influenced by women's suffrage and later, partially in defiance to prohibition, many women of her generation had become much less inhibited. June had been too busy trying to make ends meet as a widowed mother to concern herself with the trend. When she arrived in the rural desert town, Las Vegas seemed to be unaffected by the rage as far as she could see. Amy appeared to be living on the fringes of the mania which rapidly began to fade following the financial crash on Wall Street last year. Typical of most small American towns, by the time the latest urban fad caught on, it might already be passé.

* * *

"May I see it?" Leanora Campbell asked of the briarwood pipe Con brought with him.

"I've already lifted the only partial print that wasn't wiped clean from it," Con mentioned as he reached into the evidence bag. I'll send it with the others to the state crime lab in Carson City in the morning." He handed it to her. He did not need to ask. The tear running down her cheek answered for her. This was Brice Campbell's missing favorite pipe.

"His cousin had it made for him and sent it from Scotland," she began, "in 1922 if memory serves me correctly. The wood is special. I don't recall why. The chip in the rim of the bowl and the crack from it down the face occurred a week after it arrived. Brice and Gary Wagner were climbing in Red Rock Canyon..." The recollection brought a pause as she momentarily relived Gary Wagner's fatal fall and Brice's severe injury while mountaineering in Switzerland a year later.

"Fairly early in the day," she continued, "Brice somehow dropped the pipe from a cliff. It fell a hundred feet or yards; the details elude me. They spent most of the day searching for it. Just before dusk Gary discovered it wedged between two large boulders. It took all their strength for the two men to move the smaller boulder of the two and retrieve it. That's the kind of friend Gary was to your father." She looked at Newt. "There was a chip in the mouthpiece too. Brice cut his tongue on it a couple of times, so he filed it down." She held it up, eyeing the profile. "You can see how the bottom is thinner than the top. There is not another like it anywhere." She handed it to Newt. "This is your father's pipe."

It did not surprise Conor Armenta that the briarwood pipe belonged to Brice Campbell. Leanora's inspection and detailed identification were both thorough and convincing. That he had overlooked the hairline crack in the bowl humbled him.

"The evidence leaves little doubt in my mind that Dutch Wagner killed Brice Campbell and kept the pipe as some sort of morbid trophy," Con resolved. "The challenge now will be convincing a jury that I was mistaken a few months ago in concluding Mr. Campbell's death was a suicide, then persuading them that I'm not again mistaken with the allegation of murder."

Katherine Wagner had written a letter to her daughter

describing, among other things, her son's hatred of Brice Campbell.

"The real question is," Armenta continued. "Will Katherine's letter to her daughter and the pipe be significant enough proof to deliver a conviction?"

Leanora and Newton Campbell both sat silently assessing how this new information contributed to understanding the chain of events that led to the death of their beloved husband and father.

As Con exchanged the pipe for the ledger book in his evidence bag, June and Amy brought out glasses of iced tea accompanied by a pitcher for refills. The courtyard was located on the east side of the house. An abundance of nearby vegetation along with shade from the afternoon sun created a cool oasis-like setting for evening relaxation. The pleasant atmosphere helped ease some of the anxiety created by the unnerving circumstances. Leanora Campbell began to regain her composure while Con opened the ledger to page four and handed it to her. Ironically, the book from Dutch's safe, strongly resembled the one labeled 'Dutch' from Brice Campbell's study.

"The 'B.C.' on the top of the page seems to indicate 'Brice Campbell,'" he told her. "The entries on the next few pages appear to mirror those in Mr. Campbell's ledger marked 'Dutch.' I haven't had the opportunity to compare them precisely. All of the other notations look to regard liquor sales and purchases."

"Will you excuse me, please?" she asked after examining the pages.

Mrs. Campbell laid the book down on the large round table and went into the house. A moment later she returned with a file-folder. Laying the folder beside the ledger, she extracted several loose pages and began comparing the documents with the annotations.

"They are identical," she announced to the sheriff. "I copied Brice's ledger before I gave it to you," she explained.

Con returned the book to his cotton sack.

"Now what?" Newton asked.

"I'll need to discuss it with Judge Tucker and the district attorney, but I think the order that the cases are presented and whether they should be lumped together or tried individually will be crucial."

"What do *you* think?" Leanora now asked.

"The ledgers and Mrs. Wagner's letter provide solid evidence for two cases of extortion. Dutch has already been arrested on those charges. I think they will want to try them first...and together," he clarified. "I doubt the prosecutor will have much trouble getting a conviction and suspect it will result in a lengthy jail sentence.

"During our visit to Dutch's Oasis," the sheriff continued, "one of Dutch's confederates thought he had been made a scapegoat in the killing of Jimmy Garza. He started spewing accusations naming Dutch in that murder. I charged the henchman for that murder, which will probably be reduced to aiding and abetting or conspiracy. An eyewitness saw Jimmy entering Dutch's office on the evening of his murder, then Dutch wiping blood from his hands when he left a few minutes later. All of this concluded with the cohort going in and carrying Garza's body out a short time later."

"What about Mrs. Wagner?" Newt inquired.

"In her letter, she described Dutch both verbally and physically abusing her," Con told him. "And she instructed, 'Call the sheriff. Dutch has killed me.'" He paused then added, "I also have hearsay evidence that Dutch kidnapped her or had her kidnapped and held her captive for several months in a remote location. Jimmy Garza was involved with part of that and probably later witnessed her murder. Both he and Katherine Wagner were killed with a gun of the same caliber that Dutch had in his possession when he was arrested. It'll be a few days before we have results from ballistics."

Con's disclosures significantly dampened the mood of the evening.

"Well, Conor." Leanora finally broke the silence. "You have certainly given us a lot to think about. I had just begun to accept that Brice had killed himself. Now it seems he was murdered. Then Katherine, and now this Indian boy; I had no idea how complicated it all was. You are a remarkable investigator to have pieced it all together."

"Not that remarkable," he replied solemnly. "I totally missed Mr. Campbell's murder."

"You were unaware of the pipe," she excused his oversight. "Soon after you knew about it, you discovered your error. That," she emphasized, "is remarkable."

Cooling air helped calm the evening's intensity and conversation became much more casual as the quintet sipped their iced teas. At eight o'clock sharp, Grace announced that supper was ready.

"I had planned to eat in the dining room," Leanora declared, "but it is so pleasant outside this evening, would you mind eating here?" she asked her guests.

"Not at all," June answered, and everyone agreed.

Amy offered her and June's services to assist Grace in changing the dining area. Soon they had moved the dinnerware to the outdoor table where Grace immediately began serving the meal. The main course was beef Wellington, which neither June nor Conor had ever seen, let alone eaten before. It amazed Con that what appeared a small serving, filled him nearly beyond capacity. It was very rich.

After the meal, while they enjoyed peach pie and coffee, Newt inquired, "So, what has become of Mrs. Wagner?"

"Her remains were turned over to Steve Rogers at Palm Funeral Home this morning," Conor told them. "Katie Brumbaugh is making arrangements. I would think the funeral will be fairly soon."

"Brumbaugh?" Newton questioned.

"Katie Wagner," Leanora interjected. "Katherine's daughter."

He nodded in agreement. "I had forgotten she was named for her mother. She was just a little girl when I left Circle Cliffs for college. It never occurred to me that she would be a married adult now."

"She and her husband run a very prosperous tomato farm at Logan. They have two lovely children, a girl and a boy. I believe she is a year older than you, Amy," Leanora stated.

Newt blushed at his mother's insinuation that Amy might be a bit too young for him with the eight-year difference in their age. On the other hand, he knew she was anxious for him to get married and provide her with grandchildren. He also realized that his sister Amelia, and her husband Robert Westcott, had been trying without success to start a family for several years. He was certain his mother was much more aware of the details of that situation than he.

It was well past nine o'clock. Darkness had fallen. Light from the foyer passed through the French doors partially illuminating the courtyard.

"It's getting late and I know June and I both have to be to work in the morning. We should be going," Con suggested.

"The meal was delicious and conversation pleasant. Thank you for inviting us, Mrs. Campbell."

"You may call me Leanora when you are here, Conor," she replied. "I have enjoyed the opportunity to let go of titles for the evening. June, I have thoroughly enjoyed your visit this evening. It has been a pleasure to have you both."

"Conor." Newt held out his hand. "It's been good to see you. We'll have to get together again."

"Newt, Amy." Con nodded after shaking Newt's hand.

"Amy," June said. "It has been very nice to meet you and have the opportunity to get acquainted. Newton, it has also been nice to see you outside of business, and Mrs. Campbell, Leanora," she corrected after receiving a scowl, "I have enjoyed getting to visit on a more personal basis. Thank you so much for your hospitality and the splendid supper, I cannot recall ever having a more delicious meal."

After a few more minutes of small talk, Con collected his evidence bag, Leanora escorted them to the front door, Con grabbed his Stetson, and they went on their way. As he held June's door, the two marveled at the star-filled sky.

"This is what I miss the most from growing up herding sheep," Con mused. "There is nothing quite as majestic as a moonless night sky when you're far away from lights of town."

June pulled herself close to him. She could feel her heartbeat as her chest pressed against his. Then she kissed him more romantically than ever before.

"Or more beautiful than you beneath it," he added.

June had difficulty controlling her breathing. She felt Con almost gasping for breath against her chest. Her whole body seemed to quiver. She stepped back and seated herself, quickly lifting her feet into the car so Con would close the door.

He climbed behind the wheel and they pulled out of the driveway without speaking. Moments after turning onto Pine Canyon Road, Newt's tan Auburn sprinted around them. Newton honked the horn and both he and Amy waved cheerily from the open cockpit as they sped past laughing and smiling.

"They seem to be in a hurry," June commented with a slight giggle.

"I think Newt is always in a hurry when he's driving that car. It seems to bring him joy."

A half mile down the road, the Auburn slowed and made the turn into the Muleskinner's Rest, Newton's own, more modest rancho. June watched the taillight disappearing down the driveway as they drove past. They both returned to silence. June stared out the window at the stars trying to control her emotions, but almost not wanting to. The faint glow on the distant horizon ahead almost resembled a halo. Las Vegas.

"You know they are intimate," June said quietly. She heard the words, but it was almost as if someone else had spoken them.

"I suspected as much," Conor replied flatly.

"Amy all but came out and said it," June added in exasperation. She bit her lip. She did not want to sound annoyed, or frustrated, or especially jealous. Why was she talking about it? Con nodded and continued to look straight ahead without commenting. *Why won't he say anything?*

"Does it bother you that we don't?" That should get a response she thought...but it didn't. They continued down the road in silence.

"I never really considered it," he finally observed.

She paused, rolling the whole notion over in her mind. She

found his remark almost unbelievable. He is just being a gentleman. He is such a gentleman. Any man would consider it. He has to have considered it. "Conor, you know that I love you dearly," she finally replied.

"Does it bother you?" he asked. "Not that you love me, that we haven't...done that?"

"When we kissed by the car," she said. "I could hardly catch my breath. I could feel your breathing against my chest. My legs were shaking. I could hardly stand. I know you had to feel that, too." Her emotions ran rampant just remembering the moment.

"Yes, I did feel that, too," he answered. "June, I love you more than anything."

"I obviously lost my virginity a long time ago," she nearly whispered, trying to convince herself that it would be okay.

Con was slow to react. June had just offered herself up to him...completely. "Did you lose your virtue then too?"

She burst into tears. "No, Conor," she babbled. "I did not. I love you like I never dreamed I could love any man. I will give myself to you...gladly. I want...I don't want you to be disappointed in me...I want to make you happy."

"You do make me happy."

5

C onor Armenta arose early and made a pot of coffee before sunrise. After pouring his first cup of the morning, he carried it barefoot to his front porch in a tee-shirt and jeans just as the first beams of light stroked the rooftops of the neighborhood. Tuesday's edition of the *Las Vegas Evening Review* laid in the seat of the worn-out chair where it landed from the newsboy's toss as his bicycle sped down the street the previous afternoon. Con had been scrubbing his car behind the house at the time. He glanced at the headline when he picked it up and sipped his coffee as he sat down.

REMAINS OF KATHERINE WAGNER DISCOVERED

The remains of Katherine Wagner were recovered last week

by the Clark County Sheriff's Department and County Coroner Dr. Harold Martin from an undisclosed location north of the city. News of the discovery was kept secret until positive identification of the body and notification of family could be made.

Mrs. Wagner had been missing since the anniversary of her late husband's birthday in September of last year. There was no evidence of foul play when she vanished from her home on Pine Canyon Road that evening. A modest reward was offered at the time by Mrs. Wagner's son, the owner of Dutch's Oasis in Block 16. There had been no information as to her whereabouts until last week. Mr. and Mrs. Wagner were long-term residents of Las Vegas and the respected owners of the Wagner Trucking Company, a prominent business on Charleston Blvd.

Palm Funeral Home is in charge of arrangements. The date and time for services have yet to be determined.

* * *

Sheriff Armenta entered the rear of the gallery in Judge William Tucker's courtroom at ten o'clock. Court had been in session for an hour and showed no signs of ending soon. He took a seat in the back row. An hour later, the gavel rang following the announcement of a two-hour recess for lunch. After the room cleared, Con crossed the room. At the door into the judge's chambers, he knocked. The bailiff answered the door, suspiciously eyeing the evidence bag tucked under the sheriff's arm.

"Come in, Sheriff," Tucker invited from behind his desk. "You can wait outside, bailiff."

Con entered and closed the door behind him.

"Had Dutch in here first thing yesterday morning with a young lawyer out of LA," the judge began. "When I set bail at two hundred grand cash, I thought the lawyer was going to choke. When the other fella you arrested appeared, he just pled not guilty and didn't ask for bail after that."

Con had difficulty suppressing his grin. Tucker did not try to.

"Sit down, Con," the judge told him. It was not an order, but he obliged as if it had been. "So, what's under your arm?" He pointed.

"From Dutch's safe," Con answered as he extracted the ledger from the bag and handed it over the desk. "Page four."

"Looks familiar, doesn't it?" Tucker commented as he scanned the pages.

"Yes, sir, it sure does."

"B.C. must be Brice Campbell," the judge added.

"That's my guess."

"What's all this other stuff?" he questioned about the other entries.

"My thought is, records for his liquor business," Con told him. "All initials and abbreviations."

"The feds will want to see this when we're done. I'll bet their boys can decipher most of it."

"And there's this."

"A pipe?"

"Yes."

"And that was in his safe?"

"Uh-huh," Con replied. "This is the golden egg."

"How so?" Tucker asked.

"When I went out to talk to Leonora Campbell last week about testifying against Dutch, she mentioned Brice's favorite pipe. She and Newt had looked high and low for it and hadn't been able to find it since his death."

"And you think this is it."

"I thought, 'Why would someone keep an old beat-up pipe in their safe?' When I dusted it for prints, it had been wiped clean except for one partial thumbprint on the bowl, up between the stem. I lifted it yesterday and sent it to Carson City."

"So, we wait."

"Yes and no. I took it out to Mrs. Campbell last evening, and she positively identified it."

"That's thin." Tucker scowled.

Con handed it to him. "Not when she described how he got it, every mark on it as well, and where and how they got there. In her words, 'There is not another like it anywhere.'"

"Like what?"

"What do you see?"

"Well, there's a ding on the top of the bowl there."

"And it isn't recent. Eight years ago, to be exact. See how it's charred?"

"Oh, yeah," he mumbled as he took a closer look.

"Do you see the hairline crack from there down to the bottom of the bowl?"

"No."

"Neither did I until she pointed it out to me and told me what had happened. Brice had just gotten the pipe from his cousin in Scotland and dropped it accidentally off a cliff while he and Gary Wagner were climbing out at Red Rock Canyon. They had spent most of the day looking for it when Gary spotted it wedged between two boulders. There was a chip in the bottom of the mouthpiece, too, but Brice kept cutting his tongue on it so he filed it off." Con waited a moment while

Judge Tucker tried to see it. "Hold it up and look at it from the side. The bottom is about half the thickness of the top."

"Well, well, well," the judge observed.

"Good enough for a positive ID?" Con asked.

"Three points of identification. That's very good," he agreed. "If we get even a possible confirmation on the partial print, that'll sew it up tight. What else did you find?"

"A little over seventeen grand cash. That, the ledger, and the pipe were all that was in the safe." Con paused a minute. "But Dutch tried to pull a .25 automatic on me when I arrested him. It and the bullets removed from Jimmy Garza and Katherine Wagner are all on their way to Carson City for ballistics and fingerprints too."

"Now, that's interesting." Tucker smiled.

"That's not all."

"You're kidding me."

Con shook his head as the judge picked up his sandwich and finally began eating his lunch.

"An eyewitness saw Jimmy Garza go into Dutch's office on the night of the murder. Saw Dutch come out wiping blood from his hands and go into the restroom. Then Salvatore Rizzo, the other guy I arrested, went into the office and packed Jimmy Garza out over his shoulder."

"Holy cow, Con. How do you get people to spill the beans to you like that?"

Con shrugged. "Oh, and the bloodstain on the rug from Dutch's office matches Jimmy's blood type."

"So why is this Salvatore guy up for murder?"

"He ran out the back when we pulled up out front."

"How'd you catch him?"

"I had Whit Ellis outside the back door with a shotgun before Jesse and I came in the front."

The judge chuckled. "Don't ever get mad at *me*." He shook his head. "But you don't have much of a case for murder against him."

"He thinks Dutch sold him out," Con said. "And Wagner probably will try to do just that. If you were facing the gas chamber and weren't guilty, wouldn't you rather get ten to twenty at Carson City for accessory or aiding and abetting?"

"You think he'll testify against Dutch to save his own neck."

"Yep, I'd bet on it and I think Dutch will try to hang him out to dry too."

"You have a good case built against Wagner, Con. I think we can slam the door on him."

"So, now what? Charge him with three counts of murder?"

"Hold on! Not yet. I'll put it in front of the DA. He's the one who'll have to convince a jury, or probably more than one jury. This could end up as four or five separate trials. We'll see what he thinks, but first we need to hear what Carson City has to say. This jewel"—he tapped on the ledger—"corroborates the letter and the other ledger..."

"And I've got another witness."

"What kind of witness?" Tucker asked in disbelief.

"Eyewitness to Brice and Katherine's trysts at the Hotel Nevada. Dates for some of it."

Tucker did not reply as he tried to swallow a mouthful of sandwich. He ended up managing to wash it down with his now-cold coffee.

"Where do you come up with these people?"

"Long story," Con answered.

"I hope you're writing all of this down before you lose track of half of it," the judge remarked almost skeptically before continuing. "We'll probably be able to bring up the murder charges as soon as we hear back from Carson City. After that, I can hold him without bail. If it looks like he'll bond out before then, we might just have to gamble and charge him before we've got all the ducks lined up in the gallery. Keep your fingers crossed until then. Now get out of here so I can eat my lunch."

"Yes sir," he obeyed as he jumped to his feet and opened the door. The bailiff nearly fell into the judge's chambers when the door disappeared behind him, but quickly caught himself.

"Con!" Tucker halted the sheriff. "Your work in putting all of this together...it's simply incredible. Your investigation has been outstanding. Good work."

"Thank you, Your Honor."

* * *

THURSDAY JUNE 19, 1930

June Sommers walked home from work. She felt tired, both physically and mentally, as she climbed the steps of her front porch. The emotional conversation with Conor on their return from Leanora Campbell's two evenings ago left her drained. Followed by two fitful nights' sleep, or lack thereof, she had yet to fully recover. As June reached the upper step, her eleven-year-old daughter, April, shrieked with excitement at her mother's arrival and dashed from Joyce's porch to meet her. When April wrapped her arms around her mother's waist, it lifted June's spirit. A boost of energy flooded through her; the fatigue became completely absorbed by her daughter's love.

June changed from her suit and heels into a housedress and flats before beginning their supper.

"Is Con coming over?" April asked as she helped her mother in the kitchen.

"I don't know. I've not talked to him for a couple of days," she replied. He usually called nearly every day, but the telephone had been silent. She suspected he might be upset by their frank discussion too. Their relationship had grown around sincerity with one another and she thought at the time, the subject needed airing. June now questioned her judgment. Had she made him think less of her? It remained the center of her thoughts for the past two days...and nights.

"You should bake a pie for him," April suggested.

"For Conor or you?" June asked.

"I would have some too."

"How about peach cobbler?"

"Mmmm" April smacked her lips. "That sounds good."

"Get the mixing bowl," June told her as she breaded chicken for the skillet. "I will tell you what to put in it."

Potatoes boiled on the stove, green beans were on a second burner and chicken sizzled beneath the cover on the skillet. June sliced peaches for the cobbler while instructing April on making the batter. All of the ingredients were ready for the oven as June finished making gravy for mashed potatoes. The cobbler baked in the oven as the duo sat down to supper at the kitchen table. Fried chicken made a sensible choice for them, June considered as they ate. In addition to being economical, one chicken could easily make, two if not three meals for them and leftovers could be served hot or cold. Though they lived comfortably now, before coming to Las Vegas they struggled. She had not overcome the habit of being thrifty and did not intend to.

It was seven o'clock when they finished their supper and June took the hot pan of cobbler from the oven. The aroma overpowered the smell of fried chicken, that even with open windows, had dominated the kitchen.

"Can I call Con and invite him for cobbler, Mama?" April asked.

"Yes," she answered before realizing he may think she put April up to it. So, what if he did. "Yes, you can." June told her his number and she raced to the telephone.

"Hello. This is Con," he answered the telephone.

"Peach cobbler," April responded.

"What?" he asked, trying to identify the voice.

"Fresh peach cobbler," she repeated.

"What about fresh peach cobbler?" he asked, after recognizing April's voice.

"I made it," she replied. "Are you coming?"

"When?"

"Right now?"

"I'll be there." Con chuckled. "Give me a couple of minutes."

"Okay," she returned and hung up.

"He's coming, Mama," and headed toward the front porch to wait for his arrival.

"That's fine," she interrupted April's enthusiasm. "We need to clear the table and do the dishes before he gets here."

"Yes, Mama," she answered in disappointment and stared at the floor as she returned to the kitchen. April filled the sink with hot soapy water while June put leftovers into the refrigerator. She knew the routine. Mama will wash while she dries. Then they will put everything away and wash the table and counters.

When they finished the chore, June rushed to her bedroom to change from her worn housedress into a slightly less casual afternoon dress. Glancing in the mirror, she ran a brush through her hair. She heard Con's car pull to a stop out front as she applied a fresh coat of lipstick.

"He's here!" April exclaimed from the front porch.

Con mounted the front steps just as June came to the door. He wore a fresh shirt and removed his Stetson with his left hand. The scent of shaving lotion drifted toward her as he crossed the porch. She wished she had thought of perfume in her haste. He put his right hand on her waist as he leaned forward and kissed her softly on the lips before speaking a single word. April sat silently on the porch swing as she watched them.

"How are you?" he asked quietly as their lips separated.

"Much better now," she whispered.

"And how are you?" Con asked cheerfully as he turned to the blushing April.

The sudden change in his tone broke June's momentary trance.

"I'm fine!" April answered with a beaming smile.

"So, you baked fresh peach cobbler. Just for me?"

"For all of us," she clarified. "Mama helped."

"I cut up the peaches," June explained, "and dealt with the hot oven. Other than that, she did most everything else by herself," she praised.

"Well, I can hardly wait to try it." Con smiled approvingly.

"It just came out of the oven when I called you," April replied excitedly. "It should be cool enough to eat by now."

"Would you like coffee with it?" June asked. "I put a fresh pot on when April said you were coming."

"That sounds great."

Con followed the two into the house and hung his hat on the tree near the door as he passed it. He glanced around the two-bedroom bungalow. He had admired it before. It felt clean, comfortable, and inviting. Taking a moment, Con compared it to his own one-bedroom house. Though smaller, he also kept his own house clean and tidy. June's furniture was newer and less worn, he assessed, but his was not shoddy. His house was a good place to live, he decided…but it wasn't a home. This was a home.

"Have a seat, Conor," June suggested. She poured steaming cups of coffee for each of them as he entered the kitchen.

A glass of milk sat before the empty chair across the table. April busied herself scooping generous portions of cobbler from the pan on the counter into three bowls, as June set the cups on the table and sat down adjacent to Con. She reached over and placed her hand on his without talking. He gently lifted his thumb and stroked her fingers in silence. April positioned two bowls of peach cobbler in front of them and returned with a third bowl to take her own seat.

Con did not hesitate to dig in, nor was he short on compliments to the cook. Certain April had prepared the dessert under her mother's watchful eye and careful instruction reconfirmed what a splendid cook June was. Fresh black coffee made the perfect counterpart for the cobbler. When their bowls were emptied, June refilled their cups.

"That was absolutely perfect, Miss April," Con told her as he sat back from the table sipping his coffee. "It could not have been more delicious."

April glowed with happiness. She finished her cobbler and began clearing the table.

"That's okay, sweetheart," June told her. "I will clean up. It's nearly nine o'clock, you should get ready for bed."

April skipped her way from the room.

"I would like to sit a while on the porch swing, Conor. Would you care to join me?"

"Yes, I'd like that."

"More coffee?"

"No, thank you. It's good, but I've had plenty."

The sun had set with darkness rapidly approaching when they sat down on the swing. June lifted Con's arm and slid up close to him beneath it.

"I love you, Conor. I want you to know it," she said as she snuggled against him.

"I know that you love me, June."

As he said it April came to the screen door in her nightgown. "Will you tuck me in, Mama?" she asked.

"Of course, I will," June answer as she stood. "I will be right back," she told Con.

"I really enjoyed the cobbler, April," Con told her. "Thank you for inviting me over."

She giggled. "Good night, Con."

"Good night, sweetie," he responded as she disappeared into the darkness of the house.

June returned a moment later and again snuggled beneath Con's arm. "She loves you too, you know."

"And I love her," he said. "She is a wonderful girl. You should be proud of her."

"I am. I can't imagine what my life would be like without her."

They sat a while in silence as dusk dissolved into darkness. Crickets abounded in chorus around them consuming the quiet stillness.

"You know that I love you, June," he said softly. "I never understood what love was like until I met you. I would never have believed I could care so much for someone."

She turned and kissed him, delicately, lightly. He returned the kiss just as tenderly. The sensation was new. It surpassed the physical desire she wished to succumb to two nights ago. She knew he had felt the same passion. He told her so, but Conor maintained better self-control; he backed away and would not allow himself to yield to the craving. Katherine Wagner described the feeling in the letter to her daughter as an addiction. This gentler display of affection felt easier, more controllable than before. They had reached a new plateau in their love for each other, surpassing physical craving with sincere love.

"I will learn to control my passion with tenderness and sincerity, Conor Armenta. That's a promise...no, a vow."

"And I will do the same, June Sommers."

"Katherine Wagner's funeral is Saturday," she said as the thought flashed before her in her reverie.

"I know," Con replied, surprised by the radical change of subject.

"Will you take me?"

"Of course."

"She called it an addiction."

"Yes," he agreed, realizing the connection.

They sat in silence for a long time, occasionally exchanging a gentle kiss.

"You were named for the month you were born?" Con asked, breaking the silence.

"Yes. Why do you ask?"

"What day?"

"Tomorrow," she answered modestly.

"How old will you be?"

"They say it is bad manners to ask a lady that question," June evaded the issue slightly.

"But I'm just a dumb cowboy with a gun," he responded. "I don't know any better."

"I will be thirty-three. Do *not* bring me a cake full of candles."

"What if I take you and April to dinner tomorrow at the Hotel Nevada instead?"

"She will love that...and so will I," June accepted. "Now you."

"Now me, what?"

"When is your birthday?"

"My birth certificate says August thirteenth, but Mama says the twelfth."

June's questioning expression was not visible in the darkness. "Explain."

"Stewarts' Rancho was the center for people in the community back then and Mrs. Stewart helped families with things like birth certificates. Mama says that Papa headed to the rancho the day after I was born. He stopped at every rancho and camp along the way to brag that he had fathered a son. Some of them offered him a drink in celebration. He got increasingly drunk and didn't make it to the Stewarts until the next day. Papa didn't speak much English then and couldn't write it at all. Mrs. Stewart wrote the letter to the state for him. When she asked what day, he didn't realize that he had drank one whole day away and told her, 'Yesterday,' which was the thirteenth."

"And?"

"And what?"

"What year?"

"Ninety-four. I'll be thirty-six this year."

"So, where were you born?"

"Their homestead. Where Patrick lives now."

"Your brother. The same house?"

"There wasn't a house yet when I was born. Just a sheep camp with a ten-by-ten-foot tent. Papa built a floor and walls halfway up before winter. The next summer, he made it into a regular cabin. It grew with the family from there."

They continued to chat occasionally as they held each other and swayed gently on the swing for another hour.

"It is really getting late," June finally said, "and I have not slept well these past two nights."

"Neither have I," Con confessed. "Seven o'clock for supper?" he asked as he stood and helped her to her feet.

"Yes, that will be perfect," she agreed.

She opened the screen door and retrieved his hat. Con pulled her close as she handed it to him.

"I love you, June," he told her, and kissed her more romantically than he had all evening.

She returned the kiss. As her breathing became more difficult, June pulled herself away.

"I have to stop." She gasped. "I promised." June quickly escaped into the house and held the screen door between them. "Good night, Conor. I love you."

* * *

FRIDAY JUNE 20, 1930

At five minutes past eight, Hazel called to Con from her desk. "Judge Tucker!" she said, holding up her telephone.

"Good morning, Your Honor," he greeted when he picked up his phone.

"Nothing good about it," he blurted out. "Get your butt over here. Pronto!"

"What is it?" Con asked in surprise.

"Dutch's lawyer just walked into the clerk's office with a suitcase full of money. He's waiting for me to sign the release so he can yank Dutch from the county jail. I'll have the warrant for murder filled out by the time you get here."

"Yessir!" Con exclaimed, nearly missing the carriage with the receiver as he ran out the door. He dashed next door to the courthouse and into Tucker's chambers.

"Get over to the jail and get him charged, Con," he said, handing him the warrant.

* * *

Sheriff Conor Armenta entered the door of the Clark County Jail with a warrant in hand seven minutes after he had received the call from Judge Tucker.

"Bring Dutch out," he told the officer behind the desk.

"To the holding room?"

"The visitation room will be fine."

Minutes later a guard appeared at the door to the visitation room. "He's ready, Sheriff."

Dutch sat smugly at the table in handcuffs when Con entered. The guard closed the door behind him as he left the room and could be seen through the small, reinforced window in the door.

"Gary D. Wagner, Jr.—" he began when interrupted by a knock at the door.

The guard cracked open the door. "There's a man out here with papers to release Dutch," he said.

"Send him in," Con told him.

A man in an expensive-looking gray suit entered the room. He seemed in his midforties and a couple of inches taller than Con, though the sheriff doubted the man outweighed him.

"Walter G. Tibbitt," the man introduced himself with an extended hand. "I am Mr. Wagner's attorney."

"Sheriff Conor Armenta," Con replied without accepting the handshake. "Have a seat, Mr. Tibbitt."

Con slipped the tether from the hammer of his Colt 1911 as the man sat down beside his client. Dutch noticed and whispered, grinning to Tibbitt as he nudged him with his elbow.

"Are you afraid of me, Sheriff?" Tibbitt asked through the side of his mouth with a mocking grin.

"Not in the least, Mr. Tibbitt."

Both the lawyer's and Dutch's facial expressions remained unchanged.

"Excuse me, Sheriff," Tibbitt continued. "I have posted Mr. Wagner's bail. I have the paperwork for his release."

As Tibbitt reached into his inside pocket for the document, Con's right hand moved to the butt of his Colt.

"I believe you, Mr. Tibbitt," Con's commanding tone drew Tibbitt's attention back to the sheriff. He instantly noticed the placement of his hand on the gun. "If you will humor me for just a moment." He gave the warrant, still in his left hand a slight wave. "This document was signed shortly before the one in your pocket."

"By all means, Sheriff." Tibbitt's arrogance dimmed significantly. "Please. Go right ahead."

"Gary D. Wagner, Jr.," he began again, "you are hereby charged with the murder of Brice Campbell on or about the second day of April in Clark County, Nevada in the year 1930. You are also hereby charged with the murder of Katherine Wagner on or about the fifteenth day of April in Clark County, Nevada in the year 1930. In addition, you are hereby charged with the murder of Jimmy Garza on or about the thirty-first day of May in Clark County, Nevada in the year 1930. Considering the seriousness of these crimes, you are being held without bail until the conclusion of the subsequent trials on these charges."

Dutch Wagner's face was nearly purple with rage. His eyes bulged from their sockets. The veins protruding from his forehead were larger than any Con could recall seeing before. If it had been someone else, he probably would have feared for the man's life. Not Dutch. Not now. He did not care.

"Mr. Wagner, do you understand these charges brought against you?"

"This is bullshit!" he growled.

"I'll take that for a yes." Con turned to the lawyer. "Mr. Tibbitt, if you will come with me, please."

"I would like to speak with my client, Sheriff."

"You will be allowed to. Right now, you are required to leave this room."

"Why?"

"Protocol. Are you familiar with the term?"

"Of course."

"If you wish to speak to your client, you'll follow it. I'm sure that it will be an enlightening conversation." He held the door for Tibbitt to exit.

"What's the meaning of this?" he demanded once they were in the lobby.

Con held up his index finger to the attorney. "Guard, take Dutch to holding and search him. His prisoner status has been upgraded to dangerous, and he is now being held without bail. He had physical contact with Mr. Tibbitt in the visiting room. If there is anything out of the ordinary discovered, return him to his cell.

"Mr. Tibbitt is now requesting visitation with his client. Search him to ensure that Dutch did not pass anything to him earlier. If anything is found on either attorney or client, visitation is denied. Otherwise, instruct Mr. Tibbitt on visitation protocol for a dangerous prisoner and continue as spelled out in your procedures manual."

Con turned to Tibbitt. "What was it you were asking?"

"Never mind. Can I see that?" He indicated the warrant.

"You can look at it. You cannot touch it."

"Why?"

"Protocol. Memorize that word. Do you want to look at it or not?"

"Yes."

Con spread it on the corner of the desk and held it for Tibbitt to read, which he did. Tibbitt then scribbled into a notebook.

"Satisfied?" Con asked.

"Yes. What's with all this protocol crap?"

"You came into the room. I told you to take a seat. You slid your chair up next to Dutch where you could play pattycake under the table. Dutch kept his hands in plain sight. You didn't. Keeping separated from a prisoner is standard procedure in any jail. You knew that but thought I wouldn't. Don't underestimate me, Mr. Tibbitt. I have two solid cases of extortion and three for murder against him, one of which was his own mother. I *will* attend Mr. Wagner's execution."

* * *

Con drove his pickup to his parents' Mesquite Café on Fremont Street. The morning had swept past with the warrant and turmoil connected with it at the jail. The clock read eleven thirty when he walked in and hung his Stetson on the rack near the door. He started toward a seat at the counter when someone hailed him.

"Over here, Sheriff. I saved you a seat."

Con spotted an older, somewhat rotund man seated in the corner with open collar and sleeves rolled to his elbows. District Court Judge William Tucker waved his hand beckoning.

"I saw your truck still in front of the jail," he greeted. "Figured you might stop in here afterward. How did it go?"

"All right, I guess. I thought Dutch might save us the trouble for a minute."

"How so?" Tucker asked.

"The way the veins were sticking out on his head, I thought he might blow a gasket and bleed out right there in the visitor's room."

"That'd be tough to explain." He chuckled.

"Not with John B. Lawyer sitting right next to him playing pattycake under the table."

"Did you catch him?" Tucker asked in disbelief.

"Guards were searching both of them when I left. I don't think Walter G. Tibbitt will try to pull anything very soon."

"Don't bet on it."

"High dollar lawyer out of LA thought he might pull a fast one on us. Didn't work. I think he's done." Con scoffed at Tucker's lack of confidence.

"Wally Tibbitt isn't from LA, he's out of Chicago. Works for the big boys. Doesn't lose many cases."

"I thought you said he was from LA?"

"That was some kid they sent in for the plea. This guy doesn't mess with the piddly stuff."

"You know him?" Con asked.

"I made some calls. He doesn't charge by the hour. He's on salary for one of the biggest racketeers in Chicago. His boss doesn't like to lose."

"This guy's that good?" Con asked.

"If he can't buy the jury, their families start disappearing until somebody changes their mind."

"So how does Dutch fit in?" Con asked. "A couple of months ago, he was sweating making a payment on a bunch of new trucks for Wagner Trucking and sold his mother's house to do so. Now he can dish out two hundred grand like it's small change?"

"My guess is he's been running numbers out of the Oasis and washing the cash through the trucking company. The boys in Chicago are behind it."

"The seventeen thousand in his safe was probably part of that." Con surmised.

"Most likely," the judge agreed.

"Las Vegas isn't big enough for those guys to even bother with. Why would they be spending so much to save Dutch's keister?"

"He's in on the ground floor. Work the bugs out now; he'll be all set for the big bucks when it hits."

"When what hits?" Con asked.

"When ten thousand workers hit those camps at Boulder next year and can't wait to get to town with more money than they ever saw before," Tucker exclaimed. "Ripe as cherries for the picking."

"They came into town with a lot of cash to get Dutch out of jail quick and back to running their numbers racket before it dries up and blows away?"

Tucker nodded. "Or one of their competitors comes in and sweeps it out from under their feet."

"But now their golden boy just made the leap from extortion to murder," Con added, "and Dutch's neck is stretched thin as a goose across the chopping block."

"Yessir," Judge Tucker commented. "Now the price of poker just went up...and you just threw a great big monkey wrench into their machinery. The question is, will they stay behind him or find another small-town hustler and leave this one flapping in the breeze?"

6

Thankful for the cooler days of fall, Sheriff Conor Armenta struggled in the waning afternoon to make sense of the bizarre death of movie star, Matt McCoy.

"How far apart were they standing?" he asked the coroner.

"I don't know," Hal replied, disappointed in himself for the oversight. "Nobody said."

"Jesse?"

"I never asked anyone that question."

"See if you can chase down some of the crew that knows. Cameramen maybe. Send them back in here," he added as he puzzled over the question. "I'd like to talk to them."

Jesse headed toward the door. "Hold up a second," Con halted him. "I'll go with you."

* * *

The white canvas commissary tent occupied a portion of the flagstone parking area just outside the courtyard. With the sides of the tent rolled up and fastened, it provided diners with shade at the picnic tables and opportunity to catch a slight, if only occasional breeze while they relaxed. After questioning had delayed most of the cast and crew from a timely lunch, the tables were full. Con found an empty seat at one of them where a half-dozen crew members were seated. One was the young woman who previously had told him he had a phone call.

"I'm Sheriff Armenta," he introduced himself as he sat down. "I know that it's been a stressful day. I'm sorry to interrupt your already late lunch, but could any of you show me about where Mark McCoy stood when the accident took place?"

"I can," a man answered, who Con recognized from earlier as one of the cameramen. "Within a foot or two anyway."

"That would be great," Con thanked him as the man started to stand. "No, don't get up. Finish your lunch. I'm not in that big of a hurry."

Con glanced around the area as idle chatter slowly resumed. "Which tent is Hugh Parker's?" he asked the group in general.

"This one right here." The girl from the telephone call pointed to the nearest tent.

"I don't see his car," Con noted.

"Molly left with it a little while ago," one of the men explained.

"Molly?"

"Molly Mansfield," telephone girl replied. "The leading lady."

"Does she normally drive Parker's car?"

"Sometimes. The studio actually owns it. They're both on salary, so I think it's okay."

"Yeah, probably so." Con tried to sound nonchalant about the subject. His problem was, where Parker's car was now? And why did this Molly take it?

"Come back over to the house when you're finished eating," Con told the cameraman.

Jesse had been talking to a group at another table and also rose when he saw Con standing. Con walked to Hugh Parker's tent and Jesse followed.

The walls were down and three ties on the flap held it closed. Con loosened them and they entered. Also made of white canvas, this tent was about fifteen feet square. Inside were a cot, a small table with two chairs and a wall locker.

"You need to get out of here!" a gruff voice sounded from behind them.

Con turned to face a rather large man about his own age, but half a foot taller and fifty pounds heavier.

"Parker is going to be hot when he finds out you've been in here," the man added.

Con carefully pulled the search warrant from his pocket. "Anything within a quarter mile of Matt McCoy's body is considered part of the crime scene," Con replied as he unfolded the warrant. "Anything not falling under that jurisdiction is covered by this," he added as he handed it to him.

"Sorry," the big man replied as he read it. "Nobody's in charge around here right now. I figured I better mind the store."

"No offense taken," Con affirmed. "Sheriff Armenta," he said and offered his hand.

"Bobby Hansen," he said, accepting the handshake. "Gaffer."

"Gaffer? I'm not familiar with the term."

"Lighting and electrical."

Con nodded, still unsure of what that might involve. "Who watches this place at night?"

"Security guy. Usually gets here about six and stays until somebody shows up in the morning."

Jesse stood silently aside, not wishing to anger the giant. He turned somewhat angled away. Beyond the man's view, he removed the tether from the hammer on his revolver...just in case.

"Do you mind?" Con asked, indicating the wall locker.

"Go right ahead," the gaffer offered, somewhat curious himself.

Con opened the locker. The left half was a wardrobe. On the right was a series of shelves with two drawers below them. A bathrobe and two shirts hung on the left side. The top shelf had two bottles, one of scotch, the other brandy. Both wore foreign labels. Two glasses accompanied them. The next shelf had a half carton of Craven Navy Cut Virginia Cigarettes. Made in England from fine Virginia tobacco, it said on the label. Con shook his head in bewilderment. If an American had a taste for fine Virginia tobacco, why would he buy his cigarettes from England instead of Virginia. Along with the cigarettes was a bottle of cologne and a box of prophylactics. Con heard a snicker from the gaffer when he shook the box near his ear trying to determine how full it was.

The next shelf was empty, so he moved on to the upper drawer. It contained a set of silk pajamas. Beneath them were two pairs of silk boxer shorts. He opened the lower drawer to discover ladies' undergarments. He lacked the nerve to examine them more closely. Con closed the doors and turned around. Jesse and Mr. Hansen both stood red-faced behind him.

"I've seen enough," he said. "Tie the flap back shut when we leave, Jesse." He walked out with the others right behind him.

As Jesse tied the tent flap, Con turned to Bobby Hansen. "Do you know about where Mark McCoy was standing when Matt was shot?"

"Yeah," he answered. "I set up the lights for the scene."

"Can you show us?"

"Sure."

*　*　*

When they crossed the courtyard, the cameraman and telephone girl stood talking to Hal, who had repositioned himself on the bench in the shade. Jesse slipped the loop back over the hammer of his pistol as he followed.

"I'd like for you to come in one at a time," Con told them. "I want your individual recollections, not affected by what one of the others might have remembered."

They all nodded in understanding.

"Ladies first?"

Telephone girl stepped forward. Con motioned her to lead the way while he, Hal, and Jesse stepped in behind. She stopped several feet from the blanket covering Matt McCoy's body.

"I'm sorry, miss," Con said, "but I haven't caught your name."

"Emily," she answered. "Emily Scott, but everyone calls me Em."

"What is your position with the studio?" Con asked, suspecting Jesse already had this information in his notes.

"I am Mr. Parker's assistant."

"What does that entail?"

"Kissing his ass mostly," she bluntly replied and instantly regretted it. "I shouldn't have said it that way," she blushed, "I run errands, chase down actors or crew members who are involved in the next scene, bring coffee or his scot—his drinks, and pretty much follow him around picking up the aftermath from his tantrums."

"So, you were present when they filmed the scene."

"Yes, I stood right here."

"You watched Mark shoot Matt?"

"Not exactly. I was looking down at my clipboard." She glanced at the sheriff's questioning look. "Following the script," she clarified. "If an actor makes a mistake in his lines, Mr. Parker has me read it back to them correctly."

Con nodded. "Where was Parker?"

"Sitting in his chair right here." Emily indicated an area a little bit forward and to the left of where she stood.

"What happened to his chair?"

She pointed to the half-collapsed folding chair laying near the wall behind them. "That's where it landed when he kicked it."

"He kicked it?" Con asked incredulously.

"Yes, when Matt fell, he thought Matt had blown the scene. He yelled, 'cut,' then kicked his chair over there and threw his script in the air as he stormed out ranting."

"Is that typical, Miss Scott?"

"Yes."

Con shook his head, staring at the floor. No wonder Wayne Garrard had said nobody likes him.

"So where was Mark standing...before you looked down to follow the script?" he added.

Emily Scott looked at the position of the lights, then around the room. Then she walked over and about ten feet from Matt McCoy's corpse, turned to face it. "Without the cameras, it's a little bit hard to tell exactly," she said, "but right about here."

"Hal," Con beckoned.

Dr. Martin pulled a stick of chalk from his pocket and drew a very small X on the floor at her feet.

"Thank you, Miss Scott. You've been very helpful." He paused a minute as she started to leave. "Where can we find you if we have further questions?"

"If I'm not here, I'm usually at the hotel."

"The Hotel Nevada?"

"No. Only the big dogs get to stay there." She snickered. "The rest of us are scattered around town. I'm staying at the Union Hotel."

"Molly Mansfield?"

"Oh, she's definitely staying at the Nevada," Emily replied, a bit sarcastically.

"Thanks."

The cameraman was more precise in calculating Mark McCoy's position when the fatal shot was fired.

"My job," the cameraman explained, "was to film Mark's entrance into the foyer, pivot my camera precisely in time with the actor so that the light behind him shining on Matt was blocked from the camera's view as Mark passed closely in front of it. The speed of the camera swing had to look smooth and end up peering over Mark's shoulder at Matt while avoiding the second light aimed back toward Mark."

Con had him explain it twice to make sure he understood

what the cameraman described. "So, your final view was of Matt over Mark's shoulder?"

"Not quite," he explained as he stood where his camera had been stationed. "Mark walked past me. If I did it right, when he stopped, I've got him from his right ear down to about his knees in the left half of the frame. The edge of the frame should just about split his back in half and Matt's full silhouette should be filling the right half."

"That must be quite a feat," Con assessed.

"Tell Parker that," the cameraman confirmed. "Just because we make it look easy, doesn't mean that it is. Hank understands it. Parker just orders it done and we have to figure out how to do it."

Con nodded in appreciation. "Hal, how far from this camera to Matt McCoy's feet?"

Hal scrambled through his notes. "Twenty-two feet."

Con had Hal measure. The cameraman stood within six inches of the distance.

"So, how far to Mark?" Con asked the cameraman.

"Half that."

"Come over here, Jesse." Con motioned. "You're about Mark's height."

Con stood Jesse about where Mark should have been standing. "If the momentum of the fall carried him a couple feet, Matt would have been right about here." Con stopped and turned to face Jesse. "I'm about four inches shorter than Jesse. Taking that into consideration, is this about what you saw in your camera?" he asked.

The cameraman held his hands up in front of him simulating an imaginary camera view. "Mark was about a foot to the left."

Jesse sidestepped the distance. "Here?" he asked.

"Yep. Right about there," the cameraman confirmed.

"Jesse"—Con's mind was working—"you're a good shot. We're ten feet apart. Could you draw your revolver quickly and shoot me in the chest from right there?"

"Not on purpose," he answered jokingly.

"Neither could I," Con agreed, smiling.

"But you did!" Hal exuberated. "Nailed that gangster out at them bluffs last spring, twice. Dead center…in the dark."

Con suddenly became more serious. "That was different."

All were silent for a moment. "Thank you," Con told the cameraman. "This was very helpful."

Hal marked where Jesse stood as Con brought Bobby Hansen in. The gaffer provided a nearly identical position to that of the cameraman. Emily's estimation had been only about two feet away. All were within close enough proximity to make little difference.

"Go ahead and finish up in here," Con told Hal and Jesse. It surprised him; the two actors had been so close together. If Mark McCoy truly intended to murder his brother, he looked him straight in the eye when he squeezed the trigger.

Con nearly ran headlong into the tow truck driver at the door. Deputy Ben Neilly was two paces behind him.

"Sorry, Sheriff," the driver uttered in surprise. "I didn't see you."

"Max, isn't it?" Con recognized the mechanic from Desert Chevrolet.

"Yes, sir, Sheriff." He smiled. "Someone called for some cars to be impounded."

"One less than I thought, actually," Con told him. "The blue Packard Roadster is the impound. I want it inside the county shop. I'll stop and tell our mechanic to wait for you. The other is patrol car number 3 sitting by the road out there.

Just drop it off in front of our office and leave the keys with Dottie."

"Dottie?"

"The night dispatcher," Con clarified.

"Yes, sir. Blue Packard inside the county shop and car number 3 in front of the sheriff's office," he repeated back. "That's everything?"

"Nothing else for now," Con told him. He turned to Ben. "Help Jesse with the body," he told Ben, "and anything else he or Hal needs. When you get back to town, stick around with the new guy until nine o'clock. If everything is going okay, you can leave him on his own and call it a night."

"Yes, sir, Sheriff," Ben replied and went inside.

Max had the tow truck backed up to the Packard as Con walked past. "Body?" he asked in one word."

"Read about it in the *Evening Review*," the sheriff told him and continued climbing into his pickup truck. He started it up and turned toward town.

* * *

On his way to the county shop, Con drove past the Hotel Nevada. No maroon Cadillac parked out front. After a brief discussion with the mechanic at the county shop, he continued to the sheriff's office. At five thirty, Hazel and Dottie were in the midst of their shift change.

"Max from Desert Chevrolet is going to drop off Whitney's car this evening and bring you the keys," he told Dottie. "Make sure that it's locked up."

He went into his office and closed the door behind him. Sitting down behind his desk, Con dialed June.

"Hello," June answered the telephone to his amazement.

"You surprised me. I expected April," Con replied.

"She's playing outside. Are you not coming to dinner?"

"I'll be there, but I'm running late."

"Is this about Matt McCoy?" she asked. "I saw the newspaper."

"Yes," he answered. "I need to question a witness that slipped away on us."

"Just how long are you going to be?" she asked suspiciously.

"About an hour, I think."

"Seven o'clock. That's an hour and a half. Don't be late!" she scolded.

"Yes, ma'am,"

"I love you, dear," she responded. "Get to work." She did not wait for him to stutter over an awkward reply and placed the receiver in the cradle.

* * *

Con parked his pickup truck across Fremont Street from the Hotel Nevada. The maroon Cadillac was nowhere in sight. He crossed the street and entered the lobby. The fiftyish balding clerk stood behind the registration desk. Two dozen pigeon-holes containing keys, mail and messages adorned the wall behind him.

"Good evening, Sheriff," he greeted pleasantly. "What can I do for you?"

"Is Molly Mansfield in?"

"I'm sorry, sir. There is no one registered under that name."

"I didn't ask if you had someone registered under that name," Con stated forcefully. "I asked if she was in."

The clerk swallowed the lump that suddenly lodged in his

throat. "Miss Stapleton has not returned to her room since she left this morning."

"Did Miss Stapleton stop into the lobby this afternoon? Pick up messages, maybe?"

"Yes, sir," the clerk croaked.

"From who?"

"I'm not at liberty to say," he answered, beginning to regain his composure. The sheriff's patience was visibly disappearing. The clerk cleared his throat. "You might check that ashtray by the chair over there." He pointed across the lobby. "It would be on yellow paper." He held up a yellow notepad.

Con walked to the ashtray and picked out a wadded yellow paper. He unfolded it.

2 p.m.

M.M.
Be in my office first thing in the morning!

D.F.

One cigarette butt occupied the ashtray. Red lipstick marked the end of it. Just below the lipstick "Craven" appeared in blue lettering with "Navy Cut" beneath it.

"Does Miss Stapleton smoke?" Con asked the clerk as he folded the butt inside the note and placed them in his pocket.

"Yes, I believe she does."

"Did she say where she was going when she left?"

"No, Sheriff. She did not."

"Did..." Con began when the desk clerk continued.

"She did say she would be back in a few days."

*　*　*

Taking less time than anticipated at the hotel, Con drove home. When he got out of the sheriff's department pickup, he removed his gun belt and slid it beneath the seat of his car before entering the rear door to his house. He shaved and took a sponge bath over the sink before putting on a fresh shirt. He looked at his watch: six thirty. On the front porch, he found today's issue of the *Las Vegas Evening Review*. Con carried the newspaper into his kitchen and opened a Coca-Cola from the refrigerator. When he rolled out the paper, the headline read:

MATT McCOY IS DEAD.

Los Angeles. Oct. 8 (AP) – David Whitfield Fredericks, president of Unified Stars Studios announced this afternoon that cowboy movie star, Matt McCoy was shot by his own twin brother, Mark McCoy on the set of Sons of the Texas Star, near Las Vegas, Nevada earlier in the day. Matt McCoy died at the scene...

The article continued much as Con suspected it would, a mask of drama and speculations. It said nothing, but stirred emotions of the fans and thus, he supposed, sold movie tickets. The next column to the right stated:

Clark County Sheriff's Department has arrested Hugh Parker, director and producer of *Sons of the Texas Star* on charges of conspiracy to commit murder and interfering with a criminal investigation. No other arrests have been made in the case at this time. Sheriff Conor Armenta stated that the incident is under investigation by his department and no substantiated facts relating to the case will be released until all of the evidence can be evaluated.

* * *

Con pulled up in front of June's house on South 3rd Street at ten minutes before seven o'clock. The aroma of her fried chicken drifted from the kitchen to the street as he climbed from his car. He crossed the darkened porch more than an hour past sunset and knocked on the screen door.

"Come in!" April hollered from the kitchen as she helped her mother with the final preparations of their supper.

He hung his Stetson on the coat tree by the front door and entered the kitchen. June turned from the stove, wiping her hands on her apron as she met him midway across the room.

"Hello beautiful," he told her as he took her in his arms and kissed her.

"It sounds like you probably had a troublesome day," she told him as they broke from the kiss.

"Troublesome," he repeated. "That's a good word for it. How about you?"

"Typing contracts mostly," she told him. "Tiresome, not troublesome."

They chatted randomly through their meal, Con taking care not to share details that young ears might repeat out of context in the schoolyard. His promise to help June with cleanup and dishes left April free to dash into the living room and listen to her favorite radio show before taking on her homework. They soon also relocated to the couch and snuggled while watching and listening to April's giggles from across the room.

At seven forty-five, June startled at the ringing of her telephone. "Who could that be?" she asked rhetorically at the rare occurrence of a telephone call other than Conor at that hour.

"Hello?" she answered.

"Is this June Sommers?" he asked.

"Yes."

"Were you the good-looking blonde dish at the hospital the morning Con was shot?"

"Yes, that's me," now bright crimson consumed her face.

"This is Agent O'Sullivan from the Bureau of Prohibition. Dottie told me Con might be at this number for dinner. If I'm not interrupting…dessert…is he there, perhaps?"

"He's right here." She held her hand over the mouthpiece. "Conor, for you." She held up the phone.

"Who'd be calling me here?" he asked as he went to the telephone.

"Agent O'Sullivan?" June replied.

He rolled his eyes as she handed him the phone. "Hello, Mike."

"You're not too difficult to track down."

"It's hard to keep a secret in this town."

"Am I interrupting anything?" O'Sullivan chuckled.

"No. What's up?"

"Your boys got here a little while ago. They just took the film into the darkroom at the FBI office."

"That's great. When do they think it'll be done?"

"I'm not sure."

"Did Newt say when they would head back?"

"He's taking a nap right now, so they can leave around four. They must have flown getting that Auburn here as quick as they did."

"Yes. It's quite a car."

"You must have a lot of clout for the county to pay what it must have cost to have him drive those canisters down here."

"He sort of volunteered," Con told him. "A matter of civic duty."

"A plea bargain?" O'Sullivan asked. When Con failed to answer, he continued. "Well, we've got you covered, partner."

"I can't thank you enough. I owe you a big favor."

"How about I come up and buy Miss Sommers lunchbox at the next social?"

Con laughed. "No, not that big of favor." He laughed again.

"I'll kick them out of town as soon as they've got a little rest, Con."

"Thanks, Mike," he concluded and hung up.

"What was that all about?"

"Newt Campbell chauffeured Whitney to LA with the film from the movie set," Con told her. "Mike got the FBI to develop it. Newt's taking a nap and plans to leave about four in the morning, heading back here with it."

"So, what was the favor that was too big?"

"If he could buy your lunchbox at the next social that comes around."

"Oh." She turned red again.

"That's not quite as bright as he had you on the phone a minute ago," Con teased. "So, what did he ask that made you blush earlier?"

"He wanted to know if I was the blonde *dish* at the hospital the morning you were shot...finally, he told me who he was and that Dottie had said you might be here. He was asking something about interrupting when I called you to the phone."

* * *

An hour later, Con stopped near the gate to Newt Campbell's Muleskinner's Rest. He extracted his gun belt from under the seat and strapped it around his waist. He pinned his badge to his shirt as he drove onto Leanora Campbell's driveway. As he turned off Pine Canyon Road, headlights and a bright spotlight came on, glaring from beside the entrance through the wall into the outer yard. Con rolled his coupe to a stop beside the sedan displaying the lights.

"Sheriff Conor Armenta," he announced through his open window to the darkness surrounding the spotlight. "May I get out?"

"Sure thing, Sheriff," a booming voice replied from a man large enough to be the gaffer's twin brother who stepped into view. As he came closer, Con realized the man was much older. He wore a dark Stetson on his head and a revolver lashed to his hip. "Bull Hansen," he introduced himself, holding out a burly hand.

"Con Armenta," the sheriff replied, accepting the handshake. "Bull," he commented on the nickname, "it suits you."

"It's short for 'Bullet.'" The big man chuckled. "Believe it or not, thirty years and thirty pounds ago, I was pretty quick on my feet." He laughed again.

"You related to Bobby?" Con asked.

"My son. You meet him?"

"Yes, I did. He told me there was night security but didn't elaborate."

"He got me the job six years ago. I think it embarrasses him that his old man got sacked from the LA police department because he got too old and slow to do his job after forty years. They offered a transfer to the night desk, but I don't write very good. I never could have done the paperwork."

"I'm sorry to hear that." Con could understand the man's dilemma.

"Yeah, that was a different time, but it's okay. I like dressing up like a cowboy and listening to the coyotes howling at the moon." He pondered for a moment. "Can I help you with something, Sheriff?"

"Have you had any visitors, Bull?"

"A couple of cars before dark who read about Matt in the newspaper then came out hoping to see something."

"Anyone last night?"

Bull became suspicious. "Just Mr. Parker."

"What time?"

"Late. Around eleven o'clock, I think."

"Did you talk to him?" Con asked.

"He didn't stop."

"You're sure it was him?"

"His car. Short guy with a white fedora. Yeah, it was him," Bull concluded.

"Did you see his face?"

"Not exactly, but it had to be him."

"How long was he out here?"

"Twenty minutes, maybe. He parked by his tent. Had a flashlight when he got out of the car."

"You saw him walking around?" Con questioned.

"It was a full moon. I saw the car pull up by the tent. He shut it off and got out. I could see the light bobbing around as he walked around to the far side of his tent...where the flap is. Twenty minutes later, he comes back. Fires up his car, turns around, and pulls out."

"So, he got something from his tent and left."

"That's what it looked like to me," Bull answered, but was beginning to question himself.

"If he was in his tent for twenty minutes, or even ten, he must have been looking around for whatever he came to get."

"I'd think so," Bull agreed.

"Did you see the light shining around inside the tent?"

"No. I can't say that I did," he thought for a minute, "but that's pretty heavy canvas," he tried to reassure himself.

"You have a flashlight?"

"Yep," Bull answered and opened the door of his sedan. Within easy reach, he grabbed the flashlight and handed it to Con.

"I'll be right back," Con told him and strode away toward Parker's tent. He walked around the far side and held the flashlight under his arm as he unfastened the ties. Inside, he scanned around the tent as if looking for something. He opened the locker and flashed the light around inside then closed it back up and left.

As he approached the two cars, Bull spoke up. "Nobody was in that tent last night," he remarked while shaking his head in disappointment.

"Are you sure?" Con asked.

"Yeah, I'm sure," he replied in the same, almost gloomy tone. "You shined the light into that tent; even with the moon, it lit up like a movie screen. I could see every move you made."

The sheriff contemplated the jumble of tents and trucks that filled the area. "Where is the prop truck?" he asked.

Bull pointed out the square box, barely visible above the white tents.

"Which way is it pointing?"

"The doors in the back are facing away from us right here," Bull told him.

The pieces of the jigsaw puzzle were beginning to fit together. "You're still friends with LAPD?" Con asked.

"Yeah, why?"

"If you needed someone arrested in Hollywood, who would you call?"

"Who do you need arrested?"

"No one...yet."

"Captain Fred Sanders," Bull responded. "You can tell him I sent you to him."

Con climbed into his car and turned it around. "I'll send a deputy out in the morning to relieve you. No one is allowed on site unless I personally say so. After tonight, we'll cover your shift."

7

THURSDAY, OCTOBER 9, 1930

THURSDAY, OCTOBER 9, 1930

At six thirty, Con stepped into the sheriff's office. Jesse Slater sat beside Dottie's desk, drinking coffee. If Hazel arrived early to relieve Dottie, they could have breakfast together before he went on shift.

"Glad to see you're early, Jesse," Con remarked as he entered the room. "I need you to go out to Leanora Campbell's and take over for Bull Hansen. He's the security guard for the studio. Grab some lunch to take with you. Don't let anyone on location except the gardener and the housekeeper if they are there. Someone will be out this evening to relieve you. Plan on twelve hours."

He and Dottie were both obviously disappointed, but neither mentioned it. "Yes sir, Sheriff," Jesse acknowledged and rose to his feet.

"Dottie."

"Yes, Sheriff."

"I'll need you and Hazel to arrange an extra deputy for night shift to guard the Campbell estate tonight. I will talk to Hazel later this morning," he added and followed Jesse out the door.

* * *

He hung his Stetson on the hook adjacent to the black one inside the door of the Mesquite Café. Con spotted Wayne Garrard facing him from the corner table.

"If you want to reserve this table every morning, it'll cost you extra, big brother," Olivia remarked haughtily as she refilled Garrard's coffee and sat a fresh cup down in front of him. "Huevos and chorizo on special."

"I'll have the special," Con replied, "and I'll talk to your boss about the table," he added, irked by her sarcasm in front of a stranger.

"I'll have the same," Garrard chimed in, grinning at their banter. "She's a real pistol," he commented as she walked away.

"Don't let those dark romantic eyes fool you, Wayne," Con told him. "She's all fire inside. I wonder how her husband can stand her sometimes."

Wayne let the comments diffuse and turned to business. "Anything in particular you wanted to discuss, Con?"

"I searched Parker's tent after you left yesterday."

The comment drew Garrard's immediate attention. "Find anything interesting?"

"It seems our repulsive director may entertain female guests there…intimately. Anyone in particular?"

"Off the record?"

"I didn't bring my tally book," Con eluded the clarification.

"Molly is his usual bunk buddy," Wayne replied in a lowered voice, "but neither of them hesitates to hop in the sack with someone else if the mood or ambition strikes them."

"Molly Mansfield?"

"That's the one," Wayne confirmed.

"She's a pretty big star, isn't she?" Con asked but continued before Wayne could answer. "What can you tell me about her?"

"She's done pretty well for most of a decade, but she's beginning to show a little age and she knows it. She has to work pretty hard to imply her youth on screen when they cast her opposite a young guy like Matt McCoy."

"And?"

"And she's a good actress...on camera and off. She can talk as sweet as maple syrup to a kid that's a half-dozen years her junior and convince him that she's in love with him while they're filming. He'll take the bait and fall head over heels for her. When they show close-ups, he'll have that lusty look in his eye that he hasn't learned how to master on his own yet and Parker will know exactly how she achieved it"—he lowered his voice again—"by riding the kid like a green colt thirty minutes before the cameras rolled."

Con blushed at Garrard's candid assessment and rural dialect. "What about Parker? It sounded to me like they have their own thing going?"

"Molly is pretty and a good actress, but so are five dozen more just like her. They are standing in the casting line every week hoping for their big break just like she once did. They're all a dozen years younger and Molly's a dozen years older now." Wayne looked around the room. No one sat nearby so he continued. "She didn't get to where she is by going to church every Sunday and prayer meetings on Wednesday nights. She's bounced from one Hollywood bedroom to another all the way to the top and Parker knows it. His was one of them. And he's certainly not above tapping into any stimulating starlet that offers it up to him in hopes of a leading role either. They keep the carpet in the hallway between their suites at the hotel pretty well-worn. Out there on the set is another story. It's more of who can manipulate whichever player needs guidance for the benefit of Unified Stars Studios."

"So, the title of 'Director' takes on a whole new meaning in the director's tent?"

"Exactly," Wayne replied as Olivia sat their plates in front of them and refilled their coffees.

"Well then, who has needed guidance lately?" Con asked when Olivia left them.

That question brought a rosy tone to Wayne Garrard's cheekbones.

"That distinction has belonged to the McCoy brothers, as of late."

Garrard's response surprised Con and encouraged his curiosity. "What's going on there?"

"Evidently Molly's been on double duty." Wayne chuckled. "Or maybe triple duty, I suppose."

"Explain."

"A month ago, Matt McCoy had a big party at his place in Hollywood. Outdoors by his swimming pool. Most of the cast was there and others too."

"You were there?" Con asked.

"No, but I heard lots about it. There seems to have been plenty to drink and as evening approached, a few of the men had removed the shirts from their swim costumes and only kept their wool trunks. It evidently wasn't long before Molly

decided swimwear was optional and she discarded hers alto-
gether. At that point, most of the guests departed, but a few
remained." Wayne cleared his throat and took a drink of
coffee. "It seems Mark had difficulty controlling"—Wayne
cleared his throat again—"*things*, with Molly prancing around
in her birthday suit. So, he jumps into the swimming pool
until *things* settled down. Now Mark and Jenny both had
aspired to become actors and have been dating off and on for a
while. Way before this movie ever came along."

"Jennifer Vance?" Conor interrupted.

"Yes. So, *Sons of the Texas Star* was Mark's big break and
Jenny knew it. She saw what had happened to him with
Molly's show and she didn't want anything to interfere with
Mark's acting career. So, she peels off her swimsuit and jumps
into the pool with him. That diffused the situation. Molly
latched onto Matt, and before long, they were heading into the
house. Jenny and Mark were kissing in the swimming pool
and everyone else pretty much wandered on their way. That
should have ended it."

"But it didn't," Con surmised.

"No," Wayne continued. "Not only had Jenny noticed
Mark's 'condition' before he jumped into the pool, so had
Molly. Nobody said anything about it except for occasional
subtle giggles around the set. Even those had subsided until a
week ago."

"What happened a week ago?"

"After lunch each day, everyone usually takes a siesta. In
their tents if they have one or a shady spot nearby if they
don't. On this day, last Friday I think, Matt and Molly had
gone to his tent after lunch. Jenny went to the prop truck and
Mark sat in the shade at the commissary tent sipping on iced
tea along with a few of the crew. A few minutes later, Molly

returns, grumbling that Matt laid down and instantly fell asleep. This got a chuckle from a couple of the guys and that got Molly seething. So, she comes over to Mark and says, 'I know you liked what you saw at the party. I could tell before you jumped into the swimming pool. Follow me, and I'll give you some of that, if you think you can rise to the occasion.' So, Mark gets up, and she escorts him to her tent."

"That's it?" Con asked.

"Not quite," Wayne continued. "The crew guys were still chuckling over Molly taking Mark off for a little joyride in her tent when Jenny came back looking for Mark. She asks where he went, and they won't tell her. Jenny gets hammering pretty hard on them and in between giggles someone finally says they think he left with Molly." Wayne lowered his voice again. "She goes storming off and straight into Molly's tent unannounced. Jenny finds Mark and Molly playing doctor and starts screaming at them. Parker comes running from his tent and grabs Jenny out of there. He helps her back to his own tent to *console* her. Pretty soon things all get quiet again. An hour later Jenny comes out of Parker's tent looking around sheepishly, then dashes back to the prop truck. A few minutes after that, Parker's yelling through his megaphone for people to get to work."

"So, another starlet is soon to be born following a visit to Parker's tent," Con concluded.

"And that future starlet fumed around the set and didn't speak a word to Mark McCoy since then. Not until yesterday after the shooting."

Con mulled over Wayne's commentary appraising the complexity and debauchery of the movie business that he could barely comprehend. What went on in the upstairs "women's boarding houses" of Block 16 he surmised would hardly compare. Furthermore, when Jenny Vance left the sitting room at Leanora Campbell's yesterday, she did not seem the slightest bit upset. Not with Mark McCoy nor the shooting. In some ways she was nearly as haughty as Hugh Parker when Con spoke to her. She certainly had the opportunity in her position to tamper with Matt and Mark's guns. She showed no signs of remorse. And now she had motive...just the wrong guy. And she would have noticed which holster, even if she did not memorize the serial numbers like her father did.

* * *

When Con closed his office door and sat down at his desk, it was nearly ten o'clock. Wayne Garrard volunteered to notify the cast and crew that the set was closed down until further notice. Con added that they were not to leave town and to try to remain available for further questioning if necessary.

He picked up his telephone and dialed the operator. "This is Sheriff Armenta. Will you connect me with the Los Angeles Police Department please?"

"Yes, sir. One moment."

He sat listening to silence on the line followed by a series of clicks making the connection and the sound of ringing on the other end. "LAPD, Corporal Reardon speaking," the voice announced on the second ring.

"Good morning, Corporal. This is Sheriff Conor Armenta in Las Vegas, Nevada. Could I speak to Captain Fred Sanders by chance?"

"May I ask what this is regarding, Sheriff?"

"A high-profile shooting here yesterday and a key suspect

who fled the scene. It's believed the suspect drove to Los Angeles late yesterday."

"Does this have anything to do with Matt McCoy?" he asked.

"Yes, it does," Con answered.

"I read about it in the newspaper," Reardon remarked. "How did you know to ask for Captain Sanders?"

"Bull Hansen," Con replied.

"Hang on a minute."

Before Con could swallow a sip of his coffee, a gruff but friendly voice came on the line. "Sanders here. How can I help you out, Sheriff?"

Con explained the situation beginning with his arrest of Hugh Parker. He followed that by clarifying that David Whitfield Fredericks's news release was unauthorized as well as his ordering Molly Mansfield's immediate return to Los Angeles.

The sheriff's commentary drew a belly laugh from Captain Sanders. "I'd have loved to see the look on Parker's face when you pulled your gun on him." He managed to quiet his laugh to a chuckle. "You're getting to see what I have to put up with on a regular basis, Sheriff. These Hollywood folks have a lot of clout in this town and they're used to throwing their weight around. They say jump and the newsmen jump. What they say sells papers. Same's true with the councilmen and commissioners. It doesn't garner too many votes to get sideways with your constituent's heroes. It becomes a popularity contest around here."

As they discussed the options, Captain Sanders made an offer. "Let me tell you what I can do. I'll park a squad car across the street from Fredericks's office. There's a callbox right on the corner. I'll have one of the officers call me and standby on the phone until we see what floats to the top. Give me a few minutes. I'll have Corporal Reardon call you back when they're in place, then you can call Fredericks and make your play."

"Thanks, Captain."

"By the way, Sheriff," the captain added. "How is Bull Hansen doing? He sort of got a bad hand dealt to him here. I hated to lose him just as bad as he hated leaving us. But we both understood the circumstances."

"He's doing okay, I think," Con offered. "He seems to enjoy the peace and quiet for the most part. That is until this shooting came up anyway. I'll tell him that you asked next time I see him."

"I'd appreciate that. He's a good man."

"I'll be waiting to hear from your corporal." As Con hung up the telephone, there was a soft knock on his office door.

"Come in," he called out, expecting Hazel to walk in.

"Good morning, Sheriff," Judge William Tucker greeted as he stepped in and closed the door behind him. "I hope you don't mind my dropping in like this."

"Not at all, Your Honor," he replied. "What can I do for you?"

"Bill," he corrected. "I've had a busy morning. By the nature of mine, I suspect yours has been too. I started to call you, but your phone was busy so, I decided to get some air and stroll on over. From what I've been hearing, it sounds like you were going to come see me about a couple of points of law this morning anyway."

"Yes." Con cleared his throat and took a sip of his cold coffee. "As a matter of fact, that was my plan, but the morning seems to be slipping away from me."

"I'll save you the trouble. You've got Mr. Parker dead to rights on interfering with a criminal investigation. The conspiracy to commit murder will hold for now...pending your more complete investigation. I'll press the obstruction of justice charge myself, pending that result. The preliminary hearing is scheduled for Tuesday morning at nine o'clock. We'll wait until then to decide on the contempt charge, Con." Tucker waited a moment, watching his protégé absorb the information and the teacher's implied approval. "He'll be held without bail until then."

"Thank you, Your, uh, Bill," Con replied just as another faint knock came from the door.

"LAPD is in place," Hazel announced when she opened the door. "Call Captain Sanders if you need him or when you're finished talking to Mr. Fredericks. Whichever comes first."

"Thank you, Hazel," he confirmed.

She closed the door as Tucker eyed him with one raised eyebrow. "What's that all about?"

Con filled him in on his indirect dealings with David Whitfield Fredericks and his plan to strong-arm Fredericks if necessary to attain the cooperation needed to solve this case.

"May I sit in on this telephone call?" Tucker asked.

"Absolutely."

The judge nodded to affirm his consent to proceed. Con picked up the telephone and dialed the operator.

"This is Sheriff Armenta. Will you connect me with the Unified Stars Studios please?"

"Yes sir, Sheriff."

After the usual clicks of the switchboard, it began to ring.

"Unified Stars," a pleasant female voice answered.

"This is Sheriff Conor Armenta of Las Vegas, Nevada. May I speak to Mr. Fredericks, please?"

As if another person had snatched away the telephone, the

voice snapped back, "Mr. Fredericks is in a meeting and can't—"

That was as far as she got when Con interrupted, "Tell Mr. Fredericks to sit down his glass of scotch or whatever it is he needs to do so he can look out across the street, then answer the telephone."

She sat the receiver down on her desk with a clunk. He could hear footsteps receding on the hard-surfaced floor, followed by a male and a female voice. Then another female voice. He had difficulty discerning what was being said with multiple people talking at the same time. Then a second male voice joined in making it impossible to make out anything other than voices were raised and they were arguing. Fredericks, the receptionist, Molly Mansfield, and their attorney all went to the window and looked out. Across the street sat an LAPD squad car. A patrolman sat behind the wheel and a second stood at the police callbox on the corner with the receiver to his ear. As they watched, a second squad car pulled up to the curb behind the first. Then Con heard the slight metallic sound of a second phone being picked up. Probably on Frederick's desk.

"This is Dave Fredericks. What in the Hell do you want?"

"I want you and your employees to quit interfering with my murder investigation of another one of your employees. I want you and your people to quit tampering with evidence in the investigation. I want you to quit harboring a fugitive after you ordered her to flee across state lines, driving a key piece of evidence in the case. What do you think I would want?"

"You can't threaten me," Fredericks growled. "What are you going to do about it?"

"I'm going to stay right here in Las Vegas and continue my investigation. You and Molly Mansfield are going bring that maroon Cadillac sedan that Miss Mansfield transported across the state line back to Las Vegas and be sitting in my office at eight o'clock tomorrow morning."

Fredericks let out a roaring laugh. "And how do you think that will happen?" He sneered, but his laugh and his words were hollow, and Con knew it.

"I think those police officers are going to sit there across the street until I tell them to leave," Con informed him with authority. "I think the FBI will come and arrest you both on charges of conspiracy to commit murder and tampering with evidence. I think interstate flight will also be added to Miss Mansfield's charges and harboring a fugitive to yours."

David Whitfield Fredericks scoffed at Con's remarks unconvincingly. "What makes you think the FBI will get involved in this?"

"Oh, I don't know," Con replied. "You're the one who made an interstate crime out of this. Before that, they just developed your film from the shooting yesterday."

"What?" Fredericks exclaimed. "I thought..."

"Did you think that I would send the film to your studio to be developed?" Con asked but continued before Fredericks answered. "That way, you could just accidentally expose the film to light in the process and render it useless. Is that what you thought, Mr. Fredericks?"

"You think you've got it all figured out, don't you, cowboy?"

The cowboy reference did not normally bother Con. When Fredericks used the term now, his thoughts instantly flashed back to Hugh Parker's "Stupid cowboy" comment yesterday. He tried to push it out of his mind when Fredericks continued.

"How do you plan on making all of this happen?" The actor tried to turn on his most commanding voice.

"The District Court Judge is sitting five feet away from me right now, Dave. He's heard all of my half of this conversation. As soon as I indicate that you won't cooperate, he'll sign the warrants and take them to the telegraph office. It's six blocks away. The FBI and LAPD will have copies of the warrants in their hands within ten minutes. They're expecting them." Con paused momentarily to let that sink in. "Or, if I call and tell them you're cooperating, you and Miss Mansfield can get into that maroon Cadillac sedan and make yourselves visible so the officers across the street can clearly see you're both in the car. You can use Mr. Parker's suite at the Hotel Nevada when you get here. He won't be needing it and we'll be finished searching his and Miss Mansfield's rooms long before you arrive."

Sheriff Conor Armenta waited for nearly a minute without any response. He could again hear multiple distant voices on the line. Fredricks must have covered the telephone and he was hearing them talking again from the open receiver on the receptionist's desk.

"What'll it be, Mr. Fredricks?" Con nearly yelled into the receiver to make sure he would be heard if the phone was away from Frederick's ear.

"We'll be there in the morning," he replied sullenly.

"Eight o'clock. Don't be late, cowboy." Con had nearly reached his limit of patience with the lack of respect shown by every one of these movie people. Actors, he thought to himself. Why don't they try acting like human beings? "If that was your lawyer I heard talking a little while ago, you might want to drag him along too."

"Eight o'clock, Sheriff," Fredericks hung up, but the line did not break connection. The receptionist's phone was still off the hook. Con could hear footsteps nearing.

"I've got to stop by my house and pack a few clothes," he heard Fredericks say.

"I've got everything I need at the hotel," Molly followed.

Then came the attorney's voice. "I'll call my wife and have her pack a suitcase for me," he said. "She'll have it ready by the time we get there. It's right on our way out of town." He picked up the telephone from the desk and began to dial. "What the..." was all Con heard before the line went dead.

Con called Captain Sanders at the LAPD. "They took my bluff, Captain. Fredericks's attorney is joining them for the trip. I told them to make sure that your patrolmen recognized them before they left the studio in the maroon Cadillac sedan. Would it be possible for your men to tail them out of town? They'll be going to Frederick's house so he can pack a suit-case," Con explained, "then swing by the attorney's house to grab the bag his wife is packing for him."

"That's not a problem," the captain answered. "I can spare a couple of men for another hour or so. They'll like the change of pace anyway. I'd like to chat, but I need to get the change of orders to them before their prey slips away."

Con leaned back in his chair and looked at his watch. A quarter to twelve. He looked up at his guest. "If we hurry, we can slip into the café right before the noon rush," Con told the judge.

"I'll buy," Tucker told him as he came to his feet. "That was some bamboozle you fed to old Fredericks. There, at the end, you called him cowboy. What was that all about?"

"I'll talk as we walk," Con told him, and they headed out the door. "I'll need a search warrant for Hugh Parker's and Molly Mansfield's suites at the Hotel Nevada too. Mansfield is registered under the name Stapleton. I have no idea what name Parker is using."

"I don't usually take orders from a sheriff, but under the circumstances, I'll consider that a request."

"Sorry, Judge."

"You've got a lot on your plate, Conor. Apology accepted."

* * *

Two hours later, Con pulled up in front of the Union Hotel where Emily Scott, the assistant director, was staying. He had already sent Deputy Ben Neilly and Coroner Harold Martin to search the rooms at the Hotel Nevada. Judge Tucker had made out the warrant to include the entire hotel rather than chance of missing something on a technicality. The clerk at the Union rang her room and Miss Scott descended the stairs moments later.

"More questions, Sheriff?" she asked.

"Just a few," Con answered. She headed toward the chairs in the lobby. "The porch might be better," Con suggested. "Fewer ears."

"Ah, yes." Emily smiled. "Forgive my naïveté. With this crew, very little is confidential," she commented. "Or at least, it doesn't stay that way very long." She chuckled.

"Odd that you should mention that," Con replied as they took seats on the shaded front porch. "A week or so ago there was an altercation one afternoon concerning Mark McCoy, Molly Mansfield, and Jenny Vance. Moments later, Hugh Parker became involved." Con could plainly see Emily was uncomfortable with the conversation. Her face turned vibrant red. "I don't mean to embarrass you, but I suspected you would give me a less illicit rendition of the events than I might get elsewhere. Can you tell me what happened?"

Miss Scott cleared her throat. "Would you like a glass of iced tea before we proceed?" she asked as she stood.

"Sure. That sounds refreshing."

"I'll be right back."

A moment later she returned with two glasses of tea and handed one to Con before returning to her seat. The redness of her face had dissipated. She cleared her throat and began. "First, you need to know that in this business, uh, many people feel that a little roll in the hay can solve anything." She cleared her throat again and took a sip of tea. "Some women in this industry think that if they offer favors to men with influence, uh, it will improve their career. It goes the other way around too, but not as much." She readjusted herself. "Let me assure you that I do not partake in this disgusting game in either direction. Hence, I am considered an outsider by many of my peers."

"I suspected that," Con reassured her. "That's the main reason I came to you. The short version."

"Okay," she said and took a deep breath. "The short version. Mark and Jenny have had an intimate relationship off and on for about a year. More on than off. Molly started flirting with Matt as soon as they were cast together for *Sons of the Texas Star*. Matt had a party at his swimming pool about six weeks ago. Sort of a kickoff celebration for the movie. There was a fair amount of drinking and Molly stripped off naked. Mark got a little bothered and jumped into the pool so Jenny stripped off and jumped in with him. At that point I left the party. So did most everyone else."

"What about last week?" Con asked.

"Last Wednesday, Molly wanted some siesta fun. Matt fell asleep. She got mad, found Mark, and they went to her tent for a little playtime. Jenny finds out, barges in, starts ranting and raving, Parker comes in, portrays himself as Jenny's rescuer, then takes Jenny to his tent for mutual favors. What's a little adultery and infidelity among family and friends anyway, huh?" Emily took a deep breath, followed by a long sip of iced tea.

"Do you think Jenny might have been mad enough at Mark to set up this shooting," Con began, "but accidentally loaded the wrong gun?"

Emily was clearly shocked by the likelihood. "I never considered it, but it sure could be possible."

"Has Jenny's attitude changed since then?"

"She hadn't even spoken to Mark until yesterday. Jenny has spent every afternoon since then in Parker's tent and been acting as uppity as Molly Mansfield. She never used to be that way."

"Thanks for your help. Keep this to yourself if you would."

"Sure. Like I said, I don't play their games."

"Do you know where Jenny is staying?"

"At the Golden."

"Thanks again," Con offered and donned his Stetson as he stood up. "Oh, by the way. Molly Mansfield, David Whitfield Fairbanks, and their attorney are driving in from Los Angeles tonight. They have a meeting in the morning."

"Oh crap!" Emily exclaimed. "Why didn't they call me? I don't have anything prepared for a meeting!"

"Calm down. I didn't mean to alarm you," Con told her. "They're meeting with me, Judge Tucker, and the district attorney. Nothing to do with the movie...not directly anyway."

"Oh, thank you," she began. "With Hugh in jail, I don't have a buffer between me and management. Good luck with Fredericks. He's a pretty hard nut to crack."

"He's not my boss," Con told her. "If he gets too unruly, I'll just throw him in jail with Parker." He smiled.

"That'll be the day." She laughed.

Con gave her a wink and left.

* * *

Jennifer Vance sat cross-legged sipping a lemonade on a bench in front of the Hotel Golden. The low-cut sundress she wore was less modest than most ladies of Las Vegas wore. She fanned her cleavage with a handheld collapsible fan that matched the pattern of her dress. She did not turn his direction when Con pulled up and got out of his pickup.

"Good afternoon, Miss Vance."

She did not turn her gaze from straight ahead nor reply.

"I have a few questions for you," Con continued.

"I didn't see the shooting. I was nowhere near there when it happened," she snarled.

"Did I say anything about yesterday's incident?"

"No, you did not," she continued with her snobbish tone. "That is the only thing I would talk to you about, and I have nothing to say."

"You can either answer my questions now. Just you and me. Or I can get a subpoena, have you arrested, drag you into Judge Tucker's courtroom, and then you can answer them in front of a dozen witnesses. Which will it be?"

"What do you want?"

"What happened last week in Molly Mansfield's tent?"

"I don't know what you're talking about."

"I'm talking about the day last week that you barged into Molly Mansfield's tent and began yelling and screaming loud enough that two dozen people heard you." Con remained calm and patient. "I'm trying to give you the opportunity to tell me your side of the story."

"Mark and I have been dating for over a year," she began, still looking straight ahead. "She took her clothes off and danced around at that party. She got him all excited then wooed him into her tent last week and, and…"

"And what?"

"She was lying there stark naked. All splayed out with her bubs on display. She didn't even try to cover herself when I came in. At least Mark held his shirt in front of his, his…she's just a trashy little whore."

"Didn't you also take your clothes off at that party?"

"That was different."

"Didn't you go spend the afternoon in Hugh Parker's tent afterward?"

She did not reply.

"And several afternoons since?"

"What's good for the goose is good for the gander"—she turned and glared at him—"or vice versa in this case."

"Since you're quoting fables, two wrongs don't make a right, either, Miss Vance." Neither looked away. They were looking right at each other, eye to eye. "What has Mr. Parker promised you in return for the favors you've been giving him?"

"I'm going to be a star in his next picture. I'm through with all of this doling out props and cleaning up after all of these, these…" She started to cry. "A star! He promised!" she repeated, staring at him through her tears of realization.

"Thank you, Miss Vance," Con replied quietly and looked away before he began to weep himself. He felt sorry for her.

8

After dealing with Dutch Wagner and his lawyer, then lunch with Judge Tucker, the clock on the wall read half past two when Conor returned to the office.

"Dunc Blackwood called this morning," Hazel announced, waving a note between her fingers when the sheriff stepped in the door. "He said he's been losing some cattle."

"Send Jesse out to talk to him. Find out what's going on."

"He said he'd like to talk to *you*."

Duncan Blackwood had been a neighbor and friend of the Armenta family since before Con was born. In spite of animosities between some cattlemen and sheepmen, the two families respected each other and were good neighbors. His cattle ranch bordered that of the Armentas' sheep ranch on two sides. Con doubted the old man knew any of his deputies and typical of his father's generation, when they called for the sheriff, they wanted to talk to *the* sheriff. Con looked at the note Hazel handed him. It included a telephone number. He really wanted to avoid any chance of being late for his date with June. He closed the door behind him when he entered his office. Sitting down behind his desk, Con picked up the telephone and dialed the number.

"Hello," a gravelly voice answered on the fourth ring.

"Howdy, Dunc. This is Con. Hazel said you're missing some cattle."

"That's right. It's odd," he started to explain. "It's been going on since April."

"And you're just now calling?"

"Well," he began. "You'd just got shot when we noticed the first bunch missing. I didn't want to bother you." He hesitated at the excuse. "Didn't know how bad you were hurt and all."

"How many head?"

"Three that time."

"Only three? Doesn't that seem a little odd? If some fellows are going to gamble the consequences of rustling cattle, I'd expect them to open up their loop a bit more."

"The second time they only took one," Blackwood replied incredulously.

"I don't want to sound patronizing, but you're sure they didn't just get out?"

"I understand your disbelief, Con. I've felt the same way," Blackwood agreed. "I've accused my boys of everything but stealing my cattle themselves. When these last two disappeared, I thought I could figure it out myself. That was ten days ago. I rode every inch of fence line...checked every gate...twice. I've got just shy of seven thousand deeded acres ground nowadays, Con, fenced and cross-fenced. Most of it don't even got a cow track within a hundred yards of it. I know. I just got done riding every inch of it. They didn't get out."

"Well, if the rustlers didn't take them through a gate, how'd they get them out?"

"That's what I want to talk to you about...and not on no telephone. Too many ears on these party lines." There was a distinct click on the line when he said it. "Hear what I mean?"

"Yes, I did," Con confirmed. "I can't get out there before Sunday. Do you want me to send a deputy?"

"I'll wait."

"Okay, then," Con replied. "I'll be riding over from Paddy's."

"I'll stay close to home," Blackwood responded.

* * *

Today was June's birthday and tonight he would take her and April to dinner at the Hotel Nevada. He wanted the evening to be special. An occasion that would be remembered. He did not want Katherine Wagner's funeral tomorrow to overshadow the event. With that in mind, he strode into Delkin's Jewelry.

"Can I help you find something, Sheriff?" Mrs. Delkin asked as Conor peered into a case.

"What's the birthstone this month?" he asked.

"It's the pearl," she answered. "Are you familiar with pearls?"

"Round. White, right?" Con replied.

"Yes, most are white, but occasionally they are colored. Those are very rare and usually quite expensive. Are you looking for a ring? Earrings, maybe? Most of my pearls are right over here." She motioned him toward another case. "I have several strung pearl necklaces, also," she offered.

Con thought about it momentarily as he looked at the rings. A ring might imply an engagement. He couldn't remember seeing June wearing earrings. Her hair usually concealed her ears though.

"Maybe a necklace," he decided as he looked at several strings on display. Then a pendant caught his eye. "What's that stone?" he pointed at a larger, irregular pear-shaped stone.

"You have good taste, Sheriff. That's a pearl also. Sometimes nature takes a twist and they are distorted when they form." She opened the rear of the case and brought it out. "The mount and chain are eighteen-karat gold," Mrs. Delkin told him. "It won't leave a green stripe on her neck."

She laid it down on a dark blue velvet mat. Con stared, imagining it against June's skin and her sapphire blue eyes. He was afraid to touch it.

"How much?" he finally managed to ask.

Mrs. Delkin cleared her throat and swallowed. "Perhaps you should sit down."

"No. Just tell me," he said, not taking his eyes from the pendant.

"It's seventy-five," she answered. "I can let you have it for sixty."

"I'll take it," he said, looking up to meet her eyes. "I'll need to get the money. I don't carry that much in my wallet."

"That's not a problem," she managed to respond. Even at the discounted price, it was more than all she had sold in more than a week. "I will put it in a box. Would you like me to gift wrap it?"

"Yes," he answered. "Yes, please." He glanced at the clock on the wall. "I'll be back in a few minutes."

Con drove home and pulled a book by Zane Grey from the

shelf in his living room. Between pages fifty and fifty-one were two fifty-dollar bills. He tucked them into the front pocket of his jeans and dashed back out the door.

After picking up the necklace from the jeweler, Con pulled up before the Las Vegas Florist shop at a quarter to five. Inside, the florist wiped her brow as she turned from a very large floral arrangement she worked on. "What can I do for you, Sheriff?"

"I need a bouquet," he answered.

"For the funeral tomorrow?"

"For dinner tonight."

"My selection is really picked over for the funeral. What do you have in mind?"

His mind flashed on the pendant and June's blue eyes. "Blue eyes," he replied, then blushed. "Blue."

The florist smiled. "Cornflowers?"

"Sure," Con replied, having no idea what cornflowers were.

She pulled open the heavy door of a walk-in refrigerator and disappeared momentarily to return with a bundle of flowers that reminded Con of little blue daisies. "How are these?"

"Perfect," he confirmed and she began to wrap them in brown heavy paper. "Could you separate a few into a smaller bouquet?" he asked.

"For her daughter?" the florist quizzed knowingly.

There were certain things about living in a small town that never changed. One of those things, that everyone knew your business. Sometimes this anomaly was less welcome than others. Right now, it was another. Con's face lit up in a blushing grin. He chuckled. "Yes, for Princess April."

"What time?" the florist asked.

"Six thirty," Con replied with a puzzled look on his face.

"Put them into your refrigerator until you're ready to walk out the door," she told him as she handed over the two bundles.

* * *

Con felt naked without his Stetson as he climbed the steps to June's front porch with five minutes to spare. Freshly shaved and bathed, he slicked back his black hair with a light coating of pomade. He wore a white shirt and string tie beneath his jacket and the ever-present blue jeans pulled over the top of his cowboy boots. He carried the two bouquets in one hand and knocked on the screen door with the other.

April ran to the door in excitement. Her blonde hair hung in ringlets beneath the blue bow at the back of her head that matched her flowered sundress.

"For Princess April," Con announced as he handed her the small bouquet when she opened the door. "To match that pretty dress."

"Mama! Con brought me flowers!" she screeched as she bolted across the living room toward the hall.

June emerged from the bathroom still placing a small pearl stud on the second ear as she appeared. Her hair was up on her head unlike she had ever worn it in his presence before. Conor was astonished and almost disappointed at the string of white pearls adorning her neck. The momentary lapse disappeared as quickly as it arose. She looked striking in her yellow sundress. Her bouquet of flowers nearly slipped from his hand as he stared at her in awe. June stood eye to eye with him in her heels.

"You look fabulous," he stuttered as she neared him. "Absolutely fabulous."

Before she spoke, she embraced him and kissed him amorously. His arms closed behind her as he returned the kiss. They both gasped for air when they separated. June stepped back and straightened her dress eyeing Con from head to toe as she recomposed herself. The scent of his shaving lotion mingled with her perfume in the stillness of the room.

"You look quite handsome yourself, Mr. Armenta," she returned with a wink as she caught her breath.

"Happy birthday, June Sommers," Con told her as he held up the flowers.

"They're beautiful."

"They match your eyes," he managed to add as she took them. "I don't remember what they're called."

"Cornflowers, they are one of my favorites," she commented, "and they're cold,"

"The florist told me to keep them in the refrigerator until I brought them."

"I'll get them into water, then we can go," she told him then beckoned her daughter. "April, honey, bring your flowers to the kitchen so we can put them in water."

* * *

"Good evening, Sheriff," the waitress at the Hotel Nevada greeted when she brought their menus.

"Thank you, Susie," Con replied as he accepted the menu.

"Ma'am." Susie nodded and smiled at June as she handed her a menu and departed.

"You know each other?" June asked Con. Ashamed of the glint of jealousy the pretty young girl sparked in her, she wished she had not asked, but could not help herself. To her, Conor was the most eligible bachelor in town. These thin young girls, yet to experience motherhood, with their firm bodies vied for his affection, even if he failed to notice. Child-bearing had increased her waistline as much as it enhanced her bustline over a decade ago. June knew how much Conor loved her. Would it be sufficient to keep his attentions focused on her?

"A friend of a friend," Con replied, hoping to end the conversation without explaining the intricacies of how he learned of Susie witnessing Bryce Campbell and Katherine Wagner's intimate relationship. He quickly changed the course of conversation.

"You can order whatever you want," he leaned over and told April as she ogled her menu.

"Even a hotdog?" she asked.

"Absolutely," Con replied as he turned to June with a wink, ignoring her wincing at the thought.

"And ice cream?" April added.

"If you eat all of your hot dog," Con stipulated.

When Susie returned, June ordered lamb chops. They were not her favorite, but she wanted to make a point to Con that she accepted his family heritage. She assumed that lamb chops had probably been a huge luxury for his family when he was growing up and today, they were celebrating.

Con missed the subtlety of June's hint and ordered a T-bone steak. After all, today they were celebrating.

The trio all enjoyed their meal and June's lamb chops did not disappoint her. Susie brought coffee and cleared June and Con's dishes while April finished her supper.

"Are you ready?" Susie asked Con.

"Yes," he replied.

"Dessert second?"

"Yes," Con confirmed.

"What is going on?" June asked.

"Very good coffee, isn't it?" Con countered, ignoring her question.

Susie returned with Con's gift-wrapped box from Delkin's Jewelry and placed it in front of him. "Cake?" she asked only Con.

"With ice cream," Con added and winked at April as Susie again disappeared.

June sat astonished. The love of her life had made all of these arrangements since yesterday evening. Con handed her the box.

"Conor," she managed to utter past the lump that was forming in her throat. "You should not have. The dinner is more than enough."

"Happy birthday, darling," he told her as she accepted the package.

April had finished eating and watched her mother excitedly as she unwrapped the gift.

June opened the box. "Oh, my gosh, Conor," she gasped. "This is...it's...this is amazing," she whispered as a tear escaped her eye.

"Do you like it?" he asked and continued before she could answer. "Mrs. Delkin said your birthstone was pearl. I had never seen you wear them, so I thought you didn't have any." He waited a moment in silence. Tears now streamed down her cheeks. "I hope you're not upset."

"Oh God, no Conor," she found her voice. "These"—she touched the string of pearls around her neck—"they were my grandmother's. My mother gave them to me when I graduated high school. They are inexpensive, but I will cherish them forever because of where they came from." She took a deep breath. "But this. This is exquisite. It is absolutely splendid... and expensive...too expensive. You should never have spent so much money on me."

"But I wanted to," he responded. "I want to make you happy."

Her very own words from a few nights ago coming from his lips surged through her.

"You do make me happy," she repeated his reply from that night as she leaned in her chair and kissed him fervently.

"I love you, June."

"Not more than I love you, Conor. Thank you," she added as she took off her grandmother's necklace. "Help me with this?" she asked as she handed him the pendant and turned her back toward him.

April now watched intently in lieu of blushing and giggling as she had for the last several minutes. Con gazed at the back of June's bare neck and suppressed the temptation to bend forward and gently kiss it. The enticement vanished as quickly as it arose when Susie returned. She brought three slices of chocolate cake, each with a large scoop of vanilla ice cream and one with a single lit candle. She sat them in their appropriate places and turned toward June and Con.

"Holy cow!" she exclaimed. "That's what was in the box?"

June nodded.

"You gotta go to the lobby and look in the mirror!" Susie urged her.

"May I?" she asked Con.

"Sure," he grinned, "but don't take too long. You're holding up me and April's ice cream," he teased.

June rushed into the lobby with Susie hot on her heels.

"Wow!" June nearly shouted.

"You're a very lucky lady, ma'am," Susie commented.

"Yes, I am," June agreed as tears again rolled down her face.

"Sheriff Armenta is a very nice man," Susie continued.

"Yes, he is." She paused a moment. How much did this pretty young woman know about Conor Armenta. "He said that the two of you have a mutual friend."

"Why, yes," Susie replied. Caught off guard by June's comment, the memory of her once close friendship with Janet Rae troubled her. "Yes, we do. A very dear friend, but we have taken different paths and don't see each other often."

June noticed the sudden change in Susie's mood.

"It's complicated," Susie added, "and Sheriff Armenta... he...of all people...he understands." She began to cry. Two strangers stood crying together in the hotel lobby...in bliss and in sadness. June could not help but gather the younger girl in her arms and hold her. She had no idea what it was that Conor understood, but she knew he would...understand. This girl is right. Any previous hint of jealousy disappeared in an instant.

"Conor *is* a very nice man," June agreed.

"I need to get back to work," Susie announced and recomposed herself.

"And I need the lady's lavatory."

Susie pointed her in the general direction and the two went separate ways. June washed her face and noted that the touch of rouge she applied to her cheeks earlier had long since dissolved during her multiple crying sessions this evening. As she looked at herself in the mirror. There was no lack of color in her face as she wondered why she had been so emotional lately. The answer came to her without pause. "You're in love, stupid," she spoke aloud to the woman in the mirror, "and your hormones are running rampant. You want to bear this man's children!" The thought warmed her and chilled her at the same time as she applied a fresh, yet conservative coat of color to the lips in front of her.

She straightened before the mirror and admired the pendant again. It looked fabulous resting against her chest just above her cleavage. She knew she had an attractive bosom hidden below the neckline of her dress. She purchased this dress a few weeks ago with just an occasion such as this in mind. Wearing her hair up made it slightly more provocative. Alluring, but not revealing, she thought as she glanced at her profile in the mirror.

Her thoughts returned to Conor. They always did. She wondered how long it would take before the modest sheriff would propose to her. She hoped soon. Her willpower was fading rapidly and they still needed an appropriately long engagement to suppress the local gossip train from surmising a sudden *need* to wed. She primped her hair with a bounce of her palm and exited to the dining room.

Susie refilled coffee cups as June approached the table. A fresh new candle glowed from her slice of cake. Its exhausted predecessor had vanished from the table. Scoops of ice cream grew in diameter proportionately to their shrinking in height but had yet to escape the rims of the plates.

"I am so sorry that I took so long," she apologized as she took her seat.

"That's fine," Con accepted. "Susie said you two became engrossed in conversation and lost track of time."

"Yes," June did not elaborate. "I suppose I should make a wish and blow out this candle before our ice cream melts to the floor."

"Happy birthday, Mama," April chimed in as June blew out the candle.

* * *

It was well past nine o'clock when they pulled up in front of June's house. April leaned against Con as she fell asleep between them on the short ride home.

"Can you carry her in?" June whispered.

"Sure," Con quietly replied.

June opened the front door to allow them in and carefully kept the screen door from slamming as she raced ahead of Con to turn down the covers on April's bed. Con gently laid her down as June removed her shoes, then covered her, still in her dress. Con's arm naturally closed around June's waist as they stood in the dim room admiring the wonderful child rapt in slumber before them.

"She's been so excited all day about this evening," June whispered. "She begged Joyce to let her take a bath as soon as she got home from school. They came over here, Joyce washed and fixed her hair...she was dressed and waiting in anticipation when I walked in from work. Isn't she beautiful?"

"Just like her mother," Con revered.

They slipped from April's room and June eased the door closed behind them. When she turned in the darkness, Con stood immediately in front of her. He softly pulled her to him and wrapped his arms around her. She could feel the slow rhythm of his breathing against her chest...or was it her breathing. He leaned forward and tenderly kissed the side of her neck below her left earlobe. It sent a shiver up her spine.

"I've wanted to do that from the instant I saw you this evening," he said and gently repeated the action.

"Oh, Conor," June gasped. "We have to stop. You have to stop. I promised." She hesitated. "I don't want to stop, but...I don't want you to leave, but we must...we must stop." She forced herself to pull away from him as she gasped for air. "Go...sit on the front porch." She began to regain control of her breathing. "I'll bring iced tea," she said as she physically pointed him toward the front door. "Go."

* * *

"Have you ever thought of remarrying?" Con asked her as she handed him his glass of tea. In shock, she nearly let it slip from her hand. Here it comes she thought. The subject of marriage. He will ask me if I want to have more children. He will hedge around the actual proposal and then it will come. The ultimate question. Then I will answer yes and try not to scream in delight. He will kiss me and my hormones will explode. It will take every ounce of willpower I can muster to refrain myself from tearing my clothes off and ravage him right here...but I will hold back.

"Not until I met you," June replied, fighting for control over her eagerness as she sat down on the swing beside him. She stared at the profile of his face barely visible in the darkness. He looked straight ahead into the darkness, then took a sip of his tea and nodded to himself. *What is he thinking?* She asked herself in silence. *Surely, he can feel me watching him.*

Nothing compelled June to interrupt Conor's quiet reverie. She suppressed the impulse to embrace or snuggle with him. They did not hold hands, but she could feel him at every point of contact as they sat close beside one another. He drank nearly half his tea before he broke the silence.

"My parents have seldom quarreled," Con finally said.

"Even about money, after Papa was hurt," he added, "they didn't talk much about it. It just seemed natural for them to work hard and make the best they could in life from what they had."

June longed to reassure him. Tell him that her job paid well and her mortgage was small. She had no idea how much he spent on the pendant he bought for her. She feared it was far more expensive than he could afford, especially so recently after the purchase of his new car. Most importantly she did not want to embarrass him if he was in a financial pinch.

"You have a good family, Conor. You should be proud of them and yourself." She realized the conversation leaned in another direction than she had hoped or expected. "You're a good man, Conor Armenta." She leaned forward and kissed his cheek. "I love you more than you can imagine."

Con stood...rather abruptly, June thought as she scrambled to join him. "It's getting late," he said. "The funeral is at ten tomorrow."

"Would you like to join April and me for breakfast beforehand?" The concept of sharing breakfast with the man she loved at this point in their relationship surprised her. She blurted out the invitation before considering any implication a late-rising gossipy neighbor might surmise. Joyce Wright, the lady next door who often watched April would never jump to any such conclusion.

The offer surprised Con also, but he eagerly accepted.

"Eight o'clock, then?"

"Sure. I'll see you then." He looked for his hat, then remembered he had not worn it. "Uh, goodnight then," he stammered slightly before he reclaimed his poise. He then placed his hands on her waist and kissed her gently on the lips. "Happy birthday, June. I love you."

* * *

SATURDAY, JUNE 21, 1930

June awoke to the sun shining brightly in her bedroom window. She smiled to herself almost guiltily, fresh with the memory of a dream in her mind. She had awakened with Conor still asleep beside her in her bed. The dream then flashed ahead to sitting cross-legged in her robe sipping coffee as Conor sat bare-chested across the table, devouring the breakfast she had prepared for him.

* * *

Slices of bacon, diced potatoes, and biscuits, all cooked earlier waited in the warm oven. A fresh pot of coffee sat on the stove. June brushed her hair as she peered at the woman in the mirror. Conor's pendant looked magnificent against her navy-blue dress with a much more conservative neckline than the one she wore last night. She chose to wear flats opposed to negotiating the terrain of the cemetery in heels. Conor should arrive any moment. A quick dab of perfume and she was ready. His car pulled up out front as she crossed the living room.

June donned her apron in the kitchen just as Conor knocked on the screen door and April chirped, "He's here!" as she ran from her bedroom.

Conor had washed the pomade from his hair. He hung his Stetson on the tree near the door as June brought a steaming cup of coffee. "Good morning, Conor," she greeted as she handed him the cup. "Would you prefer your coffee in here or at the kitchen table while I fix your eggs?"

"The view will be more attractive in the kitchen." Con grinned as he took a sip of the coffee.

"How do you like your eggs?" she asked as she headed toward the kitchen.

"However you fix them," he replied.

"No," she insisted. "Really."

"Yes, really," he reassured her.

"Fried?"

"Yes."

"Scrambled?"

"Yes."

"Fried, it is," she said as she placed the cast-iron skillet on the stove. "April likes hers fried soft, so she can dip her biscuit or toast in the yolk," she commented as she turned to Con, now seated at what had become *his* chair watching her over the rim of the cup as he sipped his coffee.

"You're beautiful this morning," he told her.

"I bet you say that to whoever happens to be cooking you breakfast at the time," she responded cynically.

"No," Con answered seriously. "Papa wouldn't understand." He could not hold a straight face very long and began to chuckle.

"Well," she answered. "I certainly will not compare to Juan Armenta, but I can usually get everything finished about the same time." The eggs were beginning to crackle in the pan and at that moment she pulled the bacon, potatoes, and biscuits from the warm oven and sat them in the middle of the already set table.

"April," June called, amazed her daughter had not been underfoot from the instant Con arrived. "Come to breakfast." At her call, the sound of saddle-shoes running across the wood floor rang as she approached.

"This is for you, Con," she announced as she handed him a homemade card.

June fought back a tear as Con carefully unfolded it. "Pour the orange juice please, sweetheart."

April retrieved the pitcher of orange juice from the refrigerator without taking her eyes off of Con and began filling glasses on the table. Con read.

> Con—
> Thank you for taking me and Mama to dinner last night. I don't remember ever going out to a place that nice before.
> It was real good. And fun.
> Love,
> April

"Thank you, April," Con said as he refolded the card an put it in his shirt pocket. "It was fun for me too."

"Butter and jam, please." June jolted April from her daze. "Then take your seat."

June dished eggs from the stove onto the plates and returned them to the table; three for Conor, one for April and two for herself. She poured her own cup of coffee and refilled Con's before sitting down. Taking April's and Con's hands, she bowed her head.

"Thank you, Lord, for this food we receive to nourish our bodies as You nourish our souls. Please provide us with a glorious morning as we lay Mrs. Wagner to rest. May she rest in peace. Amen."

"Amen," Conor and April confirmed.

"Help yourself to the bacon, potatoes, and biscuits, Conor," June said as she reluctantly released his hand. "Take all you like."

"Thank you," Con replied as he filled his plate.

"Can we drop April off at Olivia's on our way to the funeral?" June asked as the platter passed around the table. "Stuart is at a rodeo somewhere and David went with him. April is sleeping over with Donna tonight."

"Sure," Con said. "Sounds like an all-girls party to me," he added, giving April a grin and a wink.

* * *

"Thank you for having April over," June told Olivia when they dropped her daughter at Con's sister's home.

"You know that I love having her here," Olivia replied. "She and Donna have so much fun together. Besides," she added, "it gives you two some time to be alone together."

"Yes." June blushed. Lately she appreciated April's presence when she was with Conor. It helped calm her passion. She handed April's small suitcase to Olivia. "I did not intend to move her into your house," she apologized. "It has her clothes for church in the morning."

"That's fine." Olivia smiled. "I'll hang them so they won't wrinkle."

"We will see you there," June confirmed.

"I won't be there, I'm afraid," Con interjected to both of the women's surprise. "I have some cattle rustling to look into."

"Oh." June quickly concealed being taken aback with a smile. "I shall see you in the morning."

* * *

When they arrived at the cemetery, several cars were parked alongside one of the lanes between rows of headstones. An older truck sat among them. It looked familiar to Conor, but he could not recall where he had seen it. A group of people loitered near a large mound of dirt alongside the freshly dug grave. Three men and a woman stood a short distance away, huddled in their own conversation. He recognized each of them...and the truck.

Simon Pahgoroo, a Moapa Paiute shaman drove the truck. His sister, Tomani Pete and her husband, Rayno Pete accompanied the shaman. And Luis Garza was an old friend of the Armenta family. Luis and Tomani Pete were the parents of Jimmy Garza. Jimmy had taken care of Katherine Wagner for a time and probably witnessed her murder. Subsequently Jimmy was murdered, most likely to silence him. June and Conor joined them.

"What brings you here?" Con asked as he shook Luis's hand.

"We wanted to see her off," he answered. "The woman Jimmy cared for. Simon will finish the ceremony that Jimmy began for her. Mrs. Brumbaugh said her mother would have liked that."

The couple spoke and shook hands with the other three before making their way to the graveside. A broad headstone spanned the open grave and the one beside it. "Wagner" it said in large letters across the top. Gary D., Sr. with dates of birth and death were engraved above the occupied grave. Katherine with only her date of birth adorned the other side. June began to weep at the sight of the name. The woman she did not recall ever meeting. A woman who was tortured by her love for a man who could never fully be hers. All because of circumstances neither ever expected would transpire. In the letter to her daughter, she had called it an addiction. June understood.

"Good morning, Conor." A strong male voice broke the silence behind her. June turned to see Newton Campbell pumping Conor's hand. Amy gave her a transparent hug. An effort to blend in with the sophistication of the Campbell family she hoped to become part of.

"June." Newt turned to her with sincere enthusiasm and an outstretched hand. "It's good to see you again, even on such a somber occasion. On behalf of the Wagner family, thank you for coming."

"Newton," she returned as she accepted his handshake.

"June!" came a mature female voice from the crowd of gathering people. She soon spotted Leanora Campbell motioning to her among the throng. "Come over here. There is someone you should meet." As sweet as Mrs. Campbell had recently been to her, June could not help feeling that tinge of servitude she bowed to when in the woman's presence. She scurried to obey.

"Yes, Mrs. Campbell?" June's greeting received a scowl. "Leanora," she corrected uncomfortably.

"June, this is Agnes Spencer," Leanora introduced. "She is the office manager for Wagner Trucking. But much more than that she was Katherine's dearest friend for longer than I can remember. June works for Robert," she told Agnes. "She and Sheriff Armenta are engaged to be married."

June nearly choked on the announcement. She knew her eyes must have nearly popped from her head as she stubbed her toe on a clump grass trying to pose as lawn in the barren cemetery and almost fell into the two women.

"Excuse me," she gasped as she grabbed them both for support. "I am very sorry."

"That's quite all right, dear," Agnes consoled her. "It's difficult to be ladylike when walking across a cow pasture."

"Oh, that's not what distracted me, Mrs. Spencer." June's mind raced to find proper words. "Conor and I have been seeing each other for a few months now, but we're not actually engaged." Her face flushed a brilliant red.

"I am the one who should apologize," Leanora stammered. "I...I know how you two look at one another...and comments...never mind. Never listen to gossip!" she exclaimed. "I am truly sorry, June. I never intended to embarrass you. Please forgive me."

"I am fine, Leanora," June reassured her as she searched her thoughts for the possible source of such a rumor. Amy's name soon filled the gap. Probably in an effort to urge Newton into popping the question. "Just a simple misunderstanding. I am sure whoever told you was merely mistaken."

"Well." Leanora continued to retreat. "I am ashamed of myself for spreading a tale."

The awkward moment soon passed as the hearse came up the road, followed by Katherine Wagner's gray Oldsmobile coupe.

By the time the hearse rolled to a stop, five men in the group had returned to the lane to meet it. Gus Brumbaugh and his daughter clamored out the driver's side of the crowded car as Katie Brumbaugh with Augie on her lap exited the passenger side. When Gus joined the other five pallbearers leaving Katie with two crying children to follow, Con ran toward the procession.

"Walk with your family, Gus," he ordered as he replaced him carrying the casket.

The big man did not balk. He positioned himself between his wife and gangly daughter with an arm around each of them. Augie held his mother's other hand as they followed his grandmother's casket to the gravesite.

As they placed the casket on the three round poles that spanned the grave, the pastor from the Brumbaugh family's Lutheran Church in Logan introduced himself.

"In the last few months of Mrs. Wagner's life, she became close friends with a young Indian man," he said. "It seems this young man was left the task of burying Mrs. Wagner when she passed, and he performed the ceremonies of his people to the best of his abilities. This young man's uncle is a shaman of the Paiute tribe at Moapa. At the request of Mrs. Wagner's family, he is going to complete the ceremony in order that the deceased may pass on into the afterlife according to their traditions."

Simon Pahgoroo took his place beside the casket and raised his hands into the air. He held an eagle feather in his right hand and began to sing in his native tongue. When he finished singing, he passed his hands over the casket and uttered a prayer in Paiute. He turned and whispered to the pastor then rejoined the Petes and Luis.

The Brumbaughs were given chairs and the pastor continued with a traditional Christian ceremony. At the conclusion, he introduced Newt Campbell.

"The Campbell and Wagner families have been friends for many years," Newt began his announcement. "For those of you who don't know me, I purchased the Wagner's home a few months ago and have resided there since. The place is much like Katherine left it.

"A crew has been roasting some of my prime longhorn beef out there over the barbeque pit since last evening along with all the fixings. Everyone here is welcome to come out and eat their fill in Katherine Wagner's memory. Most of you are probably familiar with the location, but if you're not, follow Pine Canyon Road until you see the sign Muleskinner's Rest right where Gary Wagner hung it when he built the place more than a decade ago."

* * *

Conor and June mingled uncomfortably with the Campbells, Brumbaughs, and Westcotts at Newt's barbeque. When Gus and Katie Brumbaugh planned to leave for home, it seemed the perfect opportunity for them to escape also.

"What is it you need to do in the morning?" June asked as they drove toward town.

"One of my brother's neighbors is losing cattle," Con told her. "I need to look into it."

"On Sunday?" she moaned.

"He called yesterday morning. By the time I got the message, it was midafternoon. I had things I needed to do." He blushed. "I couldn't avoid the funeral today." He shrugged his shoulders.

"And Jesse or one of the others could not handle it?" she asked incredulously.

"He and my father have been friends since before I was born."

"Like Luis?"

"Well, Luis is a sheepman like us and Dunc is a cattleman, but yes. Sort of like Luis."

"Dunk? Like dunk something in water?"

"Dunc like Duncan. Duncan Blackwood."

"I know him," June replied in surprise. "We did something on titles or deeds for him about a year ago. An old lien, I think. Nice old guy."

"Okay then?"

"Okay," she concluded.

They had driven a couple of miles in silence when June suddenly giggled.

"What?" Con asked.

"It sounded like I had to approve before you could do your job. I'm sorry."

"Henpecked, I think they call that," Con commented.

"Oh, Conor. Please don't think of me that way. I never meant it...I never want us to be like that."

Con changed the subject. "How'd you like to go for a ride this evening? Get away from the lights and watch the stars?"

"I would like that."

"Our bellies are full, but we'll need to change clothes and get some carrots."

"Carrots? What are you talking about?"

"For the horses."

"Huh?" She wrinkled her nose and squinted one eye in confusion. "Oh!" June exclaimed in realization. "Horseback ride?"

"Yes."

"Sure," she said. "But I need to warn you. It has been quite a while."

"Paddy has a couple of pretty gentle ones."

"I will finally get to meet him?"

"Of course."

9

SATURDAY, JUNE 21, 1930

They pulled up to the back door of a small bungalow on a corner lot, only a few blocks from her own house. She had never been there before, but the sheriff's pickup parked beside them when they pulled in assured June where they were. She asked anyway.

"This is your house?"

"Yep, bought and paid for."

"May I come in?"

"I'll just be a minute, but sure." He reacted proudly as he opened her door and led her up the back steps. Con reached past her to unlatch the back door and pushed it open for her. "Go on in," he said. "I don't think anything will bite you."

That last comment made her skeptical. As she entered the kitchen, her attitude immediately transformed to surprise. There were no dirty dishes in the sink. The table and counters were clean. A dishcloth draped over the faucet in the sink, a coffeepot on the stove, and a dishtowel hanging from the stove's door were the only things in view that were not attached. She continued into the living room. It was just as clean and nearly as neat. A week's worth of newspapers were stacked on one end of the couch and a Zane Grey novel lay on the end table beside a very large, overstuffed chair.

"The bathroom is through the bedroom," Con told her. "If you need to use it, I can wait."

"No," she said. "I'm fine."

Through the bedroom door, she could see the bed made and no piles of clothing were visible on the floor as he closed the door behind him. It seemed only minutes when the door reopened and Con stepped out in a khaki shirt and brown leather vest. As she looked closer, there were remnants of bloodstains on the vest and bullet holes, both in and out, just above the waist on the right-hand side. The sight sent a shiver up her spine. She recalled sitting that early morning in the waiting room of the hospital. It was soon after they had met. His sister, who she barely knew, was there and his parents who she had never met. His father put his arm around her as she wept uncontrollably and gently consoled her.

"He's a strong boy," she remembered Juan Armenta saying. "He'll be okay," he assured her as the doctor worked to save Conor's life. From that very moment she knew where Conor's gentle disposition came from.

"Are you okay?" Con asked. The interruption of her contemplation jerked her back into the present.

"Yes, fine," she answered and made no comment on his vest.

"I'll get some carrots," he said and returned to the kitchen.

June followed him. "Nice house," she said.

"It's small, but easy to take care of," he replied as he

chopped chunks of carrots and shoved them into his vest pockets. He filled a canteen with water from the tap and slung it over his shoulder. "Ready?"

"Yes." She smiled and they headed out the door.

"I'm afraid I will take longer than you did," June warned Con as they pulled up in front of her house. "I will hurry, but you might want to get yourself a glass of tea while you wait," June said as she trotted up the steps. "You know where it is. Help yourself," she told him and dashed into her bedroom.

Conscientiously, Con made his way into the kitchen and found a glass in the cupboard. He had eaten many meals here and watched as June and April opened and closed the refrigerator and cupboards. It still seemed uncomfortably like he was invading her privacy as he took the pitcher of tea from the refrigerator and filled the glass. He could not bring himself to sit and wait in the coolness of the house while June dressed in the next room. He stepped outside to the porch swing.

June soon came out the door. "I hope this is all right, Conor," she said showing him her outfit. "I do not have proper boots but hope these will do." She showed him the pair rather utilitarian looking shoes she wore that laced up to her ankle with a low heel. She had changed from her dress to a loose white blouse and tan riding skirt that nearly matched Con's shirt. She had tied her hair back into a low ponytail and wore a white straw hat with a modest brim. "I've not worn this skirt in years. I'm surprised it still fits."

"I can't imagine you looking better," Con told her, "and your shoes should be fine." He stood. Putting his arm around her waist and kissed her gently, perhaps for the first time that day.

June stepped away slightly taking a deep breath. "Let's go," she chirped. She took the glass from Con's hand and quickly ran it to the kitchen before allowing herself to succumb to distraction. I want to keep today casual she planned to herself. "No, I need to," she corrected the thought aloud.

* * *

There was no one in sight when they pulled in at Patrick Armenta's sheep ranch. Neither of his two dogs came out which suggested to Con he was not at home. Paddy's Model-T truck sitting in the yard indicated he might not be far away.

"Follow me," Con told June as he walked around to the rear of the house.

"This is where you grew up?" June asked as they rounded the corner of the little house.

"Yes," Con told her. "Cozy." He chuckled, remembering the family of five cramped into a house smaller than June's house, occupied by only two.

"Filled with love," she reevaluated with a smile.

"Yes, I have to agree with that," he confirmed.

Bob, Con's favorite of Paddy's horses lazily swatted at flies with his tail as he grazed in the little pasture behind the house. He snapped to attention at Con's whistle and watched cautiously before charging toward them in recognition.

"This is Bob," Con told her as the gelding slid to a stop at the fence. He held out a chunk of carrot from his pocket that Bob accepted without hesitation. "Probably the finest horse I've ever ridden," Con added. As he rubbed Bob's cheek, the horse moved closer for Con to rub his neck and behind his ears. After less than a minute, Con opened the gate and turned to walk back across the ranch yard to the barn. He grabbed

June's hand as they walked side by side across the hard-packed dirt.

"He'll just follow you?" June questioned as she peered over her shoulder at Bob, close on their heels.

"He always has so far," Con replied. He nodded toward the paddock beside the barn. "That big white mare there, with the black mane and tail," he told June. "Her name is Chalk. She's a sweetheart. Take these and show them to her." He pulled three chunks of carrot from his pocket. "If she comes to you, give them to her one at a time," he explained. "Put them on the palm of your hand with your fingers out flat like this." He showed her. "If your fingers are curled, she might mistake them for the carrot and bite them. She won't mean to, but you could get hurt pretty seriously."

June looked scared as she glanced from Chalk to Con and back again.

"Don't be afraid," Con urged her.

She held a piece of carrot in her palm as Con had shown her. "Like this?"

"Ah-huh," he confirmed. "I'll watch you."

June held up the piece of carrot between her thumb and forefinger for Chalk to see, and the mare ambled toward her. When she got close, June put it on the palm of her hand as instructed and held it out to the horse. Chalk inched toward her.

"Come on, sweet girl," June urged softly.

Chalk's nose reached cautiously to the hand and sniffed the carrot. In doing so the horse let out a brief snort which startled June half out of her skin. A sharp, "Oh!" escaped June's lips as she jerked her hand back and the carrot hit the ground between Chalk's front feet.

Con nearly blew snot from his nose trying to stifle his

laugh as Chalk casually found the carrot on the ground and devoured it.

"So, you think that was funny, huh, cowboy?" June scolded him as he tried to fight back the tears forming in his eyes.

"No." He tried to hide his grin. "Yes," he confessed. "I'm sorry, but," a snort escaped him, "that was really funny."

June's ire quickly turned to a grin. "Yes," she admitted. "I suppose that it was." She recomposed herself as Chalk watched her over the fence. "I may need the bathroom shortly," June commented. "I nearly wet myself."

Con desperately tried to contain his laughter with little success.

"Don't you laugh!" June tried to command him but broke back into laughter again herself.

"Go ahead," Con urged her on after a short reprieve. "Try it again."

The second attempt was successful and Chalk greatly appreciated her gift. June repeated the offering, and Con continued instructing her on how to let Chalk know she was her friend. "Pet and rub her on her neck and chest where you can reach. Move slowly and stay away from her face until she gets to know you. Otherwise, she might think you're going to hit her and we start all over from scratch. Watch her eyes and keep where she can see what you're doing."

As Con retrieved a halter from the barn for Chalk, Bob waited dutifully by the door. Con gave him a pat on the neck and another bite of carrot as he passed. he haltered Chalk and tied her to an iron ring near the door when he led her from the paddock. He proceeded to saddle both horses.

"Are you ready?" Con asked June when he was finished.

"Could I use the bathroom before we leave," June asked modestly.

"The outhouse is around the corner of the barn." Con pointed in the direction.

"No indoor plumbing?" she asked, hoping not to sound naïve.

"Sure, but when we're working outside, the privy saves running in and out of the house." He paused, noting June seemed to think he was joking. "There's a bucket of lime inside the door with an empty soup can in it," Con continued. "If you need to do your business, sprinkle some lime over it. It keeps down the smell."

June's face changed four shades of red. "I, uh…oh, never mind," she said as she turned and headed around the corner. The facility stunned her when she opened the door. It was the cleanest outhouse she had ever seen. "Must run in the family," she commented aloud. A fresh roll of toilet paper hung from a nail in easy reach from the seat and the bucket of lime in the corner as Conor had instructed. Most amazingly, even in the heat day, the odor remained very endurable. "The lime must work."

While June was in the privy, Con retrieved his pistol from under the seat of his car and his canteen. He had the pistol safely concealed in Bob's saddlebags and was hanging the canteen from the saddle horn when June returned.

"I am ready," she announced.

"I'll give you a leg up," he offered.

When he did, June almost lost her grip on the saddle horn. She considered herself a tad heavier than the average woman and he nearly threw her into the saddle. Conor was much stronger than he appeared to her or she had suspected. He then adjusted her stirrups and tied a lariat from the barn near the pommel of his saddle.

"Where's your brother?" June asked as they rode past the house.

"Out with his sheep, I suppose," Con answered. "There's a buckskin and a sorrel horse gone from the paddock. He left plenty of hay for Chalk, so he might not be planning on coming back for a few days.

"How big is his ranch?"

"I think he owns about two thousand acres. It's all connected, but not just one big patch. Forty acres here connects to another hundred acres that goes off another way and such, then some more ground in a different direction. It all depends on where the water is. Paddy probably leases twice that much. I know my way pretty well around most of this country. Both on his and the neighbors' places."

They ambled side by side up a trail that had been used for a road intermittently in the past.

"Where are we going now?" June asked.

"North for a mile or so then west awhile and south, then back here."

"It looks desolate," she commented.

"It sure can get that way if you don't know where you are."

"Water?" June asked.

"That's probably the most important thing. At the cabin I found where they held Katherine Wagner, there was a good spring right by it. About fifteen years ago, a fellow by the name of Clark was out there. He needed water pretty bad and couldn't find any. Probably walked ten or fifteen miles around looking for it before he died of thirst. Where he died was only a couple of miles from that spring. He just couldn't find it."

"Is that who Clark County is named for?" she asked.

"No, that was a different Clark. Railroad guy."

June watched Conor as the two horses moseyed through

the scattered brush. They left the trail they started on but could still ride side by side most of the time, only occasionally resorting to single file to navigate around some obstacle. He rode along as easily as if he had been born in the saddle.

"Bob is a pretty horse?" she verified.

"He's a good one." Con chuckled. "Riding him is like sitting in an easy chair. How are you doing with Chalk?"

"Oh. She's sweet, just like you said. Like riding a rocking chair, only sideways sort of." She laughed.

"Let me know if you need a break."

"I'm enjoying the scenery. You can see so much more from up here than down on the ground," she responded. "Where did you spend that summer when your father got hurt?" she asked.

Con clucked his tongue and with a slight turn, galloped Bob to the crest of a nearby hill. June did the same and Chalk kept along right behind them. The short sprint invigorated June and seemed to do the same for the horses as they shook their heads and manes when they stopped.

"That was fun!" June exclaimed.

Conor grinned ear to ear, elated that June did not hesitate with the little challenge. "See those red cliffs over there?" he asked her as he pointed west.

"How could I miss them?" she responded rhetorically.

"That's where Papa chased the puma. Down to the south,"—he pointed again—"is where I camped by the spring."

June scanned the vast landscape before them from their vantage point. "Does anyone else live out here besides Patrick?" she asked, seeing no signs of habitation.

"A few," Con answered. He turned in the saddle to face north. "Duncan Blackwood lives right over that second ridge."

He pointed. "About a mile and a half from where we're sitting. There are some others scattered around."

"So, this is where you feel at home," June observed. "Out here without so much as a jackrabbit to distract you for as far as the eye can see."

"Oh, there's jackrabbits and cottontails too. Birds by the thousands, coyotes, all kinds of animals out here," Con told her as he also surveyed the panorama. "This *is* my home in a way. Always will be I suppose. It's where I grew up."

"Where are they?" she asked. "The wildlife, I mean?"

"Hiding from the heat," he replied. "Conserving water just like the wildflowers that only open at night or when it rains."

"You *are* teasing me, right?"

"No. I'm dead serious. I'll show you sometime." He paused, remembering camping out here under the stars for weeks on end herding his family's sheep. "I remember one morning after a rain, there must have been a thousand wrens singing their lungs out from every bush when the sun came up. By nine or ten o'clock, I couldn't have found one for a hundred dollars." He grinned.

"Where will your brother be out there?"

Con looked to the position of the sun above them. "The sun is beginning its way down," he said, "but it's still plenty hot out. He'll have them somewhere they can find some brush for shade for a while yet. It'll be down low where we can't see them from here. When they get up and start grazing, they'll wander up the eastern and northern sidehills where the first shade of dusk will hit in about three hours. If we find them before that..." He did not finish the comment, just clicked his tongue, and started Bob off the western slope of the hill they were on at a walk.

June nudged Chalk along beside him at a half-length back.

Sheep trails crisscrossed their general direction of travel in what seemed random patterns to June. Con followed them for short distances at times as they veered in an out of their own course, but mostly they traveled on untainted ground. She noticed they paralleled a fence not far off on their right. June also saw Conor peering closely at each trail they crossed.

"What are you looking for?"

"Tracks,"

"Left by Patrick's sheep?"

"Cow tracks," Con clarified. "That's Blackwood's ranch across the fence."

"So, you're just dragging me along while you work?" June asked, feeling taken advantage of.

"Not really," Con explained, seemingly unaware of the tone in June's voice. "It's highly unlikely a rustler would move cattle across Paddy's ranch to make his escape. On the other hand, it doesn't hurt to pay attention."

They wandered along for over another mile in silence. It still peeved June to be an afterthought on what she considered to be Conor's investigation. Her mood improved as she became more accustomed to Chalk and their surroundings. Since Conor's earlier remark regarding the presence of wildlife, she watched more closely. Initially she only noticed a couple of flies annoying the horses, but since had spotted two scurrying lizards, a very small bird she could not identify, a butterfly, and what she thought may have been a roadrunner resting in the shade of a large boulder in the distance.

Conor stopped Bob at the crest of a low saddle between two hills. Evidently not sensing her earlier irritation, he turned to her with a broad smile. "I believe you're about to meet my baby brother," he told her and clicked Bob into a brisk trot.

June soon spotted a tan horse in the distance that she

assumed must be a buckskin. At the switch of its tail, she saw another reddish horse nearby. With a bit more of June's heels to Chalk's sides than she intended, the horse bolted into a gallop. Without hesitation, June sped past Conor before he realized what happened. When Con touched his heels to Bob's flanks, the big bay took flight. Chalk had no chance of catching him as Bob charged past, but Conor soon eased back on the reins as they neared the dingy white tent marking Paddy's campsite.

Both riders laughed carelessly as they slowed their mounts to a walk a hundred yards from the smoldering campfire. A Dutch oven nestled; half buried in the coals of the fire. The open front of the tent offered the only shade in sight. A pair of boots stood beside two stocking feet atop a bedroll protruding from it.

"A little late in the day for a siesta," Con hailed loudly as they approached.

The feet sprang to life and a squinting man's head beneath a crumpled hat immediately appeared from the shadows where the feet had been.

"I wasn't expecting company," the man said gruffly as he tugged on his boots. "But I must be dreaming." His voice instantly grew pleasant as he spotted June. "There's a golden-haired angel on a white horse following you."

"Yes, there certainly is, Paddy," Con responded as he stepped down from the saddle and looked back to June. "This is June Sommers, my..." he stuttered in search of words, "the sweetest, kindest, most beautiful woman in the world. And for some reason that only God knows the answer, she likes me."

June blushed at Con's praise as she slid to the ground.

Con took hold of Chalk's reins. "June, my hermit brother, Patrick,"

When she stepped forward with an outreached hand, June suddenly realized she had yet to fully regain her land-legs from the ride. "Patrick," she greeted, trying to disguise her wobbly stride. "I am so happy to finally meet you."

He walked past her hand and hugged her. "I feel like I already know you," Paddy told her as he stepped back. "Mama and Olivia told me all about you a couple of months ago. I would have recognized you from a quarter mile away," he teased as he added, "even if you hadn't brought my dead-beat brother along with you,"

June liked Patrick instantly. Perhaps an inch or two shorter than Conor, his broader shoulders reminded her of Juan, their father. He was much more at ease around her than Conor had been early in their relationship. Patrick was perhaps a bit more worldly when it came to women than his older brother, even though he presently lived a life of soli-tude. The family resemblance of the two men was unmistak-able, though June thought Patrick less handsome. Perhaps Conor had inherited slightly more of their mother's facial features.

"Have a seat on my bed," Patrick offered. "It's the only shade around here."

"Thank you," June replied, "but I've not ridden in several years and should walk around a little bit right now."

Patrick chuckled cheerfully. "I noticed when you got down from Chalk, but I didn't want to say anything."

"I believe the term is Greenhorn," June suggested. She spied the slightest tint of crimson showing through Patrick's weather-beaten complexion.

"I would never say that," he tried to withdraw.

"But you *did* think it," she accused him as she laughed at herself. Con and Paddy both chuckled with her.

"Come on," Con told her. "There's a spring over here. The water is ice cold."

He held the reins of both horses in one hand and gently kissed her before taking June's hand in his other as they led the horses to the spring. The sheep had muddied the water of the little stream that trickled from the ground three dozen yards before dissipating into the desert. It remained cold and clear near the source. June knelt, washed her face, and drank of nature's elixir while Conor watered the horses a few yards downstream.

He watched when she stood up from the edge of the rivulet. Her riding skirt was wet and dirty from her knees down. She reached down and shook the loose grass and mud from it and never took a second glance. No less the lady than he had come to know and love, he considered, perchance she is less bound by city society than he previously surmised.

When they returned to his camp, Paddy had rearranged his tent and folded his bedroll to form a cushion atop a crate of his supplies.

"For you, ma'am." He motioned to June.

"My name is June," she said. "Everyone else in your family calls me by it, Patrick. I would like you to do the same."

"June, would you like to sit down, ma'am?" Paddy asked awkwardly as he motioned to the chair he had fashioned.

"Thank you," June replied, forcing back the urge to laugh.

"I only have one plate and cup," he said as he dished a plateful of beans from the Dutch oven.

"We ate before we came out here," June informed him as he handed her the plate and a spoon.

"It's just beans and coffee," he replied. "I have plenty."

Patrick filled the cup with muddy-looking brew. It had been coffee when he made it that morning but sat in the sun in the enameled pot since then. He handed it to her as if he had not heard her earlier comment and began filling a tin can with beans which he handed to Con with a spoon. He followed that with another tin can filled with coffee for his brother and repeated the process for himself.

June ate her beans. They were delicious. Probably the way their father had made them forever. The coffee was disgusting, but she graciously sipped at it without complaint. The two men talked casually as they ate. June listened. Patrick took her empty plate and the tin cans that he had served the beans in. He refilled her cup before she could stop him and did the same for Con and himself.

The sun began to set over the red cliffs to the west as Con and Paddy conversed.

"Dunc is losing some cattle," Con told him.

"Yes, he's told me," Paddy responded. "Been going on for quite a while. I've been watching, but haven't seen anything."

"I'm coming back out in the morning," Con continued. "I'll ride Bob over there and do some serious looking around."

They continued to talk about the cattle rustlers and the discussion gradually rolled back to Bob.

"You should buy him from me," Paddy finally suggested.

"I'd love to," Con told him, "But it'll have to wait for a while. I really don't have much cash right now."

"I understand," Patrick answered, grinning. "New girl-friend, new car, spending a little more now than you used to," he ribbed his brother. "I get it."

"No, it's not like that," Con tried to explain without saying anything. He looked at June who seemed to be watching the horses. "I've got the money. I just need to hold off for a while."

"It's not a problem," Paddy answered. He saw his broth-er's glance at June. Con was embarrassed. He had always been miserly and kept an adequate savings account. Lately he was probably burning through that money at a rapid pace. "I can wait," he concluded and let the exchange end there.

"We should be going," Con resolved as he poured half his can of mud into the weeds.

June looked on in shock as she stood up. The nerve of him. She drank all of her coffee without any complaint...twice. She thought he had better manners than that.

"Thank you for supper," she told him as she handed Patrick her cup. "The beans were delicious."

"Papa taught me how to make them when I was little," he confessed proudly. "I still do it the very same way."

"Well, you certainly learned well. They are wonderful."

June again offered her hand as she prepared to mount Chalk. This time Patrick accepted in an awkward handshake. His hands were badly misshaped. She noticed it when he served their supper. The fingers of his gnarled right hand barely bent as he tried to grip hers. Now she understood why he had hugged her when they met.

"Conor did not tell the whole truth when he introduced us," June whispered.

"How so?" Patrick asked quietly.

"I don't just like him," she answered. "I love him."

"I know you do. I can see it in your eyes. I know him probably better than anyone other than Luis, maybe. And he might not have said it to you yet, but he loves you too. You are both very fortunate to have each other."

* * *

The westward sky turned a brilliant array of colors as the sun made its final descent behind the red cliffs. Streaks of yellow to violet and every shade of red and orange imaginable between adorned the horizon behind them. June turned frequently to peer back over her shoulder at the panorama as stars began to appear ahead of them. A moonless star-filled sky had hung above them for over an hour when Conor came to a halt atop the last hill above the house, barn, and corrals that marked Patrick's home. The moon would not rise until after midnight. A dim glow of light showing over the horizon told of Las Vegas in the distance. She rode up close alongside him and stopped stirrup to stirrup. He reached over and took her hand.

"This is what I miss," he said. "What I miss about not being out here every night. What I miss about living in town."

"It is beautiful," June replied, feeling the warmth of his calf against hers and the soft touch of his hand.

"Will you share it with me?" he asked.

There was the slightest twitch in his grip when he asked it. June's heart nearly leaped from her chest. What did she hear? What did he just ask her? She could not breathe. She tried to inhale. The air would not come. Nor could she exhale. She looked at him in the darkness. A pale blue profile of his face against the blue-black sky dotted with a million tiny lights. Suddenly her body realized she was about to faint and drew in a gasp of precious oxygen. It seemed like a hurricane of air abruptly rushed into her lungs. He must have heard the explosion, but his gaze remained straight ahead. Maybe he had not heard it. Maybe he was so lost in a trance, he did not notice. Maybe...no. It could not be. Maybe she was dreaming. Maybe he never asked...anything.

"Wha...what...what do you mean?" a soft female voice asked him. She heard the voice. It had to be real. Did he hear it?

"This is my world, June. This is where I came from and I don't know if it ever will leave me. Or if I can ever leave it completely." He paused and cleared his throat. "I love you, June. This is who I am. This is what I am. Will you...you... have me? Will you marry me, June?"

"Oh, yes. Yes, oh yes." The air. She sat in a trance. "Yes, I will," she gasped with the last remnant of air left in her lungs. Then taking a deep breath, she concluded he half-spoken thought. "Yes, Conor Armenta. I will marry you and love you for the rest of my life."

She looked down to her hand. Invisible in the blackness of the night. It squeezed his tighter than she had ever squeezed anything in her entire life. Exactly as he squeezed hers in return. Her fingers were numb. They both gradually eased their grip and leaned into one another. They kissed more affectionately than they ever had kissed before. She gasped to breathe through her nostrils as tears of joy flowed unrestricted down her face. She broke free and held her cheek to his, panting.

"Can we have more children?" she asked. "Boys? I want to bear you sons...as many as you would like to have."

10

Conor Armenta parked in front of the sheriff's office at a quarter to seven. A maroon Cadillac sedan with California license plates occupied the space beside the one marked 'Sheriff.' Two men and a woman sat on armless oak chairs in the outer office drinking coffee when he entered. Conor recognized David Whitfield Fredericks and Molly Mansfield from the silver screen. Mansfield sat cross-legged in an expensive-looking business suit with a calf-length skirt and a light straw fedora. Her free leg bounced nervously as she waited. Fredericks wore a tailored three-piece suit and a fedora not unlike the one Molly wore. He sat confidently sucking on a large cigar, flicking his ashes on the floor. The other man wore an off-the-shelf suit but a nice one. His tie seemed too tight. This man was unquestionably the attorney.

Hazel looked very nervously at her boss when he came

through the door. "These folks are waiting to see you, Sheriff," she announced as professionally as she could muster.

"They look comfortable," he observed as he hung his Stetson on a hook by the door. "They can wait."

Hazel looked down, attempting to appear busy with paperwork on her desk. Con was sure that she was totally mesmerized to be in the presence of the movie stars. He crossed the room to stand a few feet away directly in front of Fredericks, who then exhaled a voluminous amount of smoke.

"Sheriff." The actor nodded in recognition.

"Mr. Fredericks," Con replied. "I'm sure Mrs. Corbyn has been far too gracious to mention it, but smoking is not permitted in this office. If you wish to smoke sir, you may step outside."

The actor's pasty skin tone gradually reddened, beginning at his collar and working its way up his face. Con watched the muscles flexing in his cheeks as he ground his teeth. The action divulged Fredericks' ire.

"My apology, Sheriff," he calmly spoke as he stood. "I was unaware of the policy." He stuffed the cigar into his mouth and tipped his hat to Hazel as he exited the front door.

Con turned to Hazel. "When Judge Tucker and the DA arrive, send them on in...and open some windows."

Con closed his office door behind him and sat down at his desk to read Deputy Neilly's and Coroner Martin's reports on yesterday's search of the Hotel Nevada. Among the items collected as evidence were two fedoras from Hugh Parker's, also known as John Smith's room. "How original," Con muttered to himself. After his conversation with Bull Hansen, the sheriff specified that any fedoras found should be considered evidence. One round was missing from the box of smokeless .45 Colt cartridges from the Peters Cartridge Company. It also came from Parker's room.

Con rose and went to the door. "Is Ben on the board today?" he asked Hazel.

"Yes, sir," she answered. "He's gone out to relieve Whit at the Campbell's. Whit should be back here any time now."

"And Jesse?" Con asked.

"He's at breakfast." Hazel blushed knowingly. Jesse and Dottie should be eating together at the Mesquite Café about now Con silently surmised.

"I want to see Jesse privately as soon as he gets in."

"Yes, Sheriff."

The clock on the wall showed seven thirty when he closed his door and returned to the reports. A photograph showed the box of cartridges in the bureau drawer where they discovered it. He looked at Hugh Parker's mugshot. Con appraised the insolent expression on Parker's face.

"Above the law," he mumbled to himself. "Just like his compadres outside."

He turned to the back of the picture and the physical description of the suspect. Five foot, four inches tall, one hundred ten pounds, etc.

"They forgot to weigh his ego," Con muttered to himself. A knock at the door interrupted his one-sided conversation. "Come in," he beckoned.

Judge William Tucker and District Attorney Donald D. Davis entered and closed the door behind them.

"Good morning, Sheriff," Davis greeted with an extended hand. By the time the three had exchanged handshakes and hellos, another knock came from the door.

Con opened it. "Come on in, Jesse," he told him and closed

the door behind him. "You've met Judge Tucker," he said, "and Mr. Davis, who you saw in court a few months ago."

Already starstruck by the visitors outside, Jesse had barely regained his poise for two of the most prominent men in the county who were shaking his hand when he turned to Con.

"What did you need, Sheriff?" he asked.

Con picked up the box of cartridges. "These were found in Hugh Parker's hotel room. He probably bought them locally in the last few days. Get a copy of his mugshot from the jail. Find out when and where they came from."

"Got it, Sheriff," Jesse replied and repeated back his instructions.

Con accompanied Jesse to the door. "Report back to me personally. If I'm not here, Hazel should know where to find me."

"Got it, Sheriff," he again responded, nodding. As Con opened the door, he glanced at the clock on the wall of the outer office, Eight thirty-five.

"Won't you folks please come in?" he asked the restless trio in the outer office. As David Whitfield Fredericks grudgingly rose to his feet, Con added, "Bring your chairs, if you would. I don't normally have more than one or two visitors in my office at a time."

Fredricks gasped in disbelief that he should be required to carry his own chair to the meeting. The attorney just followed the directions without hesitation. Molly Mansfield stood for a moment waiting for either of the two *gentlemen* to offer to carry her chair for her, but since both of them were well under-way, she reluctantly picked it up herself and followed.

"Miss, gentlemen," Conor spoke as they entered the room, "This is District Court Judge William Tucker." Tucker came to his feet. "And Clark County District Attorney Donald D. Davis."

"Dave Fredericks," he introduced himself. "My attorney, Emerson Pollard. I'm sure you recognize Molly Mansfield."

After a few moments of small talk, Con interrupted. "If you'll bear with me, I forgot to make a phone call. This will just take a minute."

He picked up the telephone on his desk and dialed Desert Chevrolet.

"Good morning. This is Sheriff Armenta. There's a maroon Cadillac sedan in front of our office. It has California license plates. I need it towed to the impound yard at the county shop." He paused, listening. "No, it doesn't appear to be damaged," another pause, "yes, thank you." He hung up the telephone.

"Excuse me," Mr. Pollard began as he stood and stepped toward the door. "There are things I need from the car before it's towed away."

"I'm afraid that's not possible," Con stopped him. "The car and everything in it are impounded as evidence."

"But you can't do that. Those are my personal lawbooks in that car."

Con held up a search warrant.

"You filed a search warrant on that car this morning?" Pollard looked at Judge Tucker accusingly.

"No," Con interjected as he glanced at the warrant. "This search warrant was issued on Wednesday. It's for the Campbell estate and everything on it. That car was on the property at the time this warrant was served."

"Are you sure that it's the same car?" the attorney asked with a smirk.

"It had better be, or you will all be arrested for tampering with evidence," Con replied.

David Fredericks jumped in to change the subject and attempt to turn control of the conversation in his and his associates' favor. "I suppose, Sheriff, that box of ammunition on your desk is meant to intimidate us. Implying that your form of frontier justice will be served so to speak."

"No, Dave," Con replied sarcastically as he half perched, leaning against his desk. "This box of ammunition is evidence. It came from Mr. Parker's hotel room. Or should I say John Smith's hotel room. That's the alias he registered under. This"— he touched the grip of the .45 automatic strapped to his waist— "is meant to intimidate and ensure that justice will be served."

David Whitfield Fredericks was a tall man. A good half-foot taller than the sheriff. He was used to towering over most men; intimidating and dominating conversations with his stature, if not his eloquence. Conor Armenta was very familiar with the ploy. He allowed Fredericks no opportunity to rise from his chair, while remaining himself partially standing and looming over the actor. William Tucker was also acquainted with the tactic. He observed the sheriff with appreciation of how expertly he performed the maneuver. Fredericks clearly felt uncomfortable looking up to the sheriff.

"David Whitfield Fredericks," Con began. "You are hereby charged with interfering in a criminal investigation. This is a felony. At this time, you will not be incarcerated. You are however, prohibited from leaving Clark County, Nevada until these charges are resolved."

"You can't do this!" Fredericks blurted out. "I have a business to run!"

"You should have considered that before ordering Miss

Mansfield to steal evidence in a murder investigation and move it across state lines," the sheriff replied flatly.

"I did nothing of the kind!" Fredericks denied.

Con retrieved a somewhat crumpled yellow piece of paper from the desktop beside him. Molly Mansfield gasped when she saw it. "And I quote," he began before reading the note aloud.

2 p.m.

M.M.
   Be in my office first thing in the morning!

D.F.

"I didn't write that note," Fredericks replied smugly.

It amazed Con how quickly he recovered after seeing the shock on his face upon the note's disclosure. "No," he said. "You dictated it to the clerk at the Hotel Nevada."

A soft knock at the door interrupted the conversation. Con crossed the room and opened it. Deputy Whitney Ellis stood outside. "Sorry to interrupt, Sheriff," he said. "I saw the tow truck hooking up to the Cadillac outside. I thought you'd want to know."

Con closed the door behind him as he stepped into the outer office. "I'd want to know what?"

"Those two men and that woman in there. At one-forty-five this morning, they came out to the Campbell's. The big guy. That's David Whitfield Fredericks, isn't it?"

"What did they want?" Con asked.

"Fredericks was driving. He said the woman had left something out there and they wanted to get it. I told him that everything was off limits because of a murder investigation. He got pretty pushy. I told them to leave. He asked what I would do if they just went on in. I told him I would shoot him. He laughed and put the car in gear. I pulled my gun and told him I wasn't joking. I couldn't hear what he said then, but he slammed the car in reverse and spun it around and left."

"Is that all?"

"It's all in my report, license plate number, everything."

"That's good work, Whit," he praised. "Thanks for interrupting."

Con reentered the room and resumed his perch on the desk. With Judge Tucker and the DA in the room, the trio had remained silent in his absence.

"Miss Mansfield," Con began. At mention of her name, he had her full attention. "What was so important you left at the Campbell estate that it warranted a special trip out there just before two o'clock this morning?"

Automatically, she started to answer without thinking. "A cig— . . ."

"Shut up!!" Fredericks growled in a fury.

Molly Mansfield's face was brilliant red, partially from embarrassment of her near miscue, partially from fear of David Fredericks's short, but severe, disruption that saved her exposé.

"A cigarette butt, Miss Mansfield? Hastily discarded in an anxious moment perhaps?" The color drained from her face faster than pulling the plug from a kitchen sink. Con had nailed it. Her reaction proved it. He knew it...and she knew it.

"It wasn't this one?" He opened a small envelope on his desk and removed a cigarette butt with bright red lipstick on the end. "Craven Navy Cut," Con read from below the lipstick stain. "This is the one you left in the ashtray in the lobby of the

Hotel Nevada Wednesday afternoon," he said as he studied the trio. Emerson Pollard's facial expression had not changed since he entered the room. David Fredericks's countenance flashed between grinding his teeth in semi-controlled seething to ferocious anger. Molly Mansfield's demeanor progressed from nervous apprehension to near panic. "It accompanied..." Con let the comment dissipate into silence as he held up the crumpled yellow note he had read earlier. "You were so distracted, Miss Mansfield, or should I say Miss Stapleton, that you left immediately for Los Angeles." He paused. "You didn't even go up to your room."

Molly Mansfield looked away, unable to face her accuser. She was a good actress and knew it. She could have done it on screen, but this was different. That was make-believe and this had suddenly become very real. She took a deep breath. Regrouped and with regained poise, she returned her gaze to the sheriff. You can do this, she silently reassured herself. It's just words, lines in a script, even if Matt is dead.

"But that's not the cigarette butt we're looking for, is it?" Con continued. He dropped the butt back into the envelope and he leaned across the desk behind him, taking an identical envelope from his top desk drawer. Opening the envelope, he retrieved a second cigarette butt. He held it up and read the small blue print. "Craven Navy Cut. This cigarette came from the floor of the prop truck, Miss Mansfield. No one is allowed inside the prop truck except for Joe and Jenny Vance." Con turned his attention to her boss. "Isn't that correct, Dave?"

"Why, yes," Fredericks answered, suddenly brought back into the conversation. The sheriff had been the only one to speak since he had interrupted Molly in the brink of time. "Yes, that's the policy."

"That's not my cigarette," Molly spoke up. "Lots of people

smoke that brand," she lied knowingly. Hugh Parker was the only person she had ever seen with the disgustingly harsh smokes. "There's not even any lipstick on it," she suddenly realized. Maybe she could pull this off after all.

"No," Con corrected. "It's not a common brand. They are made in England. They cost three times what American cigarettes cost, and that's only when you can find them. There isn't a single tobacco shop or store in Clark County that sells them." He could almost hear the wheels turning in her head as he watched her. "You and Hugh Parker are the only two people around here that smoke them."

"Jenny's been spending a lot of time with Hugh lately." Molly quickly shifted gears. "Maybe it's hers."

"But Jenny doesn't smoke. Neither does her father." Con kept his eyes on Molly Mansfield. "I want you to look straight at me, Miss Mansfield," Con told her. "Do you still have Hugh Parker's keys to the prop truck?"

"No, I..." She could not believe herself. She'd just admitted to...no, wait, she hadn't. "I've never had Hugh's keys," she lied.

Con turned to David Fredericks. "David Whitfield Fredericks, will you give me the keys to the car you drove here today?"

"No, no, I won't," he announced with a sardonic smile.

"David Whitfield Fredericks, you are under arrest for withholding evidence and conspiracy to transport evidence across state lines in a murder investigation." Fredericks looked pleadingly toward Pollard, whose expression had yet to change but sat there, shaking his head. Judge Tucker struggled to subdue a chuckle while District Attorney Davis sat listening and observing as stoically as Mr. Pollard. Con noted to himself that playing poker with either of the attorneys would not likely be an enjoyable event. "Please stand and turn around, Mr. Fredericks. Place your hands behind your back."

David Whitfield Fredericks stood and turned around. "Wait, wait, wait," he said, throwing his hands in the air. "I'll give you the keys."

"Am I to understand that you have changed your mind and have chosen to fully cooperate with this investigation?"

"Yes, yes, okay," he said, nodding. "I will cooperate."

"Fully," Con growled.

"Fully, I will cooperate fully."

"Hand me the keys."

David Fredericks handed Con the keys.

"You may take your seat, Mr. Fredericks."

Con held the key-ring in his hands and carefully inspected each key on it. Two keys bore the iconic Cadillac logo another was a door key. He studied each of the remaining four keys, all bearing the Master Lock logo.

"Are these Mr. Parker's keys?" he asked Fredericks.

Fredericks cleared his throat. "I believe they are the keys to studio property that Mr. Parker carries."

Con scowled at him. "Fully."

"Yes." Fredericks buckled under the implication. "They are the keys assigned to Hugh Parker by Unified Stars Studios."

"Where did you get them?"

"Miss Mansfield gave them to me yesterday morning."

Con turned to Molly Mansfield who shrank under his gaze. "You've never had Hugh Parker's keys?"

"I...uh...I..."

"Where did you get them?"

"He...uh...he must have left them in the car."

"Do you have your own keys to that car?"

"Uh, yes," she answered softly, avoiding Con's face.

He held out his open hand, motioning her to give them to him. She dug into her purse and obliged.

Con turned back to Fredericks. "Are there any other keys to that car, Dave?"

"There should be another set kept at the studio."

Con laid Molly Mansfield's keys on his desk and held up Parker's keys by the door key to Fredericks.

"That should fit Hugh's office at the studio," he replied without being asked.

"And these?" Con fanned out the four Master keys.

"One should fit the back of the camera truck, one the back of the prop truck, another will be for the gun chest in the prop truck and the other for the cash box in the back of Hugh's car."

Con sat Parker's keys on his desk alongside the others and peered at the two fedoras from the hotel atop his file cabinet. Silently, he stood and crossed the room to them. The first was a light-colored straw like those worn by the two actors. Looking inside, he examined the sweatband that bore the name of a London haberdashery. The size tag, fifty-four, represented some sort of European system he could not identify. Smaller than size seven, he guessed.

His actions brought a snicker from Dave Fredericks. "That doesn't seem to fit your style, Sheriff," he commented sarcastically.

"Nor my size," Con replied, smiling. Seemingly undisturbed by the remark, he placed it momentarily on his head where it perched comically like a child's party hat. Returning the hat to its place, he turned back to Fredericks. "I've not spent much time in California," he began. "Around here it's considered poor manners for a gentleman to wear his hat indoors."

Embarrassed by the insinuation from the hick-town sheriff,

David Whitfield Fredericks removed his hat and red-faced, sat it on his lap. "As it is in California. I beg your pardon."

"May I?" Con asked, reaching for Fredericks's hat.

Appalled that the sheriff would ask to try on his hat, but under the circumstances, he handed it over to him.

"Seven and a quarter," Con remarked as he looked inside. "My size."

Just as Dave Fredericks started to complain about trying on his hat, Con placed it atop the other two fedoras on the file cabinet. "What's the meaning of this? Do you find it amusing to confiscate visitor's hats to adorn your office?"

"No. As you said, 'Not my style.' I prefer Stetsons." Con resumed his position of dominance half leaning, half sitting on his desk. "Where were you on Tuesday night, Dave?"

"At home. What difference does it make?"

"Witnesses?"

"What do you mean, witnesses?"

"Credible witnesses. When did you leave work? Who saw you? What time did you come to the studio on Wednesday?"

"What are you saying?"

"Tuesday night at eleven o'clock, someone wearing a white fedora in a maroon Cadillac sedan drove to the Campbell estate. They loaded Matt McCoy's pistol and switched holsters with Mark McCoy's pistol. Twelve hours later, Hugh Parker called and told you Matt McCoy was dead. You immediately called the newspaper and told the world. You already told me that you have a set of keys for the car at the studio. The car was parked across the street from the train station. Rumor has it that Matt McCoy loved to throw illicit parties and was diffi-cult to control. You constantly were forced to call in *favors* with law enforcement to keep his name out of the headlines." Con's volume had steadily increased until he was nearly yelling. He stopped, took a deep breath, and clarified, "Do you have witnesses as to your whereabouts between two o'clock Tuesday afternoon and nine o'clock Wednesday morning?"

David Whitfield Fredericks's face had lost all color. He was hot, perspiring profusely even though Con's office still held the cool of morning. He desperately wanted to remove the jacket of his tailored suit but knew it would expose his sweat-soaked shirt that had lost its starched elegance. He was being accused of murder.

"I...my maid...she's worked for me for twenty years."

"Credible witnesses...not in your employ...not someone who would greatly suffer if you were to be convicted of murder, Mr. Fredericks."

"Don't say anything, Dave," Emerson Pollard interrupted calmly with the exact same expressionless face he wore since his arrival in the office.

11

SUNDAY, JUNE 22, 1930

The sun beamed brilliantly through June's bedroom window as she awakened. It had been quite late when Conor dropped her off the night before. She forced herself not to invite him into her empty house…and her bedroom. They kissed fervently on the porch in the darkness when he walked her to the door. She bade him goodnight and quickly escaped inside. Leaning against the closed door behind her, she gasped for air.

She smiled to herself now. She could not stop smiling as the joy reverberated through her heart and soul. When June went to bed last night, she had lain awake what seemed hours repeating in her mind the events of the evening. It was all true. Conor had asked her to marry him…and she accepted. It thrilled her. There could not possibly be a happier woman in all of Las Vegas. All of Nevada. She thought momentarily that she had not slept, though she felt rested.

Then she remembered her dream from yesterday. It had repeated itself this morning. Fresh with the memory of it in her mind June subconsciously reached across the bed anticipating Conor still asleep beside her. His absence snapped her back into reality.

Only this time he would not be arriving an hour from now for breakfast. Conor would have risen early and was probably drinking coffee at Duncan Blackwood's kitchen table by now. That, after already riding Bob over from Patrick's ranch.

"Oh, my goodness!" she spoke aloud with abrupt realization of the hour. "I'll be late for church."

June's attempt to leap from bed became interrupted by aching pain from her inner thighs to lower back and every muscle between when she moved. She groaned with the effort as she maneuvered herself into a sitting position. Hobbling her way to the medicine cabinet in the bathroom, she shook a double dose of aspirin from the bottle. After turning the water on in the bathtub, she made her way toward the kitchen to start the coffee pot on the stove. June soaked for as long as she dared in the tub of hot water and Epsom salts. As the treatment penetrated from the outside, the aspirin reached the inside and gradually the pain began to subside.

June sat at her kitchen table hurriedly consuming a cold biscuit and fresh cup of coffee, then rushed to dress. She dashed down her porch steps with her purse on her arm and gloves in her hand. A block away, the soreness in her legs had nearly disappeared as the church bell began to ring beckoning the parishioners to its calling. She quickened her step as she slipped on her gloves.

Olivia and the girls were just taking their seats as she entered the sanctuary. Conor's parents were not present. June hurried up the aisle.

"You look particularly cheerful this morning," Olivia commented as June sat down beside her.

"I am very happy," June offered as calmly as she was able while trying to force her gaze straight ahead.

"You had a pleasant day yesterday?" Olivia pressed.

"Yes. Very pleasant," June replied.

"And?" Olivia elbowed her lightly in the ribs.

The poke brought a slight twinge. June had not realized the soreness reached that high, but it did not interrupt her smile.

She turned, whispering very softly into Olivia's ear. "Conor asked me to marry him."

Olivia's gasp brought heads turning from all directions. Her face reddened as she shrank slightly on the pew. She looked straight ahead awaiting the congregation to return to order.

"And you said yes?" Olivia whispered out the side of her mouth without looking at her.

"Of course!" she answered less quietly. "We'll talk after…"

After sitting on the hard pew without the opportunity to move around throughout the service, June's aches and pains returned. Though less intense than earlier, her stiffness did not go unnoticed.

"So, what has you all stoved up?" Olivia questioned as they exited the church.

"A long ride," June answered innocently without intending any double meaning.

Olivia eyed her accusingly. "Before or after the proposal?"

June's face flushed. "Horseback ride," she clarified. "Our discussion was near the end of it."

"Where?" she asked.

"We went riding at Patrick's."

"So, you met Paddy?" the questions kept coming.

"Yes. He was camped by a spring."

"Where did Con propose?"

"On the hill above the ranch yard. It was dark. No moon. Just the stars and a faint glow of the Las Vegas lights in the distance."

"Wow," Olivia exclaimed. "I know the place. You can see nearly all of Papa's original homestead from there. I can hardly believe my brother could be so romantic."

June raised the pearl pendant around her neck to Olivia's attention. "He gave me this Friday evening for my birthday."

"It's not fake?"

"It was in a box from Delkin's Jewelry," June reassured her.

"Isn't it pretty?" April chimed in at that moment bringing to both ladies' attention that two pairs of young ears had been hanging on every word for at least a few minutes.

"Yes, it is," Olivia agreed.

"Does this mean Con will be my daddy?" April asked her mother.

"If you want him to be," June answered as a tear escaped down her cheek.

* * *

Con swung his leg over Bob's saddle just as the first crescent of sunlight glimpsed over the low hill across the road from his birthplace. He wore civilian clothes carrying a canteen of water, two lariats, and his rifle in the scabbard. His 1911 Colt automatic hung on his right hip and badge in a vest pocket. Two pairs of handcuffs, his field glasses, and equal handfuls of carrots and lamb jerky rode in the saddlebags along with a flashlight...just in case.

He rode out of the ranch yard and turned north on the

intermittent trail he and June had begun their ride on the previous afternoon. A half hour later, Con passed through a gate in the fence separating the Armenta and Blackwood ranches. After another twenty minutes, he rode into Black-wood's ranch yard to the clamor of two barking dogs that soon reformed to yips as they greeted him with wagging tails. Duncan Blackwood stood on his front porch with a cup of coffee in his left hand by the time Con dismounted and dropped Bob's reins over the picket fence surrounding the house.

"Come on in, Sheriff," the tall gray-haired rancher called. "The coffee's hot and fresh."

"I'll take you up on it," Con replied as he accepted a firm handshake.

"You're looking good, Con. All healed up from that ruckus down by Luis's place?" he asked as he slapped his own chest.

"Yessir," Con answered with a smile. "Not nearly as serious as the newspaper made it sound. Took a little hide off was about all."

"Well, maybe." Dunc peered down his nose at the younger man. "Doc Anderson told me one bullet clipped an artery not too far from your heart and you lost quite a bit of blood. Said you were nearly dead when the deputy brought you into town."

"So, you talked to Anderson?"

"One of my boys got his hand hung up in a dally and broke it a couple of days after your scrape. I was going to talk to you about the first of the cattle I had lost while I was in town. Doc told me you weren't back to work yet. Said it'd be a week or two. I decided to wait."

Con blushed at being caught making light of the incident but made no further comment on the matter. He followed the older man inside. As they entered the house, it occurred to Con that he had never been inside before. There was nothing extravagant about the interior of the home, but it was obviously better built than Paddy's house and considerably larger. He knew Paddy and their father had been here about ten years earlier when negotiating a land trade. Con did not recall the details, but Juan Armenta was involved because the land traded to Blackwood was still deeded in his name. In exchange, Patrick received a parcel that included Clear Spring, where Con and June had found him yesterday.

Con took out his tally book and pencil as Dunc sat a steaming cup of strong, black coffee on the kitchen table in front of him.

"Start at the beginning," Con began, "and tell me what's happened with the missing cattle."

"The first three disappeared in April. I had the yearling heifers grazing in the valley at Kiel Spring. Nothing had been in there for quite some time. The red brome grass was drying out and I wanted to get it grazed down while the cattle would still want to eat it."

"Do you know when in April?" Con asked.

Blackwood left the room and returned shortly with a tally book of his own. "We moved them in there on the tenth," the rancher read from his notes as he sat down across the table. "They were missing on the thirteenth. Bobby broke his hand the next day in a roping accident." He looked up. "That's when I found out you were shot."

"And you decided to forget about it?"

"Well, not forget about it," Dunc answered indignantly. "Just wait until you were feeling better."

"Okay. So, what happened next?"

"Another one came up missing."

"You're sure you hadn't miscounted from the first bunch?" Con clarified while trying not to sound condoning.

"No, this one was a yearling steer. Had a twisted left horn," Blackwood explained. "I'd just seen him myself a couple of days earlier...and this was a month after the first three vanished."

"You have any dates in your book?" Con asked.

Blackwood thumbed ahead several pages. "Pete noticed his absence on May fourteenth," Dunc confirmed. "I'd seen him on the tenth."

"Same place?"

"No, I've got a well over on the school section by the old Wagon Road. It's got a windmill on it. Pretty close to the wash. There was sixty-two head of yearlings in there grazing along the wash." He continued to elaborate. "Crooked-horn was right by the well when I checked it on the tenth. When Pete made a count on the fourteenth, he come up short so he started at the well and kept widening his circle, but never found him. If it hadn't been that particular crooked-horned steer, we'd never known which one it was."

"You're sure Pete didn't just miss him?" Con questioned.

"All three of us rode back out there the next day and scoured every inch of ground within a mile of that well. We looked in every nook and cranny and under every bush and boulder. He wasn't there then and none of us has seen hide nor hair of him since," Blackwood concluded in a tone that began to lose its pleasantness.

"Don't get mad, Dunc. I'm just trying to make sense out of all of this," Con tried to reassure him. "If some fella was desperate enough, and needing to feed his family, I'd think he'd shoot one of your big calves near a road. Small enough where he could load and make off with the carcass pretty quickly. I can't see a true rustler risking the consequences for steeling one steer, or even three heifers. Same penalty for stealing one or twenty. What do you suppose that steer weighed?"

"Eight, nine-hundred pounds maybe."

"And no tracks anywhere around."

"Well," Dunc hedged. "Pete spent quite a while searching that first day and by the time we got serious the next day there wasn't much of anywhere close that didn't have a horseshoe print within ten feet of it. We were pretty much looking for the steer and not his tracks."

"Okay." Con rubbed the slight stubble showing itself on his chin as he mused over the chain of events thus revealed. The light massage along his jawline revived a hint of yesterday morning's aftershave to his nostrils and that brought a smile to his lips. Last night he asked June Sommers to marry him. He had not planned it. They were just sitting horseback under the stars looking at the distant lights of Las Vegas. He had been talking about growing up out here and then he asked her, almost before he realized it and she answered yes without the slightest hesitation. She told him how much she loved him and talked about wanting more children. Their conversation roamed over a dozen topics and continued all the way to her front door in town. There, he told her he loved her more than anything in the world...and they kissed. It had been a kiss unlike any other they had ever experienced. She slipped suddenly from his arms and the door closed in front of him almost before he realized she had disappeared. He could see her golden hair through the glass and could hear her heavy breathing through the door as her back leaned against it. A trickle of perspiration dashed from his temple down his cheek. His shirt felt suddenly damp.

"Con!" the gruff voice startled him. Duncan Blackwood stared with concern from across the table. "Are you all right?"

"Yeah. Sure," he replied as he returned his thoughts to the present. "I was just thinking."

Blackwood refilled their coffee cups.

"You told me on the telephone," Con resumed, "that you lost more livestock."

"Two more," Duncan specified. He shook his head without making eye contact. "I'm not sure when. Sometime in the last couple of weeks up on the mesa. We did a count." He thumbed through the most recent pages in his tally book, "on the sixth. Two eighteen-month-old steers. Ready for market in a couple more months. Big boys, thousand pounds or better. Bobby noticed them missing this past Tuesday. I started out Wednesday morning. Rode every inch of fence line I have. Got back Thursday night. Never found a thing."

"You told me you couldn't talk about it on the telephone. What do you think?"

"Conor, you grew up out here and spent the night in a lonely sheep camp hundreds of times over them years." He paused. "When you're out on your own like that..." He didn't finish the sentence. "You're gonna think I'm plumb crazy, Con."

"What in heaven's name are you talking about?" Con asked in confusion.

"It ain't in heaven, Con. The furthest thing from it. On them lonely nights out in the desert. Every now and again, you get this feeling. Makes your hair stand right up on end. Sends a cold sweat all over you. Do you remember getting spooked like that? Like somebody's ghost just walked up to the fire and blew a winter wind right through you?"

"Ghosts. Ghosts stole your cattle?"

"I don't mean it like that." Dunc was certain the sheriff did not believe him. "Crazy, right? Totally damned loco old man. That's what you think, don't you."

"Now, Dunc. Calm down."

"You never felt it, Con? Even when you were a kid? All them lonely nights when your pa got hurt and you spent a whole summer by yourself with only a couple of dogs to keep the wolves away from the sheep. You never had the wind come up and blow your fire out then disappear into the desert night leaving you shaking in the dark, silent stillness?"

"Yeah, Dunc. I've been scared before. Listening to the coyotes howling up close and wolves in the distance. Knowing Papa should have been back to camp two days before. Afraid that the puma and her cubs that had been killing our sheep had probably killed an eaten him. Too afraid to sleep in camp. Taking my canteen and jacket to lay out among the sheep. Using my canteen for a pillow and nearly hugging the life out of old Ranger for protection. I've been scared half to death, Dunc, but no ghosts ever came along in the middle of the night and wisped my sheep into the sky."

"You think I'm daft! Gone completely out of my mind, don't you!" He was disgusted with himself. He wished he hadn't told the kid anything. He should have known better. "You ever hear the stories about Stampede Mesa over in Texas?" he finally asked Con in a calmer voice.

"No. I haven't," Con told him and grinned. "Not too many cowboy stories get told around the fire in a sheep camp." He chuckled.

Duncan Blackwood let a chortle well up from inside of him. "No," he said. "I don't suppose that they do. Well anyway, the story goes like this. Back in the eighties, a fella named Sawyer had a herd of cattle he was trailing to the railhead to sell. One evening a thunderstorm starts to brewing. This trail boss is trying to get his herd up over this mesa and down off the other side where there's water and such to bed them down away from the storm. When he gets up top there's a brand new homesteader's cabin where none had been before. For reasons unknown to anyone, Sawyer goes nuts and stampedes his herd right through the middle of the cabin and off the other side. His riders all take flight trying to stop the stampede, the thunder and lightning commences, and all hell breaks loose in the rain and mud and darkness. Most of the cattle run off of cliffs to their demise followed by the cowboys chasing after them in the darkness.

"The next morning there're hundreds of dead cattle and horses, not to mention several of his hands and presumably the homesteader and his family. A few of his hands have survived and they begin rounding up the couple of hundred cattle that made it through the night. They herd them on and sell them, Sawyer pays off his hands and they return to Texas. None of the hands will work for him after what happened and pretty soon, this Sawyer fella becomes a drunk and disappears.

"The next year another herd of cattle are bedded down atop that same mesa on a clear star-filled night. For no apparent reason, in the wee hours of morning that herd stampedes off the same cliffs and several more cowboys lose their lives. That trail boss is overcome with guilt over the deaths. He also turns to liquor and is soon never heard from again either. A few more tried that trail with similar results and before long it became known as Stampede Mesa and shunned by all cattlemen.

"Some folks say if you go up there at night at a certain time of year, you can see ghost riders herding cattle through the dark skies and hear the screams of terror from the victims of those stampedes. They say that Satan hisself is the trail boss and his demons rustle cattle along the way to replenish his herd. Sometimes they take just a few. Sometimes whole herds. When they come, the cattle just vanish without a trace."

Con forced himself not to smile. "Well now, Dunc, that is one story that I have never heard before."

"Now, Con," he began. "I'm not saying that's what happened to my cattle, but it sure fits the setup."

Con stood and pulled his Stetson firmly onto his head. "And I'd bet the rustler or rustlers would sure like to make me think that's what happened. I'm going to look over each of the places where you've lost cattle to see if I can see something in common that would make it easier for the cow thieves to operate. In the meantime, if you could make regular counts on all of your bunches of cattle to get a better timeline it might be helpful."

He downed the last of his coffee and headed toward the door. "Also," he added, "if you're missing any livestock, call me immediately. That way I can look things over before anything gets blotted out or moved."

"Anything else?" Blackwood asked as Con approached his horse.

"If you see any demons around here, you're on your own." With that, Con stepped into the saddle and rode north leaving Duncan Blackwood shaking his head. He followed the trail headed toward the school section near the Wagon Road.

When out of view from the ranch house, Con stopped and dismounted. He retrieved a carrot for Bob and a piece of lamb jerky for himself from the saddlebags. As he fed Bob his carrot and patted the horse's neck he commented aloud, "What do you suppose the commissioners would think if I requisitioned a couple of boxes of silver bullets? I'd be looking for a job before I got the words out of my mouth."

* * *

When Con topped the ridge overlooking the windmill, he stopped to survey the landscape. A quarter mile down the wash from the well, a four-strand barbwire fence meandered across the valley. Straggling traces of the old Wagon Road appeared randomly another quarter mile beyond the fence. Considering its visibility, Con suspected the old road to still be passable in a car or truck if the driver used some discretion. He kept his seat while reaching back to recover the field glasses from his saddlebags.

His position provided a good view of the valley below for perhaps a mile in either direction. He spent most of a half hour scanning the area through the glasses. He did not expect to discover any evidence in particular from this distance. A month and a half had passed since the crooked-horned steer had disappeared. More than anything he wanted to get a feel for the lay of the land, the course of the wash down the center of the valley and where it twisted and turned. Noting direction and terrain of the hills that bordered both sides, the fence seemed to follow the section line for the most part but deviated as convenient to accommodate the topography.

He did not count them, Con but suspected there to be sixty-one steers scattered below foraging on patches of grass among the brush.

Hanging the field glasses from his saddle horn, Con left the trail and followed the crest of the ridge to the fence. The strands of barbwire were tight. He leaned over in the saddle, grabbed the top of the nearest post, and shook it. It resisted the disturbance and appeared to be solid. He turned along the trail paralleling the fence line. Worn by years of cattle investigating their boundaries and cowboys maintaining the barrier, the path revealed a single set of tracks. Hoofprints of a shod horse. A few days old. He followed it to the bottom of the valley.

"Duncan Blackwood," Con commented aloud to Bob and himself. "When he said he rode every inch of his fence line, he didn't exaggerate. We're miles from where the latest cattle disappeared."

When he reached the wash, it was larger than it had seemed from the ridge. Ten to twenty yards wide at the top and half that in depth. There, the fence departed from its course and followed a small ravine to the dry bottom of the wash. Remnants of grass and debris clung to the bottom two strands of barbwire left by previous rains that had brought the creek to life. Downstream a short way, the fence climbed a mild grade up the far side. From the edge of the wash, greenish stubble was all that remained of the grass that blanketed the bottom of the valley. Now cropped close to the ground, the four-legged mowing machines worked their way out from the wash as the strip of sod gave way to bunch grass whose clumps became more and more scattered among the brush as they climbed the adjacent hillsides. The valley appeared to be nearly grazed out. Con knew that sheep could nip the blades closer to the ground, but suspected the rancher would soon be moving his cattle to a new location.

In the distance, to his left, the windmill turned lazily with the soft morning breeze. The rod below stroked slowly up and down to the pump. Hidden from his view by some of the taller brush between him and the well, a spurt of water dumped into the first of a series of wooden troughs each time the rod reached its top. What water escaped the mouths of thirsty cattle and wildlife spilled over the edge of the last trough to quickly immerse into the sandy desert soil.

A dozen yards from the wash a wire gate interrupted the fence line to Con's right. It appeared to have been unopened for quite some time as a three-foot-tall clump of rabbitbrush grew through the wires midway between the posts on either end. Well drillers getting their equipment to the site had probably made the gate he gathered. Later the crew installing the pump, windmill and troughs would have used it too. Halfway to the gate, something caught Con's attention. He dismounted and patted Bob's neck as he dropped the reins to the ground. Walking beside the trail, he carefully examined the tracks left by Blackwood's mount.

The horse had continued walking at the same pace right past the gate. What caught the sheriff's eye was the clump of rabbitbrush. The narrow little leaves on three of the branches were wilted, brown and dying. Upon closer scrutiny he could see the twigs were broken; one completely off from the bush and stuffed down among the others. Someone opened the gate damaging the branches in the process. They then disguised the injury by propping the limbs back into the bush. It probably looked perfect for several days afterward until the leaves began to wither.

Con opened the gate and led Bob through it. After stretching the enclosure back into place, he stepped into the saddle. "Satan's ghost riders wouldn't need to open any gates," he mused to Bob as he urged him on to resume the search.

From his perch atop the ridge, it appeared the wash made several sharp turns below the fence. Con followed the twisted edge of the wash scanning the area for more clues. He saw several places where the bottom of the wash could easily be accessed, but nothing worthy of further investigation. A quarter mile below the fence the wash split into two forks creating an island in the midst of a sudden turn. The main channel looked much like the rest of the wash with a small narrower channel on the other fork. He continued to ride the edge. It surprised him not to have reached the old Wagon Road yet when he suddenly spotted it following the bottom of the wash beside him. In a few more yards the road made its rutted way up a relatively steep bank before him. He pointed Bob down the bank.

The road showed no signs of recent use. As he rode back up the bottom of the wash the soft sand soon turned to mud. Con decided it seemed too difficult to keep from becoming stuck in either the mud or the sand to make it a likely choice for a vehicle to travel. When he reached the spot where the two channels rejoined each other, the narrow channel seemed choked with tall dense brush. As he drew closer, it appeared the water source that muddied the road emerged from the narrower channel. A pair of rutted tire tracks materialized from beneath the tangle of brush and turned onto the road ahead of him.

12

"Six o'clock and we're still on the set," Molly Mansfield huffed under her breath as she negotiated the maze of ropes and stakes between the tents. Hugh insisted on meeting with the cameramen one more time to yet again instruct them exactly how they were to shoot the critical scene in the morning. The narrow pathways and disorganized layout eliminated any opportunity for a breeze to penetrate the hot and dusty compound. Lightweight sundress or not, every inch of her body stuck to itself or her clothing with sweat. She was certain she smelled like a wrestler after a match. A faint metallic sound coming from within the prop truck caught her attention.

She stalked to the open door at the rear of the truck and peered in. Jenny Vance kneeled over the box that held the guns. She had a revolver in her hand and was placing a bullet into the cylinder. Jenny listened, counting the clicks as she rolled the cylinder over, closed the little door where she had inserted the bullet, then skillfully released the hammer and let it close. As Jenny slid the gun back into the holster, Molly slipped out of sight.

Just as she returned Matt McCoy's revolver to its slot in the firearms box, Jenny heard the scuff of a footstep behind her. Her head snapped around to glimpse a shadow on the tent behind the prop truck disappear. She jumped to her feet and rushed to the rear of the truck just in time to see a similar shadow evaporate from between the two tents beside her.

* * *

"You're sure it was Matt's gun?" Hugh Parker asked as they pulled to a stop in front of the Hotel Nevada.

"Positive," Molly answered. "Mark's holster has that scrape on it from when his horse fell with him climbing the riverbank on the cattle drive."

Hugh Parker mulled the new information over in his mind. Matt McCoy's rapid rise to stardom had brought with it some difficult issues for the studio. The young star's passion for throwing wild parties brought nearly constant monitoring of his activities. Paying off newspapers to expurgate unwanted publicity that accompanied the illicit nature of his fiestas was becoming a normal expenditure. David Whitfield Fredericks had emphasized to Parker that it was his responsibility to keep McCoy's offscreen behavior in check while filming this current project.

Most recently, Matt McCoy had also confronted Fredericks that his increased fame and popularity warranted a significant increase in weekly salary and royalties. It did not go well. Mr. Fredericks had controlled his temper but made it clear that

McCoy would have the opportunity to renegotiate his contract when it expired at the end of the year.

When he entered the hotel lobby, Hugh Parker checked in at the front desk. No messages.

In his suite, he called the Hotel Golden. "May I speak to Miss Vance please?"

"It will take a moment," the clerk informed him.

"I'll wait."

The clerk patched the call through to the telephone in the upstairs hallway and raced up the stairwell to her room.

"You have a call, Miss Vance," he told her when she answered the door, motioning to the telephone midway down the hall.

"Who is it?"

"A gentleman, miss."

She hurried to the telephone. "Hello?"

"Hello, dear," Parker cooed from the other end of the line. "Would you like to join me for dinner in my suite?"

"That sounds wonderful," Jenny answered.

"Eight o'clock?"

"That will be great."

"I'll be waiting," he replied suggestively.

She had three-quarters of an hour Jenny calculated as she hung up the phone. Her father had taken their car to Block 16 in search of beverages more soothing than lemonade. It did not occur to her how demeaning it was that Hugh Parker had failed to offer her a ride.

A half hour later, she descended the stairway of her hotel in her most revealing dress. With an extra splash of lavender to mask her anticipated perspiration from the five-block walk, the aroma wafted ahead of her. Unaware of how her appearance might be perceived, she strutted out the door and up the sidewalk.

The clerk at the Hotel Nevada nearly gasped when Jennifer Vance entered the lobby. The provocatively dressed young woman was nice looking. The dominating presence of her perfume gave away what he presumed to be one of the higher-priced working girls of the town. He had not seen this one before.

"May I help you, miss?" he asked.

"I'm here to see Hugh Parker," Jenny replied.

The clerk picked up the headset from the small switchboard behind the desk, plugged a cord into the board, flipped a switch and waited.

"A young lady here to see you, sir." He paused momentarily. "Yes, sir."

He turned to Jenny. "Mr. Smith is expecting you. Top of the stairs, second door on the right. There's a B on the door."

Hugh Parker answered the door on the first knock. He wore a silk smoking jacket over what she suspected were silk pajamas.

"Good evening, Jenny. You look lovely," he said, standing aside to motion her in.

Jenny had never been inside a suite. Even though Las Vegas was a small town, this was undeniably its most sumptuous hotel. The bed was located in an alcove. The blankets were turned down, she noticed. In the dim light through an open door, she could see a large bathtub with shiny fixtures. She looked wide-eyed at the linen tablecloth beneath an array of covered plates.

"I hope you don't mind," Parker began. "I ordered for both of us."

"Not at all," she answered, blushing naïvely.

"Perhaps you would like to get more comfortable before we eat," he suggested. "I bought you a couple of things. They're in the bathroom."

"Well, uh," was all she managed to utter as she entered the bathroom.

When she turned on the switch, a room larger than her own hotel room came to life. The porcelain sink looked like a giant seashell. She read magazines. She had never seen a sink like this one. Then she saw her *gift*. A very sheer pink nightgown and equally transparent robe, if you could call it that, hung from the back of the door. She had been sweating profusely since she arrived. This did not help settle her anxiety.

Jenny turned on the faucet to fill the sink and let her dress slip from her shoulders and fall into a soggy stinky pile around her feet. In lieu of a washcloth, she found only a very large natural sponge. It felt soft and luxurious as she washed herself from head to toe in front of the mirror. The damp sponge reactivated her perfume somewhat and helped disguise some of her nervousness. She slipped the gown over her head and let it drop into place. Jenny looked at herself in the mirror. The fabric left nothing to the imagination. Hugh had seen her naked before, but this was…this was almost like posing for him. She had not felt this self-conscious since… since she stripped naked in front of the entire cast and crew at Matt McCoy's party. She looked again at herself in the mirror. No, this was worse. At least she was drunk at the party. She slipped the robe on over her gown. It did nothing to subdue the view.

* * *

At ten o'clock, Molly Mansfield crept down the creaky stairs at the rear of the Hotel Nevada. She wore dark slacks. Her shapeless jacket with turned-up collar covered the ponytail pulled tight at the back of her neck. An ivory fedora, the only one she had, pulled low in front, covered her head and part of her face. No one was in sight when she peeked around the corner of the building. She made a dash for Hugh Parker's Cadillac.

An hour later Molly wheeled the big car off of Pine Canyon Road toward the movie set. The sudden bombardment of headlights and spotlight from Bull Hansen's car flooded the driveway and blinded her at the same time. She pulled the brim lower on her hat and eased ahead slowly enough for Bull to identify the car and fast enough to not be recognized herself.

She rolled the car to a stop beside Hugh's tent, slipped on a pair of doeskin gloves, grabbed her flashlight, and walked around the corner of the tent as casually as she could. Out of Bull's view, she hurried through the maze of tents, ropes, and stakes to the prop truck. With Parker's keys, she unlocked the large door at the rear of the truck and eased it open as carefully and quietly as she could.

Once inside, she located the firearms box and unlocked it. Carefully examining the gun belts and holsters, she identified the two used by Matt and Mark McCoy. She switched the pistols and placed Matt's back into the box. When returning Mark's gun belt to the box, she noticed a cartridge missing from one of the loops. It must have been the one that Jenny loaded into Matt's gun. Carefully placing everything back as she found it, Molly hurried back to the car. Once inside she forced herself to slow her pace. Methodically she backed the Cadillac out and turned it around, then eased it past the watchman and out the driveway.

As she motored down Pine Canyon Road toward Las Vegas and out of Bull Hansen's view, Molly again located the pack of Craven Navy Cut cigarettes Parker left in the car. She did not smoke often, but desperately needed a cigarette now. She was shaking so badly with fear and excitement she could barely get it lit. She had made it. She snuck in, did her job, and escaped undetected. She took a long drag from the cigarette and coughed as it burned her lungs and throat.

"These things are disgusting," she said aloud as she rolled down the window.

She took another drag on the cigarette, more slowly as she inhaled its harshness. She nearly wrecked the car realizing her error. She had not pulled off the perfect ruse. She smoked one of these awful cigarettes as she pulled onto the set; partially to ease her unsteady nerves and partially to cement her disguise as Hugh Parker to the watchman. When unlocking the firearms box, she held the cigarette between her lips and the smoke had gotten into her eyes. In frustration, she crushed out the cigarette in the prop van. She would be caught.

The maroon Cadillac weaved back and forth down the deserted roadway as Molly Mansfield's fingers scrambled in search of Hugh Parker's flask of Cognac he kept hidden beneath the front seat.

* * *

Wednesday, October 8, 1930

Unaware what time Jenny Vance may have left Hugh's suite, Molly waited until morning. At seven o'clock she knocked on his door. Fully clothed, he answered it.

"Care for coffee?" he asked, inviting her in.

"Objective complete," Molly announced as she poured herself a cup from the silver server on the table.

Parker wiped his face with his napkin between slurps of nearly raw poached eggs. "Very good," he replied.

"I noticed something though," Molly added.

"What's that?" he asked nonchalantly.

"On Mark's gun belt," she began. "I don't know if it makes any difference, but there's a bullet missing."

"It shouldn't," he answered confidently, then retracted. "Better safe than sorry. Run down the street to the hardware store and pick up a box of .45 Colt cartridges."

"Don't you think it would look a little bit suspicious for a woman to be buying bullets at seven in the morning?" Molly asked incredulously.

"I suppose you're right," Parker said as he stood and tossed the napkin onto his plate. "Be ready to go in a half hour," he ordered as he slipped on a sport jacket and headed out the door.

"I'll be in the lobby," she answered to his back as the door closed behind him.

* * *

The sheriff's pickup truck sat parked in front of the Mesquite Café across the street and halfway to his destination as Hugh Parker marched the two blocks down Fremont Street to the Las Vegas Hardware Company. He found the ammunition displayed on a shelf behind the counter.

"A box of .45 Colt cartridges," he told the clerk as he placed two crisp new two-dollar bills on the counter.

The grizzled clerk took the money and eyed the city slicker questionably as he pushed down the keys of the cash register.

"Rabbit hunting," Parker finally blurted out struggling to think of a viable need for the purchase.

"Watch out for rattlesnakes," the clerk advised. "They're moving back to their dens this time of year."

"Thank you. I'll do that," he stuttered as he grabbed the box and hurried his escape out the door before becoming further engaged in awkward conversation.

He slowed his pace as he approached the Mesquite Café, but the pickup was gone when he passed. As his pulse rate receded, Hugh Parker realized he had left his change on the counter at the hardware store. As stingy as he might be, he had no desire to return for it.

* * *

At ten thirty, Hugh Parker had the cameras set exactly where he wanted them.

"Shooting at eleven o'clock," he yelled. "Sharp!" and marched out the door to his tent for a shot of scotch.

As soon as he was out of sight, the cameraman on number two moved his camera in about three feet. The positioning was critical in order to have Mark McCoy's body block the view of camera number one precisely as he walked past and for camera number three to remain outside the frame when he stopped. There had been no point in arguing with the director over the issue. The crew knew how to obtain the result the director wanted even if he did not. Emily Scott, the director's assistant grinned knowingly as she observed the procedure.

Everyone arrived on set and they shot the first take precisely at eleven. After two mistakes on Mark's behalf and one on Matt's, they were on take four at eleven-fifteen.

"I'll take my share now, Clay," Mark McCoy snarled as he drew the six-shooter from his holster.

Matt McCoy drew his gun a tenth of a second faster. Both guns fired almost simultaneously as the two brothers fell on the tile floor of the foyer.

"Cut! Cut! Cut!" Hugh Parker screamed, "Get these doors open and clear the smoke out of here! Get up off the floor, Matt, so we can shoot this again! You won this gunfight! Don't you remember anything? How can you forget the whole damned plot?"

"Wayne!" Parker yelled, "I thought you coached these idiots! I don't have time for this!" Parker ranted throwing his hands and script into the air as he stormed out.

Emily Scott collected the scattering pages as Parker paced the floor of the sitting room. He'd played the part perfectly. He had not acted for over ten years but remembered the glory of how well he had done in his years on stage in New York. No one here would ever guess that he knew what had happened. His heart raced with pride of his flawless performance. He needed another shot of scotch. He needed to call Dave Fredericks. Suddenly Mark McCoy came in. He was crying.

"I killed my brother," Mark sobbed. "How could I?"

"It's okay, Mark," Hugh Parker spoke consolingly. "It wasn't your fault. It was an accident. Come on. Let's go to the commissary tent and get something cold to drink."

"Wayne told me to stay in here," Mark said.

"Okay," Parker said. "At least take off your gun belt, and I'll go get us something."

Mark McCoy removed his gun belt and handed it to him. Parker could hardly control his shaking hand as he received it. Turning his back to McCoy, he slipped the cartridge from his pocket and into the vacant loop in the belt then laid it on the coffee table in front of him. His excitement was nearly unbearable as he crossed the room to the door.

"I'll bring back something for you to drink," he told Mark soothingly as he closed the door behind him.

Hugh Parker could barely contain his smugness. Everything was going superbly. In the foyer, he looked over Wayne Garrard's shoulder as he covered the lifeless body of Matt McCoy. Garrard turned and glared at him.

"Make yourself useful, Parker, and call the sheriff," he growled the command.

"The nerve of him," Parker muttered under his breath as his excitement turned to rage. He could not believe the stupid cowboy would dare to order him around. "He'll regret his arrogance when I fire him," he mumbled. "And I'll do just that the minute this is over with."

He lit a cigarette as he entered the study. *The trouble with making Western movies was dealing with all of these stupid cowboys,* Parker relented. Looking around the room he found no ashtray and tossed the spent match onto the floor. He picked up the telephone and dialed the operator. Once connected to the sheriff's office, Hazel answered the call.

"This is Hugh Parker, producer and director of *Sons of the Texas Star*. We're filming on Pine Canyon Road and there's been an accident," he told her. "One of the actors has been shot and killed." Without allowing so much as a second for clarification on any aspect of the emergency, he hung up and called Unified Stars Studios.

When Hazel tried to call back to the Campbell estate, the line was repeatedly busy.

* * *

David Whitfield Fredericks was beyond angry, beyond furious, beyond any word in his vocabulary capable of describing the level of seething rage that boiled within him.

"What the hell were you thinking?" he yelled into the receiver after hearing the chain of events that began nearly twenty-four hours ago.

"Calm down, Dave. I've taken care of everything. There's nothing to worry about."

"What do you mean, 'nothing to worry about?' You, Molly, and this prop girl will all be in the penitentiary or waiting your turn for a center seat in the electric chair," Fredericks yelled at the top of his lungs. "And I'll be right there with you if I don't turn you all in!"

"Dave, please, listen to me. It's the perfect scenario." Parker had been certain that Fredericks would be pleased with his actions. His certainty was beginning to fade. "Look, the bimbo prop girl who got her feelings hurt won't be riling the waters anymore and we both know that Molly's popularity is declining with age. Both of them will take the fall for this. And most importantly, we're rid of Matt McCoy, the troublesome partying kid who's been gouging you for more money."

"Rid of Matt McCoy?" Fredericks had been yelling so loud his voice began to crack. "Matt McCoy is the biggest star this studio has ever seen! His last picture made more money than my top three movies combined! Have you completely gone mad? You've murdered the goose that laid the golden egg for God's sake!"

"But...but I thought Matt McCoy was trouble. You're always having to deal with the newspapers to keep them from dragging him and his parties through the mud. You told me yourself to keep him out of trouble. I thought..."

"Murder is not an acceptable method of keeping someone out of trouble!" Fredericks interrupted.

"These Bedouin cowboys will never figure it out," Parker assured him.

At that moment, Dave Fredericks heard another male voice in the background.

"Who are you?" the authoritative voice demanded.

"I'm on the telephone," Parker answered.

"Hang up," the voice ordered.

"Dave, it'll be okay. I promise."

"Now!" the voice commanded.

"This is business!" Parker tried to claim his authority.

A moment later David Whitfield Fredericks heard the sound of the receiver on the cradle followed by a dial tone. He mulled over all Hugh Parker had told him. He had argued with Parker for nearly an hour. Fredericks picked up the telephone and dialed the *Los Angeles Daily News*...then called the Hotel Nevada...followed by his attorney.

13

"Gary D. Wagner, Jr.," Judge William Tucker began, "the District Court of Clark County, Nevada, has found you guilty on one count of felony extortion against Brice Campbell, deceased. I hereby pronounce sentence of $93,000 in restitution to the heirs of Brice Campbell and ten years of hard labor in the Nevada State Prison at Carson City on that charge. You were also found guilty on one count of felony extortion against Katherine Wagner, deceased. I hereby pronounce sentence of $67,000 in restitution to the heirs of Katherine Wagner, excluding yourself and ten years of hard labor in the Nevada State Prison at Carson City on that charge. These prison terms are to be served consecutively. Let it be recorded that a lien of $160,000 has been filed by this court against all property, real or otherwise belonging to Gary D. Wagner, Jr. until restitutions on these two charges are met."

* * *

"Four agonizing weeks since I arrested him," Con muttered as he sat across from Judge Tucker in his chambers after the sentencing.

"It could have taken four months to reach a verdict," the judge scolded the sheriff's impatience, "and would have, if not for the case you had built against him. It sure didn't hurt us any when his own sister and Leanora Campbell both took the stand to testify against him."

"What now?" Con asked.

"The DA prefers to hold three separate trials on the murder charges. It may cost the county a little more money to do it that way, but it reduces the chance of a not guilty verdict on all three cases when a question of innocence arises on any one of the cases. Opening remarks on the murder of Jimmy Garza begin at nine o'clock next Monday morning. Mr. Rizzo hasn't asked for a plea agreement yet, but Davis has things pretty well laid out. I think we'll be okay."

* * *

WEDNESDAY, JULY 16, 1930

District Attorney Donald D. Davis entered his office at seven thirty sharp. He carried his briefcase in his right hand with his suit jacket draped across his left arm. Even at this early hour the temperature already rose far beyond comfort for wearing a jacket.

Salvatore Rizzo, was being held for the murder of Jimmy Garza in the Clark County Jail. The same charge Dutch Wagner faced whose trial was scheduled to open in five days.

Yesterday afternoon, the prosecutor received a request marked "Urgent" from Rizzo for a meeting. Davis suspected that it was. Mr. Rizzo had yet to secure an attorney. The DA scheduled an interview at nine o'clock this morning and asked Sheriff Armenta to accompany him as a witness.

"What did you want to talk about?" Davis asked Sal when the jailer brought the handcuffed prisoner into the visitation room and seated him at a long table.

"What's he doing here?" Sal motioned with his head toward Con, who sat at the far end of the table.

"I asked Sheriff Armenta to join us," the DA, who remained standing, began, "both as a witness and for your protection."

"To protect me from what? You?" Sal chuckled at the concept.

Though Con struggled to keep a solemn face, Donald Davis did not. "To protect you from injustice, Mr. Rizzo. To keep me from coercing you into some type of agreement that may not be in your best interest. I also suspect he may wish to ask a question or two of his own regarding this case, or perhaps another. I understand that he has not spoken to you since your arrest."

Sal scratched at his neck as if there were a few days growth of beard irritating him while he considered the attorney's explanation. Con noted his freshly shaven face and slicked back hair. Sal had done his best to portray a respectable image in his prison uniform. "Okay," he finally answered. "I get it."

"What is it you wished to discuss, Mr. Rizzo?" Davis repeated.

"I never killed Jimmy," he stated flatly. "Dutch did it."

"Can you prove that?"

"I was working The Pit that night—" he began, but Davis interrupted.

"The Pit? What exactly is that?"

"The bar and tables downstairs," Sal offered. "It's just what we call it."

"This *Pit* is located in the basement of Dutch's Oasis?"

"Yeah."

"The tables are for gambling?"

Sal looked at Con then at the floor. "Some of them," he replied.

Davis turned to Con, "You know about this *Pit*," he stated. It was not a question.

Con sat up a little straighter in his chair. "Yessir. I haven't heard it called that before, but it fits."

After a pause, Davis responded. "This isn't the time..." He allowed his words to diminish into momentary silence. "Please proceed, Mr. Rizzo," he continued at a normal volume.

"Jimmy came in early that evening, sat at the bar and ate dinner, then went upstairs."

"To the ground floor?"

"No. Upstairs. To the rooms."

Davis nodded in understanding.

"Dutch came down about an hour later. He steps up to the end of the bar and talks to Bob a minute, then motions me over to him."

"Who is Bob?"

"The bartender." He waited until Mr. Davis nodded, then proceeded. "I walk over as Dutch is lighting up one of his big Cuban cigars. Bob sets a tall glass of whiskey, no ice, in front of Dutch and leaves. Dutch downs about a third of the whiskey and sucks a long draw on his cigar. Then he hands me the keys to his car, blows a smoke ring into the air and says he has an errand for me to run. I look around the room, it's Saturday night, the sun's going down and the room's filling up. What about this place? I ask him and he says he'll take care of it until I get back." Sal paused. He had begun to perspire. "Can I get a drink of water?"

"Sure," Davis answered. He motioned to Con who rose and went to the door.

"Guard?" Con beckoned at the door. "Can you get us some water?"

A moment later the guard returned and knocked at the door. He handed the sheriff a tin pitcher and three tin cups. Con filled a cup and offered it to Davis who declined, then gave it to Rizzo. He poured another for himself and returned to his chair.

Sal drank most of his water and sat the cup down.

"Tell us more, Mr. Rizzo," Davis told him.

"I asked Dutch what I needed to do. He says there's something on the floor of his office. He needs me to take it to the railroad station. I ask what it is and he says I'll know when I see it. I said the depot was closed. Where do I take it? He says to tie it up under one of the rail cars right before the train leaves. I'm looking at him like, 'What the hell are you talkin' about?' He sees the look on my face and says to tie it up kinda loose like, so it'll come undone somewhere out in the desert and fall off. I'm thinkin' he's got a screw loose or something. Then he grabs me by my collar and jerks me right up into his face. Then real quiet so's nobody else can hear, but real mean he says, 'Do it!' and shoves me away."

"So, what did you do then?" Davis asked.

"I went upstairs," then Sal added, "the ground floor. Pearl was eating a sandwich at the bar."

"Who is Pearl?"

"Pearl Lewis. She runs the upstairs." He cleared his throat. "The *real* upstairs."

Davis nodded.

"I went into Dutch's office. It was dark and I started to turn on the light on Dutch's desk, but ran my foot into something on the floor. I went back to the door and switched the overhead light on. It was Jimmy…"

"Jimmy Garza?" Davis interrupted.

Sal nodded. "I never knew his last name 'til I seen it in the paper. He was kinda layin' on his side then, but I could tell he'd been on his knees all curled up like a baby. I seen it before in Chicago. There was blood on the back of his head and his jacket. He'd messed his pants. I could smell it when I straightened him out to pick him up."

"Then what did you do?" the DA asked.

"I hoisted him up over my shoulder and walked to the door. I shut off the light and opened it real quiet and looked around the room. Nobody was there but Pearl and the bartender and they were both looking the other way. I ran out, down the hall, and out the back door. I put Jimmy in the trunk of Dutch's car then looked around and found a ball of twine. I got in the car and drove to the U.P. Park. When nobody was looking, I took Jimmy out of the trunk and laid him in the shadows by a tree. He was already starting to stiffen up so I laid him out real straight. I got back in the car and parked it down the street, where I could see the park and the station. When I saw the train coming, I put the twine in my pocket and snuck back to the park on foot. While I waited there in the dark for the crew to unload and reload freight from the train, I tied twine around Jimmy's ankles and wrists and left extra twine on each to tie him to the train.

"I waited and watched the trainmen search the train from

one end to the other looking for hobos that might have snuck aboard while they were stopped. When they went by the second time, I grabbed Jimmy up, he wasn't very heavy, and ran to the train. I got him up under a boxcar and tied him up as fast as I could to the rods under the car. I had both arms tied when the brakes released with a blast of air. I only got one ankle tied when the train started to move. I dove out from under it and under the platform just as the wheels of the car passed. I nearly messed my own pants.

"I waited quite a while after the train left, then made my way back to Dutch's car and the Oasis. When I got back, I went into the backroom and brushed dirt from my jacket pants and shoes. I put on the spare clean shirt that I keep there and returned to The Pit. It was after midnight by then. I went to the bar and told Bob to bring me a whiskey. He started to pour a glass of moonshine and I stopped him. I told him I wanted the good stuff that Dutch was drinking. He hesitated, then did as I asked. Dutch had been eyeing me since I came in. When Bob brought my drink, I took the keys for Dutch's car from my pocket and made sure Dutch saw me lay them on the bar. He waited a minute after I picked up my drink and crossed the room, then went over, and slipped the keys in his pocket. Bob refilled his glass. A little while later, Dutch climbed into the elevator and went upstairs."

Donald D. Davis stood in silent contemplation with crossed arms for more than a couple of minutes. He went to the table and picked up the third tin cup and pitcher. He filled Sal's cup and then his own before returning to his former position a few feet away.

"You realize that you have just confessed to accessory to murder after the fact, a crime punishable by up to twenty years in prison?"

"I never killed that kid," Salvatore Rizzo resounded. "I ain't gonna fry in no electric chair for Dutch Wagner."

"Nevada no longer uses the electric chair, Mr. Rizzo," Davis told him. "We now have a gas chamber. Someone has determined it is more humane."

"That's reassuring." Sal smirked.

* * *

MONDAY, JULY 21, 1930

At eight forty-five, Sheriff Conor Armenta solemnly took a seat in the front row of the courtroom gallery. Pearl Lewis and Janet Rae, both dressed in conservative business attire, were seated in the second row. They held an intermittent conversation in nearly silent whispers. Janet nodded an acknowledgment to the sheriff when he entered the room. A moment later, bartender Bob Cook entered the courtroom. Wearing a tan business suit with a white shirt and black string tie, Con would not have recognized him if not for his curly strawberry-blond hair and ruddy freckles. He did not smile nor speak as he sat down behind Armenta.

A man in a business suit that Con presumed was Dutch's attorney came in with a briefcase, crossed through the bar and sat the case on the table to Con's left. This was not Walter G. Tibbitt, the man who represented Dutch on the extortion charges. Much younger. Perhaps the Los Angeles attorney who had been present for the bail hearing. He fished around in the case and brought out three folders which were placed on the table. The attorney then moved the briefcase to the floor. Seating himself at the table he began to peruse the files.

A moment later Deputy Jesse Slater entered the room

escorting the handcuffed Dutch Wagner. In spite of the hand-cuffs, Wagner wore an expensive-looking suit. Slater brought Wagner to the table. He unlatched the left cuff, brought the prisoner's hands in front of him and relatched it. He helped Dutch into the chair beside the attorney and took a seat imme-diately in front of the bar behind them.

At five minutes before nine o'clock, Deputy Whitney Ellis ushered Salvatore Rizzo into the courtroom. He wore a suit. His hands were cuffed in front of him, not behind his back. Whit took the seat beside his prisoner before the bar to the far-right side of the room. Dutch's face paled in shock or fear when he saw Sal enter the room. It reddened into a silent rage that Sheriff Armenta had seen before as Dutch noticed his employee receiving more courteous treatment than he had been provided.

* * *

TUESDAY, JULY 22, 1930

Since the previous morning, Donald Davis had run a string of witnesses across the stand establishing Dutch Wagner's alleged murder of Jimmy Garza. Wagner's attorney, Carlton White had cross-examined every witness attempting to discredit their testimony. He questioned Bob Cook, the bartender following the prosecutor.

"Mr. Cook, you testified earlier that Mr. Garza ate sirloin steak, corn on the cob, a baked potato and drank two glasses of beer on the evening of the murder?" White asked the bartender.

"Yes, sir."

"That's been nearly two months ago. Can you be sure your recollection is correct?"

"That was the special for May."

"You served the same special every night for the entire month of May?" White asked in astonishment.

"Yes, sir," he answered, "but we only have a special on Friday and Saturday night."

The response drew a soft chuckle from the gallery.

Then he added, "but it only came with one beer. He ordered the second one separately." The chuckle grew louder and earned a medium rap of Judge Tucker's gavel and a call for order. That resulted in an embarrassed blush from Mr. White who had not yet regained his pallid facial color when he resumed questioning.

"Mr. Cook, what do you gain by Mr. Wagner going to prison?"

"Nothing," Cook replied. "I lose my job."

"Mr. Wagner has been in jail for over a month now. Have you been paid during that time?"

"Yes, sir. Every Friday."

"Even this past Friday?" he asked and continued before Bob Cook could reply. "Even after Judge Tucker froze all of Mr. Wagner's assets? Who paid you?"

That brought a resonant crash of Judge Tucker's gavel. "Mr. White, Mr. Davis, you will approach the bench."

When both men stood before him, the judge spoke sternly. "Mr. White, I have a pretty good idea where this questioning is headed. When the lien was filed on Mr. Wagner's assets, Robert Westcott was notified that business was to resume as normal at Wagner Trucking and the Oasis barring any transaction exceeding one thousand dollars. Every bank in the state received a similar notification."

"Who is this Westcott?" White stuttered.

"Robert Westcott is a prominent local business attorney. He has represented members of the Wagner family, including Dutch for several years." Tucker strummed his fingernails on the benchtop in front of him. "Who is paying you, Mr. White?"

"I am working for Gary D. Wagner, Jr.," his face began again to flush as he answered.

"Yes, I read the documents you filed when you arrived back here last week," Judge Tucker acknowledged, "but who is paying you? It isn't Dutch Wagner…and I'm pretty sure it's more than a grand."

"I'm not at liberty to say, Your Honor. Attorney-client privilege." He smirked.

"You will say, or I'll have you removed from the Nevada State Bar before you can get to a telephone," Tucker demanded.

"You can't do that." Carlton White raised his voice above the subdued quiet the trio had been speaking in.

Tucker slammed his gavel against the block startling everyone in the room. "This court is in recess until two o'clock this afternoon!" he bellowed.

"All rise!" the bailiff hollered barely before the judge reached the door into his chambers.

"Wait! Wait!" White pleaded as the judge slammed the door behind him.

"He can't do that," he stated more calmly as Donald Davis turned toward his table. "Can he?"

Mr. Davis did not reply, he picked up his files from the table and placed them into his briefcase and left the courtroom.

It was only then that Con looked at Dutch Wagner. Astonished, his mouth hung open. The ashen face staring blankly at

Judge Tucker's door. Jesse stood and began preparing to return his prisoner to the county jail until court resumed in a few hours.

Carlton White approached the bailiff and was immediately rejected. He turned to see his client being escorted from the courtroom which had already nearly emptied. As soon as White departed, the bailiff came over and whispered to the sheriff. When the last observer left, Con rose, crossed the bar and ambled to the door of Judge Tucker's chambers. He knocked.

"What is it?" Tucker grumbled from behind the door.

Con cracked it open far enough for the judge to see his face. He was on the telephone and waved the sheriff in. Con remained standing as Bill Tucker concluded his conversation and hung up.

"Have a seat, Con," he said, motioning to the chair in front of him. Tucker himself stood up and removed his robe, hanging it on the tree in the corner.

"Did you call the bar association?" the sheriff asked as the judge reclaimed his seat.

"I don't have any authority to do something like that," Tucker replied. "How'd you know what I said?" he questioned accusingly.

"A little bird told me."

"More likely a loose-lipped bailiff," the judge replied.

Con grinned. "He suggested that I see you when the court-room cleared."

"He thought I needed someone to blow some steam off to?"

"That's the impression I got," Con agreed. "And so?"

"It took three telephone calls, but I found out what I wanted to know."

"Which was?"

"Who's paying for Dutch's LA lawyer?" he answered himself. "Exactly who I thought. Walter G. Tibbitt transferred four grand into Mr. White's bank account last week."

"Not out of the goodness of his heart I'd bet," Con commented sarcastically, "so, why? Dutch is going on an extended vacation for the next several years at least and more likely taking a nap in the gas chamber. What's the point of backing him now?"

"That's what puzzles me, too," Judge Tucker supported. "I don't have anything but instinct to go on, but I think Mr. Tibbitt's employer has something very large and very sinister going on. Dutch has something to do with whatever it is and knows enough to somehow be very dangerous to this Mr. X if he were to tell the wrong people. Dutch might want to talk to the feds for example, perhaps in trade for his life."

"But if they really want to get Dutch off, why would they send the big guns back home after losing the extortion trial and hire this West Coast guy?"

"That's what troubles me," the judge surmised. "Are they just buying time for something else? Something bigger? Maybe this whole thing is just a diversion so we'll miss the big picture?"

* * *

Carlton White scurried into the courtroom at seven minutes past two o'clock. Judge Tucker had just taken his seat. Dutch Wagner and the others had taken the same positions they occupied earlier in the day.

"We're glad you could join us, Mr. White," the judge commented mockingly.

"May I approach the bench, Your Honor?" White asked.

Tucker held up his left index finger, then struck the block with his gavel. "This court is now in session," he announced. "Mr. White, you may approach the bench."

"Your Honor," White began in a subdued voice. "I spoke to the benefactor for Mr. Wagner's defense while we were in recess and…"

"And what did Mr. Tibbitt have to say?" Tucker quietly interrupted.

"He, uh," the interruption befuddled Carlton White momentarily, his face reddened feverously when he realized the judge had named the man, "the benefactor recommended we keep our previous agreement of anonymity on the basis of attorney-client privilege."

"Take your seat, Mr. White," the judge replied calmly.

"Yes, Your Honor."

When White had regained his seat, Judge Tucker made eye contact with both attorneys, "Is everyone prepared to proceed?" he asked. Both men assented with a nod.

"Good," he responded. "Mr. White, do you have further questions of Mr. Cook?"

"No, Your Honor, but I request permission to recall him later if necessary."

"Permission granted, Mr. White," Judge Tucker agreed. "Mr. Davis, you may call your next witness."

* * *

TUESDAY, AUGUST 12, 1930

For three weeks Dutch Wagner's trial for the murder of Jimmy Garza progressed uneventfully. As prosecutor Donald D.

Davis brought a string of witnesses to the stand, Carlton White continued his efforts to discredit them. The defense seemed obsessed that employees who testified against him would somehow profit from Dutch's conviction. His continual badgering of the witnesses regarding their income brought repeated objections from the prosecutor, all being sustained by Judge Tucker.

When questioning Salvatore Rizzo, White accused Rizzo of selling his testimony to the prosecution in exchange for his freedom. Sal remained calm in his response.

"I'm not sure what you consider freedom, sir," Rizzo began. "I was arrested and charged with the murder of Jimmy Garza two months ago. I pled not guilty and have been in jail ever since. When I later told the sheriff and Mr. Davis what I had done, Mr. Davis asked if I realized I had just admitted to being an accessory after the fact to Jimmy's murder. I told him I did. Later that day I was charged with accessory and pled guilty to that the next day. I have been sentenced to fifteen to twenty years of hard labor in the stone quarry at the Nevada State Prison for that. As far as I know, the murder charge is still pending. If you call that freedom, sir, I guess I'm a free man."

Clayton White looked at Judge Tucker, then at Donald D. Davis and back to Tucker. "Is that correct? He is still charged with murder?"

"That is correct, Mr. White," Tucker confirmed.

White shook his head in near disbelief. "No further questions," he concluded.

In final arguments, Donald D. Davis pointed out that even though Mr. White implied that Salvatore Rizzo's testimony was enticed, it merely corroborated testimonies of previous witnesses and other than describing some details more precisely, did not provide new evidence.

In the end, it appeared that White's tactics may have been unworthy in the eyes of the jurors. They deliberated for less than an hour following the closing arguments before delivering a guilty of murder in the second-degree verdict late in the morning.

* * *

At eleven-twenty, Judge William Tucker and Sheriff Conor Armenta took their seats at the corner table in the Mesquite Café. Olivia was already on her way with a Coca-Cola for her brother and iced tea for the judge before they sat down.

"Chicken-fried steak for me," Judge Tucker told her as she placed the tea before him.

"Twice," Con agreed.

"And bring me the ticket when we're finished," Tucker added.

"He's not worth it," she whispered to the judge loudly enough for both men to hear.

"I'll be the judge of that." He chuckled at the pun.

"Yes, Your Honor," Olivia flirted coyly accompanied with a wink.

"I'll bet she was hell-on-wheels when she was younger," he commented to Con as she headed toward the kitchen with their orders. "Quite a firecracker!"

"She still is," Con replied. "She'll flirt with every man who walks in the door, says whatever pleases her without any reservations, then goes home every evening to the husband and children she adores."

"You know she really admires you too."

"Yeah. We ruffle each other's feathers from time to time, but...family you know."

Tucker nodded. He lifted his glass. "To a job well done, Sheriff. Excellent detective work."

They clinked their glasses together and each took a drink. Conversation consisted mostly of small talk as they enjoyed their lunch together. Both ordered apple pie for dessert. Olivia delivered Con's with a single candle burning in the center of it.

"What's this?" Judge Tucker exclaimed.

"He's not told you? Today is his birthday," Olivia commented as their mother joined her in a duet of "Happy Birthday."

"How old?" the judge asked, reveling in the miniature fiesta.

"Thirty-six," Maggie Armenta interjected before Con could answer. "I just turned nineteen when he was born," she bragged. "Juan was so proud to have a son."

"And a fine man he grew up to be," the judge added approvingly.

Their pie quickly disappeared. As they prepared to leave Judge Tucker reached for the sheriff's hand. "Thank you, Conor. You may have just turned thirty-six, but you're wise beyond your years, son. It's a pleasure to work with you."

"Thank you," Con replied as he accepted the handshake. "I..." he began but could not formulate an appropriate response.

"Katherine Wagner. Opening arguments, nine o'clock Monday morning," the judge announced. "Come on," he added as he donned his palm-leaf fedora, "I'll walk you back to the office."

14

At twelve forty-five, Newton Campbell's light tan Auburn Speedster pulled up in front of the Clark County Sheriff's Office. The dark green fenders were virtually hidden beneath a heavy coating of dust that nearly matched the color of the car's body. An oily film adhered to the tapered rear deck of the car that earned it the nickname of *Boattail* among automobile aficionados of the era. Engine oil bypassing the piston-rings clearly indicated that it had been operated at a high rpm for an extended period of time. The proximity of the stain suggested that the Auburn had also traveled at sufficient speed to defy its advanced aerodynamics in the process.

Deputy Whitney Ellis uncoiled himself from the passenger seat as the car rolled to a stop. Newt Campbell jumped from behind the steering wheel and opened the compartment behind the seat to assist Ellis with the film canisters.

"Where's the sheriff?" Whitney asked Hazel as he carried in two film canisters. Newt Campbell brought in a third.

"He's at lunch with Judge Tucker," she answered. "You can set those in his office."

"What's going on around here?" the deputy asked as they emerged from Con's office.

"We're shorthanded. Sheriff Armenta has us guarding the Campbell estate around the clock," Hazel eyed Newt as she explained. "Are you up to pulling a shift tonight?"

"What time?"

"Jesse's been out there since six thirty. Will seven o'clock give you enough time for a nap?" she asked.

He glanced at the clock on the wall. "Sure. I got some sleep on the road."

She handed him the keys to his squad car and he headed out the door.

"Mr. Campbell," Hazel acknowledged. "Would you care for a cup of coffee?"

"No, no thank you, ma'am," he replied somewhat sheepishly. "I believe I'll check in at the office, then try to catch a nap myself."

* * *

FRIDAY, OCTOBER 10, 1930

"Mr. Fredericks," Sheriff Armenta began. "For the meantime, you are under home confinement instead of jail. Presently that means you will go straight to the Hotel Nevada when you leave here and remain inside there." He moved his gaze to

Molly Mansfield. "The same goes for you, Miss Mansfield. If at any time either of you are found to be elsewhere without my permission, you will be arrested and taken to jail. Is that understood?"

Molly Mansfield nodded as she stared at the floor.

"And what if you can't find me?" Fredericks pushed.

"Judge Tucker will issue a warrant for your arrest. The charge will be murder in the first degree of Matt McCoy. It will be wired to the FBI and Los Angeles Police Department as well as major newspapers. You will be arrested and confined without bail until you can be tried."

David Whitfield Fredericks kept silent eye contact with the sheriff as he contemplated his situation.

"You gave me your word, Mr. Fredericks, that I have your full cooperation. Are you having second thoughts, Dave?"

"No sir, Sheriff." Fredericks continued to look him straight in the eye. "You have my word."

"Very good. You will report to me at the El Portal Theater at one o'clock this afternoon. It's at the corner of Second and Fremont. You'll pass it on the way to your hotel."

"Anything else?"

"Mr. Pollard may accompany you." He glanced again at the actress. "Miss Mansfield will remain at the hotel."

"One o'clock," David Whitfield Fredericks confirmed and left the room followed by Emerson Pollard. Molly Mansfield also moved toward the door.

"Miss Mansfield," Con stopped her. "May I have your hat please?"

Wide-eyed, she turned to him. The guilt nearly overcame her as she handed over her hat. This man suspected her of murdering Matt, she thought to herself. A tear nearly escaped her as she quickly turned away.

"She did it," Tucker stated flatly as Con closed the door behind her.

"Yes, she did *it*," Con agreed, "but what exactly is *it*, that she did? Did she load the gun? Swap the guns? I can't quite figure out how all of the pieces fit together."

"You will figure it out, Sheriff," Daniel Davis pronounced.

The remark startled him. He had begun to accept the praise Judge Tucker bestowed upon him, but the district attorney hardly knew him. Another knock at his door diverted the sheriff's attention. Jesse Slater stood outside.

"Las Vegas Hardware," Jesse announced as he held out a sales ticket. "First thing Wednesday morning. He said he was going rabbit hunting," the deputy added as he handed the sheriff the slip and a handful of change. "He ran out in such a hurry; he left his change on the counter."

Conor eyed the ticket along with the silver dollar, dime, and nickel. "Good work, Jesse. Thank you." He closed the door and returned to his desk. Tucker and Davis watched as he scribbled a note on an envelope then dropped the receipt and change into it.

The judge looked at his pocket watch. "What's happening at the El Portal at one o'clock?" he asked.

"We see the film they took of the shootout."

"You've seen it?" Tucker asked.

"Nope."

"That might be risky," Davis surmised.

"How so? Truth doesn't lie. They'll see what happened same as us. It'll be the truth," Con emphasized.

"How do you know that it hasn't been tampered with?" Davis rolled his eyes.

"Because Dr. Martin witnessed the film being removed

from the cameras, Deputy Ellis hand carried it to and from the lab in Los Angeles, and the FBI developed it."

"How much did that cost the county?" the district attorney shook his head.

"Not one red cent," Con stressed.

"So, all that was just free?" Davis asked accusingly. His grilling began to irritate the sheriff. Only moments ago, the man commended his investigative prowess and now he chastised him.

"Yes! All free with the exception of Deputy Ellis's wages." Con raised his voice before he realized it.

Davis was about to unload on him when Judge Tucker interrupted. "Favors, Don," he said calmly.

"Favors cost money, Bill," Davis ranted. "What will it cost when somebody comes to collect for God's sake?"

"Already paid," Con answered coolly. "Two bullets from a Thompson machinegun."

"When's the last time someone shot at you for doing your job, Don?" Tucker asked. "Con's the best sheriff we've had in a long time...maybe forever. You might disagree with his methods, but as long as he keeps bringing in the kind of evidence he has so far and stays within the limits of the law doing it, I'll back him."

"Well, I..." Davis began.

"I'd like to see both of you at one o'clock if you can make it," Con invited.

"We'll be there," the DA answered for both of them.

* * *

At a quarter to twelve, Sheriff Conor Armenta delivered three canisters of film to Ray, the projectionist at the El Portal

Theater. He crossed the street and walked a block west to the Mesquite Café. Hanging his hat by the door, Con avoided his usual place at the counter when he ate alone and chose a small table near the window. A moment later retired US Marshal Wayne Garrard entered the door. He hung his hat next to Con's and scanned the room for him. When their gazes met, Con motioned for Garrard to join him.

"Not where I expected to see you, Sheriff," the marshal commented.

"I wanted to watch the street for your boss."

Garrard nodded understanding.

"I'm surprised Fredericks isn't buying your lunch at the hotel?" Con needled him.

"Don't go wrecking my appetite that way. I saw him and the lawyer sittin' in the restaurant there." Con did not reply. "So, what am I going to see on this film?"

"Matt McCoy getting killed from three different angles."

"You've seen 'em?"

Con shook his head. "I'm relying on you and Miss Scott's expertise to ensure I don't miss anything." He paused, contemplating whether to share his next thought. "Dave Fredericks's too, but I'm not sure whether to trust him yet."

"You've read him right," Garrard confirmed. "Fredericks is a smart man. Even if he didn't know a thing about it before Parker's phone call, he's got a lot of money riding on this movie. He'll be very carefully protecting his investment."

Olivia arrived with two Coca-Colas and sat them before the two men. "Mulligan stew or roast beef sandwich on special today," she told them.

"I'll have the stew," Con told her.

"Lamb?" the marshal asked, peering at the waitress.

"Of course," she replied incredulously.

"I'll have the sandwich," he told her.

Garrard looked at his lunchmate grinning from across the table. "No offense, Con. Other than the while I lived in Alaska and ate whatever I could find, I've always ate beef."

"No offense taken, Wayne. I enjoy a good steak as well as the next guy, but my grandma taught Papa how to make Mulligan stew the old Irish way and it's very good."

Shortly after their lunch arrived, Judge Tucker and the DA came in. They both acknowledged Con's presence and proceeded to the table in the corner.

Wayne Garrard noticed their arrival. "Friends of yours?" he asked casually.

"The older fellow is District Court Judge William 'my friends call me Bill' Tucker," Con replied. "I call him Bill…in private."

"What about the other one?"

"He's a bit like Dave Fredericks. That is Clark County District Attorney Donald D. Davis. He calls me Sheriff Armenta; I call him Mr. Davis."

Garrard chuckled and almost choked on a mouthful of sandwich. "Lawyers," he remarked after swallowing and took a swig of his Coca-Cola.

Conversation through the meal consisted of small talk and sharing old tales of policework. Both men avoided discussing the case at hand. As they finished their second drinks, Emily Scott strolled down the far side of the street with a notepad in hand.

"That's our cue," Con said, making jest of the movie business.

"Yep," Wayne confirmed without further comment.

As the two men crossed the street, David Whitfield Fredericks and Emerson Pollard stepped onto the sidewalk from the

Hotel Nevada. Con and Wayne walked a few paces ahead of Fredericks and Pollard to the theater where Emily Scott stood outside the door of the darkened lobby.

"Thank you for coming, Miss Scott," the sheriff addressed her. "If you will excuse me just a moment."

Con turned around just as Fredericks and Pollard walked up behind them. "Mr. Fredericks, as a matter of formality I must make this perfectly clear." At that moment Judge Tucker and the DA joined them. "As a prisoner of the Clark County Sheriff's Department, you may not initiate a conversation with anyone except your attorney and officers of the court. At the moment, those officers are Judge Tucker, Mr. Davis, and me. If Miss Scott or Mr. Garrard wish to speak to you, they may request to do so just as if they were wanting to visit you in jail."

It was apparent that David Whitfield Fredericks was seething at the indignation of the circumstances. He did not speak.

"Do you understand, Mr. Fredericks?"

He cleared his throat. "Yes, Sheriff. I understand."

"Very well, then," Con replied and turned to hold the door for Emily Scott. Wayne Garrard stepped aside. "Your Honor," he said as he motioned the judge and DA to enter the building ahead of him. He then stepped in front of Fredericks to pass through the door. As Emerson Pollard passed through the door, Dr. Harold Martin arrived.

"Come on in, Hal," Con told the coroner and followed him in.

The lobby was cool, yet stuffy. The projectionist stood at the foot of the stairway.

"Gentlemen and Miss Scott, this is Ray," Con introduced. "He will be operating the projector. We are running the film without sound initially and will add it if necessary. If at any point you wish to stop the film, holler out and Ray will stop it."

"May I add something, Sheriff?" Ray asked.

"Certainly."

"The bulb in the projector is extremely hot. If I stop the film for more than a few seconds, it will melt the film. Besides making a big mess, the film will be permanently damaged. So, what I'll do is this. As soon as I think the film is getting hot, I'll shut the light off. I can back it up and roll it again in slow motion if you want, but to see it still, it's gotta be quick."

"Thank you, Ray," Con replied. "That's good to know. We'll work around it...and Ray, thanks for coming down here in the middle of the day for us."

"Sure thing, Sheriff."

"These idiots don't even know how a projector works," Conor heard Fredericks whisper to Pollard. He ignored the comment.

"Mr. Fredericks, Mr. Pollard, let me introduce you to Clark County Coroner, Dr. Harold Martin," Con began. "Hal, you probably recognize David Whitfield Fredericks. This other gent is Emerson Pollard, Mr. Fredericks' attorney."

"It's an honor to meet you," Hal gushed as he shook Fredericks's hand.

"Judge Tucker, Mr. Davis, this is Emily Scott and Marshal Wayne Garrard, retired. Miss Scott is the director's assistant and Marshal Garrard is a technical director on the movie." They all exchanged pleasantries before moving into the theater.

As the spectators took their seats in the dimly lit movie house, Ray called out from the projection booth. "This one is marked 'camera one,' Sheriff."

"Go ahead, Ray."

As the movie began, it quickly became apparent to the sheriff that camera one was the unit operated by the cameraman who assisted in pinpointing Mark McCoy's position when the fatal shot was fired.

As the camera made its critical swing, Con hollered out, "Stop it there, Ray!"

The film came to a halt as the camera looked straight at Mark McCoy's right side. The actor was so close to the camera that only his neck to his waist was in the frame. Fifteen seconds later the screen went black.

"Did you see what you wanted?" Ray asked from the booth.

"Did you see it, Hal?" Con asked.

"Sure did," the coroner answered.

"What were we looking for, Sheriff?" the district attorney questioned.

"The first loop in the cartridge belt," Con replied. "It's empty."

Wayne Garrard shook his head as he commented, "I sure didn't catch that."

"Ray, can you back it up a bit and run it again slowly?" Con requested.

"Absolutely, Sheriff."

A moment later, the screen lit up to see Mark McCoy walking backward to the beginning of the camera's sweep, then slowly started walking forward again toward them. Con could not help smiling as it reminded him somewhat of a Charlie Chaplain movie he had seen once.

"Well, I'll be damned," Garrard muttered barely above a whisper as the actor passed across the screen.

Matt McCoy's mouth moved silently on his solemn face in

the background. Mark's cheek moved in response as he pulled the revolver from his holster. When the gun was halfway out, Matt began drawing his own pistol much quicker than Mark. The viewers watched in fascination as the scene played out in slow motion. Mark's gun had yet to come level when a burst of sparks flew from Matt's gun followed by a cloud of blue-black smoke that nearly obliterated him from view. Less than a second later, Mark's pistol bucked. It came up in his hand from the recoil as a flash erupted from the muzzle with very little smoke to accompany it. Both actors fell simultaneously to the floor.

A commotion to Con's left drew his attention from the screen as Emily Scott dashed up the aisle toward the entrance to the room. Wayne Garrard sprang to his feet quite agilely for his age and raced to her just as she bent over the trashcan near the door retching.

Unaware of the disruption, Ray stopped the projector as the end of the film slapped at the spool. "Do you need to see it again?" he asked from the booth as he rewound the reel.

"Yes," Con replied, "but wait until I tell you to restart it." He turned toward the coroner. "Mark's gun wasn't pointed at Matt when he pulled the trigger, but it kicked pretty hard. What do you think, Hal?"

"It was hard to see Matt through the smoke from the black powder," he answered, "but it looked believable to me."

"Mr. Fredericks?" Con asked.

The request for his opinion caught Dave Fredericks off guard. "Well, I...honestly, Sheriff, I was watching Matt's acting, then the perfect timing of the shootout. I didn't notice the position of Mark's gun when the shot was fired."

"I'm sorry, Sheriff," Emily Scott remarked awkwardly as she retook her seat.

"I'm the one who should apologize, Miss Scott. I should have warned you what to expect."

"I might not have eaten such a large lunch," she replied, blushing. "I'll be okay now."

"What did you see, Wayne?" Con asked.

"Pretty much like you called it," Garrard answered. "Mark was expecting the light charge of a blank to be in his gun and didn't have a firm grip on it, Con. When the full charge of the real cartridge went off, it kicked pretty hard and his hand came up fast. It looks to me like Mark shot his brother."

It annoyed David Whitfield Fredericks that Wayne Garrard and the Sheriff spoke to each other on a first name basis.

"Run it again, Ray. Regular speed until we get to where the camera turns, then slow it down."

After watching the entire sequence again, Con became even more certain that the gun in Mark McCoy's hand had killed his brother. By some freak chance the bullet struck Matt McCoy directly in the heart.

"Miss Scott," he began. "What did you see?"

"It's hard to tell with all of the smoke from Matt's gun, but I have to agree with Wayne. It looks like Mark shot him."

"Mr. Fredericks?"

"I too, have to agree with Wayne," Fredericks announced. "I've shot a lot of blanks with these guns over the years. They handle entirely differently than a regular cartridge. It looks to me like it happened just as Wayne described."

"Judge Tucker, Mr. Davis, anything to add?" Both men shook their heads.

"Mr. Pollard?" Even in the dimly lit theater, Sheriff Armenta could clearly see the man's face had significantly paled.

"No, sir," he replied.

"Can we run camera two, please?" Conor asked the booth.

"Coming right up, Sheriff," Ray responded.

"Regular speed for now, Ray."

"Yessir."

The screen soon lit up. Camera two was stationed at a side angle slightly closer to Mark than Matt but concluding in a wide shot of both actors. It followed Mark from entering the door as he crossed the room. From this view it became impossible to keep camera one, director Hugh Parker and Emily Scott from the picture as the camera rotated past them. It settled in on the two actors facing each other from opposite ends of the frame with the crew again safely out of view, blocked by Matt McCoy's silhouette. At regular speed, both six-shooters seemed to discharge simultaneously. At the same time a flash of light came from off camera to the right, somewhere behind Mark McCoy.

"What was that?" Con exclaimed to no one in particular as the film ended seconds later.

"Probably a reflection of the blast from Matt's gun in a mirror or window behind Mark McCoy," Fredericks offered. "This kind of thing often occurs when filming on location like this. Unexpected influences from objects not normally found on studio sets."

The explanation made sense to the sheriff he supposed, perhaps Fredericks's expertise may be useful after all.

"Run it again, Ray," Con told the projectionist. "Regular speed to start, then can you slow it down this time when the other camera comes into view?"

"I sure can, Sheriff."

On second viewing, the slow motion process seemed to confirm David Whitfield Fredericks' previous theory. The off camera flash appeared to occur precisely in time with that from Matt McCoy's pistol.

"The timing of the flash does appear exactly in sequence with Matt's muzzle blast," Armenta surmised. "Thank you for your insight, Mr. Fredericks."

Surprised by the commendation he sat up a little taller in his chair replying, "Glad I could help, Sheriff."

The view from camera three was inconclusive. The burst of light came directly in line behind Mark McCoy. Barely visible, it faintly haloed his body through the smoke from Matt's gun. Likewise, the position of Mark's pistol when fired was also obscured by the haze.

Without further input from the observers, Con accompanied them to the lobby. He turned to David Whitfield Fredericks. "Thank you again for your comments, Mr. Fredericks," he offered.

"Please call me Dave, Sheriff," Fredericks replied from behind an imitation smile. "We're all friends here."

Con let the reference slide. "Enjoy the stroll back to your hotel," he responded implying he should return directly to the Hotel Nevada without ordering it.

"I intend to do just that, Sheriff," Fredericks replied, fully understanding the insinuation. Straining to continue forcing a smile, he pulled a cigar from an inner pocket of his jacket. "Good day, sir," he added. Suddenly recalling his hat was at the sheriff's office when he reached to tip it, Fredericks turned and walked out the door. Emerson Pollard followed closely behind him.

Ray descended the stairway from the projection booth carrying the three film canisters. "There you go, Sheriff," he said as he handed them over.

"Thank you, Ray. You've been a great help," Con told.

"Anytime. When the boss called me, I never questioned it. I consider it my civic duty," he told them. "I'm glad to be of service," he added. "You can let yourselves out. I'll be right behind you, soon as I shut out the lights."

"Quarter to three," Judge Tucker commented, pulling the watch from his pocket as he stepped out the door. "Okay Con, what's troubling you?"

"Nothing, Judge," he replied unconvincingly.

"Something has been eatin' at you for the better part of an hour. Spit it out. What is it?"

"I've been in Mrs. Campbell's foyer a dozen times over the last few months," he finally admitted. "I just can't recall a window in the vicinity of where that flash came from...or a mirror either for that matter." Con looked at Wayne Garrard and Em Scott. "How about you two?"

Both had equally skeptical looks on their faces.

"You're going out there," the DA stated as he studied the sheriff's face.

"I've got to look again."

"Mind if I ride along?" Garrard asked.

"I'd appreciate having a second pair of eyes out there," Con replied.

"How about a third?" Emily chimed in. "I don't remember a window or mirror either."

"Not that I would mind, but three in the cab of my pickup truck would be pretty crowded."

"We can take my car," Wayne offered.

"Where's it at?" Con asked.

"In front of the hotel."

"Can you go get it and pick us up here?" Con asked. "I don't particularly want Fredericks or Pollard knowing the three of us left together."

"That's not a problem," he answered. "I'll be right back."

"There's nothing else I need to see out there," Hal Martin entered in. "I got a two-day-old corpse in the cooler needing my attention." He glanced at Emily who began to look queasy again. "You kids enjoy your ride in a hot car down a dusty road. I've got work to do in a nice cool examination room," he added as he turned and walked down the street.

"Let me know what you find out there," Tucker requested as Wayne Garrard pulled up in a Dodge sedan.

Con held the rear door open for Emily Scott, then climbed into the passenger seat adjacent to Garrard.

When Wayne turned off of Pine Canyon Road at Leanora Campbell's driveway, Ben Neilly sounded a short burst from the siren of his squad car. The deputy climbed from behind the wheel as the unfamiliar vehicle approached.

"Marshal Garrard!" Ben greeted in surprise as the big sedan eased to a stop beside him. "Oh, Sheriff Armenta! Sorry, I didn't recognize the car."

"We're going to have another look in the house, Ben," Con told him. "Anything else going on?"

"Fella waved when he put mail in the box out on the road around noon. Haven't seen another soul before or since. I read four chapters in the book I brought with me," he added. "That's about it."

"That's the way I like it," Conor remarked. "It makes filling out your daily report easy, too." He winked at his deputy.

"Yessir," Ben replied as the car proceeded toward the courtyard.

The tall front doors opened at the sheriff's hand. He left them to stand ajar as the trio entered the cool foyer. The lights remained in place as they had been on the day of the shooting.

Chalk on the floor marked the placement of cameras and positions of the actors.

"I should sit down," Emily stated as she unsteadily held
the arm of a chair near the wall.

"Are you all right?" Con asked.

"I don't know what's come over me. I feel light-headed,"
she added as she eased herself into the seat. "Everything
seems so, so final now. I didn't notice it so much on
Wednesday."

"Shock," Wayne concluded. "On Wednesday, you were in
shock. Your brain shut off the effects of the situation and put
your body into survival mode. Now, that's passed. When
reminded, you're feeling the full impact of what happened. I'll
get you some water." He glanced around unsure where he
might find it.

"The kitchen is down that way," Con pointed.

Wayne Garrard looked at him in surprise. Amazed by the
sheriff's familiarity with the opulent residence, he turned and
made his way down the hallway.

The doors to Brice Campbell's den and the sitting room
had remained open since Wednesday. The stale, lingering odor
of cigarettes and gun smoke still nauseously filled the area.
Con opened the French doors to the rear courtyard and
windows in the adjoining rooms. Even in the heat of late afternoon the slight breeze was refreshing.

Wayne returned with a glass of water for the director's
assistant. Con studied Hal's markings on the floor. Wayne
joined him and the two lawmen began aligning the direction
of the light source that appeared on the two films. Con stood
over the chalk marks showing where camera number three
had stood. From there to Mark McCoy then beyond, a large
painting of the Grand Canyon hung on the wall.

Con moved to where Matt McCoy stood and looked at the painting. "It just doesn't make sense," he commented to neither of his associates in particular. "Even if the painting could have reflected the flash from Matt's muzzle blast, the angle is all wrong. It would have showed on the wall behind the second camera, not toward Mark and camera three."

"Mmm-humm," Wayne Garrard mumbled in agreement as he stood in front of the painting. Emily Scott had regained her composure and watched the two men intently from her chair as they visualized reconstruction of the scene.

"Just as you and I remembered, Sheriff, there is nothing here resembling a window or mirror that could have reflected the source of the flash," she alleged.

As they each silently contemplated the possibilities the telephone in Brice Campbell's study began to ring. No one was expected to be here and the trio attempted ignoring the intrusion in silence. When the caller failed to hang up after the third or fourth ring it became annoying. On the eighth ring, Emily could no longer tolerate the imposition.

"Would you like me to answer that?" she asked Armenta.

"Sure, okay." Being pulled from his thoughts, he responded, squatting on his haunches studying each of the chalk marks.

Her heels rang on the tile floor as she crossed the room. He could hear her subdued voice as she spoke to the caller.

"Who?" she asked. "Just a minute."

"Sheriff." She beckoned from the other room.

"Yeah?"

"It's Dr. Martin. He says it's important."

Con picked up the telephone. "Yeah, Hal. What's going on?"

"We've got it all wrong," Hal announced.

"What do you mean?"

"Mark didn't shoot his brother."

"What do you mean? We all watched it on film...from three different angles."

"He didn't shoot him. I just dug the slug out of Matt McCoy's chest..."

Con waited listening to the silence on the telephone. "Are you still there?"

"Yeah."

"Well?"

"Lead bullet. No copper jacket. Never clipped a rib or hit a bone. Perfect condition..."

The telephone went silent again.

"Tell me."

".38 caliber."

"What?" Con nearly yelled.

".38 caliber. Not .45. You need to find a .45 caliber slug in a wall or floor or somewhere out there. This bullet never came from Mark McCoy's six-shooter."

15

SUNDAY, JUNE 22, 1930

Creosote brush and rabbitbrush were only two of a wide variety of native shrubbery in the area that could easily be mistaken for dead when they actually thrived. These were the primary materials of choice used by the rustler, or rustlers to fashion a woven fence across the narrower fork of the wash. Conor rode Bob to it, following the rutted tire tracks. The horse sank ankle-deep in the muddy bottom hidden under the grass that flourished in the wet soil. Con dismounted where the ruts disappeared beneath the brush. Bob munched on the tall grass around him when he dropped the reins.

Examining construction of the makeshift scrub fence, he discovered the creator had woven it together from branches of nearby vegetation. They secured it on each end to examples of the same species growing from the banks on either side of the wash. A few scraps of baling wire strengthened the obstruction where necessary and held a six-foot wide removable section in place at the center of the barrier. Loosening one end of it, Conor let himself through.

The rutted tire tracks ended abruptly at the fence. An indentation in the soft ground a few feet beyond marked where the base of a ramp had rested to load the missing steer into the truck. A similar brush-fence crossed the ravine a dozen yards above where he stood. A quarter of the way up the righthand wall of the gully a small rivulet of water emerged from a spring, the cause of the spongy earth beneath his feet. The banks on either side were impassable to most livestock, but Con saw evidence where wildlife had scaled it.

As he led Bob to the spring for a drink, he noted the number of residual cowpies and how the grass within the enclosure had been foraged. Though recovered since its occupancy by time and water, he estimated Duncan Blackwood's missing steer had grazed here for at least a couple of days before being transported. Someone had done a lot of preparation to heist a single steer. He had seen a much grander version of the makeshift corral once before. It had been used to trap wild mustangs on a much larger scale and held perhaps a hundred horses at a time.

When he mounted back up on Bob, Conor left the section of the fence open allowing wildlife easier access to the spring. They took the wider main course of the wash and followed it back toward the gate in Blackwood's fence. As they passed the upper end of the smaller fork of the wash, Con peered back down the narrower ravine. A bend in its path hid the upper fence of the enclosure from view.

When he spotted a gentler incline up the bank, he pointed Bob to it. The horse picked up his pace as he scrambled to the top. They paused there a moment while Armenta considered the options for his route. Kiel Spring was about five miles away he guessed and within about a mile of the old Wagon Road. If he entered the gate and followed the trail up the fence line, he would make a right turn at the section corner about four miles up. The trail made it a little further to ride and rougher terrain to cross. He decided the Wagon Road would be the most direct route.

He retraced his path atop the embankment until the road ascended up to intersect his path. Swinging left onto the remnants of the old Wagon Road; Con put Bob into his smooth, ground-eating lope. A half hour later as the road climbed a grade, it disappeared almost completely. With soil and sand washed away by previous torrential rains the road became a maze of rocks and boulders. Slowed to a cautious walk, Conor urged Bob ahead, picking his way through the web of obstructions. As rugged as the terrain became, some hardy soul had moved enough of the boulders to crawl along the route in a wheeled vehicle. Obliterated by time, the sporadic tracks among the rocks were unidentifiable.

After crossing the eroded rubble field, the Wagon Road again offered the smoothest course toward Kiel Spring. Bob immediately returned to his even-gated lope up the gradual incline of the road. With Charleston Peak straight ahead, Con brushed Bob's rein across his neck turning him up the canyon toward the spring. The narrow canyon made a sweeping turn to the northwest before widening out into a small valley after a quarter mile. Just before reaching the bottom of the valley, the canyon became choked with brush.

Looking for a trail through the dense brush, it suddenly began looking very familiar as the sheriff neared it. Another rustler's corral had been built across the canyon. It took only moments to locate the gate and open it. Much like the one he had discovered earlier, the walls of the holding area were too steep for livestock to scale. The small underground stream that trickled from the spring above momentarily surfaced for a dozen yards before vanishing again below the terrain. The three heifers that were held here had all but eliminated the forage during their stay. The grass had yet to recuperate.

Conor had not seen any tracks from a truck like he discovered earlier, but concluded they had dissolved since the theft, nearly three months ago. He continued on through the back of the corral, while keeping a fervent eye out for any clue that might help identify the cagy cow-thieves. As he rode, Armenta surmised the rustlers were likely responsible for the crude repairs to the road.

He had ridden over a mile from the road before he reached Duncan Blackwood's fence. Unlike the wash between the school section and the Wagon Road, the fence had no gate as far as Con could see in either direction with his field glasses. He had grabbed a pair of fencing pliers from his brother's toolshed when he saddled Bob at dawn. Better to be prepared, in case it became necessary at some point to pull the staples from several posts and lay the barbwire on the ground to walk his horse over it. He hoped he would not need them. As he studied the valley above, he judged the spring to be another half mile away or more. Further from the road than he recollected earlier in the day.

The steepness of the hill up the fence line to the north offered an easier climb for Bob. Con urged him up, parallel to the fence. A hundred yards along were signs where a small group of cattle had slid on their haunches down the slope. The age of the disturbance fit with the time of the theft. Tracks above and below it had completely disappeared.

Almost immediately, the slope became more gradual.

Within a few feet, the barbwire disappeared through the branches of a juniper tree. The strands seemed slightly looser here than elsewhere. Conor dismounted for a closer look. Within the boughs of the tree, the wires had been cut, then spliced back together with newer galvanized segments. He smiled. The rustlers were making it easier to navigate their back trail, even if they left no tracks.

In short order, Con dissembled the fence and led Bob through. In a few minutes the passage was repaired and he stepped back into the saddle. He removed his Stetson and peered up at the sun as he wiped the sweat from his brow on a shirtsleeve. Past midday, he contoured the sidehill and made his way toward Kiel Spring up the valley.

The steep bluff on the south side of the valley provided a narrow strip of shade where the spring emerged at its feet. When dismounted, he loosened the cinch on Bob's saddle, then removed his bridle and hung it from the saddle horn. Conor fed him a carrot as he rubbed around his ears where the bridle had been, then retrieved a handful of lamb jerky for himself before Bob ambled to the cool water escaping from its source before him. He stretched out his legs and leaned against the cliff mulling over the evidence he had uncovered thus far while slowly chewing his jerky.

Coupled with what he learned from Duncan Blackwood, he felt he was getting to know his quarry. These rustlers were far from stupid. Their methods required a great deal of planning and preparation. Furthermore, they were calculating and cautious. They did not seem to be interested in making a big haul all at once. If they had only stolen the three heifers, he might suspect a small rancher trying to increase his breeding stock. The three market-aged steers taken on the other two occasions, suggested otherwise.

One thing for certain, the rustlers knew the area very well.

Back astride after a short rest, Armenta pointed Bob up a narrow game trail over the steep incline to the south. He paused peering across the panorama where the track crested the broad saddle atop the rim. Four or five miles to the southeast and lower in elevation, the flat top of the mesa appeared over the broad valley between them. Plotting the route in his mind, he urged Bob down the gradual slope into the valley. A half hour later, they began their ascent up the crest of the narrow ridge that would spill out onto the mesa at its summit.

Conor estimated thirty to forty steers dotted the top of the plateau when they reached it in midafternoon. A few grazed sporadically, but most sought out scant bits of shade beneath a dozen pinyon trees scattered across the top of the bluff. Their roots sought out narrow cracks beneath the thin layer of soil covering the surface of the massive block of stone that formed the butte. A surprising volume of water collected from infrequent rains in two natural stone tanks near each end of the mesa. At present, Blackwood's cattle were not depleting it, but the rancher kept close watch to ensure it lasted as long as the grass that fed them.

A half mile long and quarter mile wide near the center, the butte provided about forty acres of arid land for forage and high enough elevation for the grass to still be green from spring. After thoroughly examining the ledge on both sides, Conor determined access to the top was limited to either end of it. He found no sign of a makeshift corral on the north end when he rode up it nor any remnant of road that would provide a point of approach for the rustlers' truck. He paused to allow Bob a drink of warm water from the second pool before continuing on. As he surveyed the peaks and ridges to the east, Conor could name nearly all of them. Though he could not recall ever being here before, he knew exactly where he was. A quarter mile from the south end of the mesa, a miniature version of it rose as a pinnacle at nearly the same elevation. An east–west barbwire fence crossed the saddle midway between them with a wire gate at the summit. He rode to it.

A well-worn trail meandered inside the fence in either direction. The trail to the east dropped off a steeply. To the west, the slope was gentler. The fence and the trail angled off along the face of the mountain. The shod tracks of Duncan Blackwood's horse came from the east and continued west. He had dismounted at the gate and walked around examining it. Con did the same. There were no visible cattle tracks nearby and no evidence of the gate having been opened recently. The nearest vegetation was several yards away leaving little to study other than the ground around it. This was the most recent theft; less than three weeks ago. Other than Blackwood's minimal tracks, there had been no disturbances to the scene.

Leaving Bob standing at the trail, Conor crossed the fence two spans from the gate and carefully began searching for tracks. As he approached the gate from the far side, he looked intently for any indication it had been opened and laid down while the steers had been driven through it. If it had, the rustlers had been careful to cover their tracks…then he spotted it. The smallest tuft of red-brown hair on a barb on the bottom wire on the gate. He leaned down for a closer look. Only a few strands about an inch long. Approximately what could be expected from the leg of one of Blackwood's Hereford-longhorn cross steers. One of them had walked over the opened gate as it lay on the ground and brushed their leg against the wire. It would be difficult to prove how recently the event occurred, but nevertheless was noteworthy.

Conor slowly stood erect, careful not to take another step and possibly obliterate even the slightest clue. His eyes methodically swept the area, beginning at his feet, working his way outward. He spotted no disturbances to the soil. Soon he was scanning an arc thirty feet away. Little chance he would see anything at that distance he thought to himself. Cautiously, he turned and traced his steps back to where he crossed the fence. He calculated a path to walk an arc the same distance away around the gate and back to the fence. It would bring him within a few yards of the nearest sage and rabbitbrush. With eyes to the ground, he began his first circle past the gate.

Just west of center and thirty feet out from the gate, Conor spotted a disturbance in the dry soil. It looked almost as if someone had used a broom to brush out a track. He challenged himself. *Could it be made from the tail of a squirrel, or even a porcupine as they crossed his path? No, there would be tracks to accompany the mark. The tail or wing of a bird in flight maybe? Perhaps a hawk or an owl swooping down on its prey? If it made the strike, there would be indications of a struggle, no matter how slight. If a near miss, there would be tracks, most likely of a rodent. A far miss? Possibly.* Without further evidence, he made a mental note of the spot and continued on.

At the far end of his arc, Armenta moved out another fifteen feet and began making a larger circle around the gate. As he neared the area of the brush mark, he stood among a scattering of knee-high brush. Twenty feet outside of his circle something green stuck out from beneath a bush. He watched the ground closely as he left his course and worked his way toward the object. Two steps later, he spotted a cow track. More probable, a steer track. Then more. He followed them several feet. They headed straight down the side of the hill into the trees. They walked at a slow pace, nearly single file making it difficult to discern exactly how many. What troubled him; it looked to be three distinct sets of tracks. There were only two steers missing. Where did the third one come from?

Distracted by the sudden appearance of the tracks, Con stopped and returned to the green object that initially caused the detour from his arc. It took a moment to find it. A bow from a pinyon tree. The tips of the needles were conspicuously covered with dust. The branch had been hewn from its tree with a hatchet or axe. He contemplated his quarry as he walked back to his horse. The theft may have occurred up to three weeks ago, but even at that the rustlers had done an amazing job of hiding their tracks. Con had not seen a single track since the top of the mesa; a quarter mile away.

That's a lot of tracks to brush out, he considered to himself. And not just brush out, but sprinkle dust over the brush marks to hide them, too. Even if there were two rustlers, it still must have taken at least a couple of hours. And who's minding the steers while they're doing all of that? If they were horseback, which they must have been, what about the tracks they left up on the mesa? Did they brush and dust them, too? He'd ridden all the way around the top of the rim himself and never spotted a single horse print other than his own.

Conor opened the gate, led Bob through and closed it behind him. "Well, Pard," he told the horse as he stepped into the saddle, "let's go find us some rustled steers. I know you can go anywhere they can."

Not far into the trees, they came up to a single strand of barbwire nailed to the trees about three feet off the ground. It veered to the right keeping parallel to the fence above them. The three sets of tracks, now less often in single file, kept above the barrier. They were easy to follow since the steers often slipped on the steep sidehill as they angled down it. After a half mile they came to the remnants of an old road that contoured the hill. Here the steers followed the road. The barb-wire had been cut where it crossed but continued along the road on the downhill side. Tire tracks covered the steers' tracks as it rounded a bend into a steep ravine where the road ended abruptly.

A tiny rivulet of water cascaded down the gully from an unknown source above. The gaping hole in the far side of the ravine framed with timbers marked the entrance to a mine-shaft of bygone years. Two rusty steel rails extended from the ominous entrance the few feet across the gulch to the near side on four heavy planks. From there they continued another twenty feet to a minecart tipped onto its side at the edge of the massive tailings pile that marked the end of the road. Three sets of steer tracks disappeared onto the plank bridge.

When Con stepped down, he reached into his saddlebags retrieving a carrot for Bob and a piece of jerky for himself. He had worked fifteen years in a gypsum mine, but never under-ground. Con chewed on the jerky as he tried to reassure himself that Duncan Blackwood's ghost stories were just tall tales of cowboys trying to scare their younger counterparts around the campfire. He reached up taking Bob's bridle off and hung it from the saddle horn. Digging into the saddlebags he found his flashlight. The horse stood there faithfully as Con rubbed the side of his face.

"Maybe Dunc's right. Maybe ghosts *are* stealing his cattle. I don't have any silver bullets." He turned to look Bob in the eye as he pulled his Colt automatic from its holster. "If you hear gunshots, you might want to get the heck out of here."

Sheriff Conor Armenta skeptically crossed the plank

bridge. At the entrance to the mineshaft were two sets of hoof-prints and a set of boot-tracks exiting. He slipped the .45 back into its holster and continued. Fifty feet into the side of the mountain, the tunnel opened out to a room. The rusty rails continued through it into another passageway. Planks lined the ceiling held up by a forest of timbers. Several cowpies adorned the floor. Water dripped from the ceiling into a pickle barrel cut in half for a water trough. The other half of the barrel held remnants of hay a few feet away. He shined his flashlight around the room without discovering anything that might help identify the rustlers. There were no ghosts, but the cool surroundings were far from comforting.

Bob knickered when Con reappeared from the mine. He placed the flashlight back into the saddlebags and Bob gladly accepted the bit when given it. Within minutes, they were trotting down the unfamiliar road. It was a smooth gentle slope winding around the contour of the mountain. They were headed east in general and making good time as they descended. After four or five miles of twists and turns they broke out into the open and Con could finally see for certain where they were going. They would hit the old Wagon Road in about eight miles. He added up in his head where they had been and figured he had ridden about twenty miles so far and would be a little over thirty by the time they were back at Paddy's barn. They still had about five hours of daylight.

* * *

Avoiding an elongated conversation with Duncan Blackwood, Con cut across his ranch from the Wagon Road straight to his brother's sheep camp. Patrick's dogs announced his arrival as Conor loosened Bob's cinch before releasing him near the spring. With canteen and the remainder of his jerky in hand, he walked to the campfire.

"If you're going to show up for supper every evening," Paddy mocked, "I'll be out of beans by Tuesday."

"I brought jerky," Con offered.

"Papa's?" the younger sibling queried.

"Of course."

He nodded, grinning. "Been out chasing rustlers?" he asked.

"Yep," Conor offered with a nod.

"Any luck?"

He nodded again as Paddy handed him a tin can full of steaming coffee. "It's fresh," the younger brother added, recalling the muddy dregs he shared on the last visit.

"I didn't complain."

"I thought June was going to choke," Paddy apologized, grinning in embarrassment.

"Don't ask me for her forgiveness." Conor blushed. "That's between the two of you."

"You love her?"

"More than you could imagine." His face reddened even more.

"I could see it." A silence fell between them. "I told her so," he finally added. "She has the same look." He waited for a reaction from the man he idolized who stared into the fire.

"I asked her to marry me," Conor finally responded.

"When?" Paddy asked in surprise.

"Last night...when we sat on top of the hill behind your house, watching the stars."

"And?"

"And what?"

"What did she say?"

"Yes."

"Woohoo! Congratulations, big brother!" he responded excitedly in a mixture of Spanish and English. "When?"

"I don't know. Soon I think."

"We'll have a grand fiesta!" Paddy exclaimed.

"I suppose so," Conor agreed, suddenly realizing the stir their engagement would create in the gossip mill of Las Vegas. Paddy turned his attention to the pot of beans by the fire as his brother returned to silent contemplation.

"So, what about the rustlers?" he asked as he handed Con a plate of beans.

The question snapped the sheriff back into the present. "It's interesting," he began, then told his younger brother about the two corrals woven from sticks and branches, then about the tire tracks in the mud near the old Wagon Road. He concluded that the rustlers must be bringing their horses in a truck, then herd their captors into the corrals.

"They leave the cattle in the corrals while they take their horses back to wherever they come from and return a couple of days later, load up the cattle, and disappear." Patrick hung on every word in amazement as his brother unveiled the evidence and formulated it into the scenario of how the outlaws were getting away with their ill-gotten merchandise. It all made sense.

Conor then continued by describing their latest heist and how expertly they had hidden their tracks over the large area. He shared how Duncan Blackwood had told him he had two steers missing but must have miscounted because there were three sets of tracks that he followed down the hill and into the mineshaft. He concluded with how they must have backed their truck to the very edge of the plank bridge and laid their ramp up to the entrance of the mine to load the cattle.

"What about their horses?"

"They must have come down the hill somewhere else and loaded them into the truck down the road somewhere," Conor explained, but realized it did not make sense. To further his doubts, he retraced the ride from the mineshaft down the mountain through his head. He had not noticed anywhere that horses had come down the bank to the road or indications of where the truck may have been parked to load them. Maybe the experts had obliterated those tracks too.

"Even with the strand of barbwire to guide them," Paddy puzzled, "why would the steers just walk themselves down the hill, across the bridge, and into the abandoned mineshaft?"

Con stopped chewing on the spoonful of beans in his mouth. "They wouldn't," he sputtered without swallowing. The bewildered expression on his face remained, as he gazed blankly at his brother and slowly resumed chewing the mouthful.

* * *

It was nearly dark when he rode Bob into the ranch yard. He fed the horse the last of the carrots while unsaddling him. It had been a long ride and Bob seemed much less affected by the exertion than his rider. Conor scooped oats from the bin and sat the bucket in front of him as he brushed the salt and sweat from his back. After leading Bob to the pasture behind the house, he stopped for a moment to rub and pet the big white mare in the corral.

"Sorry darlin', I didn't save you any carrots," he consoled her before returning to the barn.

He slid his rifle under the seat and loaded the rest of his gear into the Sheriff's Department pickup truck. Continuing to ponder over the evidence at the mesa and the mine below as he slid behind the wheel, Armenta drove to town. He had to have missed something. He intentionally avoided sharing Duncan Blackwood's ghost theory with his brother. He saw no point in initiating rumors.

A thumbtack held a note noticeably on Con's back door when he pulled up.

Conor—

Call me when you get home. Even if it is late.

June

16

MONDAY, AUGUST 18, 1930

When Sheriff Conor Armenta entered Judge William Tucker's courtroom on yet another Monday morning, it seemed as if he had expended an entire lifetime there. In reality, he had spent several days of the past two months testifying in two separate trials involving Dutch Wagner. This would be the third, with yet one more to follow. Though one day on each trial should have been sufficient, Dutch's attorneys had deemed it necessary to call him back in, no less than three times for each trial to explain some minute detail that should have been clarified during their initial questioning.

At first the inconvenience was merely annoying. During the most recent trial, the murder of Jimmy Garza, it felt intentional. The sheriff suspected Mr. White deliberately distracted him from other responsibilities in order to keep his attention away from some unknown illegal activity of his employer.

Although Gary D. Wagner, Jr. appeared on the court clerk's paperwork, Armenta, Judge Tucker and the district attorney all knew the money that paid Carlton White's legal fees came from outside the state.

Opening arguments for the murder of Katherine Wagner were concluded before Judge Tucker recessed for lunch. That afternoon, Salvatore Rizzo testified describing his role in the abduction and transportation of Mrs. Wagner to Dutch's moonshine hideaway at the Valley of Fire. Afterward, Wagner was charged with kidnapping and assault in addition to the murder charges already held against him.

* * *

Tuesday, August 19, 1930

Sheriff Armenta studied through the pile of reports on his desk filed by his deputies yesterday. He had not yet been called to the witness stand when Judge Tucker adjourned the proceedings the previous afternoon. Conor came into the office at six this morning in order to get as much work done as possible before the court reconvened at nine. He glanced up to see the clock on the wall of the outer office through his open door, eight-fifteen. Fortunately, he found nothing requiring his immediate further attention.

At ten minutes before nine o'clock, Armenta followed District Attorney Donald Davis into the courtroom. Davis passed through the bar and took a seat at his assigned table. Dutch Wagner and Carlton White were seated at the other table whispering between themselves. Jesse sat just inside the bar a few feet behind them. Whit Ellis led Sal Rizzo into the room just as Conor seated himself in the gallery. They took seats against the wall opposite the jurors.

At precisely nine o'clock, the bailiff bellowed, "All rise," and proceeded to declare Judge Tucker's arrival.

Tucker took his seat behind the bench and after a series of formalities struck his gavel to the block and declared the court in session. Rizzo was brought back to the witness stand and detailed events of several visits to the hideout over Mrs. Wagner's extended stay there.

"Mr. Rizzo, when did you last see Mrs. Wagner?" Carleton White asked under cross-examination.

"April."

"Do you remember when in April?"

"About the middle of the month. A Saturday morning."

"At the cabin in the Valley of Fire?"

"Yeah."

"And what was the reason for your visit?"

"I brought the trunk out there," Rizzo answered. "From the garage by her house," he added.

Dutch Wagner said something to White under his breath.

"Do you mean Mr. Wagner's house?"

"No," Sal answered. "Dutch lives at the Oasis."

Even from behind, the sheriff could see Dutch Wagner's face reddening. He knew this side effect of Dutch's temper. The back of his neck and ears glowed as he hissed some inaudible order to the attorney.

"Who told you to take the trunk to the cabin?"

"Dutch did. He told me to go out to his mother's house and get the trunk out of the garage and take it to her. He said she sold the house and the new owner was moving in on Monday."

Armenta knew if Dutch faced him at that moment, he would see the veins protruding from the man's forehead as if ready to explode. Conor could also tell that Carlton White was desperately trying to portray to the jury that Dutch, the loving son was just having his mother's belongings delivered to her vacation cabin in the Valley of Fire. When the attorney turned to see Dutch's face, all color left his own. He quickly tried to regain his composure and hopefully divert the jurors' attention to the witness.

"And what was Mrs. Wagner's reaction when she received the trunk?" he asked Rizzo.

"Oh, she was excited when she saw it. She didn't have no clothes to speak of. A couple of old dresses Jimmy found at an abandoned homestead, and one he bought for her at Overton. She could hardly wait for me and Jimmy to pack it into her cell and get it open."

"Her cell?" White gulped as a murmur of whispers spread through the jury box.

"Yeah," Rizzo replied. "One end of the shack was partitioned off into a cell. It made it easier for Jimmy than handcuffing her to the bed all of the time." Con heard one of the ladies in the jury gasp.

"I was under the impression that Mrs. Wagner's accommodation was quite pleasant," the attorney continued as he desperately tried to gain control of the interrogation.

"Oh, yeah. Jimmy put up wallpaper over the boards and bought cloth that Mrs. Wagner made curtains out of. She had a dresser and mirror. She adored Jimmy, and he liked her, too. She was a nice old dame when you got to know her a little. Nothin' like Dutch made her out to be."

"No further questions, Your Honor," White concluded. The plan had been to make Jimmy look like the bad guy and murderer, while Dutch had avenged his mother's death by killing him. The exact opposite result had been realized.

"Any other questions, Mr. Davis?" Judge Tucker asked the DA.

"Yes," he answered, opting to take advantage of the current mood in the courtroom.

"This house, Mr. Rizzo, the one where the trunk was," the prosecutor verified. "Is that the same house that the defendant was convicted a few weeks ago of extorting from his mother?"

"I don't know anything about that, he always just called it his mother's house."

"No further questions, Your Honor," Davis stated.

* * *

When the court reconvened after lunch, District Attorney Donald Davis called Sheriff Armenta to the witness stand. After giving a detailed synopsis of his search for Mrs. Wagner, resulting in the discovery of her corpse, the DA moved his questioning to the autopsy.

"What was determined to be the cause of Mrs. Wagner's death?"

"A .25 caliber bullet wound at the base of her skull just above the spinal cord. The same type of wound as killed Jimmy Garza," Conor continued. "When the ballistics report from the state crime lab in Carson City arrived, they determined that Jimmy Garza and Kathleen Wagner were killed with the same .25 caliber firearm."

"Was there other evidence attributing to the nature of Mrs. Wagner's death?"

"A letter from Mrs. Wagner to her daughter written three years ago with instructions to be delivered upon her death. It also stated that Dutch Wagner had been blackmailing her and Mr. Campbell, and that she feared he would kill her."

"What did you do then?"

"Based on this evidence, Judge Tucker issued a warrant and I arrested Mr. Wagner on extortion charges."

"But now the defendant is charged with murder," the DA stated. "How did this come about?"

"When ballistics tests from the crime lab established that the bullets responsible for both deaths were fired from the pistol taken from Mr. Wagner at the time of his arrest, Wagner was charged with their murders."

"No further questions, Your Honor."

"Your witness, Mr. White," Judge Tucker announced.

"Let me get this straight, Sheriff. Based on hearsay, you spent three days joyriding around in the desert. In the meantime, you left the county-owned vehicle assigned to you at your brother's disposal while the county paid this same brother for your use of his horse and truck?"

"Objection, Your Honor," Davis interrupted. "Sheriff Armenta is not on trial here."

"Sustained," the judge confirmed. "Mr. White, it may appear that you stepped into the Old West when you arrived here. Let me assure that I expect you to adhere to the same decorum you would in any Los Angeles courtroom. I will not tolerate further sarcastic insinuations."

"Yes, Your Honor," the red-faced attorney replied.

"You may proceed, Mr. White."

"Sheriff Armenta, Mr. Wagner says you held your gun to his head when you arrested him."

"Objection, Your Honor, hearsay."

"Sustained. Rephrase your question, Mr. White."

Perspiration beaded on the attorney's forehead as he ran

his finger around the collar of his shirt. "Did you hold your gun to Mr. Wagner's head when you arrested him for extortion?"

"Yes."

"Hardly a capital offense, Sheriff. As Judge Tucker so eloquently indicated a moment ago, this is not the Old West." Carlton White continued accusingly. "Did you find such a display of deadly force necessary?"

"If it had been the Old West, sir, the sheriff would not have held Mr. Wagner at gunpoint after he attempted to draw the pistol from his pocket to shoot him." Conor explained. "The sheriff would have pulled the trigger."

* * *

Wednesday, August 27, 1930

"Mr. Foreman, have members of the jury reached a verdict?" Judge Tucker asked.

"We have, Your Honor."

"What say you?"

"On the charge of assault, we find the defendant not guilty. We didn't feel the evidence was sufficient to prove Dutch was the perpetrator of Mrs. Wagner's injuries."

The statement drew a loud buzz from the crowd which brought two quick raps of Judge Tucker's gavel.

"You need not explain the reason for the jury's decision, Mr. Foreman," the judge clarified. "Please continue."

"On the charge of kidnapping, we find the defendant guilty," the foreman announced. "On the charge of murder in the second degree, we find the defendant guilty."

"Very well, Mr. Foreman. Gary D. Wagner, Jr., you have

been found guilty of kidnapping and murder in the second degree of Katherine Wagner, your mother, by a jury of your peers. You will be held in the Clark County Jail without bond until sentencing on a date yet to be determined. This session of the District Court of Nevada is now adjourned." With a rap of the gavel Judge Tucker stood.

"All rise," the bailiff bellowed as the judge exited the courtroom.

Conor spotted Katie Brumbaugh and Leanora Campbell departing the rear of the courtroom when he turned. Both appeared to be crying. He could hardly imagine Mrs. Brumbaugh's range of emotions under the circumstances. Leanora Campbell held her by the arm as they left.

* * *

Tuesday, September 2, 1930

"What's he doing here?" Dutch Wagner asked his attorney when he entered the courtroom.

"Alfonso Drago?" Carleton White clarified seeing his client's focus.

"Yeah."

"Witness."

"They brought him all the way from Carson City?"

White glanced at a document from the file on the table in front of him. "Evidently. Should we be concerned?"

"He used to work for me...stole a truckload of whiskey," Wagner told him.

As the trial for the murder of Brice Campbell began, District Attorney Donald Davis introduced several key pieces of evidence. He held up an affidavit from Johann Berger, the

Austrian Mountaineer who led the climbing expedition that Gary Wagner, Sr. had died on.

"The defendant's father died in a climbing accident," he announced before beginning to read the heading on the document aloud describing the catastrophe. Davis then apologized in advance for the graphic nature of Mr. Berger's testimony before proceeding with his reading of it. When finished, several members of the jury were pale.

"For seven years, the defendant has blamed the victim for his father's death." Davis waved the affidavit in the air. "Nothing could be further from the truth."

For a fleeting moment, the expression on Dutch Wagner's face showed the realization of his error and remorse. Remorse for the killing of Brice Campbell. That led to killing his mother for falling in love with Campbell. She should have been mourning his father's death instead. As the dominoes began to fall, Jimmy Garza, a peon willing to sell his soul in the white man's world for a hundred dollars or tell that world all he knew, had to be silenced. Anger soon replaced Wagner's remorse. Anger for being caught. If not for killing the stupid Indian, he would not be here now. He did not blame himself for the blunder, he blamed those who caught him. Especially Sheriff Conor Armenta, a lowly shepherd in Dutch's appraisal, landed into a position of authority by a populous, even more ignorant than the man they had elected. His blood-pressure rising with his anger shown in the crimson hue of his face. He sat silently staring at the handcuffed wrists resting in front of him.

"...Call the sheriff. Dutch has killed me..." Mr. Davis read the conclusion of the letter left to his sister. It jolted Dutch back into the present. The letter had already been used to help convict him of his mother's murder and now to avenge the death of her lover.

Donald Davis called Al Drago as his first witness. "You were formerly employed by Mr. Wagner?"

"Yes."

"How long did you work for him and in what capacity?"

"About five years. At first, I was a bouncer at the Oasis. Later I helped with the moonshine, too."

"What did you do with that phase of Mr. Wagner's business?"

"Made deliveries mostly," Drago answered, "but I picked up supplies, packed firewood, worked around the still...pretty much anything they needed."

"How often did you talk to Mr. Wagner?"

"Almost every day."

"Did he ever express a dislike of Brice Campbell?"

"Only every day." Al Drago chuckled. "Dutch knew I'd worked for Fremont Construction before and held a grudge against Campbell for firing me. He always bitched that Campbell killed his old man to seduce his mother. He hated him."

"No further questions, Your Honor."

"Mr. White," Judge Tucker responded as he scribbled a note on his pad. "Your witness."

"Mr. Drago, you stated that you worked for Mr. Wagner about five years?"

"That's right."

"When did you leave his employ?"

"When I got caught running a truckload of moonshine for him. He framed me. Told the cops I stole the truck and that it was my whiskey."

"But you were arrested for killing livestock."

"That was his doin' too. He told me to shoot this old man's

sheep anytime they were gettin' close to the road. He didn't want the old guy findin' the still."

"Did you tell the sheriff all of this when you were arrested?"

"Eventually."

"But you were still convicted of these crimes."

"I couldn't prove otherwise." Drago smiled sardonically.

"What do you gain by testifying here today?"

"A vacation from making little rocks out of big rocks at Carson City, a train ride, better food. That's all I can think of."

"No one has offered a reduced sentence? No cash?"

Al chuckled. "I get to watch Dutch sit there on his butt and fidget. After he screwed me over. That's enough."

Dutch jerked in his seat with intent to jump up and slug the witness before overcoming the reflex and settling back into the chair. Carlton White saw the reaction. So did the jury.

"No more questions, Your Honor."

* * *

Thursday, September 4, 1930

It had become clear during the weeks of trials that Dutch Wagner was a violent and deadly man. At first, he seemed able to control it. As the weeks passed, he appeared ready to explode into a violent rage at any moment. It became more and more difficult to avert the jurors' attentions from the defendant's mood swings. This fourth and final trial progressed rapidly. Though it would be difficult to admit to his employer, Carlton White could hardly wait for its conclusion. The prosecution had just called the widow of the victim to the stand. He disdained the prospect of cross-examining her. She seemed so distinguished and kind. His client had murdered her husband almost beyond any possibility of doubt. He could not bear to hurt her feelings, to disrupt her mourning. The entire case disgusted him. Mr. Davis now held a small briarwood pipe in his hand from the exhibit table. He handed it to the witness.

"Mrs. Campbell, can you identify this pipe?"

"Yes, it belonged to my husband. It was his favorite because it fit nicely into the pocket of his trousers."

"Purely for the record, by your husband, you are referring to the late Brice Campbell?"

"Yes, sir."

"Mrs. Campbell, there are many pipes very similar to this one. How can you be certain that this particular pipe belonged to your late husband?"

"It was custom made in Scotland from a specific type of briar. I cannot recall the name of it. Brice's cousin had it made for him there. There is a chip inside the rim of the bowl and a hairline crack all the way down to the bottom of the bowl from it. The damage was caused when Brice dropped it from a cliff during a climb when the pipe was nearly new, about eight years ago. There also was a chip in the mouthpiece from the same incident, but it cut Brice's tongue so he filed it down," she held the pipe up to see its profile. "You can see how the bottom is much thinner than the top." A tear streaked down her cheek. "This is my husband's pipe."

"Let the record show that Mrs. Campbell identified three unique markings and characteristics of the pipe. It is also on record that Sheriff Armenta pulled a partial print from between the bowl and stem of the pipe which has been identified by the state lab as coming from Brice Campbell's right thumb," Donald Davis noted. "Mrs. Campbell, when was the last time you saw this pipe?"

"The evening that Sheriff Armenta brought it to me to identify. About three months ago."

"On June seventeenth?"

"That sounds about right. I can say for certain when I check my calendar at home."

"That won't be necessary," Davis responded. "When before that?"

"The evening of April second, about eight p.m."

"What makes you certain of the time and date?"

"It was the last time I saw Brice alive." Tears now streaked down both her cheeks. Donald Davis handed her his handkerchief.

"No further questions, Your Honor."

Judge Tucker cleared his throat. "Mr. White?"

"No questions, sir."

"Mrs. Campbell, you may step down," Tucker told her. "The court will now take a ten-minute recess," the judge proclaimed as he struck the block with his gavel.

"All rise," the bailiff called as Judge Tucker left the courtroom.

* * *

Friday, September 5, 1930

Defense Attorney Carlton White had little hope of a not guilty verdict in this third murder trial of Gary D. Wagner, Jr. In a last-ditch effort, he had convinced Wagner to take the stand in his own defense. After bringing the court to order at nine o'clock, Judge William Tucker called the attorneys to approach the bench.

"Gentlemen, are both of you prepared to present final arguments?"

"I'd like to call one more witness for the defense, Your Honor," Mr. White requested.

"Which witness do you wish to reexamine?"

"Not reexamine. A new witness, Your Honor."

"But all of the witnesses have already testified. You can't bring in a new surprise witness this late in the game."

"I'm going to call Gary Wagner to the stand."

"You're sure?"

"Yes."

"You realize that you're leaving your defendant wide open for cross-examination by Mr. Davis?"

"Yes, Your Honor."

"Go ahead," Judge Tucker obliged with a rap of his gavel.

"Mr. White, please call your witness forward."

"I call Gary D. Wagner, Jr. to the stand."

A rumble through the crowd brought two sharp raps from Judge Tucker's gavel. Deputy Jesse Slater snapped to attention in his chair then stood to escort the defendant ahead. In front of the witness stand he unlatched Dutch's right handcuff while the bailiff swore him in then relatched it. Dutch ambled up the step and sat himself straight up in the chair.

"Gary Wagner, can you share with the court your whereabouts on the evening of April 2, 1930. I was working at my business, Dutch's Oasis, it's a gentleman's club."

"It was a Wednesday. What were you doing on that particular night?"

"Drago was attending to other duties, so I was covering the floor downstairs."

"Was business slow? Crowded?"

"We were pretty busy for a weeknight, but nothing like a Friday or Saturday. The girls had a full night upstairs."

"Anything particularly noteworthy?"

"Things were pretty well dried up by midnight downstairs. An associate of mine came in from working outside of town to discuss some matters. That was after midnight, probably one thirty or so. The last of the customers left from upstairs around three. We locked up and I went to bed."

"What about the next morning?" White continued.

"I got up around nine o'clock, shaved, dressed, and went to the Hotel Nevada for breakfast. That was where I first heard about Brice Campbell committing suicide."

"What time would that have been?"

"Around ten, I think."

"So, then. You were nowhere around the home of Brice and Leanora Campbell or that of your mother between the hours of midnight and seven o'clock on the morning of April third?"

"No, sir."

"I have no more questions, Your Honor."

Sheriff Armenta had moved to a seat directly behind Donald Davis and the two men were engaged in a quiet conversation across the bar.

"Your witness, Mr. Davis," the judge informed him.

"In those hours soon after midnight, you said you met with a business associate. Is that correct?" Davis asked.

"Yes, sir. Around one or one thirty."

"You also said that this associate had been working outside of town and came into town to discuss something with you. What sort of work was the associate doing outside of town that night?"

"I don't know," Dutch responded.

"What was the associate supposed to be doing?"

"Objection. The prosecution is asking the witness to speculate."

"Sustained," the judge agreed. "Please continue, Mr. Davis."

"Was this associate Joseph Mariano?"

Dutch's face began reddening. The prosecutor watched as Dutch mulled the options of his next answer over in his head.

"I remind you that you are under oath, Mr. Wagner," Davis added.

"Yeah," he finally replied. "Yes. Yes, Joe Mariano came to talk to me."

"Objection, Your Honor. How is this line of questioning pertinent to the case at hand?" Carlton White exclaimed.

"I'll permit it," Judge Tucker asserted. "I want to see where this is going. You will answer the question, Mr. Wagner."

"Did Joseph Mariano operate a moonshine still southeast of Las Vegas at the time of Brice Campbell's death?"

"I don't know," Dutch answered.

"What did Mr. Mariano discuss with you so urgently at that hour?"

"I don't recall."

"I have no further questions of the witness at this time, Your Honor," Davis stated, "allowing permission to call him back later, if necessary."

"The defendant is the final witness, Mr. Davis," Tucker replied with a puzzled look on his face.

"I would like to call Mr. Alfonso Drago back to the stand, Your Honor."

"I will grant that. The court will recess for thirty minutes for Sheriff Armenta to arrange Mr. Drago's return to the courtroom." Judge Tucker made a quick rap with his gavel.

"All rise," the bailiff ordered as the judge rose and entered his chambers and Conor darted out the door.

* * *

Sheriff Armenta escorted Al Drago into the courtroom just as Judge Tucker returned to the bench. Lacking sufficient time to change back into the suit he wore earlier, Drago wore a prison uniform. William Tucker allowed them time to be seated before calling the court back to order.

"Mr. Davis," he addressed. "You may call your witness."

"I call Alfonso Drago to the stand."

Conor brought him forward and the bailiff met them in front of the witness stand. "Mr. Drago, do you understand that you are still under oath from your previous testimony."

"Yes, sir."

"You may be seated."

"Mr. Drago," the DA began. "Could you tell the court where you were on the evening of April 2, 1930?"

"I was working for Mr. Wagner at the moonshine still southeast of here."

"Was Joseph Mariano there that evening?"

"Yes, he was in charge."

"Did you see Brice Campbell there that evening?"

"Yes, sir."

"Was there an altercation that night between Mr. Campbell and Mr. Mariano?"

"Yes, sir."

"Can you describe for the court what took place?"

"Campbell showed up and confronted Joe wanting to know where Mrs. Wagner was. He told Campbell it wasn't his job to take care of her. Campbell said something else and then

Joe…We couldn't hear what they said, but Joe punched him in the face and Campbell went down like a sack of taters. Then Joe told us to take Campbell and make sure he never came out there again."

"You said 'us' and 'we.' Who was with you?"

"Wesley. Carl Wesley. We worked together for Dutch."

"What happened next?"

"Carl knew a trail up to the top of the cliffs. We took Campbell up there and told him his only way out was down the cliff to where his car was parked below. He made it about halfway down and fell. We could see him lying down at the bottom in our lantern. We thought he was dead and scrambled back down the trail to see. When we got there, Campbell was driving away in his car. We went and told Joe what happened and that we didn't think Campbell would be back. Joe said that Dutch needed to keep his personal life separate from business. We went back to work and Joe left a little while later."

"No further questions, Your Honor."

"Your witness, Mr. White."

"No questions, Your Honor."

"You may step down, Mr. Drago," the judge told him as he looked at the prosecutor. "Call your witness, Mr. Davis," he declared, suspecting he would call Wagner back to the stand.

"I call Gary D. Wagner, Jr. to the stand."

After confirming his oath, Dutch Wagner climbed into the chair on the witness stand.

Donald Davis picked up the briarwood pipe from the exhibit table. "Mr. Wagner, can you tell the court what this is?"

"It's Brice Campbell's pipe."

"You took this pipe from Mr. Campbell after you killed him?"

"No, I never saw it before Mrs. Campbell identified it yesterday."

"You never saw it before, but it was in the safe in your office on the day you were arrested on extortion charges. Can you please tell the court how it got there?"

"I don't know. I never saw it before."

Mr. Davis returned the pipe to the table and picked up an eight by ten black-and-white photograph. He handed it to Wagner.

"Do you recognize this photograph, Mr. Wagner?"

"Never saw it before."

"It's a photograph of the inside of the safe in your office, Mr. Wagner. It was taken by Clark County Coroner Dr. Harold Martin a few minutes after your arrest. You had just opened that safe in compliance with a search warrant issued by Judge William Tucker that same day. Does it look more familiar now?"

"I've seen the safe, just not the picture," Dutch replied smugly.

"Look carefully at the photograph, Mr. Wagner. There is a ledger book tilted up to one side because it is laying on top of that very pipe. Do you see it?"

Dutch swallowed. "Yes, sir."

"That ledger book has entries of every extortion payment Brice Campbell made to you. It also has hundreds of other entries. A handwriting expert has sworn that every single entry in that book was made by you. Do you recognize it?"

"Never seen it before in my life."

Davis sighed. "Do you see the money stacked on top of the ledger book? Seventeen thousand three hundred and sixty-four dollars, to be exact, in cash. Do you recognize the money, Mr. Drago?"

He tried to swallow the frog in his throat again. "Ain't never seen it before in my life," he croaked hoarsely.

"So, you won't mind if the county just deposits that into the general fund?"

"No, sir," he managed to reply.

"Can you explain to the court how any or all of the contents of your safe got there?"

"I don't know. Someone else must have put them there," he answered with some regained swagger.

"How many people besides yourself have the combination of that safe?"

"I don't know."

"No more questions, Your Honor."

"Mr. White?"

"No questions."

"This court will recess for lunch and reconvene at one o'clock for closing arguments."

"All rise," the bailiff ordered, following the ring of Tucker's gavel.

* * *

In closing arguments, the prosecutor told how the left-handed victim had broken his left wrist in the fall from the cliff. Mr. Mariano had confronted the defendant to take care of his personal matters and keep them from interfering with business. Wagner had gone to the home of Brice Campbell and assaulted the older and injured man, retrieving the victim's revolver in the process. He then held the gun to Mr. Campbell's right temple and killed him. In posing the victim as if he had committed suicide, he discovered Mr. Campbell's briarwood pipe, and stole it as a morbid trophy of the event. Davis voiced his opinion clearly that beyond reasonable doubt, Gary D. Wagner despised Brice Campbell resulting in Wagner's planning and murdering Campbell in the first degree.

Before going into deliberation, Judge Tucker addressed the jury.

"It has been a tiring and emotional several weeks for this court," he began. "None of you have participated as witness nor juror in any of the previous trials, though they have been thoroughly publicized by our local newspapers. It is not your responsibility to judge whether Mr. Wagner is innocent or guilty of any crime beyond the murder of Brice Campbell on the morning of April 3, 1930. It is your duty, to the best of your abilities, to ignore other crimes that may or may not have been committed by the defendant and focus only on the crime which he is being tried for today."

In less than an hour, they had reached a verdict.

"Gary D. Wagner, Jr.," Judge Tucker began, "you have been found guilty of murder in the first degree by a jury of your peers. You will remain without bond in custody of the Clark County jail until sentencing at a later date yet to be determined. This session of the District Court of Nevada is adjourned," Judge Tucker decreed with the ring of his gavel.

Dutch Wagner sat sullenly behind the table. The same chair he had occupied through many days of the past several weeks.

"Don't worry, Mr. Wagner." Carlton White leaned over and spoke under his breath. "Sheriff Armenta will never get you to Carson City."

17

"Miss Scott," Sheriff Armenta queried, "could you move your chair to its approximate location on Wednesday?"

She stood and slid the tall folding chair closer to the array of chalk markings on the floor.

"Please be seated," the sheriff told her as she stood beside it.

"Where were you, Wayne?"

Garrard moved behind the light positioned to the rear of the marks where camera two had been. Conor crossed the room and stood a few feet in front of the painting of the Grand Canyon that adorned the wall.

"Who stood here?" he asked them.

"I don't know," Wayne replied. "I was watching Mark and Matt."

"The gaffer," Emily answered. "Bobby Hansen."

"How far do you suppose it is from here to Matt McCoy, Wayne?"

"Twenty feet, maybe?"

"He's our man."

* * *

SATURDAY, AUGUST 30, 1930

Bobby Hansen sipped a glass full of tonic water heavily laced with gin as he lounged bare-chested in the late afternoon sun by the swimming pool. A tall man, just over six feet, he acquired his sculpted physique from years of carrying the heavy equipment required to film movies around the sets. Not at all homely, his well-proportioned body often attracted the attention of more than a few female members of the crew; even an occasional rising starlet. In his midthirties, he had been around the industry long enough to have seen a half-dozen young men like Matt McCoy rocket into stardom before fizzling into the obscure background after a short-lived period of glory. That did not slow Bobby from taking advantage when these youngsters chose to blow vast amounts of their new-found wealth on lively parties.

"Nice party." He raised his glass in salute to the staggering host when he walked past, arm in arm with Molly Mansfield.

Molly, much more sober than she portrayed, helped Matt remain upright as they socialized their way around the pool. Closer to his own age than Matt McCoy's, she had lost some of the firmness in her figure from a decade earlier but remained slim. There was a time past, when they had spent time together, before she began pursuing relationships more benefi-cial to advancing her career. Now, as she gradually slipped past her prime, Molly worked hard to prolong her youthful appearance on the screen. Before long she would be being cast as a middle-aged mother. Bobby was certain the concept repulsed her.

He glanced around, surveying the eligible women among the crew. Emily Scott sat beneath the umbrella of a table on the far side of the pool. She drank orange juice through a straw, most likely mixed with vodka or rum he thought. She talked and laughed with two middle-aged cameramen and one of their wives that shared the table. Em was pretty and nice, but prudish. She had a good figure, but seldom wore attire that showed it. Today was no exception, her swimwear being more modest that anyone else there. Bobby had taken her to dinner a couple of times and never made it past first base.

His gaze roamed to the prop girl, Jenny Vance. Though tomboyish at times, she was perhaps the sexiest woman here. Her bathing suit barely covered the shapely body inside it. Jenny however, clung to Matt's twin brother Mark like an octopus. Mark was co-starring in this coming picture and hoping to duplicate his brother's success.

As Bobby assessed the unlikelihood of recruiting any interesting female companionship from among the guests at the party, Matt and Molly made their way back around toward his lounge chair. Matt had removed his shirt as he circled the pool. From years of working on his father's ranch, he showed off a well-developed physique of his own.

"How ya doin', Bobby?" he slurred. "Getting' enough to drink?"

"Yeah," he lifted his half-full glass to show him. "I'm doin' fine."

"Gotta keep the workin' class happy," Matt bragged as he waved his glass around to the crowd.

Bobby ignored the remark and smiled. "Yeah, somebody's gotta do the dirty work."

"Lucky for you, your dad got you a job at the studio."

Molly Mansfield's eyes nearly popped out of her head as she stood red-faced, staring in disbelief. Bobby Hansen maintained his composure.

"Well, it was before your time, but actually, I lined up the job for my old man."

"Yeah, sure," Matt McCoy mocked him.

Bobby Hansen jumped to his feet ready to pop this mouthy kid, no matter who he was. Suddenly he realized Molly Mansfield had shed her swimsuit and was prancing around naked to a chorus of whistles and catcalls from many of the mostly male crew.

Mark McCoy stared at Molly shamelessly until the need to adjust his swim-trunks became apparent and he opted to take a quick dip in the pool. Jenny Vance noticed her boyfriend's embarrassing predicament and wiggled out of her bathing suit, made a quick pirouette to the pleasure of several onlookers, and jumped into the pool with Mark.

"Don't you think we should go inside, sweetie?" Molly coaxed as she led Matt away by the hand.

Most of the guests then began leaving. Mark and Jenny were necking in the pool. Bobby Hansen downed the rest of his drink and went to the hosted bar for a refill, which disappeared quickly. Getting another for the road, he walked out the side gate.

* * *

FRIDAY, OCTOBER 10, 1930

"What about Mark?" Emily Scott asked.

"We need to find the bullet shot from his gun," the sheriff replied.

"It killed Matt," she replied in disbelief.

"No. A .38 caliber bullet killed Matt. That's what the coroner called about. The bullet from Mark's gun hit somewhere else," he told them. "The flash we saw on the film? That was from the gun that killed Matt."

"So where did Mark's bullet go?" Emily asked.

"Either the floor or the wall behind Matt," the retired marshal answered for the sheriff. "With this tile floor? I'm guessing the wall."

"Right," Armenta confirmed. "Let's start looking."

All three started scanning the wall.

"Probably below our waists," Con suggested.

"Right," Garrard agreed. "I think I've got it," he chimed back in a moment later, drawing the attention of his companions. Wayne Garrard found a splintered hole in the mopboard behind where Matt McCoy had stood and four inches off the floor.

"You have a flashlight in your car?" Armenta asked him.

"Sure do," he said and headed out the door.

"What do you think?" Conor asked Wayne a few minutes later as the two men lay on the floor peering into the hole.

"The hole looks about the right size," Wayne considered. "It went clear through."

"Do you think there will be enough left of the bullet for a ballistics match?"

"Nobody had hardly heard of ballistics when I was working. I have no idea."

"We have a telephone"—Conor looked at the open door into Brice Campbell's study—"we can find out."

After multiple telephone calls, the experts in Carson City doubted the bullet would be in good enough condition for a match but would do their best if it was recovered. Sheriff Armenta chose to abandon probing further for the meantime.

On their return to town, the trio discussed the case.

"Miss Scott," the sheriff addressed. "You understand that what we discussed today is strictly confidential."

"Yes, sir."

"I mean absolutely no discussions beyond talking to me."

"I understand, Sheriff," she confirmed. "I don't spread gossip, but I can scarcely believe Bobby Hansen would shoot Matt McCoy. Beat him up maybe, but not shoot him."

"Where is Bobby staying?"

"The Northern Hotel."

"And Bull?"

"Adjacent rooms. Bull's in a suite. It's quieter so he can sleep in the daytime."

The sun had nearly set when Wayne Garrard's Dodge rolled into Las Vegas. They dropped Emily Scott at the Union Hotel then Garrard drove Con to the sheriff's office.

"What do you make of all this, Wayne?" he asked as they pulled up.

"Bobby Hansen is no bully. He's big enough, but that guy is as calm and easygoing as they come. What's the motive?"

"Sometimes those big quiet guys are the ones holding something inside that needs to get out. I keep hearing that Matt McCoy could be a loose cannon."

"He had his moments," Wayne admitted. "Got too rich, too fast I think."

"And he liked parties."

"He liked to drink and couldn't hold his liquor too well either."

"Not a good combination. Anything going on recently?"

"Not that I'm aware of, but the boys have been staying with their dad. I'm not sure they've even been to town since we got here."

"Thanks, Wayne. You've been a great help." They shook hands.

"My pleasure, Con. It feels good to get my brain back working on something more worthwhile than how quick some kid can get his gun out of the holster without dropping it." He laughed at himself as he released his grip.

"I've got a couple of calls to make before I can call it a day," the sheriff shared. "Have a good evening, Wayne."

Conor stood on the steps watching Wayne Garrard drive away. As the car rounded the corner, he wondered if he should be so trusting of the retired lawman, then turned and entered the door. After checking messages, he called the Northern Hotel.

"May I speak to Bull Hansen?" he asked the clerk.

"I'll put you through to his room."

"Hello," the deep voice answered.

"Hello, Bull. This is Sheriff Armenta. I need to talk to you concerning couple of things."

"What about?"

Conor thought the question unusual. It stirred his suspicion. "Is this Bull?"

"Uh, no. He's taking a nap."

"Who am I talking to?"

"This is Bobby Hansen. Uh, we met on the set."

"Who are you talking to?" Con heard from a gruff voice in the background.

"Uh, the sheriff. He wants to talk to you."

"Well, give me the damned telephone." Con heard a slight rustling over the receiver.

"Bull Hansen here. What can I do for you, Sheriff?"

"I've got some hats I need you to look at. I wonder if you could drop by my office in the morning?"

"Sure. What time?"

"Early or late?" Conor asked.

"After not working for a couple of nights, my brain is all mixed up. It doesn't know when to be asleep or awake. Maybe a little later."

"Will nine o'clock work for you?"

"I'll be there."

* * *

SATURDAY, OCTOBER 11, 1930

Sheriff Armenta arrived at the office at seven thirty. Hazel made coffee as he came in. Being short-staffed while having a deputy on security at the Campbell estate, she volunteered to work through the weekend. At a quarter to nine, Bull Hansen came through the door and hung his hat on the peg beside the sheriff's. He looked just as Con remembered him, minus the Smith & Wesson that had adorned his right hip at their previous meeting.

"Good morning, Bull. Thanks for coming in." He welcomed the visitor with a handshake halfway across the outer office. "Cup of coffee?" he offered.

"Sure...Black," he added as Con grabbed a clean cup and filled it.

"Bull, this is Mrs. Hazel Corbyn. She's the one that keeps all of us in line around here," he teased her.

Hazel blushed as Hansen grinned at Conor's tormenting.

"Hazel, Bull Hansen. He's security for the movie company."

"My pleasure, ma'am." The big man took a slight bow. "I'll try not to cause you any extra work."

"Come on in," Con invited, closing the door behind them.

The guard eyed the stack of fedoras atop the file cabinet. "I can tell you from here, unless you got another one with that same shiny, blue-green feather, it's the hat on top there."

"Make yourself comfortable, Bull," Con said, motioning him to a chair as he took the stack from the cabinet. He handed Molly Mansfield's, the top one, to Hansen. Then sat down behind his desk and reexamined the one from Hugh Parker's room, clearly at least a quarter size larger.

"You're certain that was the hat the person wore who came out to the movie set Tuesday night?"

"Positive. I didn't recollect it the other day, but now I remember that shiny feather reflecting in my spotlight when the car drove by."

Armenta considered Bull Hansen's disclosure. It confirmed his own deduction. Molly Mansfield was in the prop truck the night before the shooting. She absent-mindedly snuffed out her cigarette by the gun chest. She had a key to get into the chest and all of the evidence points toward her doing just that. How did Matt and Mark's guns get switched? And when? The bullet was missing from Mark's belt, but the gun was Matt's. Hugh Parker did not purchase the box of cartridges until the morning of the murder. He did not replace the missing bullet in Mark's belt until after the shooting. He had to have done that when he consoled Mark in the sitting room. Why then?

All of the conspiring, preparation, tampering with evidence Con contemplated, only to be beaten to the draw by Bobby Hansen. The thought brought him back to the man's father.

Bull Hansen sat quietly in the chair across from the desk, allowing the sheriff time to consider the evidence. He had finished his coffee and held the empty cup in his lap.

"I'm sorry, Bull. I got side-tracked itemizing the points of evidence in my head."

"I figured as much. That's why I just sat here and let you figure it all out."

"I wish it were that easy."

"I understand. I may have just been a sergeant on the street by the end of my forty years, but I worked on my own share of tough cases during that time." He paused, reminiscing over a few of them. "Sometimes they just don't make sense. I could never figure out for the life of me why some people do what they did."

"That's where I'm at. By what I've seen and what Captain Sanders told me, you were a good cop. Honest to a fault," Conor thought about how to ask his next question. There were no alternatives. He needed to just plunge ahead and let the chips fall where they may. "If I ask you some tough questions, Bull, will you give me honest answers? Tell me the truth?"

"It sounds like I might not want to answer your questions."

"But you'll know not answering might be answer enough. There is no easy place to start."

"Well, go ahead then," Hansen answered with a frog in his throat.

"Does Bobby shoot?"

Hansen let the question and a dozen possible reasons the sheriff might have asked it roll around in his head. None of them were good.

"Yes."

"Is he a good shot?"

The question was tougher, not the answer, but answering it.

He held his breath. "Yes." Then let it out with a bit of a whistle.

"How good?"

"You'll find out sooner or later anyway." He took a deep breath and let it out. "A hundred out of a hundred on the LAPD pistol range ten years ago. Before he went to work for Mr. Fredericks."

Con knew the questioning had to be tearing Bull Hansen apart. "Would you like a glass of water?"

"Yeah." He nodded. "That would be good."

Con stood up from behind his desk and went to the door. "Hazel, could you bring us some water?"

He then walked to the window and opened it. When he turned around, Hazel was setting a pitcher of water and two glasses on his desk. She left the room without speaking or looking up and closed the door behind her. Con filled both glasses and handed one to Bull before sitting back down. This wasn't an interrogation. Bull Hansen had done nothing wrong. He wanted to look at the man at eye level. Bull drank down half of the glass of water. He knew there were more questions. And they would get tougher.

"I'm ready."

"Does Bobby have a gun?"

"No."

"Does he have access to yours?"

"Yes."

"What caliber is your revolver?"

".38 Special."

"Where is it now? In your hotel room?"

"No. The owner doesn't like me bringing it inside the hotel. It's under the driver's seat of my car."

"Could Bobby have taken it to the set on Wednesday without you knowing it?"

"He drives my car to the set every day. When he gets back, I go out."

Conor Armenta could barely manage to complete his questioning. He nearly broke down himself in the process. Wayne Garrard had described Bobby Hansen's gentle nature to him. He saw now where the son acquired that trait.

"You know what comes next."

"You take my gun, then you arrest my son," he resolved.

Con stood. "Shall we go get it?"

"I'll get it," Bull answered. He finished his glass of water and sat it on the sheriff's desk, then stood and walked out the door. A moment later, the sound of a gunshot rang through his open window. Conor ran to it and stared down at the street. Bull Hansen lay beside his car in a pool of blood. The car door stood open. His pistol lay on the street beside him. The sheriff rushed through the outer office.

"Call Hal!" he yelled to Hazel as he passed.

18

June dozed on her couch. The telephone rested on the end table. Her head, wedged uncomfortably between a decorative pillow and the arm of the couch nearby. The clock began striking ten as she counted it off in semi-consciousness. *I must be dreaming,* she thought, as the clock added new random notes intertwined with the chime in a strange order that did not quite fit. The confusing symphony finally awakened her sufficiently to realize the phone was ringing.

Conor waited as the telephone rang the sixth time, adding anxiety with each monotonous trill. Just as he pulled the receiver from his ear in provision of rushing to June's house, it quit ringing.

"Hello, sweetheart," she answered, trying to clear the cobwebs from her head.

"Are you okay?"

"Not entirely," she replied as the fog began to lift.

"What's wrong? Your note said to call, no matter how late. You weren't answering. I was beginning to worry, thinking something terrible might have happened."

"I'm so sorry," she replied, finally awake. "I didn't mean to scare you. I've just been so excited all day. We are going to be married, have children. And I was lonely. I missed you. I wanted you to know that. I want to make you happy. I will be yours forever, just like it says in the wedding vows, 'til death do us part. I am filled to the brim with my love for you. I cannot wait to share it."

There was silence. "Are you there?" she finally asked.

"Yes…yes, I'm here."

"Do you understand how I feel."

"Oh yes, I do. I understand perfectly. I feel exactly the same way. I just don't have the right words to express it."

"Yes, you do, Conor." She sniffled as yet another flood of tears flooded her face. "You do have the right words. You just said them."

"I love you, June. I never knew what love was before I met you. I feel like I could explode."

"I know. I know just what you are saying," she expressed, as another thought rushed into head. "Oh, I need to tell you, too. I told Olivia this morning in church. And Donna and April. April wants to know if you will be her daddy?"

Conor paused, overwhelmed by the concept. "I could never replace her father," he struggled speaking the words.

"You already have. There has never been a man in her life before you, a father. She has only seen photographs of him. He was killed before she was born. You love her, and she adores you. You will be her daddy."

Conor was overcome with emotion. He needed a lighter subject. "You told Olivia?"

"Yes, I hope that's okay with you."

"Yeah, sure. Now we won't have to send out invitations. By tomorrow morning, everyone in Las Vegas will know."

"She's not that bad." June giggled. "Well, maybe. I told Joyce too. And I called Leanora Campbell."

"Leanora Campbell? Why?"

"Yesterday morning at the cemetery, she introduced me to a friend of Mrs. Wagner as your fiancé. I nearly choked and explained that there was not an engagement...yet. She was embarrassed and apologized profusely for spreading a rumor. When I called, I told her that now she could spread the story however she saw fit and know that it was true."

June and Conor carried on their conversation for nearly an hour before bidding each other goodnight.

* * *

TUESDAY, AUGUST 12, 1930

After having lunch at the Mesquite Café, Judge William Tucker and Sheriff Armenta strolled toward their offices in casual conversation. When they approached the sheriff's office, Judge Tucker stopped and reached out his hand.

"Happy birthday, Conor. Enjoy the rest of it," he exalted as they shook hands. "I suspect it will include a pleasant dinner with your bride-to-be. Ah, the many joys of youth. If only I were your age again," he reveled before continuing to the courthouse.

When he walked in, Hazel handed the sheriff a note. *Call June at home!* He looked at her somewhat surprised.

"I told her you were at lunch with Judge Tucker when she called."

"Why's she at home?"

Hazel shrugged innocently as Conor entered his office. He left the door open and dialed the telephone as he sat down at his desk.

"Hello, Sommers residence," April answered as if she were a receptionist.

"Good afternoon, miss," he replied, joining in the game. "Is Mrs. Sommers in?"

"Can I call you Daddy yet?" she whispered.

"I would love it, but you should wait 'til after the wedding."

"Ohhh-kaay," she sulked before holding the phone away and calling out, "Mama! It's Con."

"Hello, sweetheart." June's voice soon came over the telephone. "How was your morning?"

"The jury found Dutch guilty of murdering Jimmy," he answered. "Why are you at home?"

"I took the afternoon off from work," she beamed. "We are celebrating. You can pick us up at three o'clock."

"But I'm still at work," he reminded.

"Hazel said you were not busy and it would be fine. It is only one thirty. You have an hour and a half."

"So Hazel is the boss now?" he mocked. Conor did his best to glare at her as she grinned back at him through the open door before looking away.

"Fill your car with gasoline," June added.

"Oh?" Con questioned.

"We are going for a ride," June explained. "Happy birthday!" she added and hung up.

"So, Mrs. Corbyn," he addressed her firmly, "what's going

on around here?"

"I have no idea what you're talking about." Hazel giggled slightly as she pretended to be engaged in a stack of papers on her desk.

"Okay," he surrendered, taking his Stetson from its peg. "I'll see you in the morning."

* * *

In a fresh shirt at five minutes before three, Conor scaled the steps of June's porch two at a time. She caught a whiff of lotion from his clean-shaven face when she met him at the door. The yellow flowers on her cotton dress complimented her blonde hair as well as the blue pearl pendant adorning her neck set off her eyes. The dress flowed so perfectly over her form without being snug, it could have been sewn together around her.

"You look wonderful," he told her as their lips met.

Before he could step back, a pair of young arms embraced him around his waist.

"Happy birthday, Con!" April greeted with glee.

"Thank you, sweetie," he replied as he lowered himself to her level to return the hug. "You look as lovely as your mother today."

"Shall we go?" June suggested. She snuck a wink to April that Conor pretended had gone unnoticed.

"Where are we headed?" he asked.

"I will guide you," June replied as April scurried to the kitchen, returning with a small, gift-wrapped box.

"I'll ride in the back," she declared.

"Well, okay then," Con accepted and walked ahead to open the rumble seat of the coupe. He held April's hand as she negotiated the steps from the bumper to the fender then into her place. June looked on until her fiancé held the car door for her. It had been his gentlemanly custom since they first met.

"Where to?" he asked when he started the engine.

June pointed, grinning ear to ear.

Conor backed the car out and turned it south.

"Turn right," she said, still smiling, her first words spoken since their departure.

Con rested his right hand on the shift knob as they motored west on Charleston Boulevard and out of town. June positioned her left hand atop his. The engagement ring he ordered from Mrs. Delkin had arrived only a few days ago. The two small diamonds glistened alongside the blue pearl set between them. It matched the color of the pendant he bought for her birthday…and her eyes as he had admired.

When June directed him down Pine Canyon Road, he suspected they might be headed to Leonora Campbell's, but soon they ventured onto yet another side road. Having never been together on most of the roads they toured in near silence, it surprised him she knew they existed, especially since she did not own a car.

"Are you lost?" he asked her once.

"Of course not." She continued to smile.

They now were approaching his brother's ranch, driving back toward town. "We're almost to Paddy's," he told her. "Would you like to stop?"

"Why not," she replied.

He slowed the car. Not until they turned down the driveway did he notice it. Both his parents' and his sister's cars were parked at the house.

June watched his face as he came to the realization. "Are you surprised?"

"Yes, I certainly am."

"I've been planning for weeks. Olivia swore I would never get you all the way out here without you figuring it out." She laughed with delight. "I win!"

Conor chuckled. "Congratulations, darling! It isn't easy to best my sister."

She leaned over and kissed his cheek as the car came to a stop. He turned and kissed her more seriously.

"It's a good thing we're not alone," June responded, more to herself than Conor, as she caught her breath. He did not comment, but took a deep breath also, as he climbed out of the car.

"There's the birthday boy!" Maggie Armenta shouted from the shade of the trees surrounding the house.

Conor held the door for June, then hurried to assist April as she descended from her perch. He turned just in time to see Paddy hugging June.

"Happy birthday, big brother," he bade as he took Conor in his arms. "That lady"—he glanced back toward June without releasing him—"she is your gift from God."

"Yes," he agreed. "I do think you're right."

"Come to the fiesta!" Patrick cheered as they sought the nearby shade. Then he saw the feast. A platter of sliced ham, bread, potato salad, cantaloupes and peaches covered makeshift tables of boards on sawhorses. A cake with a host of candles sat near the end of the table and melting ice dripped from between the slats of the ice cream freezer on the porch.

"I was going to make fried chicken," Juan announced, "but I've heard it would fall far short of that made by your future bride." He reached up and hugged his son. "Happy birthday, son!"

The comment both flattered and embarrassed June.

"Who would have told you such a tale?" she asked Juan but looked accusingly at Conor.

"Luis. He told me about the picnic you and Con brought to him…and your fried chicken. He said it was better than any chicken I ever made!" Juan beamed as he told the story.

"Well, I am flattered by Luis's praise, but I have eaten enough meals at your café to suspect it was unwarranted."

April still carried the small box with ribbon tied around it. She and Donna were whispering and giggling by the porch as Maggie and Olivia surrounded Conor. They both hugged Con tightly as Olivia teased him about being an old man. She even gave him a quick peck on the cheek. He looked from one to the other accusingly.

"So, you two were both plotting this"—he looked over the layout—"the whole time I was having lunch with Judge Tucker?"

"And you never suspected a thing, big brother. You're not such a hotshot detective as you think you are," Olivia taunted.

Olivia's son David waited behind his mother and grand-mother for his turn. At the age of thirteen, he held out his hand wishing to be considered and adult. Conor accepted it and exchanged a firm handshake.

"Happy birthday, Uncle Con," he offered sullenly.

"Thank you, David. I didn't see your father," he commented.

"He's working. Had to take a load up to Salt Lake." David sulked. "He won't be back 'til Friday."

"Just in time for the St. Thomas Rodeo on Saturday," Conor observed.

David's frown quickly broadened into a smile. "Oh, yeah!" he nearly cheered. "I never thought of that."

Six chairs were positioned around Patrick's kitchen table in the shade beneath a large cottonwood tree. Two opened bottles of Coca-Cola sat at one end. June placed a plate heaped with food beside them.

"For the guest of honor," she said, pulling out the chair as Conor glanced around. "That's you, dear," she clarified. "You may enjoy one of your drinks while the rest of us fill our plates," June told him as he took his seat. The adults soon surrounded him. The youngsters sat nearby on pillows around Patrick's coffee table that had been brought out onto the porch.

"Will you say grace, Papa?" Maggie asked.

Juan paused, reflecting for a moment what this house had meant for his family. He sat at the far end of the table from Conor with Maggie and Olivia to each side. He reached and took their hands as did the others around the table, then bowed his head.

"Thank you, Father, for bringing us together to celebrate our first son's birthday and his engagement. We outgrew this house you provided for us, but we haven't forgotten it. We want our grandchildren to remember it, too. Bless the food we're gonna eat, in Your Son's name, amen."

A tear rolled down June's cheek. "How long has it been since all of you have been here together?"

"Fourth of July 1910," Patrick answered. "Right before we all moved into town."

"That's right," Juan reminisced. "Luis bought the last of our sheep, we rented the café and a house in town."

"My gosh," June exclaimed. "Twenty years ago."

"Yeah. Con helped Luis herd the sheep down to his place. He worked the rest of the summer for him," Juan recalled. "The rest of us loaded everything we could into a wagon and hauled it to town. By the next time we saw Con, he'd turned sixteen, the café was goin' pretty good and we's all settled in."

"I *was* settled in," Olivia interjected. "The house had two bedrooms. Mama and Papa in one, I was in the other. Paddy slept on the front room floor," she explained. "When Con came back, he and Paddy got the bedroom and I got the floor."

"Until somebody gave Con a couch that made into a bed that he brought home for Olivia," Juan clarified.

"It was a futon, Papa," Olivia corrected.

"And Con bought it," Patrick added.

"No, a lady gave it to him from a boarding house over on 4th Street," Juan assured them.

"It was a boarding house all right, but not on 4th Street," Patrick retorted as his brother ate in silence. "I watched Con pay her a dollar for it and helped him pack it home from Block 16." At that, Conor slapped his brother on the arm while never lifting his eyes from his plate.

Patrick quickly realized that Conor had lied to the rest of the family about the origins of the couch for nearly twenty years.

Olivia stared at her older brother in disbelief. "Do you mean, I went through puberty sleeping on a futon that came from...from a...a..." She could not bring herself to finish the question.

June's face shone a brilliant shade of crimson as she quietly munched on a mouthful of potato salad without looking up.

Maggie tried very hard to stifle a chuckle without any success. "Now I understand why you've always avoided the subject when anyone brought up your brotherly kindness in getting your sister the couch." She managed to complete the assessment before bursting into laughter and tears at the same time.

Juan's anger at his son's deceit ebbed when he recognized the humor behind it.

Olivia failed to revel in the comedy the rest of her family seemed amused with. "Now, I get it." An old memory flashed into her thoughts. "I finally understand Jimmy Butler's rude comment at the school dance when I was fifteen."

"What did he say?" her mother asked, fearing her daughter had suffered some immoral allegation that scarred her for life.

"I don't remember it exactly and wouldn't repeat it if I did."

"What did you do?" Maggie continued with genuine concern.

"I slapped him. It was so severe and loud that everyone in the gym was staring. Then I kicked him in the crotch as hard as I could."

Con looked at his sister guiltily, sorry that he had unknowingly brought her shame all those years ago.

Olivia, holding her fork at half-mast, stared into nothingness in the distance, unaware that she held every adult's gaze. Then she giggled.

"He deserved it anyway," she finally shared with a grin, which brought her to look around at the table of concerned faces. "Well...he did."

Unaware of the world around them, some antic at that moment brought a round of laughter from the trio on the front porch. A similar chorus soon erupted from the table in the yard.

The diversion from the festivities by the tale of the couch dissipated and April appeared at Conor's side to hand him her package.

"Perhaps you should wait to open that until after we have had cake and ice cream," June suggested. She rose and headed toward the cake while Patrick jumped to prepare for serving ice cream. Meantime, Maggie and Olivia cleared the table. A small bonfire mounted from the thirty-six candles ablaze on the chocolate cake June carried toward the table. She baked it last night and her future in-laws delivered it to the party for her. As she approached, Conor's family broke out singing "Las Mañanitas" concluding with cheers and applause.

April watched intently as Conor blew out his candles. "What did you wish for?"

"For today to never end," he told her.

Her smile dissolved. "That won't come true," she responded in disappointment.

"It will in here," he told her as he patted his chest over his heart and embraced her.

June again burst into tears on her seemingly unending rollercoaster of emotions. Maggie put her arm around June's shoulder as her own eyes overflowed.

"Can he open my present now?" April asked her mother, breaking the spell of the moment.

"He sure can," June replied as her daughter pushed it toward him on the table.

He picked it up and shook it as he held it to his ear. It was somewhat heavy for its size and rattled profusely. "What could this possibly be?" he asked rhetorically yet in sincere curiosity.

"Open it!" April exclaimed.

Removing the ribbon, he tore open the wrapping paper and opened the box inside. It contained two carrots, cut into six pieces. He looked puzzled.

"They're for Roberto," April explained.

"You mean Bob?"

"Aunt Olivia says his name is really Roberto."

"Should we give them to him?" he asked April and

glanced at June. She wore the same broad smile in silence that she had throughout the afternoon.

"Mama showed me how!" April cried out as she tugged Conor's hand until he came to his feet.

He followed her around the corner of the house with June on his heels. The rest of the family were close behind. Bob stood by the gate with a large red bow fastened to the halter he seldom wore.

"You?" he began to ask when he turned to June. Her arms were already entwining around his neck as their lips met passionately.

"Happy birthday, Conor." She gasped when they separated.

"You bought him?" he asked in disbelief.

"Your sister says that I stole him actually," she corrected.

He glanced at Paddy.

"I gave her the family discount."

"You'll have to excuse me while I change clothes," June told him.

"Why?" Conor asked, still muddled by the rapid progression of events.

"So I can go with you when you take Bob out for a spin around the block," she replied cheerfully and dashed in the back door of the house.

Con opened the gate and rubbed Bob's neck. He handed one of the carrots to April and watched carefully as she held it out to the horse on her open palm. She giggled when his soft lips tickled her palm as he accepted it. April stayed at his side as her future father led Bob to the barn.

Paddy brought Chalk out from the corral as June joined them at the barn wearing her riding skirt and a new pair of boots. He tied Chalk's lead rope to one of the iron rings mounted near the door and brought a blanket and saddle from the tack room.

"Let me do it," June insisted when he laid the blanket across the horse's back. "You will have to help me, but I need to learn how to do this."

April followed Con's every move as he saddled Bob. He let her carry the bridle from the tack room and showed her how to hold it with the bit up to Bob's mouth.

"Let him take the bit in his mouth," he explained, "then pull it on up and slip it over his ears." She watched and listened intently. "Do you wanna try it?"

"Sure!" she said.

Conor slipped the bridle back off and handed it to her. She held it as high as she could with the bit near his mouth. Bob watched the young girl who treated him with carrots. The mild-tempered gelding leaned forward and took the bit in his mouth, then lowered his head so she could reach over his ears with the bridle.

"Now pull his forelock out from under it." Con told her.

"His what?" She looked at Con.

"His bangs." He smiled. "On horses they call it a forelock. The lock of hair on their forehead. It pulls their hair if it's caught up under the bridle."

Bob lifted his head back up when she turned away, now higher than her reach. April gave an exasperated sigh.

"Don't get upset," Con told her calmly. "He will sense it and do the same." Knowing Bob's good nature, he continued. "Take his reins and gently pull down. He should lower his head for you."

Bob did. As she carefully drew the hair from under the bridle, Con added, "rub behind his ears while his head is down, then pet his neck and he'll know it's okay to raise it back up."

April watched in amazement. "How did you know he'd do that?"

"Horses are a lot like people," he told her. "They usually respond well to kindness and praise." He handed her another carrot. "Now you can give him that to say thank you. He can't answer, but if you pet him while he eats it, you're telling him, 'You're welcome.'"

Bob lowered his head again as she petted. "What does that mean?"

"Scratch behind my ears again," Con replied in a deep voice and chuckled as he spoke for the horse.

April giggled and obliged.

While Con tutored April, June received a similar lesson from Paddy. Conor kept track of her progress out of the corner of his eye with admiration. She swung the saddle over the blanket on the second try, then slid it forward as Paddy showed her where it should ride on Chalk's withers. He held his hand under it as she tightened the cinch strap and told her when to stop. Then he had her put her own fingers in its place so she would understand how tight it should be. She became distracted watching and listening to Conor coaching April.

"Like that?" she asked Paddy when she saw him bringing Chalk's bridle.

He grinned and nodded. "Just like that."

She followed the example with success on her first attempt. Chalk had balked ever so slightly when the bit touched her lips, but June waited patiently without forcing it and the mare complied.

She walked over to Conor. "I need a carrot."

He turned, reached around her waist with one arm and

planted a moist kiss on her lips. "Will that do?" he asked, grinning wryly.

Quickly recovering from the surprise. "Yes, that works just fine, but what about Chalk?"

"You could do the same for her," he replied, still grinning. "But she'll respond better to this." He handed her the carrot.

* * *

An hour later, Conor and June rode side by side at a leisurely walk through the hills behind Paddy's house.

"It was so kind of your parents to take April home with them this evening," June began. "I was surprised she chose that option over your sister's house."

"She may be longing for grandparents as much as they love grandchildren."

"I had not thought of that."

Several minutes passed in silence. "I like it," June remarked.

"What?" Con asked, startled awake in the midst of a daydream.

"I like your life."

"Okay," he came back, unsure of the correct response.

"You grew up here," June clarified. "You said it was a part of your life that would never leave you. Then you asked if I would share it with you. Marry you. I said yes without even thinking...because I love you more than I ever thought possible, and I wanted to share that love with you and nothing could ever change that. I didn't fully realize that I was agreeing to share *your* life with you. Today, now, for the first time, I understand what that means. I like your life, Conor. I will learn more about it and someday…someday I hope to love it as much as you do…as much as I love you."

"I'm proud of you," Conor told her, "proud of the way you worked, learning to saddle Chalk, proud of who you are…and thankful too. Thank you for Bob. I've been so overwhelmed; I don't think I ever thanked you for him. What a gift! Thank you for being part of my life…for being *all* of my life. I love you and I'll do my very best to make you the happiest woman in the world."

"I already am."

19

SATURDAY, OCTOBER 11, 1930

At a quarter past eleven, Sheriff Conor Armenta climbed the stairs at the Northern Hotel. Bobby Hansen's room was second to the last on the right. The clerk downstairs said he might be in his father's suite next door. With his hat in his left hand, Conor rapped his knuckles on Bobby's door. He heard footsteps a moment before the door opened. His face showed surprise. The sheriff had forgotten how large the man was. About his own age, a couple of inches taller than his father, and very physically fit.

"What can I do for you, Sheriff?" he asked. His expression had transformed to anxiety after seeing Armenta's serious mien.

"Your father shot himself."

"Accidentally?" he questioned in disbelief. "Is he okay?"

"Intentionally," Con answered. "No. He's not okay."

"You mean..." He did not need to finish the question. "Why?"

"You must know the answer to that better than me."

"Well," he said. "Thank you for coming to tell me." He began to close the door.

"That's not all I came to see you about..." Armenta stopped while putting his hat back on, "Robert Hansen, you're under arrest for the murder of Matthew McCoy."

All color left Bobby's face. After the arrest of Hugh Parker, he was confident no one had noticed where the bullet came from. When Fredericks and his attorney showed up yesterday, it bolstered his assumption.

"How'd you know?" he asked, staring at the floor like a chastised schoolboy.

"The muzzle blast from your pistol. It showed up on the footage from two of the three cameras." The sheriff brought a pair of handcuffs from his rear jeans pocket. "I hope these aren't necessary, but I can't take that chance."

"I understand," he said, placing his hands at his back.

"In front will be fine." He was barely able to secure the cuffs around Hansen's large wrists.

Sheriff Armenta followed his prisoner down the stairs and out to his pickup truck parked in front of the hotel. He opened the passenger door and Hansen climbed in. With a second pair of handcuffs, he linked the first pair to a bar beneath the dashboard of the truck. When he closed the door, David Whitfield Fredericks sat in the shade in front of the neighboring Hotel Nevada. He looked away quickly and took a puff on his cigar.

* * *

The sheriff entered the lobby of the Hotel Nevada a half hour later.

"What room is Miss Mansfield in?" he asked the clerk

"We don't have—" the clerk began, when Armenta interrupted.

"Miss Stapleton," he corrected.

"Top of the stairs, second door on the left."

When he knocked on the door, the sound of the footsteps he heard approaching were that of someone considerably heavier than Molly Mansfield. He took a step back as the door opened.

"Come in, Sheriff," David Fredericks greeted with a smile.

Through the open door of the suite, he could see Emerson Pollard seated on a sofa. Molly Mansfield leaned against a side table across the room. She sipped on a glass half-full of an amber liquid without ice. He entered the room.

"I saw that you had one of my employees in custody earlier. Is there something I need to do? Post bond, perhaps?"

"That's not why I'm here." He turned to the lady across the room. "Mary Ann Mansfield, you are under arrest for conspiracy to murder Matthew McCoy."

She fainted and fell to the floor. Dave Fredericks rushed toward her.

"Stop right there, Fredericks!" he ordered as he pulled back the hammer on his .45 automatic.

Fredericks stopped in his tracks.

"Dave," Emerson Pollard spoke calmly. "Don't do anything stupid. His pistol is pointed at the back of your head. He's six feet away. It's cocked."

"Mr. Fredericks." Conor spoke with equal coolness. "You are still a primary suspect in this murder. I will not give you the opportunity to slip Miss Mansfield a poisoned pill or any other method you have invented to murder her before she can testify to what parts you and Mr. Parker played in this conspiracy.

"I have positive identification that she drove the maroon Cadillac to the set at the Campbell estate the night before the murder. She parked by Hugh Parker's tent. Someone left the car with a flashlight but did not enter the tent. Someone crushed out a Craven Navy Cut cigarette beside the locked gun chest in the prop truck. Miss Mansfield drove the car away from the premises twenty minutes later. You, sir, are only half a step away from joining her in prison. I will be fully justified in performance of my duty, should your actions make it necessary for me to pull this trigger.

"That will not be necessary, Sheriff," Fredericks muttered. "May I turn around?"

Molly began to stir.

"No, sir. You will keep your back to me while moving to your left and then to the door. When you reach Mr. Pollard, he will stand and join you. You will both go to your suite, close the door, and stay there for not less than one hour. You will not use the telephone nor entertain guests in any way during that time. Do you understand?"

"Yes, Sheriff."

"Do I have your full cooperation?"

"Yes, you have my full cooperation."

As Fredericks and Pollard left the room, Molly Mansfield regained consciousness.

"What happened?"

"You fainted."

"Where are Dave and Emerson?"

"They are in Mr. Fredericks's suite." He bent over to help her. "Can you stand now?"

"I think so."

He helped her to her feet. "Do you remember what I said before you fainted?"

"Yes, I'm under arrest for conspiracy to murder Matt."

"Yes. Can you walk on your own?"

She nodded. Conor handcuffed and escorted her to his pickup. At the jail he had her placed in a solitary cell for her own protection as well as privacy from the male prisoners.

* * *

WEDNESDAY, SEPTEMBER 24, 1930

At nine o'clock, Judge William Tucker called the court to order. Dutch Wagner sat without expression alongside Carlton White, his attorney, behind the table assigned to the defense. District Attorney Donald D. Davis occupied the only chair at the table designated for the prosecution. Sheriff Conor Armenta perched on the uncomfortable, pew-like bench in the first row of the gallery.

"Gary D. Wagner, Jr., you have been found guilty of murder in the second degree of Jimmy Garza by a jury of your peers. You also have been found guilty of murder in the second degree of Katherine Wagner by a separate jury of your peers. In addition, you have been found guilty of murder in the first degree of Brice Campbell by yet another jury of your peers. Is there anything you would like to say to this court before I pronounce sentence of punishment for these crimes?"

He shook his head.

"Your Honor," White burst in as he jumped to his feet. "I would like to make a statement on my client's behalf."

Judge Tucker rapped his gavel. "You're out of order, Mr.

White. You have been given ample opportunity to express your opinions during closing arguments in each trial of these cases. Mr. Wagner has indicated he has nothing to say. Your request is denied, sir," he concluded with another rap of his gavel.

"Gary D. Wagner, Jr., it is the opinion of this court that you have shown no remorse in causing the death of your victims. The circumstances in the death of the late Jimmy Garza were of a most heinous nature; particularly the desecration of his corpse. It is therefore the decision of this court that you shall be put to death, much more mercifully than your unfortunate victim, by poisonous gas at the Nevada State Prison in Carson City." He turned to the next page of papers in front of him.

"For the murder of Katherine Wagner, it is the opinion of the court that the conviction should have been for first-degree murder. In the victim's own words, she expected her demise at your hands for several years. The jury found you guilty of kidnapping however, found insufficient evidence that you specifically planned to kill her on that particular day, thus chose the second-degree conviction. It is the decision of this court that sentencing for the kidnapping charge is diminutive and therefore inconsequential. For the murder of Katherine Wagner, you shall be put to death by poisonous gas at the Nevada State Prison in Carson City." The judge turned another page.

"There is no question that Brice Campbell's murder was planned. He was more than twice your age with a broken wrist. That you overpowered him and killed him with his own revolver merely provided the opportunity for you to disguise it as a suicide. It may have worked had it not been for discovering the morbid trophy stolen from the victim and found in your safe. It is the opinion of this court that if this crime had not been so easy, the other two may never have occurred. You have been found equally guilty of all three crimes by three separate juries. For the murder of Brice Campbell in the first degree, it is the decision of this court that you shall be put to death by poisonous gas at the Nevada State Prison in Carson City.

"I find no pleasure in decreeing to end someone's life. In truth, I find the duty sickening. I have had to choose this sentence a number of times during my forty-year tenure behind this bench. During that entire time, Mr. Wagner, I have found none more deserving of the punishment than you.

"This court is adjourned," he concluded with the resounding ring of his gavel, then stood and departed the courtroom.

* * *

MONDAY, OCTOBER 13, 1930

At nine o'clock, Bobby Hansen stood in handcuffs before Judge Tucker's bench.

"Robert Hansen, you were arrested for murder in the first degree of Matthew McCoy. Your arrest took place on October 11, 1930, at approximately eleven fifteen. Are you aware that your father took his own life earlier that same morning?"

"Yes, sir."

"Is your father's death or any other circumstance inhibiting your mental faculties to a sufficient degree to make you incapable of entering a sensible plea to the charges brought before you at this time?"

"No, sir."

"On the charge of murdering Matthew McCoy in the first degree on October 9, 1930, how do you plea"

"What does 'in the first degree' mean?"

"A legitimate question, Mr. Hansen. There are three categories of murder recognized by the State of Nevada. If you unintentionally took the victim's life, that would be third-degree murder, sometimes referred to as manslaughter. If some event occurred at the time that caused you to intentionally take the victim's life, that would be second-degree murder. If you planned in advance to take the victim's life, then carried out those plans, that would be first-degree murder. That is the charge brought before you today.

"Mr. Hansen, did you plan to take Matthew McCoy's life, then carry out those plans?"

"I did, Your Honor."

"Robert Hansen, do I understand you correctly, that you are pleading guilty of murdering Matthew McCoy in the first degree?"

"Yes, Your Honor."

"Mr. Hansen, the Clerk of the District Court will prepare a document to that effect for you to sign. This is a very serious charge. Read it carefully. If you do not understand everything that is in that document, don't sign it until you do. Is that clear?"

"Yes, Your Honor."

"The deputy will escort you to the clerk's office, then back to the Clark County Jail where you will be held until sentencing."

"Yes, sir."

* * *

At ten thirty, Deputy Jesse Slater escorted Molly Mansfield into the courtroom. Emerson Pollard followed a few paces behind, then took his place beside his client before Judge Tucker's bench.

"Mary Ann Mansfield, you are charged with conspiracy to murder Matthew McCoy. How do you plead?

"But we didn't kill Matt," she said.

"If you had, the charge would be Accessory Before the Fact. Your plea, Miss Mansfield?"

"It's Mrs., actually. What's the maximum sentence?"

"Have you consulted with your counsel, Mrs. Mansfield?"

"If I may, Your Honor?" Emerson Pollard interrupted.

"Go ahead, Mr. Pollard."

"I did not have access to a set of lawbooks over the weekend, Your Honor," he told the judge, "and it's been some time since I represented a case in your state, sir."

"I understand, Mr. Pollard. Under the circumstances, you may request a continuance if you need to research a point in question."

"If I might exercise that option later, if need be, we can continue now."

"Very well. The typical sentence would be anywhere from ten to twenty years up to twenty-five years to life imprisonment. Under extreme cases, the death penalty has been enforced."

Molly Mansfield remained surprisingly calm, though her face paled.

"What about a plea bargain?" she asked.

"You and Mr. Pollard would need to discuss that matter with District Attorney Davis. Let me warn you before anything like that occurs, Mrs. Mansfield," Tucker added, "perjury carries a penalty of ten to fifteen years in addition to any other conviction."

"Is that before or after the death penalty?" she managed to get out before Pollard stepped sharply on her toe.

William Tucker fought back a smile.

"I would like to request a continuance before the plea, Your Honor?" Pollard asked.

"Granted. Mrs. Mansfield, you will be held in the Clark County Jail until we reconvene on Thursday at nine o'clock. This court is adjourned."

* * *

TUESDAY, OCTOBER 21, 1930

Sheriff Conor Armenta and his prisoner, Dutch Wagner, boarded the train bound for Salt Lake City with connection to Carson City, Nevada at four-fifteen in the morning. He carried an old-fashioned carpetbag containing his razor, suit jacket, and a change of clothes. Two days there, execution on Thursday, then two days back home. A lone passenger car attached to the rear of the express car led more than a dozen freight cars on this working man's train. Conor guided Dutch to a seat on the right near the front and directed him to the window. He unlatched Wagner's left handcuff and connected it to the framework of the seat in front of him. The smug expression on Dutch's face in the dimly lit car caught the sheriff's attention.

"The less you have to say, Dutch," he told him, "the better we'll get along."

One other passenger occupied the car: a man dressed in miner's gear with dirty overalls. He sat near the rear on the left-hand side. Con sat across the aisle, one row back from

Dutch. As he watched the brakeman checking the outside of the train, the conductor entered the rear of the car.

"Got your ticket there?" he asked the miner who handed it to him.

"You're on the wrong train, sir. This train won't leave for another couple of hours," he told the man.

"Sorry," the man said as he jumped to his feet.

"Better hurry," the conductor told him as the car lurched and began to move.

Con watched the man bail off the rear of the car and dash across the platform out of sight into the darkness. The conductor ambled his way up the aisle toward them. He handed the conductor both tickets.

"One round-trip ticket to Carson City," he noted as he punched holes in it. "And one one-way." He glanced knowingly at Dutch, cuffed to the seat in front of him. "Enjoy your trip, Sheriff," the conductor added as he handed the tickets back to him.

A LOOK AT BOOK FOUR:
ALTAHA

BLOODSHED, BULLETS, AND THE GUNSLINGING ROAD TO JUSTICE.

Sheriff Conor Armenta's routine prisoner transfer turns deadly when an assassin's bullet kills his captive and narrowly misses him. Determined to track down the shooter, he enlists the help of his Moapa Paiute friend, Rayno Pete, setting off on a treacherous manhunt across the unforgiving Mormon Mountains.

Their trail leads to Altaha, a fearsome Chiricahua Apache known as the last true warrior of his people. His legend stretches across the Southwest, built on his deadly skill and cunning. But as Conor and Rayno close in, they find themselves facing not just the perilous terrain, but a relentless adversary who seems to always be one step ahead, turning the hunter into the hunted.

In a deadly game of survival, Conor must trust his instincts, his partner, and a surprising new ally—Rayno's once-wild Indian dog. With every step drawing them closer to a final showdown, one question remains: will they bring down the elusive Altaha, or will he vanish into the dusty frontier once again?

AVAILABLE DECEMBER 2024

ABOUT THE AUTHOR

Jefferson Glass grew up near the Klamath Indian Reservation in the ranch country of southeastern Oregon. Influenced by the stories found in his grandfather's collection of Zane Grey novels, his young imagination went wild in these rural surroundings. At an early age, he often hiked with his dog over countless miles of public land that bordered his family's property. The only rule was to be home by suppertime. As a teenager, his wanderlust gave way to working the hayfields of a nearby ranch.

In 1981, Jefferson moved to central Wyoming where he began his writing career. He has written numerous articles on Western history for *Annals of Wyoming, True West Magazine* and WyoHistory.org. His non-fiction books, *RESHAW: The Life and Times of John Baptiste Richard* and *Empire: The Pioneer Legacy of an American Ranch Family*, won a Western Writers of America Spur Award and a Will Rogers Medallion Award respectively.

Jefferson began research in 2020 on his Conor Armenta Mystery series, set in 1930s Las Vegas. While exploring Clark

County, Nevada, and surrounding areas, he and his wife stumbled across Kanab, Utah, where they purchased a home and relocated. The magnificent view of The Grand Staircase-Escalante out their back door is certain to inspire years of future writing.